The Pilot's Wife

The Pilot's Wife

Cynthia Anderson

First published in the UK in 2025 by

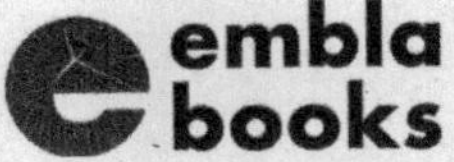

An imprint of Bonnier Books UK
5th Floor, HYLO, 105 Bunhill Row,
London, EC1Y 8LZ

A CIP catalogue record for this book is available from the British Library.

ISBN: 9781471419058

Also available as an ebook and an audiobook

2

Typeset by IDSUK (Data Connection) Ltd
Printed and bound in Great Britain by Clays Ltd, Elcograf S.p.A.

The authorised representative in the EEA is Bonnier Books UK (Ireland) Limited.
Registered office address: Floor 3, Block 3, Miesian Plaza, Dublin 2, D02 Y754, Ireland
compliance@bonnierbooks.ie
www.bonnierbooks.co.uk

For Sacha, Noé, and Ivan, with love
and
for Mom and Dad, you are missed

Permissions

The author acknowledges with gratitude the permission to use the following materials:

T.S. Eliot, *Four Quartets* by permission of Faber and Faber Ltd. and HarperCollins Publishers

Shot from the Sky by Cathryn Prince, by permission of the author

'Website of the Independent Expert Commission on Administrative Detention' by permission of the Swiss Federal Department of Justice and Police

1

Gina

Colorado Springs, Colorado
September 2018

On the sixth-month anniversary of Mom's death, I make more crème caramel than my grandmother and I can eat. We sit side by side in her kitchen, three ramekins filled to the brim on the Formica table. A whiff of vanilla lingers on my fingers from slicing the sticky bean lengthwise and scraping out the seeds to add to the milk and cream like Mom taught me.

My grandmother, or Mamie as I've always called her, slips her spoon into the pale yellow custard, releasing a warm, syrupy scent.

"Perfect texture," she says.

We eat in silence, the only sound our spoons raking the porcelain clean. Her bony shoulders curl forward as she glances at the untouched one. She doesn't speak, but I know what she's thinking: time to move on.

All the books say normal grief goes away. Six months post-loss, I'm meant to emerge with a new identity—a survivor, fearless and strong. But the reality is I continue to feel unmoored since Mom died, drifting like a boat in a storm, trying to find an anchor in the things she loved, like crème caramel.

Mamie reaches across the table for my hand. "I miss her too," she says.

I gently touch her bruised, paper-thin skin, then reach up with a napkin to wipe a speck of custard off her mouth.

"I've decided to take a trip," she says softly.

"Where to?"

"Switzerland."

My hand draws back, knocking a spoon to the floor. I was expecting her to tell me about a day trip organized by the Spring Village Assisted Living Center, where she lives. But Mamie's talking about going home. "After all this time—"

"You and your mother always wanted me to return."

My memory flashes back to the year I graduated from high school when Mom tried to talk Mamie into a girls' trip to Switzerland—just the three of us. Mom wanted to see the house where Mamie was born, the forest nearby she often talked about, and the lakeside town where she went to university. But Mamie said there was nothing left for her in Switzerland. We went to Santa Fe instead. That was two years ago; a lot has happened since then.

I reach down to pick up the spoon.

"I want you to come with me," she says.

My eyes go to the loose wedding band on her ring finger. She's losing weight again. She should stay here, where it's safe. I slide Mom's ramekin over to her. "You better eat this one too."

"Will the restaurant give you time off?"

I waitress at Le Chat Noir, the only decent French restaurant in town. I lift my shoulders. "It's our busy season."

Shouldn't she be asking if the doctor will clear her to fly? Mamie has glaucoma. In one eye, she's lost all sight; in the other, the lower lid turns out like a pomegranate pith. An operation can correct it. But she's ninety-three, and the risk from surgery is too high.

"Just a week," she presses.

Since Mom was an only child, Mamie is the last link to my maternal side. Of course, I want to know more about my Swiss roots, but now isn't the right moment to go far away. In the weeks after Mom's death, I could still hear her voice in my head, and that helped to lift my sense of uncertainty and brokenness. It was like she was still here. And then her voice went quiet. I've been hoping and waiting for her to come back. If she does and I'm in another country, maybe I won't hear her.

"Could you bring something from my bedroom?" Mamie says, nodding to the hallway. "There's a box in the bottom drawer of the nightstand."

I put the ramekins in the sink and head down the hall.

Her bedroom has a musty smell. I want to open the window, but it's sealed shut. On the nightstand sits the silver-framed black-and-white photo of my grandfather. He died before I was born. I smile at him, like I always do, wishing there was some way to break through the invisible barrier that blocks me from knowing him. I've never been in love, but I can tell Mamie's still in love with Grandfather because even after all this time, her voice rises like a musical note when she says his name.

I bend down and open the drawer. There's a small faded green leather box inside. It's heavy and old, the leather on the corners ragged and torn. This is the first time I've seen it, which is odd since I packed all Mamie's things to move her here after Mom died. Did she slip it into her handbag so I wouldn't see it?

I bring the box to the kitchen and place it on the table.

"I was your age when I left Switzerland. Just after the war in Europe ended." A shadow from the window above the sink crosses her face. "Open it."

I lift the lid. Inside is a watch. Mamie indicates that I should take it out. Scratches scar the glass cover. The dial is black with big phosphorous numerals, and the patina is glossy like a gorgeous night sky. Beyond the hour markers, gold numerical scales rim the dial's edge, which only the long second hand can reach.

"It was your grandfather's."

My eyes are drawn to the strap. At the last adjustment hole, the leather is ashen and cracked. I run my finger over it and feel a faint spark on my skin. Could my grandfather have left some charge behind that's waited all these decades to come to life? I turn the watch over. My fingers tremble as I touch a dark burgundy stain on the leather underside.

"How come you never showed it to me before?" I say, looking at her. She doesn't answer. "Did you show Mom?"

She shakes her head. "On the dial," she whispers, "Rolex Oyster Chronograph and Fab Suisse."

"Where's the Fab—"

"Below the six."

I find the tiny letters poking up like coral along the watch's bottom rim. "What does it mean?"

"Fab is short for *fabriqué*: made in Switzerland."

Mamie was born in Switzerland and met my grandfather, an American army pilot, there during the war. They fell in love, and she followed him to the United States. Growing up, I never considered why she wasn't interested in returning. I figured it was because Mom and I were all that mattered. Now that it's only Mamie and me—is that why she wants to go back?

"Why now?" I say.

"There's someone . . ." She sits very still. "The watch doesn't belong to me. I need your help to go back and find her."

"Her?"

"My daughter . . ."

I freeze. Oh dear, maybe Mamie hasn't been coping as well as I thought she had. I reach forward and cover her hand with my own. "Mamie, your daughter died of cancer. Remember?"

She stares at me for a moment. "Not your mother." Her voice trembles. "I'm talking about Elizabeth."

"Elizabeth?" I echo in disbelief.

"My lost child."

I clap a hand over my mouth and my heart races.

"Yes, I had a daughter before your mother."

I feel light-headed, unbalanced. "With Grandfather?"

She nods.

I can't believe this. "Did he know? Did Mom know?"

"I never told anyone . . ." Mamie's eyes water ". . . until today."

The world stops for a moment. Mom has a sister. I have an aunt. But why would Mamie have abandoned her? I shake my head, unable to make sense of what she's just said. "What happened?"

She straightens her back as if an invisible seam is being pulled inside her chest. "I told you, I lost her." She looks at me. "I need to find her." She points at the watch. "I want to give it to her."

I do a quick calculation. It's been over seventy years. "Do you know if Elizabeth is still alive?"

She shakes her head. Hard-to-ask questions swirl in my mind. The wind knocks the branches of the old oak against the glass. I turn to the window. The afternoon's blue sky is tipping toward gray.

"Have you ever done something wrong?" Her voice hardens. "Truly wrong, when thinking about it hurts, and you hate yourself every time you look in the mirror?"

I gently place Grandfather's watch back in the box. Yes, I hate myself on some days. Yes, there's something I wish

I could redo. And, yes, sometimes, I can't stand to look in the mirror. Mamie stares at the watch and shivers. I get the sense it's pulling her back to a terrible time. I want to comfort her and make the hurt disappear, but I don't know how.

"I owe it to Elizabeth and your grandfather to try and make things right. It's taken me a lifetime to figure this out. Now, I might have only months left."

"Don't talk like that. The doctor said you're fine."

"He said I could fly and told me what precautions to take. I'll need you to put the drops in my eyes."

I try to imagine Mamie in the Denver airport going through security. Can she manage the bathroom on the plane? What if something happens to her mid-flight? And what will we do in Switzerland? Besides, will she know how to locate Elizabeth? Nothing about this sounds easy. But if Mom has a sister, wouldn't she want me to go and find her?

I hesitate. I promised Mom I'd look after Mamie and keep her safe. What if something happens to her while we're over there? "Dad's pushing engineering school. I'm waiting for an interview. The timing isn't good." Even to me, my excuse sounds weak.

"I thought you didn't want to go back to university?"

"I don't. I've tried to tell Dad—"

"It's none of my business, but you should do what your heart tells you."

How can I when it only tells me what I don't want? Don't want Mom dead. Don't want to go back to university. Don't want to be afraid. Life is a blur—if only I could turn back time to how it was before.

"I shouldn't pressure you," Mamie says, leaning across the table and cupping her hands around my face. "But there's no one else I can turn to for help."

Catching the smell of vanilla on her breath, I watch her lips turn into a smile as her hand slides down and straightens the yellow scarf tied around my neck.

"Getting away will be good for you," she says. "Help you see the world with fresh eyes. Who knows what you'll discover out there waiting for you?" I glimpse a great sadness on her face, and then a smile sweeps it away. "That was one of your grandfather's favorite sayings." She touches the Rolex. "Did I mention that my hometown, Le Brassus, has been a watchmaking center for centuries?"

"No." I'm beginning to realize there are many things Mamie hasn't told me. My gaze drops to the box. I feel an odd pull toward the Rolex as if the dial is calling out, urging me to go. Could Mamie be right that this trip is what we both need to emerge as survivors after Mom's death? But it all sounds too crazy to be true. And yet, the watch exists. Maybe Elizabeth does, too. What do I have to lose? "Can you tell me more about her?"

"Not until we're in Switzerland. It's a part of my past I've had to bury deep inside." She reaches for the tissue box. I fear she's going to cry. Instead, she lifts it and reveals a blue passport underneath. She slides the passport to me and opens it to her picture page. A red credit card slips out. "Take these and buy the airline tickets on your computer. Isn't that how it's done these days?"

Mamie's square color photo flashes at me, her name to the right: REARDON, HEDY.

"Is there enough in my account to cover a week in a hotel?" she asks.

I nod but don't tell her there likely won't be anything left from the balance of five thousand dollars after paying for international airfares and hotel costs. It's the last money from Mom's estate, meant to be Mamie's emergency money.

"There is only one place to stay in town," she says, "Hotel de la Lande. Can I leave the arrangements to you?"

"I've got to talk to Dad first. I need a little time."

She darts a glance at the watch. "The one thing I no longer have."

2

Hedy

Le Brassus
May 1944

The church stood behind Hotel de la Lande. Despite being late for the service, Hedy felt compelled to stop.

"I'll take one," she said to the girl standing outside the church's front door alongside a table with a box of terra-cotta milk bowls. The red cross on the girl's white scarf glowed in the afternoon sun, a beacon of hope amid the darkness of war. A large poster of a malnourished child with lifeless eyes swung from the edge of the table, the phrase SAVING THE UPCOMING GENERATION printed in bold letters across the bottom. It was the slogan used by the Swiss Red Cross to raise money to feed and shelter thousands of children left orphaned by war in Europe.

"*Merci, mademoiselle,*" the girl said, her voice soft and polite. She lifted a white ribbon tied to the milk bowl's handle. "Shall I pin it on your collar?"

Hedy nodded and bent down so the girl could reach her collar. The contrast between the girl's plump cheeks and the gray jowls of the child in the photo made Hedy's stomach turn. She'd been fourteen when the war started, and couldn't help but reflect on the five years of devastation it had brought to nearly every country in Europe—except her own.

The pealing of the church bells echoed overhead, and she stepped inside. The congregation sat on wooden pews arranged in a horseshoe across from the dais where Pastor Rolle stood. Hedy slid onto the bench in the second row next to her mother. Her mother handed her the pound cake she'd baked the night before, and Hedy placed it on her lap. Glancing to her left, she waved at her father, standing with the men in the choir on the balcony.

"God is light. God is love. God is spirit." Pastor Rolle's voice boomed through the small hall. Though shorter than Hedy's father, the dais made him appear taller as he stared down at the congregation. "Awaken to the power of the Word of God and the Holy Spirit." Hedy shifted her weight, and the bench creaked.

"Beware those who refuse God's grace." Maybe Hedy imagined it, but she felt his razor-sharp eyes settle on her. "Because they still remain under his judgment."

The windows were high, and the pastor never allowed them to open. The air was thick and stale without a breeze, and a clammy, sick taste rose at the back of her throat.

"Many in the faith have been led astray," he continued, "seduced by the writings of our famous citizen Rousseau."

Pastor Rolle disparaged Rousseau, Voltaire and other Enlightenment thinkers during every Sunday sermon. Hedy suspected he held a personal grudge against them because they were well-read and educated. A part of her wondered if that grudge could extend to her, too, since she was the only woman from her class to go on to study at the University of Lausanne.

"With injustice and suffering worldwide, many are touched by Rousseau's argument that God is distant and uncaring, and his urging of individuals to follow their hearts to judge right and wrong."

God *did* feel distant, Hedy thought. How else to explain why he'd let the war go on for all these years with so much death and destruction?

"But the Bible warns that hearts are deceitful. Jesus says that from the heart comes evil thoughts: murder, adultery and sexual immorality. We must never forget that we are born sinners." He held his hands up to the sky. "Jesus calls us not to follow our hearts but to follow him. He is the only way, the only truth and light."

By the time the sermon ended, Hedy was melting from the stuffiness and heat. When she stood, beads of moisture at the backs of her legs made her dress stick to her skin. All she wanted was to get outside and breathe fresh air. She handed the cake to her mother and motioned that she was heading for the door. As she turned away from the bench, the pastor's voice called her name.

"Mademoiselle Borel, a moment, please."

Turning back, she glimpsed him advancing toward her, and forced a smile.

"I'm glad you could come and listen to the Word of God today," he said.

Hedy hadn't attended the service last week, and she wouldn't have come today if her parents hadn't insisted. Her mother handed her the cake she'd baked to make amends. He kept a list of those who failed to attend Sunday service.

"My classes," she mumbled. "I had a lot of work last week." She offered the cake to the pastor. "Mother and I made this for you."

He thanked her and motioned to someone in the crowd. "There's a fine young man I want to introduce you to, if you'd be so kind as to wait."

Hedy wished she could sneak away but that would only make matters worse. She pinched the skin between her thumb and index finger and concentrated on the light from outside. Her mother always said that Pastor Rolle could read people's thoughts. Hedy let her mind go blank so he wouldn't see how much she disliked being here.

"This is Franck Glauser," Pastor Rolle said.

"From the Glauser family, who have the dairy farm at the Chalet de la Thomassette?" her mother said.

"Yes, I'm the eldest." Under one arm, he carried *Le Mois Suisse*, a paper known for praising Hitler's crusade against Bolshevism. His eyes slid toward Hedy. "We were at primary school together. Do you remember?"

"Of course," she lied. He must have had a bad case of chicken pox as a child because his face was scarred with pockmarks. "Nice to see you again."

"Since they're the same age, I thought they should get reacquainted." Pastor Rolle smiled.

"It's very kind of you to think of Hedy," her mother said. "Franck, please come for dinner one evening."

Hedy wanted to elbow her mother to get her to retract the offer, but she felt the pastor's beady eyes on her.

"I'd like that," Franck said, tucking his hands in his pockets.

"Good. I'll stop by the dairy farm with a date once I check the calendar at home."

Franck nodded.

Hedy slipped a hand through her mother's arm. "We better get going. Goodbye."

Once outside the church, Hedy whispered, "Why did you invite him?"

"It was expected. We need to keep Pastor Rolle as a friend."

"Can't you see what he's up to?"

"Of course. But if you reject his introduction to a prospective suitor without spending an evening in Franck's company, then the pastor will think you've done it out of spite. He's a powerful man. You need to be careful."

That night, after dinner, Hedy's father, a luthier, set off to his workshop near the house. Many of the men who sang in the church choir with him also purchased his violins. Since the war hadn't slowed the demand for musical instruments, he often worked at night. Hedy washed the dishes while her mother dried them.

"When I was your age, I thought I knew everything too," her mother said.

"I never said I know everything."

"The way you act around Pastor Rolle isn't wise."

Hedy sensed she was about to receive a lecture and wondered how to get out of it.

"You should be more careful. I've told—"

A sharp knock at the door saved her. Wiping her hands on a towel, she ran to open it . It was their neighbor, Madame Jadot.

"Where's your mother?" She frowned.

"In the kitchen. Please come in."

Broad in the hips and belly, Madame Jadot wore a blue apron and wooden clogs. Hedy had to turn sideways so she could pass her in the hallway.

"Hedy has forgotten the blackout blind again!" Madame Jadot said.

"Have I?" Hedy folded a hand over her mouth and went to her room to check. Madame Jadot's clogs rapped on the floor behind her. Yes, she'd forgotten! She reached up and closed the curtain, then turned around. "I'm sorry."

"It's not the first time." Madame Jadot crossed her arms over her chest.

"Does one window in the village make all that much of a difference?" Hedy said. Her mother stood beside Madame

Jadot, silent. She wished her mother would defend her, but since she didn't, this spurred Hedy on. "I don't understand why we must black out the windows."

"General's orders." Madame Jadot shot a glance at Hedy's mother.

"But we're not at war," Hedy said.

"What about Schaffhausen?"

"That was a mistake. The paper said it was a navigator error." Hedy had read about the American plane that bombed a Swiss town on the German border last month.

"In daylight?" Madame Jadot shook her head. "Thirty of our citizens lost their lives!"

Hedy's gaze dropped. There was no point in trying to argue with Madame Jadot. Like most people, she worshipped General Guisan, the commander of the Swiss Army. They treated him like a king, his portrait hanging in most living rooms across the country, and none dared speak against him.

"I'm afraid your daughter lacks discipline." Madame Jadot's voice hardened. "I must report this infraction to the Commune. I hope you'll take this matter seriously."

"Yes, we will," her mother said. "Goodnight."

After she left, Hedy turned to her mother. "I didn't mean to cause trouble."

"Then stop this nonsense."

"What nonsense?"

"Madame Jadot, Pastor Rolle: they can make your life, our lives, difficult."

"All I did was forget to put up a blackout blind." Why did Madame Jadot and her mother make a big deal about such a little thing? "It's all nonsense. You've heard the rumor that Hitler ordered the general to black out the country so the Allied bombers can't find the Rhine border at night."

Her mother raised her hand as if to slap Hedy but stopped herself. "I suggest you learn to hold your tongue. It is foolish to repeat rumors that could cause you trouble later."

Hedy wrapped her arms around her middle. She couldn't believe her mother was acting like this. All the frustration building inside her for months suddenly gushed forth. "Why do you have to be like everyone else? *Don't say anything bad about the Germans. Be quiet. Be neutral.* If that's even what we are. *Then we'll be safe*," Hedy mimicked her mother, who regarded her impassively, making Hedy even angrier. "What if Nazi Germany wins? What will happen to all of us then?"

"They won't win. And the war won't last another year."

"That's what you said last year." Hedy's temper flushed hot in her cheeks.

"You have your whole life ahead of you."

"How can you just sit by and let it all happen? Don't you want to do something?"

Her mother drew her hands together at her chest as if to calm herself. "Once you have your degree, you won't have to stay here. You could live and teach anywhere. Your education will give you choices and make you free. You're the only one in the family to have such a chance. Don't throw it away for something you can't control and which has the power to hurt you." She took a breath. "You're smart. Act like it."

"You mean I should look after myself like the general and the politicians look after Switzerland, standing by and doing nothing while others suffer? That's not a world I want to live in, and I can't believe you think I would." She stormed to her room.

Later in bed, Hedy couldn't stop thinking about how Pastor Rolle and Madame Jadot were always watching and judging her. Why couldn't she be left alone to think and act as she felt was right? Maybe it was because she lived in a small town.

She felt freer in Lausanne, where she attended classes. There, no one watched her; people were busy with their own lives.

And yet she regretted arguing with her mother. It wasn't fair to expect her parents to understand. They'd never gone to university, never had the chance to study the way she did. Their lives were narrow and confined to this small town, which they rarely left. Almost every day, Hedy went to Lausanne, which had a synagogue and a thriving Jewish community. Many of her classmates were Jewish, and she sometimes talked with them about the war. She could see that they tried to hide their frustration at the few Jewish refugees allowed into Switzerland. She sensed their desperation, overhearing some say neutrality was a policy that benefitted the tyrant, not the oppressed.

Hedy was exposed to more ideas and people than her parents, yet they'd always loved and supported her. Without them, she might never have made it to university. She knew they were good and regretted the mean words she'd hurled at her mother. Unable to sleep until she made amends, she got up and tiptoed down the hall.

"Maman," she whispered outside her parents' bedroom, trying not to wake her father. Her mother was a light sleeper and, like Hedy, was probably mulling over their argument. "I'm sorry I yelled at you."

Hedy stood still, waiting.

"Maman, are you awake?"

The door was open. As her eyes adjusted to the darkness, she saw the bed was empty. Her mother must be in the workshop with her father. She kept his books and ordered supplies. Hedy went to the front door and opened it. Cold air streamed inside. The night was dark, without a sliver of moon. Though the workshop was a short walk downhill, she would need a candle because the village was cloaked in blackout blinds. She wanted to apologize and tell her parents she'd been wrong, but she feared a light would draw Madam Jadot's scrutiny and only make matters worse. Deciding she would say sorry in the morning, she closed the door.

Back in her room, Hedy settled into bed. Again, she couldn't sleep. There was one Jewish classmate, Joseph, whom she'd seen raising money to help Jewish refugees escape Europe. She figured he likely worked with those admitted into the country. Maybe Hedy could work with them, too. Doing so would help calm the voice deep inside that made her uneasy about the constant stream of pro-German articles she read in the newspapers, the enforced darkness at night meant to confuse the Allied bombers, and her mother's overreaction to Madame Jadot.

No one spoke about what would happen if the Germans won the war. She couldn't understand why everyone wasn't volunteering to support an Allied victory. Wasn't their cause worthy enough for her country to fight? She would talk to Joseph, find out what the refugees needed and what she could do to help. She was tired of observing and complaining. She needed to act and make a difference, and the prospect that she would filled her with excitement and hope.

Hedy closed her eyes. She felt lighter, as though a weight had been lifted from her chest, and she knew what it was—the weight of neutrality.

3

Samuel

Harrington Airfield, United Kingdom
May 1944

Second Lieutenant Samuel Reardon checked his watch: 2200. The three-room Nissen hut reeked of cigarettes and sweat. He and the navigator, Lieutenant Thomas Roy, reviewed tonight's flight plan. They were the only two among the B-24's six-man crew who knew where the plane would fly tonight.

"We cross the French coast at an altitude of 4,000 feet to stay above possible machine gun fire at Calais," Roy said, pointing at the map. "South of Lille, we'll descend to 600 feet and track along the Somme River into Reims, zigzagging our way around the flak." He'd drawn boxes indicating known German guns. "Then on to Dijon and the target." He tapped a pencil on the table. "Tailwinds should get us back early, by 0530."

"I like the sound of that." Samuel removed his cap and ran a hand through his hair. Though only twenty-two, the war had a way of accelerating time, turning one year into ten, so he was considered old among the crew. Maybe that's why he was losing his hair, finding pale chunks on the pillow and around the drain. He thought it might be the food—it was hard for a farm boy from Wichita to get used to powdered eggs. His mother always said the good Kansas air and sun kept his hair the color of summer wheat.

In England, there wasn't much sun. As Samuel flew at night and slept during the day, he wouldn't see it anyway. Over these last weeks, before going on a mission, he'd remove his cap and run his hands through his hair like his mother did when he was a boy. He did it for good luck. It was silly. But this was his twentieth mission, and he didn't want his luck running out so close to reaching the magic twenty-five missions, which would allow him to go home.

He went to the room where Sergeant Banks, the dispatcher, helped a Joe into a green-and-brown mottled jumpsuit.

"I'm the one who will tell you how to jump and when," Banks said in his slow southern drawl. "This will be my fifteenth trip over yonder, which means I'm halfway home to Georgia." He saluted Samuel. "Isn't that right, Second Lieutenant?"

"That's right."

Banks had been a part of Samuel's crew when he commanded an antisubmarine plane in the Bay of Biscay. Then they'd been dropping munitions on Boche subs. Now, they dropped agents, radios and guns into enemy territory to strengthen the Resistance before the big offensive everyone sensed was coming.

The Joe, who went by the code name Odeon, looked like an underwater diver in his jumpsuit. Banks adjusted the straps on the parachute before testing the release mechanism. He patted Odeon on the back.

"This chute is the best one we have. Made of silk. Opens quick and easy."

"You'll be hearing from me if it doesn't." The Frenchman laughed.

It was good that he was joking. Samuel knew from experience that the quiet Joes held their fear tight inside. Fear wasn't a friend. It could freeze their legs up when the green light flashed, and the Joes had to swing into the jump hole.

"I'm the pilot," Samuel said to Odeon. Not all the pilots bothered to introduce themselves, but Samuel knew that the Joes were facing the greatest risk of all the people on the plane tonight. He wanted to recognize them and let them know someone cared. "Once you get on the ground, tell your reception committee we'll make two more runs to drop the packages. The first will come about eight minutes after you're in. If it's safe, we'll circle back and make another."

Odeon gave him the thumbs-up. Samuel went to the next room, where Captain Grenell issued orders to a young American agent code-named Rabbit. The agent seemed like he should be in high school playing football rather than dropping into enemy territory.

"Carry these crystals for the radio set in front of your jumpsuit," Grenell said, reaching into his pocket and pulling out packets of blue and white capsules. "The blue ones are Benzedrine Sulfate to overcome fatigue. The white ones are knock-out drops that will make you unconscious for six hours. They're both useful. Just don't get them mixed up. White like a pillow to sleep, OK?"

Rabbit nodded. "Got it."

Samuel wanted to warn him to stay away from the blue ones because he'd seen plenty of men get hooked on them. But Grenell was filling the kid with so much information he didn't want to add to it.

He checked his watch: 2215. "Let's go."

Outside, the full moon's gray light splintered the darkness. The agents moved awkwardly in their bulky jumpsuits and parachutes. In the distance, the engines whirled from the many B-24s starting up on the airfield. Colonel Fiske, the commanding officer of the Carpetbagger Squadron, had briefed forty pilots for tonight's missions. Each plane would fly alone without fighter protection to a different enemy target on the continent.

A car brought them to the hardstand where the *Silver Wolf* waited. Lieutenant Nicoll, the copilot, had already taken his seat on the flight deck. Samuel made his way to the plane's front and touched the thick black paint on the side of the nose that hid a prancing gray wolf in a tux holding a champagne coupe in one hand and a cigar in the other. He did it before every flight for good luck.

Banks stepped forward and pointed to the bomb bay. "We're loaded to the ears, sir. Twelve containers to get rid of after we drop the Joes."

Samuel hoped he could make the drops in two rounds because a third one would increase the chance of alerting German radar.

Rabbit and Odeon shook hands with Grenell, then clambered into the plane through the hole in the bottom of the fuselage. The same hole through which, roughly three hours later, they would jump into the darkness over France.

Samuel glanced at his watch. It was 2220. He told Grenell he'd see him back here for breakfast and climbed into the flight deck.

A soft red light glowed inside. The first time he flew a B-24 solo, he feared he wouldn't be strong enough to get her off the ground. With four powerful engines, no pressurization, open windows in the belly for the gunners and the cold night air streaming in, it had been like a shot of adrenaline straight to his heart.

"Good evening, Lieutenant Nicoll," he said.

"Welcome aboard, sir." Nicoll saluted.

Samuel sat on his parachute—there was no place to put it in the cramped flight deck, and the silk cushioned the cast-iron seat—removed his cap, crushed it in his pocket, and then put on a helmet with earphones and mike attached.

"Engines good?" he asked.

"All running smoothly, sir," Nicoll replied.

The navigator settled into the seat just outside the flight deck. Samuel swiftly went through the checklist. Then, the flare went up on the runway, and he lined the *Silver Wolf* up to the taxi strip. Setting the brakes, he pushed the throttle to get the engines running at maximum. He loved this part—the rattle of every nut and bolt, rivet and tube as he released the brakes and rolled down the strip, picking up speed.

"Flaps at twenty degrees," he instructed Nicoll.

At the end of the runway, Samuel pulled the nose up. The B-24 resisted, as it always did. *Come on, old wolf. Folks are waiting for us.* He cleared the tree line. Nicoll raised the landing gear and brought up the flaps.

Samuel's ears popped. The mandatory radio silence during take off remained in force until the plane was over the Channel. Roy took their position every five minutes to confirm they were on course. As they reached open water, the sky clouded over. Cruising at an altitude of 4,000 feet, Samuel looked through the blister in his side window but couldn't see much. He squeezed the wheel, took a deep breath, and kept an eye out for German bandits sweeping through the clouds.

After crossing into France, the fog lifted. To avoid artillery guns, he dropped down to 600 feet. He could see the Somme River winding like a ribbon below. Even if the searchlights shone on the B-24, the black camouflage paint and red flight deck lighting made it impossible to spot at night.

"Turn five degrees west," Roy called on the radio as he guided Samuel in the first of many zigzag maneuvers to avoid German guns on the ground.

"Ten minutes to target, Bobsled," Roy announced on the intercom.

Samuel reduced the flying speed from 300 to 130 miles per hour—the slowest the plane could go before stalling. He had to hold it like that to prevent the parachutes from getting pulled into the plane's draft.

"Banks, how are the Joes?" Samuel asked on the interphone.

"Good, sir. They've got butterflies in their bellies, but I told them I get 'em too every time I jump."

"Lights blinking over the target. Action stations," Roy said on the intercom.

Five seconds to reach the drop zone; time for the Joes to swing their legs into the hole.

The light flashed green. "GO," Roy shouted.

Samuel held his breath and waited. The world went quiet. Even the propellers seemed to still for a few seconds before Banks returned to the intercom. "Two chutes opened. All good."

Samuel exhaled. No word he knew could express the enormous relief he felt that the two men under his watch, especially the kid just starting out, had made it through this first stage of their mission. He banked to the left to come back around and drop the packages.

"Smooth as silk. Looks like we might be on a milk run," Nicoll said.

In a few hours, they'd be back at Harrington having breakfast with Grenell to debrief him on the mission.

"Sir, lights out; the reception committee's signal is gone." Roy's voice rang with panic.

The mood in the flight deck shifted.

"What's the wind speed? If they're using torches, they might have been blown out."

"No significant wind, sir," Roy replied.

Thirty seconds away from the drop zone, Samuel followed procedure. "Abort the drop. Set the course—"

Flak shattered the cockpit window. Short breaths. Dense cold air in his lungs. Blood spattered on the wheel and his gloves. Was it his blood?

Nicoll fell forward against the instrument panel.

"Nicoll, you OK? Hang on, buddy, we're gonna—"

The plane jerked and mushed down. Samuel tightened his hands on the wheel, pulled up and righted the nose.

"Flak hit number-three engine," Banks shouted on the intercom.

On Samuel's left, the engine threw oil and smoked badly. He could see it was losing oil pressure fast at the controls, but it was too late to feather the propeller. The engine became a windmill, reducing the plane's power to little more than one engine. A single thought in his head: could they get back over the Channel with only one engine?

"Drop all the containers," Samuel ordered. The plane vibrated fiercely. "Anything loose goes. Lighten the load."

"Losing altitude," Roy barked.

Samuel's stomach lurched. A rush of yellow flashed at the corner of his eye. Number-three engine burst into flames. He would have tried to put it out with a rapid descent if he had more altitude, but he was too low.

"Mayday! Mayday!" He choked on the burning fuel and smoke. "Deploy destructors." He breathed hard and loud. "Bail out and good luck. I'm turning toward Switzerland."

4

Hedy

Lausanne
May 1944

After class, Hedy told Joseph she would like to talk with him. He suggested they meet the next day at the cathedral in La Cité—the medieval part of town that overlooked Lausanne.

As she waited for him, her eyes adjusted to the shimmering light on the rooftops and the sparkling blue waters of the lake beyond. It was a beautiful day, and people came to La Cité to enjoy the view. She knew her mother would disapprove of her meeting a man alone, even a classmate, in a public place, but Hedy had no intention of telling her mother.

"I'm here," Joseph said breathlessly, cheeks bright red and his forehead beaded with sweat. "Sorry I'm late . . . ran up the Escaliers du Marché."

There were hundreds of steps in the Escaliers du Marché—the wooden covered staircase that started at Place de la Palud in the center of town and curled up to La Cité.

"Come out of the sun," Hedy said, guiding him into the shade cast by the giant leaves of a horse chestnut.

Pinkish-white flowers grew upright and glistened like candles on the tree's branches, their tangy, woodsy odor cutting through the air.

"I got delayed at the refugee camp," he said, hands on hips, catching his breath. "I was trying to calm a frantic mother who didn't want her son taken away."

She lifted a shoulder slightly. "Taken where?"

"All refugee children, at six, are transferred out of the camps. It's for their benefit." His dark, solemn eyes fixed on her. "If you saw a camp, you'd understand."

She had seen one, but on the outside. Every day on the train, she passed a camp in Cossonay, its rooftop visible over a tall wooden fence, but she'd never thought about what life was like for the families inside. All she knew was what she'd read in the paper—how the camps had been set up two years ago after the border was overrun by Jewish refugees. Initially, the government had refused to let them in. But seeing the desperate state of the refugees, Swiss citizens took to the streets to protest, insisting the government help them.

A compromise was reached. Women and children under six were granted temporary asylum, but men would need a visa, which was nearly impossible to obtain. The government argued the men would work for low wages and mass unemployment would follow if they were allowed in. At the time, it seemed the government had made the right choice. "Tell me more about the refugee camps."

"They're military work camps," Joseph said, wiping the sweat from his brow. "Barracks with beds on straw."

"To house women and children? What about schools and playgrounds?"

"There's nothing like that, which is why the children are transferred to group homes or families."

"Surely a mother can go with her child?"

"The government insists the women pay for the cost of the camps, so they must stay and work. People say the army makes a nice profit from their labor."

Despite the warm spring day, Hedy shivered, thinking about how much the refugees had already lost on their way to the Swiss border. It was too cruel to take away their children, too. And yet, weren't they the lucky ones? To be given a place of shelter, even at a work camp, was to be saved. Hedy hated war. It shattered all that was good in people and brought out only the bad. She felt a ball of anger rolling up from her belly to the base of her throat. She couldn't believe her government separated mothers and children to profit off the former's labor. But hadn't she been here when all this was decided? She never spoke up but yelled at her mother for not doing anything. It wasn't enough to wish the war would end; she should do more, like Joseph.

"I'd like to help refugees. That's why I wanted to speak with you today." She knitted her fingers and held them close to her chest.

Tipping his head sideways, Joseph glanced around. "Let's walk."

Leaving the shade, gravel crunching underfoot, they elbowed through the crowd to reach the far side of the cathedral. When they arrived at the southern nave's stone wall, adorned with a stained glass window in the shape of a rose, they could go no farther.

"There are other camps," he said, turning to her.

"I don't mind traveling." She expected Lausanne with its large Jewish community had enough volunteers, but other towns might need assistance with their refugees.

"Not refugee camps." He snapped her a fierce look. "Prisoner-of-war camps holding American and British airmen."

She blinked. "I don't—"

"Allied bombers whose planes have been hit. Unable to return to England, they make emergency landings here." He drew a breath. "Or they've mistakenly entered Swiss airspace, and our army has shot them down."

The blackout curtains flashed in Hedy's mind. Maybe the rumor that Hitler had asked the general to adopt the policy to confuse the Allied pilots was true. Her stomach clenched at the possibility that it was more than that. Was her country, by shooting these Allied planes down, conspiring with the Germans? "I didn't know. Where are these camps?"

"In mountain towns—Wengen, Adelboden, Davos. The more remote, the more problematic for the pilots to escape."

"They're escaping?"

"They're trying. I belong to a network that helps them." His eyes narrowed on her. "We need more individuals to join us."

She stepped back and turned away from him, fear clawing at her stomach. She craned to get a better view of the lake. The color of the water shifted, a pale green near the shore and a deep blue farther out. White waves crested the surface. She remembered the day her father tried to teach her to swim when she was seven. She'd followed him into the Lac de Joux near her house, but her limbs turned to stone once the waves bounced about her chin. He urged her on, encouraging her to be brave, but fearing she'd be swallowed by the unseen darkness below, she froze. Stuck, she was unable to move, and her father had to carry her out of the lake. Hedy never went in again, and the experience had left her feeling ashamed and empty, as if she was nothing. She'd let her father and herself down.

"Every day a crew remains in a camp is a lost day," Joseph said, his voice taut and sharp like a train's whistle drawing close. "It's urgent that the Allies continue bombing Germany to bring the war to an end."

She turned back to face him. "I want to help the women and children, the refugees."

"The best way to help them is to free the pilots."

She shook her head, and the exact words she'd told her father as he carried her out of the water came forth. "I can't."

"We need people like you."

There were others he could ask. Men. They knew how to do such things. Why her? Then, the answer clicked in her mind. "It's because I speak English, isn't it?"

"That's part of it. And as a woman, no one will think—"

"I've got the nerve to smuggle pilots?"

He smiled. "Correct."

She wanted to tell him she *didn't* have the nerve, just like she was unable to conquer her terror of the water all those years ago. But a faint voice in her mind said she was no longer a child.

"I'd considered seeking your help before," he said, "but to protect the network we must be careful about who we approach. Yesterday, when you asked to meet, I knew my instinct had been right and you were one of us."

Did Joseph see something in her, like her father had, that she couldn't see in herself? His belief that she could do it, that she wouldn't freeze and fail, intrigued her. "What's involved?"

"The pilots must navigate through our cities. You would act as a guide to get them from one point to another."

"And if caught, the consequences would be—"

"Severe."

Her family would be disgraced. The village would turn against her mother and father. Hedy's body angled away from Joseph and back toward the lake. The wind picked up; the waves became stronger. An uneasy silence settled between them.

"If you prefer not to get involved," he said, his voice clipped. "Maybe I've misjudged you."

"Are you sure there isn't something I could do for the refugees?" She wanted a way out and hoped he would give her one.

"Your skills are needed to assist the pilots. You'd be making a huge difference."

She *wanted* to make a difference. The possibility that she could made her heart beat a little faster. Reading between the lines in the paper, she sensed the Allies were gaining strength, but it had taken Hitler ten years to conquer Europe—what if it took the Allies as long to defeat him? How could she live with herself if the war lasted another five or eight years and she hadn't taken this opportunity to right the balance in the Allies' favor? But what if she failed like she had that day in the lake? Was she strong enough to overcome her fear to help someone else? White waves rippled over the surface of the lake. A few boats launched their sails into the wind.

Here was her dilemma: to join the network could possibly put her parents in danger because, if caught, society would shun them. No one would buy her father's violins, and they would struggle to survive. But to not help the pilots would conflict with the compassionate person she aimed to be. And because her country had been indifferent to the innocent victims of this terrible war, even profiting from their labor, she felt an extra duty to act. Could she try with one pilot? Just one. If she succeeded, she would continue. If she found it beyond her, she would stop.

Hedy angled back to Joseph. "Tell me again, what's involved?"

"The pilots don't speak French. They're often caught by the police in train stations when they're stopped and can't respond without giving themselves away. We need people who can escort them from the station in Lausanne or Vevey to certain places along the lake where boats wait. Your job would be to get them safely to the boat. Then they will row on their own to cross the lake and reach the Free French side, where a Maquis network helps them return to England. I've done it a few times. It's not complicated." He looked intently at her. "But you must be brave and a quick thinker."

Hedy pinched the bridge of her nose. She wanted to be brave, to prove to herself that she was no longer a child, that she could make a difference, maybe even help turn the tide in the Allies' favor. Then her mother's words came to her. *Don't say foolish things that will cause you trouble later. The war is almost over.* Her mother would never forgive her for doing this. But Hedy couldn't go on complaining about others while not doing anything herself. Until now, she hadn't had a chance. If she was careful, she wouldn't be caught, and her parents would never find out.

"I'll do it," she blurted out, hardly recognizing her voice.

Joseph smiled. "Somebody will contact you. A meeting will be arranged. It will likely be at night, so you'll need an excuse ready for your parents. To protect the network, you'll rarely meet the same person twice. They're good people who you can trust with your life."

"All right." Her voice shook a little.

He stepped away from the nave and glanced up at the wall. "The rose window is remarkable. Do you know it?"

She shook her head, stepped back and regarded the window. Although she must have seen it a hundred times, she'd never given it or the church a second thought, not after listening to all those disappointing sermons by Pastor Rolle.

"After Notre Dame in Paris, this is one of the finest examples of medieval stained glass in the world," Joseph said. "It represents the Imago Mundi or Image of the World. All inside the circle is human action in time and space. It may surprise you to know that a Jew can be enamored with Christian iconology, but I am. I look at this, and it gives me hope."

The glass was dull gray to Hedy, like street gutters washed out by rain. Maybe inside the nave, the light reflected through the glass and brought the colors to life, but not from where she stood on the outside. "I don't see hope," she said.

Joseph pointed at the window. "The circle. No beginning or end, it's an ancient symbol of truth like a compass reminding us that even the darkest human experiences can be overcome by doing what is true and right." He tilted his head. "People like you give me hope."

A moment of easy silence fell between them.

"I won't lie and tell you everything will go smoothly," he said. "Just be strong and remember the circle, and you'll find your way through."

5

Samuel

Switzerland
May 1944

A tar-like blackness carpeted the ground, making it hard for Samuel to tell if he'd already crossed the border into Switzerland. In his mouth, an acrid taste swirled. The reek of fuel leaking from the plane's left wing tank and flames sputtering off the engine on the right wing warned he was running out of time. Once the fuel vapors hit the fire, the plane would explode.

All the crew had bailed, and he would have joined them if not for Nicoll slumped forward in his seat, flight suit splattered with blood. Samuel tried to hold the wheel with one hand long enough to reach over and check if Nicoll had a pulse, but the plane heaved and slowed to the point of nearly stalling, and he was forced to bring his hand back to steady it. His copilot hadn't said a word or made any movement, but if there was a chance he was still alive, it was Samuel's duty to get him to safety.

Clouds covered the full moon, but enough light radiated to spot what appeared to be a strip of level ground ahead.

Samuel's throat thickened with the possibility of all that could go wrong. One mistake, and he'd smash the plane into a mountain or forest. But staying in the air—with the number-three engine on fire—wasn't an option. He reached for the lever to lower the landing gear. Hesitation. A single spark from dropping the wheels and *boom*. Flames hot, smoke dense, Samuel blazing like a log in a fire. He was running out of time. His gloved finger gripped the lever and struck it down like a match.

Ka-thud. The ship hit the ground hard. The impact hammered Samuel's skull. He banked too far to the left and gripped the wheel to prevent the plane from flipping. Pumping the brakes, he brought it to a rattling, rolling stop. His hand punched through the windshield, already shattered by flak. He maneuvered Nicoll on his back and jumped to the ground. Ignoring the burning in his right ankle, he dragged his copilot away from the plane.

Sweat rolled down his face. He removed his gloves and felt Nicoll's neck for a pulse. None. The moment he closed Nicoll's eyes, the plane exploded.

Samuel watched the flames, his face and hands burning from the heat and crack of the fire.

Something hard jabbed at his back.

"*Levez-vous*," a voice commanded.

Where the hell was he—still in France? Raising his arms, he stood and turned, shifting his weight onto his good ankle.

A soldier in a gray uniform pointed a Tommy gun at Samuel's chest. Something moved at his side. An Alsatian dog lunged. Shrill barking pierced his ears. Luckily, the animal was on a lead and was pulled back. The soldier stepped forward, and in the light of the flames, Samuel recognized the patch sewn on his uniform: a red square with a white cross in the middle. Switzerland. He felt a surge of relief and lowered his arms.

The soldier poked the gun at his chest. "*Les mains en l'air!*"

"I'm an American," Samuel shouted.

A glint, like steel, in the soldier's eyes. "*Les mains en l'air!*" he repeated.

Samuel did as he was told. The soldier searched him and confiscated his compass, map and the small knife in his boot.

"*Pour vous, la guerre est finie*," the soldier said.

Samuel didn't understand, but it felt like he'd gone from one fire into another.

He was brought to a building about a thirty-minute drive away and placed in a room with two military officers who spoke fluent English. He requested to see a doctor for his throbbing ankle. None came. But there were plenty of questions.

"Squadron name and unit number?"

"What type of plane do you fly?"

"How many crew? What happened to them?"

"Was your target in France or Germany?"

"Is this the first time you've flown into Swiss airspace?"

He provided the same answer each time. "Samuel Reardon. Second Lieutenant. Serial number T7125984."

He was confident he would be released. An American army pilot couldn't be kept as a prisoner of war in a neutral country. But as the hours wore on, doubt began to grow. It worried him that they'd confiscated the crucial items he would need to find his way back to England. And they didn't seem to care that he was injured. He'd told them he was hungry and was given a glass of water. The longer he sat alone in that cold, sterile room, it dawned on him that maybe it had been a mistake not to bail out with the rest of the crew. He imagined the crew had all landed safely and were being helped by the French Resistance. Something didn't feel right here. He resolved that no matter what happened, he would ensure Nicoll got a proper burial.

He must have fallen asleep because he awakened to the squeak of the door. Rays of light shone in from the window.

It struck him that if everything had gone to plan, he'd be eating breakfast with Grenell now.

A middle-aged man dressed in civilian clothes and small-rimmed glasses entered. He placed a leather briefcase on the table.

"My name is Monsieur Jenzer. I'm sorry to wake you," he said slowly, as though to be sure Samuel would understand. "Would you like a coffee?"

"Sure would." Samuel rubbed his eyes.

The door was left open, and Jenzer spoke French to the soldier outside.

"Are you the doctor? My ankle's bad."

"I wasn't informed that you required medical attention." His glasses slid down his nose as he wrote something in a notebook. "I'll make sure a doctor is called. I'm from the Swiss Red Cross." He sat down. "Would you like to send a telegram to your family notifying them that you're interned in Switzerland and safe?"

Samuel sat upright. Why hadn't Colonel Fiske warned the pilots and crew about internment in a neutral country? Maybe he didn't know. Or perhaps he did, and it was still better to be interned in Switzerland than taken prisoner in Germany or France. "How does it work—being interned in a country that isn't at war?"

The man pushed his glasses up. "The Hague Convention grants a neutral power the right to intern troops belonging to belligerent armies who arrive on their territory."

A nutty odor wafted in the room. He turned his attention to the door. A soldier brought a tray with coffee. Samuel's mouth watered. It had been fifteen hours since he'd had anything other than water.

"*Merci*," he mumbled. It was the only French he knew. He added sugar and milk to the coffee to ease his growling stomach.

"How long will I be here?" he asked.

Jenzer gave a tight smile. "Until the end of hostilities."

His mind spun. That could be a year, maybe longer. What the hell would he do here? Colonel Fiske and the Carpetbaggers needed him. So many hours of training had gone into him being able to do his job. If he belonged anywhere, it was with the squadron.

He wrote the name and address of his mother in Wichita. "I would like to speak with the American military attaché."

Jenzer nodded. "You'll be quarantined for two weeks before being sent to a military camp for officers. The American Legation has already been informed of your arrival and the hotel where you will be quarantined. They'll come and see you there."

"What about my copilot? Who's taking care of him?"

His glasses again slid down his nose. He looked out over the lenses. "The body was transferred to the American Legation for burial."

Samuel looked at the pines outside the window. He seemed to be on the edge of a forest. He thought about the rest of the crew. There was no knowing what had happened to them. Though things hadn't turned out as he expected, he was alive. Beyond the trees stood a jagged mountain range; one rose above the others, its snow-capped peak shimmering in the morning light like an arrow tip. Something about that majestic peak gave him hope. Maybe because it resembled the Indian arrow tips he often found as a boy at home. If he could get a postcard of that mountain, he would send it to his mother and let her know he was safe. He was lucky to be able to think of such things. Maybe the men he'd been flying with just a few hours ago had been less fortunate, like Nicoll. He wouldn't let the luck that had brought him here go to waste.

One week later, there was a knock on the door of Samuel's room at the Auberge de Guillaume Tell. He figured it was the waiter bringing lunch. On crutches and unable to carry a tray, he shouted for the man to open the door.

A man in civilian dress entered. "How's the ankle? I heard you jumped through the windshield!"

Samuel grinned. He sure was happy to see another American. "It's getting better. Just a sprain. Who are you?"

"I'm Lieutenant Jones from the American Legation in Bern." He held out his hand and shook Samuel's. "Sorry it took time to get to you, but we've had pilots landing daily this week, mostly in the east along the German border." Jones was tall and lanky. Samuel wondered why a lieutenant was permitted to dress in civilian clothes. "You're the only one who came into Geneva from the French side. What happened to the rest of your crew, besides the copilot, who didn't make it?"

"They bailed out while we were still over France."

"Not you?"

"I couldn't abandon Nicoll—in case he survived an earlier hit by flak. What's happened to him?"

"He was buried in an American cemetery outside of Bern."

Samuel exhaled. It wasn't right that Nicoll had been put to rest by strangers without a single person who knew him present. He should have been there. But he held his tongue. No point in arguing over something that couldn't be undone. "How did you get here?"

"I was shot down by the Swiss in '43."

"Shot down?"

"My landing gear jammed. I couldn't lower it. The number-two engine was smoking, but the Swiss military thought I was ignoring their request to land, so they made sure I did." He laughed. "It's what they call armed neutrality. You'll find out all about it."

"Doesn't sound very neutral to me. Have they shot any Boche down?"

"Once. German retaliation was swift and savage. Never tried it again."

Samuel wanted to ask why the Allies wouldn't do the same, but his experience of the military was that questions were rarely welcomed. "Then you joined the Legation?"

"General Legge needed help with all our pilots diverting to Switzerland." Jones threw a stack of *Life* magazines and a pack of cards on the table next to Samuel's bed. "Something to keep you busy."

"That's swell, thanks." Samuel wasn't allowed to leave his room. All he had to keep him occupied was a Swiss radio and watching the world through the window. "Where you from?"

"Florida panhandle. Flat as a pancake. I never saw mountains until I came here." He moved the towels from the chair to the floor, sat down and opened a file. "Wichita is flat too, ain't it?"

Samuel nodded. "This place sure is different." He couldn't get used to how unfriendly everyone appeared. Living around jagged peaks seemed to carve a stone heartedness into them. "What happens now?"

"At the end of next week, your quarantine will be over. Swiss soldiers will escort you by train to Davos, a mountain village in the far east of the country. Once you've settled in, either General Legge or I will come to see you to assess the situation. Don't be surprised at the sound of bombs dropping. Davos is only a few hours from Munich. It will take a while to get used to the hotel rattling."

"I didn't realize I'd be so cozy with the enemy."

"We're in the center of Europe, so it's hard to avoid them. You'll receive fifteen francs every ten days. Twice a day, the guards permit internees to walk through the town to drink in a café or buy something in the local tourist shops. There's a nightly curfew at 2200 hours on weekdays and 2230 on Saturday nights. Failure to comply with the curfew or any other rules will result in punishment." He looked at Samuel directly. "General Legge expects all rules to be obeyed, including the mandatory rendering of salutes to Swiss officers."

Samuel frowned. He didn't try to mask his dismay. "I'm not planning on staying, just so you know. I've got to get back to my squadron."

Jones recoiled, clearly not liking what Samuel had said. "On the orders of General Legge, there will be no escape attempts. Anyone caught escaping will be punished by the Swiss authorities. We will not intervene."

"I'm in the 801st Bomb Group. They need all the pilots they can get. We're on special missions. Tell General Legge to call Colonel Fiske in Harrington, England. He'll explain to the general what we've been doing, how few pilots can fly the B-24 so low and slow like I've been trained to do."

"We all think we're irreplaceable," Jones said, laughing. "But in war, everyone is expendable." He stood. "General Legge has stipulated that any internee who attempts to escape will not only be punished by the Swiss authorities but will also be court-martialed by the United States Army and receive a dishonorable discharge. I hope I've made myself clear?"

"Crystal." Samuel could have added more, but he'd said too much already. He couldn't go anywhere with a bad ankle for a few weeks. In Davos, he'd discuss the situation with General Legge. Once the general understood the mission of the 801st, Samuel was confident he'd help him return to England.

6

Hedy

Switzerland
June 1944

The week after meeting Joseph, Hedy rode the train home from class. She was deeply engrossed in her homework, translating the opening poem in T.S. Eliot's new book, *Four Quartets*, into French. The sharp and bony lines didn't seem to fit together. Concentrating hard to get their meaning, she barely noticed what was happening around her.

At some point, the woman sitting beside her must have pulled the rope to request a stop. After she disembarked and the train thrust forward, Hedy noticed a brown leather book left on the seat. She took it, intending to give it to the conductor, but then her gaze fell on a slip of paper sticking up from the pages with her name written on it in tight black letters. The woman hadn't forgotten the book but had left it intentionally for Hedy to find. Joseph said somebody would contact her. Was this how the network—?

"*Mademoiselle*," a man's voice.

She jumped and turned to find the conductor staring down at her.

"*Billet, s'il vous plaît.*"

Hedy put the book down, reached into her bag for the rectangular yellow ticket and handed it to him to clip.

"*Merci, Mademoiselle,*" he said, moving past her down the aisle.

She let out a breath and glanced around the half-empty carriage, but none of the passengers seemed to pay attention to her. She tilted forward, opened the book and read the three lines below her name.

Tomorrow.

10:00 p.m.

Vevey train station.

She snapped the book shut and looked out the window. Her mouth went dry with the weight of what she was embarking on. It was one thing to tell Joseph she would help but another to take the first step. Now, the moment was upon her. She could no longer waver between protecting her parents and the duty she felt to counter her country's apathy. An airman needed help. Luckily, she'd heeded Joseph's advice and taken precautions to prepare her parents in advance, telling them that Mrs. Amacher, a university lecturer, had asked Hedy to assist at an upcoming morning seminar. Since the trains didn't run that early from Le Brassus, Mrs. Amacher had suggested she register to use one of the student dorm rooms. Initially hesitant, her parents eventually agreed, understanding the importance of Hedy's studies. Since she'd already seeded in their minds that she would be away for a night, she would tell them the seminar would occur on the day after tomorrow.

She slipped the paper back into the book. Outside, the world rushed by in brown, green, and blue hues. She would have to find a way to unwind the coiled fear that tightened her chest.

The next night, Hedy stepped off the train at Vevey station. The platform was dark except for a dim light overhead. She took the stairs up to the ticket counter and the main hall, then glanced at the clock above the front doors: 9:55 p.m.

She had timed her arrival well. But what to do now? All the passengers on her train wended their way to the station's front doors or down to other tracks. No one stood in the hall except her. The man behind the ticket counter cut her a cold stare. Was it odd for a woman to be alone at night, or did it feel that way because the Vevey station was sparser and smaller than the one in Lausanne? A row of windows, covered in blackout curtains, faced the street. She craned to see the front double doors, confident that someone would walk through them at any moment and she would know it was her contact. Instead, all she glimpsed was her reflection in the glass panes that had no blackout blinds.

A man, his features obscured by the wide brim of his hat, passed in front of her. He must have come up from the tracks below because she hadn't seen him enter through the front door. He carried a book under his arm. Recalling the book left on the train, she decided to follow him. Her flat heels clicked across the tiles. She worried the man at the ticket counter would notice, and the old urge to be still crept over her. *Keep moving*, she whispered, pushing herself forward. She would feel better outside and away from the man's watchful gaze.

It had rained earlier, and the smell of asphalt mixed with gas fumes hit her as she stepped onto the street. The man with the book under one arm crouched on the sidewalk to tie his shoe. He stood, raising his body slowly. Hedy read it as a signal and followed him across the street to a parked car. He opened the back door. She held her breath and got in.

He sat up front. There was no introduction or confirmation that she was correct to follow. A red flash and a sulfur smell inside the car as he lit a match.

"At 10:15, a train will arrive," he said. "You'll be waiting on platform number three, a white coat on your arm."

She could see only the rough line of his chin and jaw illuminated by the red glow of a burning cigarette.

"Once all the passengers disembark, turn and walk up the stairs to the main hall and out to the car, as we did just now. Not too fast. Not too slow. The airman will know to follow the white coat. Then you both get in the back seat." As the man inhaled, the red glow expanded. The burning odor of tobacco spiked her nose. "Repeat it back to me," he said sharply.

"Train arrives at 10:15. I'm on platform three with a white coat on my arm. Once the passengers disembark, I walk up the stairs. He will follow, and we both get in the car."

"Correct." The man shot pale gray smoke rings in the air. "Without letting on that you're doing it, if you see what I mean."

"But I don't have a white coat."

"We will give you one."

"What happens once we're in the car?"

"One step at a time." He checked his watch. "Come." He got out, opened the trunk, and lifted a white coat from inside, which he draped over her arm. "Good luck."

Simple. Go in the station and come back out with the airman. That was all. But Hedy's heart was hammering, and she felt a rush of dread as if the waves of the lake were striking her shoulders. Fighting through it, she shifted her thoughts away from all that might go wrong. When she crossed the street, her limbs started to wobble like an unsteady fledgling peeking over the rim of a nest to the ground below. She might drop the coat or stumble and fall. Then she'd draw the attention of the man at the ticket counter. *Be calm*, she willed. A line from Eliot's poem came to her: *at the still point of the turning world.* She didn't know what it meant, but she liked how the words sounded one after the other, and she found that by repeating them, she could quell the trembling in her legs and the thrashing of her heart long enough to make her way up the stairs to the station, across the hall and down to platform three.

The 10:15 train was on time, rushing into the station with a gust of warm air that lifted the ends of the coat from her arm. A family of four, an older couple and a man stepped off the train onto the platform. Hedy guessed the short man, wearing a hat low on his forehead, was her pilot. She didn't dare make eye contact with him but held the coat out a little from her body to make sure he would see it before turning to the stairs. Not too fast. Not too slow. Once she reached the hall above, she caught her reflection and the man with the hat behind her, in the front door's glass panes and let out a breath.

The station's front doors suddenly opened, and a girl and a man rushed in. Smiling and laughing, they ran past Hedy to the family who had been on the platform a moment ago and was now behind her. After the doors swung shut, Hedy saw only herself reflected in the glass. She blinked. Where was the pilot?

She couldn't have lost him. It hadn't even been a minute. She stopped to look down at her bag and adjust the coat while angling her body to get a clear view of the hall. She spotted the family hovering at the front door and the older couple at the ticket counter. Eyes darting, she searched for the man as her heart kicked against her ribs.

Logic told her he couldn't be far. She retraced her steps to the staircase that led down to platform three. It didn't make sense that he would return to the platform. He had to be on this level. *Think!* A noise, like a wounded animal, drifted toward her. She turned, and her gaze fell on the men's room. On the opposite side of the hall was the women's, barred by a door that required a half-centime to unlock. But the men's room was open. Advancing, she glimpsed the white urinals lined up in a row and an acrid smell wafted in the air. A splash of water, a flush, and then a dry heaving told her the airman was in a stall, retching. Her whole body hummed with nervous tension as she stepped inside.

"Monsieur?"

The jarring smack of the station's front doors opening and closing careened across the hall to reach her. Hedy turned and saw a policeman entering the station. The hair on her arms stood up as though the air was charged by a volt of electricity.

"Sir," she said, switching to English. She hoped no one else was in there, but she had to ensure the pilot understood the danger. "Hurry, police."

Water ran. A metal door slammed. The pilot came to her, his face whiter than snow.

The policeman's heels clacked across the tiles, drawing closer as Hedy's knees shook with uncertainty. Standing inside the men's room, she drew the policeman to her like a moth to a flame. If she left, would the pilot have a better chance? But Joseph had said this was how the airmen were caught, alone and confused, unable to speak.

"Madame?" The formal, official tone of voice told her who it was. "Is something wrong?"

A puzzle. Forward to the pilot. Backward to the police. Outside to the car. Seconds to solve it. Hedy's mind raced. She had to act fast.

"*Mon chéri*," she said, stepping farther inside and putting an arm around the pilot.

She could feel his body tense as if he feared the worst. Hedy felt the same but didn't give in to it. She pulled him alongside her and reached the officer at the entrance near the urinals. She looked him in the eyes, as her teachers had taught her to do when anyone of authority entered the classroom.

"I'm afraid my husband is ill with food poisoning. It must have been the fish at dinner."

"Madame, let me assist you. Where are you going?"

"Home," she pushed out the word, her fingers clammy at the pilot's waist. "I've parked across the street from the station." *Keep moving, one step after another.* She was no longer in the men's room but in the hall. *Just make it to the front door*, she told herself.

"I will help you bring your husband to your car," the policeman said, walking alongside her.

"That won't be necessary." Her mouth was grainy with fear as she shouldered the front door open, and the policeman came alongside to hold it for her.

"Are you sure you'll be fine on your own?" he asked.

"Yes. Broth soup, rest, and my husband will be good by morning." The cool night air on her face and the darkness boosted her confidence. "Thank you, and goodnight." She guided the pilot down the steps.

Once they were in the street and out of earshot, the pilot whispered, "I wouldn't have gotten out of that pickle without you."

"Pickle?"

"Slang for mess."

She opened the car door, glanced at the station doors to check the policeman wasn't watching, and slid into the back seat with him.

"What the hell happened in there?" the man in the front demanded. He turned around to look at them, the whites of his eyes glimmering cold and hard like shards of ice.

"He was sick. I pretended he was my husband so he wouldn't have to speak with the policeman."

They drove on in silence along the lake road. Was the man angry with her? Should she have acted differently? She stared at the light from the full moon shimmering on the lake's surface. A short time later, they arrived at a home that bordered the shore. The driver parked the car and turned to Hedy.

"Tell him we've arranged for a boat that he will row across the lake. But ask if he's too sick to make the trip."

She passed the message.

"He said he feels better now that he got everything out of his stomach."

The pilot signaled as much with both thumbs up.

"Once he reaches the shore on the other side, the French Resistance will take over. They've got good smuggling routes to get him back to England. He must watch out for the Swiss Army patrolling the lake. If he sees a boat with lights, he should stop rowing and lie flat until they pass. It's a cold night, so we've got a blanket to keep him warm. And a compass. Tell him to head east, and he'll reach the other side within four hours, well before sunrise."

After Hedy explained all this to the pilot, the man in the front row said that once they got out of the car, they must be silent so as not to alert the attention of patrols. He asked if the pilot had any questions.

"Just thank you all for helping. I'll never forget it." He looked at Hedy. "First time a Swiss girl's rescued me in the men's room."

Hedy smiled. "You're my first pilot, so I'll remember you too!"

He tipped the brim of his hat.

Before they left the car, the man in front turned back to her. "You did well back there. I'll tell the network you're ready to go it alone."

A warmth spread across her chest, reminding her of when her father had given her a glass of pear schnapps, and she'd gulped it down instead of taking a sip. Her face had turned red, and her ears popped. She smiled and nodded, grateful he'd recognized her effort.

They stepped outside the car and walked to the wooden boat waiting on the shore. The pilot climbed in, and the other man handed him the wool blanket, compass and flashlight. As Hedy helped to slide the boat into the lake, her leather shoes sank in the pebbly sand. Water seeped over them. Pushing down the old fear, she listened to the waves splashing softly. While the airman disappeared into the darkness, Hedy realized she'd taken the first step in a new life and resolved to take many more.

7

Gina

Colorado Springs, Colorado
September 2018

By the time I leave Mamie's apartment, it's late afternoon. The sky is leaden as if it might rain. I turn on I-25 in the direction of Dad's.

It's Monday, and the restaurant is closed. I wish there was a place to go other than Dad's house. I'm grateful that he doesn't make me pay rent, but he lives with Helen, the woman he divorced Mom to marry, and it doesn't feel like home. My friends from high school have all moved on, either to university or jobs out of town. Over the summer, I saw a few, and they all assumed I'd be going back to university, too. I let them think that because it was easier than explaining why I'd chosen not to. While Mom was ill, no one asked about my plans because everyone understood I'd put my studies on hold to look after her. Now that she's gone, it's different. As Dad says, no one who gets a perfect score on the SAT becomes a waitress. But I like Le Chat Noir's open dining room, no hidden spaces to get caught in, and the memories it holds. Sometimes, I imagine Mom at a table in the corner, smiling as I bring out the menu du jour, and the hollowness inside eases for a while.

Up ahead, I see the exit for the Garden of the Gods Park. Lifting my shoulders, I glance at the rearview mirror—the lane is clear—and turn off the interstate. Driving along Mesa Road, I reach the park's entrance. On my left, a red sandstone taller than a skyscraper, known as North Gateway, greets me like a warm smile.

Even on a gray day, the towering red rocks, circled by ponderosa pines and juniper trees, are stunning. The last time I came was in January. Light snow dusted the ground. Mom had asked me to bring her to a beautiful setting to celebrate the completion of her first round of chemo. Restaurants and cafés were out—the cancer had carved a small hole in her esophagus, so she could no longer eat or drink, except through a tube in her stomach. Thin and pale, she sat in the passenger seat wearing gray sweatpants, padded boots and a quilted down coat. We stayed in the car, heat blasting, watching the red rocks, blue sky and white ground. She adjusted the yellow silk scarf across her forehead and smiled at me. I'd bought the scarf when she started to lose her hair. Sunflower yellow for warmth, light, hope. I smiled back, trying to hide what was going through my mind—Mom was running out of time.

Now, holding her scarf that I carry with me like a talisman, I bury my face in the smooth silk, wishing I could be with her again.

After a while, I set the scarf on the dashboard. Gray clouds swell in the distance. I recall the summer Mom and I took a guided hike on the trails along these rocks, both of us marveling at the slender shadows they cast on the ground. The guide explained how whole worlds—insects, birds and plants—exist inside the tiny gaps carved by the wind and rain on the surface of the sandstone. In a way, that's what I'm doing now, living in the narrow spaces from the past.

Now, Mamie wants me to step out and leap into a vast world I know nothing about.

Tap, tap, tap like soft footsteps on the metal overhead. It must be raining. No, not rain, but hail. Little white balls roll off the windshield and fall to the ground. I don't understand what happened in Switzerland before Mom and me. How Mamie lost Elizabeth, and why she kept it a secret all these years. If I can't figure out my life, I'll never be able to help Mamie fix hers.

The hail stops, and everything goes quiet.

I hear Dad's voice, sensible, logical, reasonable. *You can't fly with a half-blind ninety-three-year-old woman across the Atlantic Ocean to a country you've never been.*

But then my own voice rises. *Switzerland isn't Somalia. I speak fluent French, which I learned all those afternoons from Mamie, who took care of me after school while Mom was working. And we will be going to her hometown, a place she knows.* Mom's yellow scarf reflects in the windshield. Maybe I can do it.

My phone rings. It's Dad.

"Are you lost?" he jokes.

The sky is nearly dark. I check my watch. I've been here for two hours.

"I stopped at the mall on my way home from Mamie's." I shouldn't lie to Dad, but I don't want to tell him I'm crying in the Garden of the Gods.

"How is she?"

"Good." Another lie, I think, as I remember the deep sadness on her face when she told me about Elizabeth.

"There's a letter from the School of Engineering. I bet it's the news you've been hoping for."

I wait a beat. "OK, I'm on my way."

"Helen's made burgers for dinner. We won't start until you're back."

Hanging up, I feel like a coward. I never should have let Dad believe that I wanted to return to university. I pretended that architecture didn't suit me because it was easier than telling him the truth. He's convinced that I'm going to be an engineer like him. It's strange how quickly one lie leads to another, and soon, you're buried under them and can't find your way out. Is that what happened with Mamie and Elizabeth? Maybe she's right that this trip will be good for us. A week will give me a break from Dad's pressure about university. Then, when I return, I'll tell him I want to continue working at Le Chat Noir.

I tuck the scarf in my purse and turn the car engine on.

There's the sound of ice clinking in a glass as I enter the kitchen. Dad's making his customary after-work vodka tonic. The envelope, sharp-edged like a steel-framed trap, waits on the granite counter.

"Hi, sweetie," he says. A tang of lemon hits the air as he slices a wedge and drops it into the glass. "Did you get what you needed at the mall?"

"Yes." More lies. Little ones, like all those hailstones, piling up.

He reaches for the envelope and hands it to me. "Why don't you open it now?"

I read the return address printed in institutional black ink: *Office of the Dean of the School of Engineering and Applied Science, University of Colorado.*

Dad takes a gulp of his drink. I consider telling him I don't want to go, but Helen enters the kitchen. She's wearing shiny leggings and a bouncy sports top. Seeing the envelope in my hand, she smiles and puts an arm around Dad. They're both watching me. I open it as slowly as possible, turning the envelope over and sliding two fingers under the paper to break the gluey connection before unfurling the letter.

I want to put the paper down, but Dad comes beside me and reads over my shoulder. My head throbs.

"What does it say?" Helen asks.

"If Gina passes an interview next week, she'll be accepted into the engineering school in January." He pats me on the back. "Congratulations. I knew you'd make it."

I fold the letter and put it back in the envelope.

"Don't worry. You'll pass the interview." Dad smiles. "Then you'll be back where you belong."

I force a smile and push the letter out of my mind. If I think about it, then I remember what happened, and it gets hard to breathe.

"Let's eat," Helen says.

We gather around the table and exchange polite conversation.

"How's your grandmother?" Helen asks. "It's nice you visit her every week."

"She talked about her past today. Told me something I didn't expect."

"What's that?" Dad leans forward.

"Mom has a sister."

He inclines his head sideways. "Your mother never—"

"She didn't know. Mamie kept it a secret."

He puts the fork down and leans back. "A sister? Where?"

"In Switzerland. She wants me to go there and help find her."

He shoots a sharp glance at Helen. "She sounds confused. I can't believe—"

"She was unequivocal. Showed me a watch that belonged to Grandfather. She wants to give it to Elizabeth."

"Who is Elizabeth?" Helen asks.

"The daughter Mamie left behind in Switzerland."

Dad frowns. "This doesn't make sense." He rubs his palms together. "What did you tell her?"

"That I have to talk with you first."

"Good girl." He exhales. "I hope you're not considering it. Even if the story about Mamie having another daughter is true . . ." he rolls his eyes ". . . and I find it hard to believe, but let's pretend. It's been, what, seventy years since your grandmother left? How on earth will she find her?"

"I don't know, but Mamie will."

He shakes his head. "You've got to prepare for your interview, right?"

"Mamie doesn't have anyone else."

"Why is that your problem? Focus on yourself. All that time looking after your mother while she was ill hasn't helped; in fact, it's put you behind your peers." Though Dad fell out of love with Mom years before they divorced, his callous words leave a bitter taste in my mouth. I put the fork down. "Mamie has no right to pressure you. She shouldn't have waited to return and find this woman."

It's not just some woman but Mamie's daughter, Mom's sister, my aunt. There's the watch, too. I want to tell Dad how I felt holding it—the connection to my grandfather, whom I never knew, and the sense that I'm not alone. But I notice the shiny digital one on his wrist that tracks the crucial things in his life—sleep, heart rate, bank balance. Since Grandfather's broken watch can't perform any of those functions, how can I expect him to understand?

"You're going to be an engineer," he says, as if his words can make it happen. "Your future is what matters, not Mamie's past." He gets up to fix another drink. "I always knew you would become an engineer. Remember the summer you turned sixteen?"

Dad won't let me forget the summer we rebuilt the engine in his 1965 Mustang. Yes, I liked the challenge of taking something apart and seeing if I could put it back together. Devising a system for remembering where each piece belonged, I created a map in my brain that told me exactly where the gaskets, seals, O-rings, springs, and friction plates went. No room for uncertainty. Figuring out on my own how it worked. That was what I loved. And being with him. But it was still *his* project. I didn't have the heart to tell him that I hated the smell of burning fumes, the heat of the flames kicking out of the exhaust, or the oil on my jeans. No matter how much time I spent with him in the garage, it wasn't something I yearned to do or dreamed about. Cars are Dad's passion—not mine.

He returns to the table. "Tell Mamie your studies take priority. After the January term, if she still wants to go, then maybe you can consider it over the summer."

I nod. It's a silent lie this time because I'll go to my room later, turn on the computer, and search for flights to Switzerland.

8

Hedy

Le Brassus June 1944

On Friday night, Hedy opened the door to find Franck holding a glass jar. Inside, pale blue and yellow eggs floated in briny water.

"Two dozen," he said. "These water-glassed eggs will keep for up to a year."

She frowned. "We don't have the coupons. I can't—"

"You're pretty tonight," he said, looking her up and down. She caught a whiff of beer on his breath as he handed her the jar.

The lime at the bottom of the jar loosened in her hands, clouding the water with a chalky gray silt. A wave of discomfort washed over Hedy. Not only was Franck disregarding the regulations on food rationing, which would get her family in trouble, but the familiar, almost intimate tone he used to address her was disturbing.

She turned abruptly to the kitchen.

"My goodness." Her mother's eyes widened as they fixed on the jar. "Where did all those eggs come from?"

Hedy slid the jar onto the counter and tipped her head back toward Franck.

"But we don't have the vouchers." She heard the strain in her mother's voice. "That amount would require four weeks of ration cards."

Franck winked at Hedy. "It's our little secret. I won't tell."

Her father entered the kitchen and shook Franck's hand. "Welcome," he said, motioning to the table at the other end of the kitchen, where they sat down. "I often see your father's truck early in the morning delivering milk. He's a hard worker."

Franck lifted his shoulders. "Soon, I'll be driving the truck."

Hedy went to the sink, where her mother stood. "I don't feel comfortable," she whispered.

"It's only one evening." Her mother squeezed her arm. "Your father and I are here. It will be fine."

Whatever her mother thought she could accomplish by inviting Franck, Hedy suspected it wouldn't come to pass. She would be civil with him, but afterward, she would have nothing to do with him. She took a deep breath before carrying the bowl of steaming potatoes to the table.

Her father poured the wine. As Hedy and her mother sat down, Franck took a slug from his glass.

"My sister Lise travels by train to Lausanne every week." He glanced at Hedy.

"Is she studying there?" her mother asked.

"Yes, midwifery." He ate the cabbage cooked with lardon, talking as he chewed. "What do you study, Hedy?"

"English."

Franck half-smiled. "Next year, Lise will become an apprentice midwife in the hospital in Lausanne."

Because of Franck, her mother had added more butter to the potatoes than usual. Hedy ate slowly, savoring the taste. "I've got another year too."

"Then what will you do?"

"Not sure."

She watched a frown trace across his forehead. "You better think about it, and if there's time to study something else, you should."

"Why?"

"After Germany wins the war, English speakers won't be needed."

Hedy's stomach dropped as though she'd been punched in the gut. Heat rose like flames in her cheeks. "Germany won't—"

"Hedy will become a teacher," her mother said quickly, cutting her a sharp look from across the table. Hedy read the warning in her eyes: *drop it, don't react.* A rancid taste rose at the back of her throat, and she had to do all in her power to stop herself from shouting that Germany would never win because brave Allied bombers were risking their lives in the skies.

"What about you, Franck?" her mother continued. "What are your plans?"

"I'm the eldest, so I'll take over the dairy farm from my father. I already do a lot of the work on my own."

"Well, please thank him for sharing his bounty with us," she said.

"He doesn't know I nicked the eggs from the storage cellar. I didn't bother to ask." A sharpness, like a knife's edge, entered Franck's voice. Hedy glanced at her mother and saw that she had noticed it too. "Papa won't dare to say a word to me." He lifted his shoulders. "He's afraid of me. I can denounce him for hoarding food." He took another slug of wine.

An uncomfortable silence followed, broken only by the sound of Franck's boot heels tapping on the floor.

"Perhaps you should take the eggs back," her father suggested with a sidelong glance at her mother. "We don't want to cause any trouble between you and your father."

"Why would I do that?" Franck leaned back in his chair and cracked his knuckles in his hands. "Our chickens have been laying eggs all spring, and my father's pocketed money from selling them on the black market. Why shouldn't I benefit too?"

Hedy watched another glance pass between her parents.

"Don't trouble yourself to bring more," her mother said. "We have all we need."

He turned to Hedy. "If you want anything, just ask." His sour, wine-soaked breath wafted over her. "I get everything Pastor Rolle needs. I can do the same for you."

She nodded, but the thought of owing anything to Franck unsettled her. She cleared the plates and helped her mother serve an almond and hazelnut cake for dessert. She and her mother remained silent while her father talked about his violins, the choir at church and hunting grouse. He invited Franck to look at his workshop. Franck hesitated as if he wanted to stay with Hedy, but her father insisted, saying she would be busy with the dishes. Once they had left, her shoulders loosened, and she finally relaxed.

"What will we do with those eggs?" Hedy asked. She wanted to suggest to her mother that they take the jar to a refugee camp, but she worried her mother would question how she knew about the conditions for the refugees. Joseph had sworn her to secrecy about the pilots, and she didn't want to mention his name or say anything that could risk exposing the network.

"I know of people in need who can use them," her mother said.

"Can you believe he said Germany will win the war!" She'd never heard someone proclaim it openly, even if they wanted Germany to win. The pretense of neutrality was a barrier most people didn't dare cross.

"He's not alone, I'm afraid. But why is he so close to Pastor Rolle?"

"I don't know. But at least I don't have to see him again."

"Unless—"

"You said only one night." Hedy pulled a face.

"Be careful not to anger him. You don't want him to turn against us."

Her mother had thought she was doing the right thing by inviting Franck into their home, but his behavior during dinner proved it was a mistake. She couldn't lead him on or let him believe there was any chance they would be together. She had to set things right. The sooner, the better.

"I'll tell him I'm busy with exams and don't have time. He'll get the message and move on to someone else."

Her mother turned and touched Hedy's cheek. "Why would Pastor Rolle suggest him?"

"Does the pastor want Germany to win, too?"

The front door opened, and Hedy and her mother went quiet. The men returned to the kitchen.

"I need to be heading back," Franck said. "My mornings start early." He looked at Hedy's mother. "Thank you, Madame Borel, for the dinner."

Then he stepped close to Hedy, and a bolt of terror rolled through her as she sensed he wanted to kiss her on the cheek. To her relief, he took her hand instead.

"Until we see each other again," he said, "goodnight."

As her father walked him to the door, Hedy felt a twist in the pit of her stomach. Maybe it was irrational or an overreaction, but her gut seemed to forewarn that getting Franck out of her life might not be as easy as she thought.

9

Samuel

Davos
June 1944

"I'm gonna steal it. You in?" Garcia asked. His hair, shiny with pomade, was parted neatly to the side.

"You bet I'm in," Bobby said.

Samuel chuckled. Garcia and Bobby were crew members from the *Baby*, a B-17 bomber that had crash-landed in April in a Swiss town near the Austrian border. They'd been in two other camps, Chaumont and Adelboden, before coming to Davos. Today, the three men sat on the porch in front of the Palace Hotel—their new home—eyeing the eagle and swastika plaque above the door of the German consulate across the street.

"What will you do with the plaque after you steal it?" Samuel asked.

"Bury it in the ground, throw it off a cliff, dump it in the lake. Anything not to have to look at it every day," Garcia said. "It will be our small contribution to our troops fighting in Normandy."

Garcia was a bombardier. The joke in the Air Corps was that the bombardiers had the best seat in the plane—a glass nose in the belly at the front providing the clearest view of the target, but also the most vulnerable to flak. Samuel counted the eighteen bombs stitched on the front of Garcia's leather flight jacket, signaling he'd survived eighteen missions. He reckoned Garcia had nerves of steel.

"General Legge might not be pleased," Samuel said, wanting to get a read from the men on the general.

"You ever talk to Legge?" Bobby asked.

"Only to Lieutenant Jones, who told me I'd be court-martialed by the U.S. Army if I tried to escape."

Bobby flexed his rock-hard hands. Gold navigator wings were sewn on the front of his flight jacket. Samuel had heard that before Bobby joined the Air Corps, he was a champion lightweight boxer.

"The American Legation in Bern needs to be investigated," Bobby said. "They don't help the internees one bit. Legge seems to carry a grudge against the Air Corps. I heard he served as a cavalry officer in the Great War and was buddies with Theodore Roosevelt's son. Times have moved on. We're fighting an air war now."

"Maybe Legge's pro-Nazi like some Swiss politicians," Garcia said.

Samuel couldn't argue with Garcia's account of Switzerland. He'd been in the country nearly a month, and there was no denying the place leaned pro-Nazi. There were plenty of German soldiers, including SS officers, who came to Davos for rest and recreation. It was more than just a shared language that made them comfortable. They wouldn't come here if they didn't feel at home and welcomed.

"I think the regular folk support us," Garcia said, lowering his voice. "A guy who works at the hotel bar helped a pilot escape last week."

Samuel straightened his back. "How?"

"Grease their palms, and you'll get civilian clothes and a train ticket," Garcia said, looking around to make sure no one was close by.

"How much?" Samuel asked.

"Don't know. But the Swiss will take watches instead of cash."

"That works?" Samuel glanced at the A-11 on his wrist.

"Sure does. I heard the pilot waited until the final check at eleven last week, snuck out of the hotel, and walked to a train station farther down the valley. Then he boarded the morning train heading west."

"What happens after that?"

"His plan was to go as far west as he could. The closer to the French border and the farther away from Germany, the better chance of finding the Maquis. The Resistance has multiple lines to get him out through France."

"Did he make it?"

"As far as I know."

Samuel's mind sharpened at the possibility of getting back to England. Being away from the war, yet in the middle of it, was the worst. All day with nothing to do. The food was terrible. Every night, potatoes. Rancid cheese. Hardly ever meat. At night, he struggled to sleep with bombs pounding across the border, knowing it was fellow Americans risking their lives. He felt like a jack-o'-lantern, all hollowed out inside. He was losing himself and couldn't stay. Now that his ankle had healed, he wanted to go back and do his part.

Garcia seemed to read Samuel's mind. "Just make sure you don't get caught. If you do, they'll send you to Wauwilermoos for ten days of punishment. And I've got it on good word it's a bad-news joint."

"You know pilots who've been there?"

"They call it the dungeon. You pray that they put you in the hole—solitary confinement—as that's better than bunking with the Russians."

Two SS officers, their suits cut sharp as knives, walked by and waved at the Americans. The muscles in Samuel's arms tightened. He sensed it was the same for Garcia and Bobby. The Germans continued to the consulate, amused that they were free and the Americans were not.

"You steal that plaque, and I'll give you five bucks," Samuel said.

"Now you're talking," Garcia said, laughing. "Keep your money. You're going to need it. Bobby and I have a plan."

Samuel guessed they would do it after General Legge's visit next week. It would be asking for trouble if they did it before. The general was coming to Davos to speak with the interned airmen since new pilots arrived daily. Samuel would make the case to Legge that he had a duty to return to his squadron. He was sure Legge would understand. If he didn't, talking to Garcia and Bobby had confirmed that he could escape without the help of the Legation. He didn't want to go alone, but since Garcia and Bobby could read between the lines of what he was saying, it was up to them to suggest if they wanted to join him.

A week later, on a scorching afternoon in a dimly lit room tucked away from the hotel's dining hall, Samuel sat on the other side of the table from Brigadier General Legge. The general, clad in jodhpurs and leather boots that creaked with every shift of his weight, seemed to belong to a different era.

"Second Lieutenant Reardon," he said, "how are you finding Davos?"

"Sir, I asked Lieutenant Jones to have you contact my commanding officer, Colonel Fiske—"

"Answer the question, Second Lieutenant."

"I don't like it at all, sir."

"Is it the food?" Legge's eyebrows lifted. "A lot of men complain there isn't enough."

Samuel detected a southern drawl—too low for Texas or Tennessee—and pinned him as a South Carolina man. His experience with Southern soldiers had taught him they had little patience for complaints.

"I don't care about the food, sir. Only about the men in my squadron, the 801st. I respectfully request assistance to return to my squadron without delay."

Legge removed a leather pouch from his pocket. "Every pilot I interview wants to return to their squadron. To each of them, I say we are bound by Swiss law. Surely you can understand the difficult position the Legation is in, but difficult or not, we do not break Swiss law."

All week, Samuel had wrestled with his thoughts, trying to find the right words to convince the general why he was different from the other pilots. But now, as he caught the sweet, pungent odor from the tobacco the general pressed into the pipe, he questioned how much he should reveal. Perhaps the general had his own agenda. Samuel's duty was to protect his squadron. He decided to tread carefully, saying as little as possible.

Legge drew a match. The sweet smell turned bitter as the tobacco burned and smoke puffed.

"Now that our boys are in Normandy," Legge said, clearing his throat, "the military strategy shifts from air to land. It may be hard for a pilot to appreciate, but the outcome will be determined by what can be achieved on the ground." He clenched the pipe between his teeth. "How many missions have you flown, Second Lieutenant Reardon?"

"Twenty, sir."

"Well, you've done your part. Now leave it to the men on the ground to push through to Paris and Berlin to finish the job."

Samuel remained silent, which seemed to irritate the general.

"If I deem it necessary for you to remain interned in Switzerland, then by God, that is what will happen." He took a sip from the glass on the table. "Our objective is to maintain good relations with the Swiss government, respecting their policy of armed neutrality. We've put considerable effort into making sure you boys are in a decent enough place and have all that you need."

Samuel resented the general's words. Why was he pretending that detaining American pilots while German soldiers were free to come and go represented neutrality?

"So, do we agree that there will be no more talk about returning to your squadron?"

"Yes, sir."

"You pilots are a stubborn lot." His eyes sharpened, giving Samuel the sense that he was being lined up in the crosshairs of a gun sight. "Infantrymen know to keep their mouths shut and follow orders."

"Yes, sir."

"Don't get any wise ideas about escaping. Without help, you'll be as easy to spot as a catfish in shallow water."

The general checked his pocket watch—another relic from the world before—and without looking up, in a gruff voice, said, "Dismissed."

10

Gina

Switzerland
September 2018

The following week, Mamie and I land at Geneva Airport. I'm amazed at how organized the country is—there's even a train station down the hall from baggage collection. On the plane, I read through two Swiss guidebooks and work out that the best way to make the sixty-kilometer trek from Geneva to Le Brassus is by train. The airport staff who meet us with a wheelchair kindly bring Mamie to the station after we collect our bags. Soon, we find ourselves on the elevator leading to the station's underground platform.

The train is a double-decker. I've never seen anything like it, and after Mamie settles on the ground level—she's too unsteady on her feet to handle the stairs—I go to the upper deck. Even in my fuzzy-headed daze after a fourteen-hour flight, I'm stunned by the scenery. As the train departs Geneva, it heads east and winds along the edge of Lac Léman. The guidebook says it's the largest lake in Western Europe with an invisible border running down the middle, as half of it is in France. The lake's crystal blue waters and snow-capped Alps, including the famous Mont Blanc, are on my right. On my left are medieval villages and cows adorned with bells and flowers. Yes. Cows. Wearing flowers. I wouldn't have believed it if I hadn't read about it in the guidebook. There's a name for it too: *désalpe*. The autumnal procession of farmers bringing their cows down from the mountain pastures where they've grazed on fresh meadows all summer. In the window, I catch the reflection of the yellow scarf on my wrist next to the watch. I wish Mom could be here to see all this, help us find Elizabeth, and stop me from fighting with Dad.

I should have told him in person, but I lacked the courage to and called from the Denver airport instead. When he answered, my throat tightened like I'd swallowed a lump of apple because I knew I was about to crush all his hope and pride in me.

"Are you at the restaurant?" he asked. "It sounds busy."

"I'm at the airport . . ." My voice trailed, giving him time to process. "Mamie and I will soon board a flight to Geneva."

"Are you serious?" He took a beat. "Tomorrow is your interview."

"I called the engineering department and told them I couldn't go."

"What? Call them back, say—"

"Dad, listen to me for a minute. I don't want to be an engineer."

Silence.

"Are you still there?" I asked after a while.

"Then what do you want?"

"I don't know."

"This is bullshit." His voice hardened. "Don't do this."

"I'm going to Switzerland for a week. Mamie needs my help, and it's a chance for me, too."

"A chance to do what?"

I wanted to say that I needed to carve something out for myself that wasn't related to him or Mom and that this trip felt like a first step. But these incoherent, half-formed ideas made easy targets for him to shoot down, so I kept them inside.

"I guess just to learn about where I came from." I leaned my hand on the column next to the window that overlooked the runway. Grandfather's watch was on my wrist, and Mom's scarf was next to it to protect it from nicks. Though the Rolex no longer worked, I didn't want to risk putting it in my suitcase. And I liked how solid and weighty it felt, connecting me to something that went before. "We can talk more when I get back."

"You're being overly emotional." He huffed. "No one gets anywhere in this world by looking back."

Arguing with Dad is pointless. I'd end up saying something I'd regret later. "I'll call you when I land in Geneva."

"Don't bother." The line went dead.

I should have seen that coming, but I didn't, and it sent a cold chill across my shoulders.

An hour later, we reach Lausanne and change trains. No longer a double-decker, this one heads north to the remote Jura Mountains. Le Brassus is the terminus. I lean back and close my eyes, expecting sleep since I've been up for over twenty-four hours. But sleep doesn't come. Instead, I'm drawn to the window and the green rolling meadows outside. A light rain falls and blends with sunlight. Steam rises from the ground. The grass is bathed in a golden glow. Everything about this place is beautiful.

In Le Brassus, we wear coats, tightening the collars against the rain. Though Hotel de la Lande is a five-minute walk from the station, I insist we take a taxi. Mamie has hardly said a word. She must be exhausted from the flight and emotionally overwhelmed. After we clean up and change clothes, I use the hotel's wireless network to check my phone.

There's a text message from Helen. *Don't worry. Your dad will get over this. Call if you need anything. Love, Helen.*

"Is everything all right?" Mamie asks.

I nod and turn off my phone. "Where should we eat?"

"Not in the hotel. The restaurant was never good, and the service slow. I can't remember any clever girls like you working here."

I'm tempted to remind her that it was over seventy years ago she was last here, that perhaps the service has improved, but I just smile inwardly and guide her across the street to a place called Chez Lily. Simple and cheap. We both order *saucisse aux choux*, which is delicious. And we talk about tomorrow.

"I'd like to drive by my parents' house," Mamie says. "Then go to the town hall, where they maintain detailed records." She drops her gaze. "The file on my family will be the best place to start to find Elizabeth."

I lean forward. "You said that once we're in Switzerland you would tell me about her."

She lifts her gaze to meet mine. "I will, but not tonight." Her voice is thin and fragile. "It's been a long journey. Tomorrow."

11

Hedy

Le Brassus
October 2018

Mouth dry, Hedy wakes in the night. She reaches for the glass of water on the table next to the bed. The cool liquid soothes her scratchy throat. Her eyes sting, but in the darkness she can bear it. It's only in the light that the burning overwhelms her. After the sun comes up, she'll ask Gina to put the drops in.

Their room is on the second floor. The window is open, and on the cool night air, she catches the sharp scent of spruce like a crisp, tart apple. Is the church still behind the hotel? Memories come at her: hard benches; musty odor; Pastor Rolle's sharp eyes, like coal cakes, staring down from the pulpit.

The church bell ticks the hour. So, it's still there. She has spent decades trying not to remember, not to think or feel. Maybe it's a natural reflex to look away from shame and pain; the human instinct to protect oneself from what hurts. But her daughter Elaine's death has spun her in a new direction. Now the question is: should she break her silence?

Not all the memories are painful. Beyond the church, she sees the meadow, the river running through it, the ground sloping and speckled with white limestone and green understory. Her father walks by her side. Together they pass birch and spruce and ash until he stops, touches an old trunk's gray grooves, looks up, and tells her this is the one.

The trees know what happened. They've seen the good and the bad, how she stumbled and fell. She'd been foolish to think she could right the balance in favor of the innocent; like a naïve child, she thought that she could make a difference. But that urge keeps returning because she's still trying to set things right—isn't that why she came back? Her fingers knot the blanket. If they find Elizabeth, how will she explain what happened and why it took decades to summon the courage to return?

Will Elizabeth believe her when she says that in her heart she's always been looking for her daughter even if shame prevented her from coming back? In every passing face, she'd try to glimpse a familiar expression or eye color, anything that might help find her. Sometimes, she'd imagine that Elizabeth was looking for her, too.

Gina turns in the bed next to her. Such a good girl. Quiet, she barely makes a sound. But she's too hard on herself. No daughter should have to watch a parent die before her time and not be able to do anything about it. Hedy knows that pain, how it drills like a screw into one's bones with an ache that never leaves. And yet, she senses it's more than that. Gina's been different since she left university. When Hedy tries to talk about it, find out if something happened, her granddaughter shuts up tighter than a clam. Maybe being here will unlock her pain. The one thing she's learned in life is that there's no sense in trying to bury the thing that hurts because it's always there floating under the surface.

In the morning, her granddaughter brings her a coffee and a croissant from downstairs.

"It's raining," Gina says.

Hedy turns to the window. Fog, like white foam, slides between the treetops. Gina puts the drops in her eyes and the world blurs.

A short time later, they drive up to a house.

"This must be it," Gina says, "9 Piguet-Dessous."

Hedy rolls down the window and squints. Her one good eye fixes on the faded poppy-red shutters, and her breath catches. "Yes."

"Do you want to go inside? I can knock on the door."

"No. But what's over there?" Hedy points to two gray boxes on the front wall.

"Looks like mailboxes."

"Two?"

"Let me get out and have a look."

Gina returns to the taxi. "There are different names on the boxes—maybe the house has been converted into apartments."

Hedy's stomach twists. "That must be it. Now, to the town hall."

They pass the green meadow on the right and the village school on the left. The rain has stopped, and children play in the courtyard, their laughter echoing with excitement and hope. Hedy was always first in her class. What good did that do her? She wants to tell Gina she shouldn't listen to her dad insisting she return to university, that a person isn't defined by what they know or the lines on their résumé, but the taxi pulls up to a gray concrete building before she can speak.

"This isn't the town hall," Hedy says, frowning. "It was an old house on the main street."

"That was a long time ago," the taxi driver says. "Too many people work in the town hall now. This building is temporary until the new one behind the train station is complete." He nods to the cranes in the distance. "It's the high demand for luxury watches—haven't you noticed the building going on?"

Gina pays the driver and helps Hedy get out of the car.

Inside, a woman with blue-framed glasses sits behind the counter. "How can I help?"

"My name is Hedy Borel. I'm here for my records," she says, taking a deep breath and steeling her voice so it won't crack. "And those of my parents, Alain and Ariane Borel." She wants to say her daughter, Elizabeth, too, but she doesn't have the right.

The woman stiffens. "Do you reside in Le Brassus?"

"I was born here."

"Then you are Swiss?"

Hedy wants to say she abandoned her country after it betrayed her, but the woman's tone warns against it. She's here to find Elizabeth; if it means lying, she will. "Yes."

"May I see your identification card?"

Hedy places her American passport on the table and opens it to the page that confirms her place of birth is Le Brassus.

"This passport identifies you as American," the woman says, pointing to a sign on the wall. "Affairs concerning foreigners are handled on Mondays and Fridays. Only Swiss citizens receive services from the Commune on Thursdays. You'll need to come back tomorrow."

The words land like a slap on Hedy's face. She can almost feel a red welt rising on her cheek. Despite the steel, cranes and concrete houses, maybe her country hasn't changed.

Gina steps forward. "My grandmother is ninety-three. She—"

Hedy holds her hand out. "Would you mind sitting down over there and giving me a moment in private with this woman?"

Gina opens her mouth to protest, but Hedy, determined to do this her way, motions to the sitting area. She feels the buried anger of seventy-three years breaking the surface. She knows what she will say, has rehearsed it in her mind a thousand times, the words on the tip of her tongue. The only reason she's holding back is because Gina stands by her side, and Hedy isn't ready to tell her what she knows she must.

Everyone she has loved is lost to her, except for Gina and Elizabeth. She's afraid to tell Gina because she might lose her too, but if she doesn't tell her, she won't be able to find Elizabeth. She can't do it alone. What are the right words to help Gina understand the terrible things she did? If only she had more time to figure it out. She moistens her dry lips and clears her throat. She had found her bravery over seventy years ago and survived; it is within her reach now to tell her granddaughter. Tonight. She will start from the beginning and leave the worst for the end.

"Go on," Hedy says, nodding at the waiting area. "Have a seat over there. I won't be long."

12

Samuel

Davos
June 1944

Samuel sat with his back to the bar and scanned the room in the hotel's basement. Low ceiling, stone walls, sticky beer-stained floor. Half a dozen pilots gathered around tables playing bridge, chess and gin rummy. Garcia was engrossed in a game of chess in the corner. When he looked up, Samuel tilted his head toward the bartender and mouthed, *He the one?*

Garcia nodded, then returned to his game.

Samuel swiveled the stool to face the bar and ordered a whiskey. He held the glass to his nose, taking in the sharp and smoky aroma. He didn't particularly like the taste of whiskey, preferring beer, but it steeled his nerves. He knocked it back in one gulp.

"Another one?" The bartender's sun-darkened skin resembled polished oak.

"Give me a beer."

The bartender took the empty whiskey glass. Samuel watched, but the man's eyes gave nothing away. Under the glass, Samuel had slipped a paper with one word written on it: *escape.*

The bartender tossed the paper in the trash and went to the back. Maybe Garcia had identified the wrong guy. Warmth from the alcohol spread to Samuel's neck and face. If this wasn't him, he'd find the right one. He couldn't sit the war out in the Palace Hotel across from the German consulate. His meeting with Legge had only strengthened his desire to get out of Switzerland. He wanted to be with his fellow airmen, doing his part to bring the war to an end.

A pint of beer appeared on the bar's copper top. Under it was a white napkin with black writing in the corner. *Meet me out back at midnight.*

Samuel came down the hotel's wooden stairs in his socks, silent as a cat. If he was caught breaking the curfew, the staff would report him to the Legation.

Outside, the uneven stones on the ground chafed his feet. He leaned against the side of the building. A full moon crowded out the stars. At this hour, his squadron was likely crossing the English Channel, coming in close to the French coast. With some luck, he'd be back in the air, flying with them by the next full moon.

He heard the bartender on the steps leading from the basement to the outside. The hinges creaked, and the door opened.

"You don't like Davos?" the bartender said, lighting a cigarette.

"Too many Germans for my taste."

"Better wait."

"Why?"

"Roadblocks. Army angry about pilot last week."

"I won't take the road."

"Mountain trails no good."

"Are the trails marked?"

"Yellow lines hard to see."

Not harder than flying a B-24 at night and looking for a drop target in utter darkness. "I'll see 'em."

"Trains stop after midnight. Better to walk the tracks."

"How long would that take?" he said, looking up at the moon.

"Pass two stations—Glaris and Monstein—then at Wiesen, no soldiers, take the train there. No walking." He put the cigarette in his mouth and raised his hands. "Bridges."

Samuel figured he meant the viaducts over the gorges he'd seen from the window on the train ride up. He didn't want to find himself crossing one of them at night. "And the mountain track takes how long?"

"Five hours. If you get lost . . ." he shrugged ". . . longer."

Since the bartender came from around here, he trusted him to know. "If you recommend the tracks, that's what I'll do. How much?"

"You need clothes, a newspaper to read on the train, a ticket from Wiesen to Lausanne . . ." he blew rings of smoke ". . . and something for my trouble."

Since Samuel only had a few francs in his pocket, which he would need once he got to wherever the train would take him, there was nothing to do but give the bartender his watch. He didn't like parting with it. Not only was the A-11 practical, but after all the times he'd hacked it with the crew's watches before going out on a mission, it had become a talisman, bringing Samuel good luck. He didn't want to throw that away, even if he wasn't sure he believed in it. But he had no choice if he wanted to be back in the air doing the job he'd been trained to do. He unhinged the strap and handed the watch over.

"Next week, all right?" The bartender flicked the cigarette to the ground and crushed it with the tip of his boot.

"Tomorrow."

"Too soon."

Samuel pointed at the sky. "Walking on the tracks by moonlight will be safer than in darkness. You got the watch. I go tomorrow night."

The bartender took a long look at him. "All right. Tomorrow night."

Samuel plumped a couple of towels under the blanket on his bed to make it look like he was sleeping. If all went well, he wouldn't be discovered missing until the curfew check the following night at ten. By that time, he hoped to be halfway across the country and, with some luck, maybe in France under the protection of the Maquis.

He carried his boots down the stairs and put them on once he was outside the hotel. He found the paper bag the bartender had left behind the willow tree; inside were civilian clothes and a train ticket. He quickly changed and put his uniform back in the bag, which the bartender had agreed to get rid of for him. The streets were quiet and cloaked in darkness from the blackout curtains. When he reached the Davos-Platz station, it took a moment for him to make out the white wooden fence to the right of the building. Climbing over it, he crossed the platform and jumped on the ground near the tracks.

The crisp night air sunk deep in his lungs. The last time he'd done this much physical activity was the night four weeks ago when he crashed the *Silver Wolf*. Adrenaline pumped through his veins. It felt good to leave the Palace Hotel, the German consulate across the street, the strange world of Legge, and the American Legation—he was taking his first steps toward freedom.

He moved at a steady pace, walking along the outside of the tracks. The Swiss had confiscated his compass and maps, but they couldn't take what was stored inside his head. During those early days in flight school, his greatest fear had been that he might wash out. All he'd wanted was to fly. If he hadn't made the cut, then navigator, sitting behind the flight deck, setting the plane's course, was the next best position. Now, he was glad he'd worked as hard on learning navigation techniques as he did mastering the B-24's controls. Celestial reckoning had been a difficult skill to acquire, but it was the one he would rely on the most tonight.

The moon's light had receded slightly, and with all the towns and villages blacked out, the stars shone brighter than last night. He stopped for a moment to get his bearings. On his left, he spotted the seven stars of Ursa Major—the big dipper—and drew an imaginary line from the two stars in the dipper's bucket to find Polaris, the north star. All he needed was to keep the North Star on his right to be confident he was heading west.

Bats twirled in the air. He ducked to avoid them. The tracks began to follow along the bank of a stream. He stumbled a few times, his boots sliding in the water. He decided to walk in the middle of the tracks but found the ties were too close together for a step at a time and too far apart to use every other one. The bartender clearly had never walked on railroad tracks. Samuel wondered what else he could be wrong about. He should have taken the mountain trail. Perhaps he still could. But at that moment, he came upon a small station—Glaris—and figured he was nearly halfway, so he kept on going.

The wind rustled the trees from the forest, carrying the sharpness of pine and larch. He tried to imagine what it must look like in the day—green meadows on one side, thick forest on the other. In the morning, he would see more at the station.

The tracks rolled into a tunnel. Pitch-black inside. The bartender should have warned him about a tunnel. Sweat dripped down his back as he kept to the slip of ground between the rock wall and the tracks. The air was stale and chalky. A sharp-edged panic hit him, and it all came back—the time he was twelve, and the wind lifted the loose topsoil from the land on his family's farm and all the farms around the state. It had been planting season. He and his elder brother, Tommy, went to school only in the mornings because they helped their father work the plow in the afternoons. All three of them were in the field when the wind started. Suddenly, Samuel couldn't see, even the wooden handle of the plow in his hand, and the horse pulling it disappeared. He called out to his brother, thought that if he walked in the direction he'd last seen Tommy, he would find him. Instead, the dust burned his eyes and filled his mouth and ears, thick like stumbling into a cement wall.

He fell to the ground and might have suffocated if not for Tommy, who found him and helped him to stand. *You gotta hold yourself like a man,* Tommy had said, *not give the wind or anything a chance to destroy you.* They huddled, hunching into one another for hours. Samuel had been a boy then. And though the air and darkness in the tunnel felt the same to him, now he was twenty-two, and Tommy was gone, his boat hit by a U-2 submarine a little over a year ago. He took two quick breaths in, one out, and let the fear leave him.

The ground shook. He bent down and touched the track. The cold metal rattled. In his gut, Samuel knew it was a train. He tried to flatten his body against the rock wall, but the tunnel was low, and the curve of the wall left no room for his head. An acrid scent of sulfur. The strident clack of metal on metal. The only thing to do was lie on the ground and flatten his entire body against the wall. He closed his eyes and counted as the train rattled past.

When it was gone, he let out a long exhalation and the tightness that had gripped his chest in a vise eased. He stood and patted his clothes down. After the dust cleared, a halo of gray showed the end of the tunnel. He hurried toward it, and once he was outside, he drank in the fresh air. One more station—Monstein—and he would be there.

After what felt like an hour of walking, the tracks forked. One went south, the other north. He had no idea which one would lead him to Wiesen, so he took a guess and followed the southern track. The farther along he went, the more he regretted listening to the bartender. He should have warned him about the fork in the tracks and told him which to take. Samuel had been too eager.

The ground along the track narrowed. He switched to the inside, stepping between the ties. Something felt different. He couldn't quite figure it out until his boot slipped on the edge of one of the ties, and instead of hitting small sharp rocks, as he'd done all the way, there was only air. The bartender's raised arms flashed in his mind. *Goddammit.* He was on a trestle above a gorge. His legs started to shake. He bent down on all fours and turned to make his way back. Once he was on steady ground, he picked up his speed. Done with the tracks and all the hooey the bartender had told him, he found an opening between the trees and dashed toward it.

All he had was a bar of chocolate he'd nabbed from the hotel. He ate it as he walked. It was darker in the forest, but he didn't mind. He heard a train whistle in the distance and was grateful he was nowhere near the gorge. The ground was soft and easy to traverse, the crunch of leaves and sticks reassuring under his sore feet.

After some time, he came upon a clearing. In the distance sat a stone house. No lights, just the moon shining down on its tin roof. Approaching, he could hear water dripping. He held out his hand and felt a long rectangular stone basin and a cold metal pipe. He bent down and drank.

A dirt track ran off the side of the house. He took it, thinking it would lead to a village or a bigger road. It sloped down steeply. He kept to the side of the tracks, preferring not to leave marks on the dirt. He'd learned in training that it would be harder for a dog to pick up his scent on wet grass than on dry dirt. And if he was close to the forest, he could quickly run in and hide.

The sky was a deep blue, and the sun had crested the hori-zon. Just as he was thinking how grateful he was to be off the railroad tracks, he came around a bend and walked into a group of soldiers manning a barricade. They shone a light on his face.

"*Halt, deine Ausweispapiere*!" a soldier said, pointing his gun at him.

There was nothing for Samuel to do but hold up his hands.

13

Samuel

Switzerland
June 1944

They brought him to a police station. He asked for water.

They laughed. "Who helped you?"

Samuel didn't answer. He wasn't going to betray the bartender.

He was left alone in a police cell overnight and given cheese and bread in the morning. At midday, the police bundled him into the back of a van. He hoped they were bringing him back to Davos. The van drove until the sun was low in the sky. Then, it stopped. He was brought out. Instead of the Palace Hotel, it was a dirt track. An officer with a gun in one hand and a dog on a lead in the other greeted him.

"*Gehen Sie*!" the officer said, poking him with the gun.

After about an hour, he arrived at a camp surrounded by barbed wire. Above the gate, he read the sign: *Wauwilermoos*.

In a narrow room, they emptied his pockets and removed his dog tags. They tried again with the questioning, wanting to know who helped get his clothes and the train ticket in his pocket. He refused to answer, so they placed him in the hole Garcia had warned him about.

The cell was no more than ten by ten feet. The stench inside was so caustic he gagged. A trench ran down one side of the wall; the door closed, then darkness. He felt around for a blanket or window. Nothing but hard cement. From what he'd heard in Davos, punishment for first-time escapes was ten days.

He was angry. Angry with the Legation for letting him rot in this cell. Angry with the Swiss for hiding behind neutrality when his time at Davos proved the country was far from neutral. Mostly, he was angry with himself for taking the wrong track—if he'd gone north instead of south, he might be with the Maquis now. But Samuel understood anger wouldn't be enough to get him through this.

He hunched into himself and went to what he knew was real. A place they couldn't take away from him and that would be there waiting after the war—the Arkansas River. It was where he and Tommy had spent their summers exploring. Samuel stepped into the cool water and washed the grime off his body. He climbed over the rocks and guided his canoe through rapids and whirlpools. He camped overnight and woke to bird songs in the early mornings. He waded in the water and threw his line until he felt the tug and reeled it in, slime on his fingers as he scaled the bass before grilling it over a fire and tasting the soft white flesh that peeled easily off the bone. There was a whole world there waiting for him. A world that he and Tommy loved. He promised himself that after the war, though he couldn't bring Tommy's ashes back to sprinkle in the river, he would get something that had belonged to his brother and put it in the water, to finally put him to rest.

He would make it through if he could hold on to that special place in his mind.

On 4 July Samuel returned to Davos.

The Palace Hotel overflowed with airmen. He was told at the front desk there were 350 men and no more single rooms. He wouldn't have minded if not for what he'd just been through. He'd gone so deep into himself he'd yet to adjust to being on the outside. His collarbone chafed his shirt, his trousers hung low on his waist, and he needed a shave after ten days. He looked for familiar faces—Garcia and Bobby—but everyone he passed was a stranger. A weight pressed on his chest. *Talk. One word. Then another. Like riding a bike.* He cinched his shoulders back and turned the room's door handle.

A man sat on one of the two beds, back against the wall, reading a paper.

"Hello, chap," he said, standing. Ginger hair cut close to the scalp, he held out his hand. "I was told I'd get a roommate today. I'm Peter Lindsay, His Majesty's Royal Air Force."

"Samuel Reardon." They shook hands. Samuel sat on the other bed and forced himself to speak. "You been here long?"

"Arrived five days ago after a two-week quarantine in a Zurich hotel. Crash-landed at Dübendorf Airfield. The British camps are chock-a-block, so they've thrown me in with you Yanks."

"What about the rest of your crew?"

"I was the only officer. They sent the enlisted men to Wengen," he said, eyeing Samuel. "Looks like you've been somewhere unpleasant."

"Ever heard of Wauwilermoos?"

"The penal camp that's more like a Luftwaffe Stalag?"

"That's the one." The weight slid off his chest. He could do this. "Believe it or not, they cleaned me up before bringing me here."

"What were you in for?"

"I tried to walk my way out of Davos."

"Blimey." He flashed a toothy grin. "Did you get close?"

"I got lost."

They both laughed.

"What's the news on the war?" Samuel said.

"Hitler sent Rommel's Panzer division to Normandy. Our boys are fighting them around Caen. I heard your side has launched an offensive against Saint-Lô. The Nazi bastard ordered his men to fight to the death."

Staccato, rapid-fire explosions came from outside. Samuel went to the window and opened it. The smell of metallic gunpowder hung in the air. American soldiers sauntered through the street, setting off firecrackers.

"What's that about?" Peter said, looking at the men on the street.

"Independence Day."

"I guess I should congratulate you."

"Save it. Nothing to celebrate until after the war's won."

The Americans made a ruckus, and smoke wafted up from the street. Some passersby smiled. Others stood with arms crossed at their chests. The Swiss soldiers were letting the Americans blow off steam. What else could they expect from 300 young fighter pilots billeted in a hotel with nothing to do? But when the Americans advanced toward the German consulate, the Swiss soldiers moved in, forcing them back to the Palace Hotel.

Through the gray smoke, Samuel looked at the lintel above the double doors of the German consulate: it was bare. The corner of his mouth curled up. Garcia and Bobby had stolen the black eagle and swastika! It was a drop in the ocean compared to the fighting in Normandy—but they'd done what they could, and it made him proud.

"Seems like something is missing from the German consulate across the street," he said with pride.

Peter's blue eyes went wide. "Two of your chaps stole the plaque! The day I arrived, it was found in the hotel cellar, hidden behind cases of wine." He ran a hand through his hair. "They caught the airmen—a bombardier and a navigator—and sent them to Wauwilermoos."

They'd be all right in the hole, just like Samuel had been.

"Got to admire men like that," Peter said. "Even if it only angers the Germans for a few days, it sends a signal."

"What do you mean?"

"Every man must do his part, no matter how small or wherever he finds himself."

Samuel agreed with that. He glanced at Peter's wrist. "That's one helluva watch. I never saw a pilot at Harrington wear one of those."

"It's very special to me," Peter said. "One day, after we get out of here, I'll tell you the story."

14

Samuel

Davos
July 1944

A week later, Sam Woods, the American economic attaché at the consulate in Bern, parked his black Opel in front of the Palace Hotel. It was a knock-you-off-your-heels kinda car—a coupé with hexagonal headlights and the model name, *Kapitän*, embossed in shimmering red letters on the steel hubcaps. All the airmen came out to admire it before joining the line outside the room where Woods would meet with them individually.

Some of the pilots referred to Woods as General Sam. Though he was the same generation as Legge, all similarity ended there. Hefty and dressed in a pale gray double-breasted suit and tie, he had a receding hairline with a few strands at the back of his crown. But it was his character that made him stand out. Finishing with a pilot, he walked him out to the hallway, shook his hand and wished him good luck. Then he turned to the rest of the men, and in a warm Texas drawl, said, "Don't worry, fellas, I'm going to get to every one of you."

Samuel suspected Woods might offer his only chance to bust out of Davos, so when it was his turn, he decided to take a chance and surprise the economic attaché.

"Sir, you've been inside all morning. Perhaps you'd like to stretch your legs and get some fresh air?"

Woods smiled. "What do you propose, Second Lieutenant?"

"How about if we go for a walk and talk? You'd have a chance to admire the scenery."

"That's fine by me."

Samuel was relieved not to be in a room where their conversation could be overheard and reported to Legge. The sky was clear, and they turned north, away from the train station and toward Davos-Dorf, the German enclave.

"I contacted Captain Fiske. He vouched for you."

"Did Legge tell you to do that?"

"Oh, dear boy, no. Legge doesn't tell me anything. But I make it my business to find things out. My question to you is, do you still want to risk another escape attempt to return to your squadron?"

After six weeks in Switzerland, including ten days in solitary confinement, someone in the United States government was offering to help. It was hard to believe, but how it filled him with hope. Finally, he was no longer alone. "You bet. Can you get me out?"

"I've built a good network, assisting over a hundred airmen escape." He lit a cigarette. "I can't guarantee all will go smoothly—it never does. But I can give you the best chance of making it a success."

"I'd be grateful, sir."

"That's what I thought you'd say. Fiske wanted me to let you know that there's a high likelihood the squadron won't be permitted to send you back out on a mission."

"What? Why?" Samuel couldn't believe what he was hearing.

"I don't know, son. You'd have to ask him."

"It doesn't make sense."

"That's war for you. Perhaps they wouldn't want to risk you landing in Switzerland again and upsetting the authorities. Ever since our boys dropped their load on Schaffhausen, the Swiss have been less than pleased with us. I'm telling you all this because every escape involves risk. You could be killed or captured and sent to Wauwilermoos for the duration of the war."

Samuel raked his hand through his hair. He didn't want to go back there, but he couldn't spend the rest of the war in a hotel doing nothing.

They continued walking in silence. Everything around Samuel took on a new intensity. Footsteps in front and behind, boys' laughter, water trickling in the stream as it ran along the main street. He noted the light—golden rays falling over a chalet nestled in the woods, amber striking the wildflowers in the meadows. It would be easy to stay. That's what Woods was trying to say. Was Samuel ready to give all this up and risk his life, or years in a prison camp, just to sit behind a desk? He would have liked to ask Woods for advice. But he knew this was a decision only he could make. He didn't have it in him to do nothing and wait the war out. Others were fighting. He wanted to do his part.

"Sir, I know the risk and am willing to take it."

Woods smiled. "Good. You never know what sort of adventure you might stumble upon. I've had a few pilots join the Maquis in France. Maybe that's in your future."

"Hard for me to see that. I'm a pilot. Flying is all I know. I won't be much use to them."

"Something's out there waiting for you. Legge thinks the war's end will come swiftly after our boys liberate Paris. I'm not so optimistic. It's going to take time. Better to be doing something than sitting around, which is the surest way to get into trouble."

"Agreed." He wanted to ask about Peter. Samuel had noticed Peter's watch, which could be useful since Samuel had given his away. "Would it be possible for my roommate to come? He's an RAF pilot."

"Yes, it's better you're two in case there's trouble."

They'd reached the train station at Davos-Dorf.

"Now that we understand one another, you see that path up there?" Woods didn't point with his hand but motioned with his chin to a pole with a yellow-shaped arrow at the tip. It was too far away for Samuel to read the small black lettering on the arrow.

"Yes, sir."

"Two nights from today, you will come the way we're walking now and cut into the forest where the yellow sign indicates. Look carefully. Note it so that you'll be able to find it in the pitch-blackness."

"Where does it go, sir?"

"It's a mountain path across the valley to Kublis."

"How long will that take?"

"Five hours," he said, turning around. As they made their way back to the hotel, Woods put his hands behind him and explained the plan. "Once you arrive in Kublis, make your way to the church on the outskirts of town. You'll hear the bells that ring the hour. Go inside. The door is always left unlocked. Sit on the bench in the fourth row."

Samuel nodded.

"Wait for someone to come and sit alongside you. They will ask what you would like for breakfast. You'll reply: *hot tea and toast with apricot jam and butter.* Then you'll be driven to Vevey. At nightfall, you'll be brought to the lake to row a boat across to the other side, where the Maquis will be waiting."

No train tracks. Samuel liked it. "What about civilian clothes?"

"I always keep some in the car. Before I leave tonight, I'll put them in a brown bag and send them to your room. Two sets, right?"

"Yes, sir."

"Very good. Any other questions, Second Lieutenant Reardon?"

He had one, but it didn't relate to the escape plan. "Sir, can you explain why General Legge doesn't help the pilots escape? None of us understand it. And frankly, sir, we all feel abandoned by him."

"A lot is going on in this war. I can't speak for Legge other than to say the general is a military man who thinks people should be machines. After they turn out to be human, it surprises him." Woods' mouth tightened. "He knows what I get up to and though he doesn't approve, he leaves me be."

"Why is that, sir?"

"Switzerland acts like a mailbox of sorts—a place where both sides in the war can communicate with one another and carry out espionage—Legge doesn't want to upset this arrangement. The Americans want to keep the Swiss authorities happy. But my contacts have useful information, so he pretends that he doesn't know what I'm up to. I'm left alone." He went silent for a moment. "Now, what I'm about to tell you is confidential, so you keep it to yourself, understand?"

"Yes, sir."

"Some time ago, I received firsthand witness accounts from two men who escaped a camp holding Jews in Poland. He said the people sent there were worked to death." He shook his head. "The things they told me were terrible."

Samuel had heard rumors of the Germans shipping the European Jews to a camp in Poland. He didn't know what happened to them there. Some guys had said people were killed on arrival.

Woods looked down at his feet. "I sent it all to Washington. They've suppressed it. I don't know why. But there's nothing I can do other than gather more information, and hopefully, one day, there will be too much for Washington to ignore."

There were so many things about this war Samuel didn't understand. The generals and politicians could order squadrons to bomb the camp in Poland. They were bombing the hell out of cities and civilian sites all over German-occupied Europe—why not a camp where people were worked to death? Maybe there was some bigger picture Samuel couldn't see. All he knew about war was that it was a deadly spinning wheel and the faster it spun the more dangerous it became for himself, Woods, Peter, Garcia and Bobby, who were just cogs on the edge.

"Sir, I appreciate the risk you're taking to help me."

"I like to think that even one small action can have a multiplying effect."

They'd reached the hotel. Samuel would have liked to stay with Woods, but other pilots were waiting.

Woods held out his hand and leaned in close. "Now, you go out there and make me proud. You hear?"

"Yes, sir." Samuel shook his hand. "Thank you, sir. I won't let you down."

15

Gina

Le Brassus
October 2018

I do as Mamie wants and sit on the avocado-colored sofa in the town hall's waiting area. Her back is to me as she talks to the woman at the desk. I don't understand why the woman pushed back, seeming to make it difficult for Mamie to access her family's files. Glancing around, I look for something to focus on while I wait.

On the white table in front of the sofa are Nordic ski maps, hiking trail brochures, and magazines. I'm drawn to the cover of a slick promotional magazine with a photograph of a spiral glass building. The photo is framed by large white lettering at the top, *Musée Atelier Audemars Piguet*, and in black italics at the bottom, a quote that compares watchmaking to architecture by Bjarke Ingles.

My jaw drops as I reach for it. Ingels is the most innovative architect in the world. The one paper I wrote at university was on the waste incinerator he designed outside of Copenhagen with an artificial ski slope, a running path, and the world's tallest climbing wall. I turn the magazine's pages, and the museum's structure unfolds—double spiral walls constructed of curved glass with a brass mesh on the outside to regulate light and temperature. How could a watch museum in Mamie's hometown lure someone of Ingels' stature?

A door squeaks, and I look up. The woman behind the desk is gone. Mamie flashes a smile in my direction. I stand, thinking she wants me to come over, but she shakes her head and signals I should remain where I am. I sit down and read about the museum's roof made of steel and covered in grass so it blends with the landscape. A little swell of happiness rises in my chest as the museum seems to incorporate all the elements that first drew me to architecture, all that I thought it was before reality struck.

"Gina?" Mamie says, motioning for me to come over at last. She's holding a clip of paper, small and white.

I set the magazine down and join her.

Her arm reaches out to mine. "My family's file is stored off site in a warehouse."

"Can we go and get it?" I ask.

Her mouth turns down. "Access to the warehouse is only for Commune employees. But with a little haggling, she promised to deliver the file to our hotel within a few days."

"Good." I hope Mamie has another lead so that we don't waste any of the time we have here. I help her outside to where the taxi driver waits.

"I didn't sleep well," she says, settling into the back seat. "Jet lag. I want to return to the hotel for a nap." Her face is white, her cheeks gaunt.

"Are you feeling OK?" Maybe the battle with the woman has tired her.

She rubs her temples with her fingers. "A lot of memories."

"Is there something I can do?"

"Being here is enough," she says, squeezing my hand. "Tonight, let's eat early and I'll tell you everything about

Elizabeth. I'll need your quick thinking to figure out how we use these next days until the file arrives."

I nod, grateful that Mamie's finally letting me into her world, like she said she would. "I'll look forward to that."

"No need to stay with me at the hotel. Go out and explore the town. Enjoy yourself while I rest."

After I leave Mamie at the hotel elevator, I go back outside. There's a chill in the air and a light wind, but I feel like walking to clear the jet lag and loosen the knots in the side of my neck from the hotel's soft pillow.

On the next block, there's a short line in front of an oyster-white nineteenth-century building. *Musée Atelier Audemars Piguet—Guided Tours.* Since I'm curious about the building and don't have another place to go, I join the queue. A sign states the tour lasts forty-five minutes. Only five people are in line ahead of me, so I'm confident I'll get in. I reach the door, and a man in a pale gray suit asks for my name.

"Gina Carlyle."

He scans the paper in his hand. "You're not on the list."

"What list?"

"The registration list."

"I didn't know you had to register. I can do it now."

"I'm afraid not," he says, stepping back. "We require advance registration for security reasons. In addition to being a museum, this is also the workshop where our master watchmakers assemble the Grandes Complications, so we can only offer tours once a week. You'll have to come back next Thursday."

I don't know what a Grande Complication is, but our flight back home is at the end of the week. Now that I know about Ingels' spiral glass museum, I can't come to Le Brassus and *not* see it. On the practical side, it's starting to rain, and I need a place to spend a few hours while Mamie sleeps.

"Could you make an exception?" Sweat breaks across my brow. "I won't be here next Thursday." I wipe my forehead, and his gaze goes to my watch.

"Are you one of our customers?" he says.

I'll lie to get in. "Yes."

He bows ever so slightly as if I've suddenly become royalty. "Come in, Ms. Carlyle."

I follow him to a room where a handful of people sit on beige sofas around a coffee table stacked with books and glossy pictures of watches. It feels like I've entered a luxurious living room rather than a museum.

"What would you like to drink?" a woman asks.

"Coffee, please."

Someone comes to collect the forty Swiss francs for the cost of the tour. I draw in a breath—that's fifty dollars or half my tips on a slow weekday night at the restaurant. But now that I'm here, I don't want to back out. I put my bag in a locker in a side room and return to the sofa, where a coffee waits with a square of fine dark chocolate covered in silver paper. Our small group includes a young couple, two middle-aged men, and a family with well-dressed teenage boys. We sip our drinks and steal glances at one another.

A man enters and introduces himself as Mr. Righetti, the in-house historian.

"Welcome to the world of Audemars Piguet. We're delighted you can join us today. I look forward to introducing you to our collection of exceptional timepieces. This is the original house where it all began in 1875. The new museum is just behind the house, where we'll go now." He glances around the room. "Do you have any questions before we start?"

I have a question that's been turning in my mind since reading in the guidebooks about watchmaking in the Swiss mountain valleys. "How did watchmaking come here? It seems an unlikely location."

Rubbing his hands together, he smiles as though he's been waiting for that question. "Two hundred years ago, the people living in the valley were dairy farmers. Winters were long and cold. For six months, schools were closed, and the roads and railways snowed in. With little to do, the farmers kept their cows on the ground floor and spent their days crafting delicate watch parts under large windows in their attics. In the spring, they would bring the parts they'd made to Geneva to sell to the watch companies. Then, a few families decided to manufacture their own watches. Two of those families were Audemars and Piguet." He releases his hands. "Shall we start?"

We step into the spiral museum, and I'm immediately struck by its beauty. The glass walls seem to merge with the green meadow outside, creating a stunning view. The historian explains that the spiral structure represents the beating engine of every mechanical watch—the mainspring. I can't quite grasp what he means. All the watches I've worn have a battery that must be changed yearly. Then he brings us to a display case containing a wristwatch and, alongside it, the hundreds of tiny parts that somehow fit inside, including the long, elegant S-shaped metal mainspring.

"The spring is loaded in a barrel. The longer the spring, the more energy and power reserve the watch has," he says, pointing to the crown on the edge of the case. "Winding the crown creates tension within the spring. The beauty of a mechanical watch is that if you wind it regularly, it never runs out of energy. In the throw away culture of the modern world, our watches are designed to last forever."

He speaks of barrels, gears, escapement wheels, levers, oscillation systems, tourbillons, sapphires and rubies, but I keep wondering at the impossibility of all those parts fitting inside a wristwatch. It could never be done by a human hand. A machine must position them perfectly in place. But hadn't he mentioned dairy farmers assembling the parts through the winter months?

"Now, let's turn to the Grandes Complications. Does anyone know what a watch must include to be considered a Grande Complication?"

One of the teenage boys raises his hand as if he's at school. "A minute repeater, a chronograph, and a perpetual calendar."

"Very good," says the historian, nodding his approval.

The boy's parents exchange smiles.

I don't know what these things are, but since everyone else seems to, I feel like I should and make a mental note to look them up on the internet at the hotel.

He leads us to the center of the building. "This is the most complicated watch ever produced: the Universelle. Made in 1899, this pocket watch comprises one thousand one hundred and sixty-eight parts and has twenty-one functions."

Everyone approaches the gold watch hanging in the display case. But my eyes shift to the glass walls beyond the Universelle, where a handful of men and one woman, wearing small magnifying glasses over one eye, are entirely absorbed in their work. The metal tools on their tall wooden desks, the way the light slips through the glass wall, their hands cradling the watch as if they're holding a newborn, hits me with a jolt of adrenaline. Not a single machine. The assembly of hundreds of parts is done by human hands.

"Now, it might surprise everyone to learn that without women, we would never have transitioned from pocket to wristwatches."

I see him move to another display case. But I'm not ready to turn away from the woman behind the glass, the instruments in her delicate hands sliding back and forth with a surgeon's precision.

"Two hundred years ago, women's dress styles did not include pockets. A watch that men carried in their vest pocket was cumbersome and impractical for a wealthy woman. In 1810, a Swiss-born watchmaker, Abraham-Louis Breguet, designed the world's first wristwatch for Caroline Murat, the queen of Naples, who was Napoleon's sister. Men felt it was too small and fragile to put on their wrists. It would take World War I's brutal trench warfare and the early days of aerial combat before men finally agreed to give up the pocket watch for the practical advantages of the wristwatch."

War and watches. I glance at my wrist. Grandfather wore this during the war. Did he need it for flying? Is that why there are all those numerical scales on the outer rim? And the scratches on the glass. I remember the stains on the leather underside. Maybe Grandfather was hurt while wearing it. It's a story I'll never know because he's gone, but some part of him remains with the watch that lives on.

The historian turns to lead the group away from the Universelle. I want him to stay a while longer, and point to the watchmakers. "What watches are they making?"

"This is the workshop of our master watchmakers. Each creates a Grande Complication from start to finish, assembling over six hundred components by hand."

"How long does that take?" one of the teenagers asks.

"Eight to nine months." There's a communal gasp.

Warmth rises in my throat. Giving birth to something that never dies. I touch the watch on my wrist. My finger and thumb find the crown and wind it. To my astonishment, it moves. In my mind's eye, I see the interior stem turning the toothed barrel as the metal spring, curled like a seashell, absorbs the tension that will slowly release the energy to propel the hands on the dial. I look down, hoping the second hand will sweep across the face. No. Too easy. Seventy-three years is a long time. I can't expect the watch to start working after winding the crown. Suddenly, guilt, like the nib of a pen, pokes at my chest as I realize I've been so absorbed by the watches that I haven't thought of Mom since entering the museum. I reach for the scarf tied around the handles of my bag. Memory is fragile. If I don't think of her, she'll truly be gone.

I look at all those dials, and an idea comes to me. Wouldn't it be magical if Grandfather's watch could be working when Mamie gives it to Elizabeth? It's a crazy notion and I feel like I'm getting ahead of myself since we don't have a single lead to find Elizabeth. But Mamie had recalled every inch of the dial as though it was sealed in her memory. All that's missing is the turning of the hands. I think she would want to see them moving as they once did and since a watchmaker could do the restoration while we're looking for Elizabeth, it just might work. I smile, imagining Mamie's expression when the gold hands are once again sweeping across the black dial.

The tour ends, and we return to the old building to collect our bags. The idea of repairing the Rolex has taken such hold that I can't let it go. I come alongside the historian and hold up my wrist. "Do you know anyone who can get this watch working again?"

His eyes light up. "A Rolex Oyster 3525. Very rare. I noticed it right away. Collectors have given that model a nickname—Monoblocco."

"Oh," I say, leaning forward. "Why?"

"The case and bezel are made of one piece—a single block, hence a Monoblocco."

Bezel is another word I don't know that I feel I should. "What's a bezel?"

He lifts an eyebrow. "A bezel is the rim that holds the glass cover on the watch. Some have special markings and can be rotated to help the wearer read other times."

"Is it here?" I say, pointing at the metal rim of the Rolex.

He nods. "If you want to get it working again, I know someone who might be able to help." As he removes a business card from his wallet, the air buzzes with an invisible charge, making my heart beat a little faster.

"He's an unconventional watchmaker, young but incredibly talented. He prefers traditional methods and works only on vintage watches. I've recommended him to our clients who collect the dead brands."

I nod, not letting on that I have no idea what that means.

"The quality of his work is exceptional. Lucky for you, he's based in Le Brassus."

The historian writes a name and telephone number on the back of the card and hands it to me.

"Be sure to use my name. He only accepts clients on recommendation."

"Thank you." The card feels right in my hand, as if it's meant to be there, though I can't explain why.

16

Gina

Le Brassus
October 2018

Outside the museum, I check the time on my phone. A little over an hour has passed since I left Mamie at the hotel. She's probably still sleeping, and I don't want to wake her.

It's no longer raining. Puddles on the road sparkle in the sunlight. I notice a building on a hill set off from the road. Light shines on the metal milk jugs outside the double doors. It must be the *laiterie*, cheese shop, that a flyer at the hotel advertises as the oldest building in town. There's a bench out front. I make my way there.

I sit on the bench and pull out the historian's card. Monsieur Righetti's name is printed on one side, and scrawled in black ink on the other: *Kai Grueinger*. Doesn't sound French or Italian. Probably Swiss-German. I have a chunk of ruffled bills in my wallet that add up to a thousand dollars. It's all the tip money I've saved for a deposit on an apartment. I don't know if Dad will allow me to stay with him now that he's no longer speaking to me. But if repairing Grandfather's watch for Mamie means delaying moving for a few more months, I can do that.

I take in the broad view of the wooded hills and the dark shadows stroking them from passing clouds. Mamie puts on a brave face, but being here is hard on her. She's quiet, like there's too much pain in her heart to speak. I want to lighten her burden and do something to make her happy.

Though truthfully, there's another reason I want to call the number on the back of the card. I can't get the elegant swirl of the mainspring out of my mind. How could something as hard as metal bend and curve to capture time? A beautiful idea made concrete. I look at Grandfather's watch. The possibility of the energy flowing back through it, and me understanding how that works, expands inside my chest, like a tiny ember warming the coldness that has been there since Mom's death.

I pull out my phone and dial the number. "May I speak with Kai Grueinger?"

"Who's calling?" A man's voice, guarded, slightly distant.

I introduce myself and tell him how I got his number.

"What can I do for you?"

"I have an old Rolex watch that no longer works."

"Which Rolex?"

I should have recorded the number the historian referenced. I look down at the dial and read what's written on it, trying to sound confident. "It's a chronograph."

"Rolex makes a lot of chronographs. What's the model number?"

All I can remember is the nickname. "It's a Monoblocco."

Silence. Did I mispronounce Monoblocco? Or maybe he's not interested. I look down at the watch, scratched with nicks and dents. It's nothing like the gleaming timepieces in the museum. But the design is just as elegant, and with those decimal numbers ringing the outer dial, it must have helped Grandfather during the war, maybe even saved his life. The silence on the other end seems to go on forever.

"I'd like to have it restored."

"I don't do restorations," he says, a knife-sharp edge to his voice.

"But Monsieur Righetti—"

"I repair watches."

"Repair, that's it." Why is it so complicated? "I just want the watch to tell time again."

"I've never worked on a Monoblocco. Only a few hundred were produced."

My pulse races. "Does that mean you're interested?"

"Yes."

"I'm in town for a week."

"Then you better come over now—3 Chemin des Noisetiers."

"Oh, great, thanks. I'm on my way."

I check the map on my phone and find Chemin des Noisetiers a few blocks from Mamie's old house. My stomach growls. I'd like to stop and get lunch but this is too important. Kai said to come over now. I'll skip lunch since Mamie and I will eat an early dinner.

It doesn't take long to reach Chemin des Noisetiers. My shoes crunch and crush the hazelnuts that have fallen from the trees and litter the street. I find number three—a wood and stone house standing out from the concrete ones around it. Two neatly trimmed boxwood plants adorn the front door. I knock.

No reply. I knock again. This time, the door clicks open. A steady beat of music drifts in the air.

"Kai?"

No answer. I step inside a narrow hallway. Men's shoes are stacked neatly on my right under a wooden bench. Coats hang from hooks on the wall above. I close the door, advance to a staircase covered in white carpet, and follow the music. Halfway up, I realize I've left a trail of hazelnut shells on the treads. Idiot. I slip off my black flats, hold them in one hand, and pick out the bits of shell lodged in the carpet. Returning to the bench, I tuck my shoes under it and stuff the shell shards in the pocket of my jeans.

Back on the stairs, the treads tremble from the percussion. The words in the music punch like fists in the air. Must be French rap because it's about selling drugs to get euros. I reach the first floor. There's an open kitchen on one side, a leather sofa, two chairs and a fireplace on the other.

"Kai?"

Still no answer. I continue up the next flight—the music so loud it bounces like a tennis ball off the walls. Reaching the second floor, I see my reflection in a massive window along with a man's form as he sits facing the window and a computer. The music stops.

"Kai?"

He turns around. "Hello."

"I knocked, and the door opened."

"I buzzed you in," he says, advancing toward me.

A large poster of a man, eyes hidden behind dark sunglasses, hangs on the wall to my left. He resembles a rap artist with multiple gold chains around his neck.

"Is that it?" He points at my wrist, the Rolex next to Mom's yellow scarf.

"Yes."

"Can I see it?" A quick shimmer in his eyes.

I unstrap the watch and hand it to him. As he examines it, I get a closer look at him. His blond hair is cut short and swept back from his forehead. He is clean-shaven with an angled jaw. Tall and lean, he wears black jeans, a close-fitting white T-shirt that curves around his well-defined muscles, and clean white socks. I'm glad I picked the shells out of his white carpet. He turns the watch in all directions, studying it carefully.

"Where did you buy it?"

"It belonged to my grandfather."

"How did he get it?"

"He was a pilot in the war."

"British or American?"

"American. Why?"

"Provenance is crucial. Are you going to tell me it's been sitting in a drawer for over seventy years?"

I nod.

He frowns. "American pilots weren't issued Rolex watches."

I shrug. "Why does that matter?"

"Trust me, it matters. Rolex supplied the British army."

"It's *his* watch."

Returning to the desk, Kai takes a loupe—the small magnifying glass I'd seen the watchmakers wear in the museum—and goes in for a closer look.

"Are you here to sell it?"

"No."

He slides the loupe off and looks at me. It's the first time I see how blue his eyes are. Egyptian blue, my favorite color.

"It's worth a lot of money," he says.

"Even with the scratched glass and dented metal case?"

"Defects give it value. There's nothing perfect about the past."

"Is that why you repair, not restore, watches?"

His gaze lingers on me and I hold it, determined not to look away. I don't want to give him any reason to believe this watch doesn't belong to my family.

"Most of these watches were worn by British pilots blown out of the sky on night bombing raids. Maybe fifty of the hundred models have survived." He shifts his weight. "It would be good to know how it came into your grandfather's possession. A Monoblocco would have a story to tell. Do you know it?"

I feel the shells' sharp edges rubbing against my thigh. "No." Or at least not yet. Though Mamie would never sell it, I ask, "You said it was worth a lot. How much?"

"Come on," he says, grinning, "you're kidding that you don't know?"

"I don't."

He examines it again. "Forty-eight thousand dollars as is, but after repairs and once you find the story behind it . . ." He looks up. "I'd add another zero to the price. In a few years, the way the luxury watch market is growing, it will probably be worth half a million."

Unable to breathe, I take a step to one side and nearly fall over. Kai grabs my arm.

"You OK? Here." He rolls out a wooden stool on wheels from under his desk. I sit, gripping my legs with my hands to steady myself.

"Someone could have stolen it. I've been walking around with fifty thousand dollars on my wrist. I can't wear it anymore."

"Not a chance. That's the beauty of vintage watches. No bling. You'd only know the value if you're a connoisseur. In which case, you'd want to buy it, not steal it. One hundred percent safe to wear anywhere." He smiles. "Although don't go swimming with it—it's not waterproof."

"Are you sure it's worth that much?"

"I bet there's a Valjoux 72 inside." His voice is soft, wistful almost.

"A what?"

"It's the movement that controls the chronograph." Maybe he can read the confusion on my face because he pauses. "Chronograph is a stopwatch. See the two sub-dials at the nine and three o'clock position? The 72 controls them. It's a workhorse, made to last." He presses the button above the crown, but none of the hands move. "There's damage in the mechanism; it might be a lever, clutch or spring that needs replacing." He snaps his fingers. "I'll get it functioning in no time."

A crack of worry opens in my chest. If the watch is worth as much as Kai says, the cost to repair it will be more money than I have. "How much to fix it?"

"Depends."

I swallow.

"Parts aren't that expensive but labor is another matter. And you want it done in a week. Rush jobs are more expensive. My fee for taking it apart, cleaning and replacing the pieces that aren't working, running the serial number at Rolex to get copies of the original papers, will make your head spin." He looks me up and down. "Am I right that you aren't loaded?"

I nod.

"What's your budget?"

"A thousand dollars." The thick wad of bills that had seemed weighty now feels insignificant.

"Right—well, that will cover parts, but not labor."

I bite my lower lip and wait for him to tell me more bad news.

"But I've never worked on a Monoblocco and I'd like to. If you allow me to take pictures of the movements and record videos for my website, I'll give you a discount on the repair cost. Some customers wouldn't want to share photos of their watches."

"I don't mind. It seems like a fair trade."

"Great. It's not for promotion. I've already got more clients than I can handle."

"Then why?" I say, curious.

"Our industry seems to believe people will always wear wristwatches. But what if, in the future, they stop? Then, the skills needed to maintain mechanical watches will be lost. Though these watches have all outlived their original owners, they too are fragile, and we need to care for them, if they are to survive." His eyes sparkle as he speaks. "After I'm gone, I want a record to remain in case some crazy kid wants to teach himself."

"Or herself," I add.

He smiles. "Exactly. I'll just charge you for the parts, which might come in under a thousand." He holds out his hand. "Do we have a deal?"

The tiny ember inside has grown into a flame. Joy surges through me. I want to ask him if I can observe as he repairs the mainspring, but I hold off. He might think I'm crazy, and I don't want to give him a reason to change his mind. I can hardly wait to return to the hotel and tell Mamie I've found a watchmaker with Egyptian-blue eyes who listens to rap music and wants to repair the Rolex. She won't believe how much it's worth. Elizabeth will be a rich woman if we can find her. I reach out my hand.

"Deal."

17

Gina

Le Brassus
October 2018

On the way to the hotel, I gently kick the hazelnut husks out of my way. It's twilight, and tangerine-rose clouds shimmer in the sky. The French song that played in Kai's house repeats in my mind alongside the mesmerizing mainspring curled like a cat's tail in the museum.

I feel different, as though Grandfather's watch opened a door into a world I didn't know existed. Is this what Mamie meant when she said getting away would benefit me? My thoughts shift to Elizabeth and how finding her will be bittersweet for Mamie. Time flows forward, so they'll never be able to recapture those lost decades apart. And yet, I remember a physics professor saying that time isn't absolute. In some corners of the universe, where gravity is strong, space and time stretch and slow. Maybe the steadfast love Mamie has carried all these decades for Elizabeth will act like a gravitational force, slowing time down for them in the present. They deserve to be together.

The hotel is up ahead. I see the last light reflected in the windows as I cross the street to reach it. I take the stairs to our room and brush the electronic key card against the door's flat metal surface. When I hear the click, I push it open.

"I'm back."

There's no light on, and the room is gloomy and dark. Mamie's in the armchair near the desk.

"Mamie?"

Silence. Her body slumps to one side, motionless.

I charge across the room. Her eyes are closed, and her face is still. Too still. Mom's last moments come back, sickening me, and I force myself to shake them away. "Please, Mamie." I come close. "Wake up, please."

But she doesn't. I stand and go to the switch near the door to turn on the light. Then, back at her side, I take her hand in mine and feel the warmth from her body. "It's Gina," I say, "can you hear me?"

I've never stared at her this close, and I realize how deep the lines are etched about her mouth and eyes, like someone has drawn them with a sharp instrument. She could be having a stroke. I'm ready to pull out my phone and call an ambulance when her eyes slit open.

"Gina?" Her voice sounds parched.

"I'm here," I say, relief like a bucket of cool water washing over me. Recalling the doctor's warning that glaucoma dehydrates the body, I let go of her hand to reach for the pitcher on the desk. "You must be thirsty," I say, pouring water into a glass and handing it to her.

Her crooked hands hold the glass as she takes small sips. "That's all," she says. "Put it on the table?"

I want to insist she drinks more, but then I recall how she hated it when the staff at the assisted living center told her to drink more water and she'd intentionally clamp her lips shut to defy them. Instead, I press her gently. "Tell me when you want more."

She straightens her back and sits up. “I must have fallen asleep. What time is it?”

“Six-thirty. Are you feeling OK?”

“Yes. A little hungry. How about you?”

“Very hungry. I missed lunch.”

“Oh.” Her eyes widen. “Shall we go back to Chez Lily and try the fondue?”

I nod. “Do you remember what you said this morning about having an early dinner and that you'd tell me about Elizabeth?” Mamie drops her gaze. I press her a little. “I can't help you find her if I don't know what happened.”

“All right.” She takes a breath. “The story will take time to tell.”

“Then we must start tonight, *n'est-ce pas*?”

She nods, and I wrap my arms around her. “I promise I won't let you down. I'll do everything I can to help you find her.”

At Chez Lily, we sit next to the window. On the table, a pot of melted *moitié-moitié*, half Gruyère and half vacherin cheese, to share. A sharp, oily aroma from the fondue fills the air.

I watch Mamie spear a small potato with the forked end of a long metal stick, twirl it in the cheese, then slide it onto her plate. She lifts the heavy wooden pepper mill from the table and grinds a fragrant mix of peppercorns, caraway and chili seeds, mustard and coriander grains over the melted cheese. She looks up at me. “The spice gives it a kick.”

I tell her about the museum tour and how I got Kai's name. “He said the watch is worth fifty thousand dollars.”

She doesn't blink. “I hope you told him we're not selling.”

I nod and take a breath. “I gave him Grandfather's watch to repair, which he promised to do for a reasonable price. I'm paying for it,” I say, insisting. “I've saved plenty from my tips.”

"Your idea to repair the watch before giving it to Elizabeth is brilliant. But you shouldn't pay for it with the money you need to get an apartment."

I wave a hand in the air. "This is more important."

She stares at me with her rheumy eyes, then reaches across the table and takes my hand. "That's very thoughtful. Thank you. Your mother would be proud."

I squeeze her hand, grateful she's mentioned Mom because I like feeling she's a part of this, too.

"What did you say the watchmaker's name was?"

"Kai."

"That's a German name."

I raise a shoulder and grind the pepper mill over the cheese on my plate, inhaling the bittersweet mix of coriander and caraway.

"Is he Swiss-German or German?" she asks.

"I don't know. Does it matter?"

"No . . ." Her voice trails off. "It doesn't. So, you like him?"

I open my mouth, surprised by how quickly Mamie has jumped to that conclusion. "No. I mean, yes." She laughs—the first time I've heard her laugh since Mom died.

"He *is* handsome." I feel warm patches creeping along my neck. "But it's not his looks—"

"We don't get to choose who we fall in love with." She smiles. "It's a physical reaction—our hearts telling us this is the one."

"What are you talking about?" I stammer. "I didn't say anything about love."

"You said he was handsome."

"I was trying to say that I like what he *does*."

"Your voice changes when you talk about him."

"It does not." I want to get her off the topic of Kai. "Have you ever seen inside a mechanical watch?"

"No."

"There are hundreds, maybe thousands of pieces, and this magic metal spiral that powers the whole thing."

"Is that what Kai showed you?"

"I saw it at the museum. It's called a mainspring, and when you wind the crown, it tightens the spring into a concentric shell and the slow unwinding of the spring powers the movement." I dip another potato in the cheese.

She leans back in her chair. "I don't remember a museum like that. It must be new. Tell me more about Kai."

I shrug. "I've told you everything I know."

"Does he live in Le Brassus?"

I nod. "A ten-minute walk from the hotel."

"Everything is a ten-minute walk in Le Brassus, except the forest."

"The forest?"

"Le Risoud. It's behind the village and Europe's largest. Half in Switzerland and half in France."

"Like Lac Léman?"

"Yes. I used to often go there." She exhales a long breath, and I feel a sadness like an invisible hand reaching across the table to touch me.

Lily, the owner of the restaurant, comes over. Her red hair is cut in a soft bob. "Oh, look." She points at the fondue pot. "You've left the best part."

I glance at the thin, crusty layer of cheese stuck at the bottom.

"Burnt cheese?" I say.

"It's called *la religieuse*." Lily picks up the pot and starts scraping it off with a fork. I glance at Mamie, who nods her approval. When Lily's done, she tilts the pot over and divides the chunks of charred cheese between our plates. "They look like nun's caps, *n'est-ce pas*? Go on, try it."

It's crunchy and flavorful, like a potato chip. "Delicious," I say.

After she takes her leave, I turn back to Mamie, hoping she will continue. "Why did you often go to the forest?"

She tightens her fingers around the fork. "I went there . . ." Her gaze shifts to the window and the darkness outside.

Does the forest have something to do with Elizabeth? Maybe that's why it's hard for her to talk. I reach over and take one of her hands in mine. "I know this is difficult, but the more you tell me about what happened, the better I can help find her."

She nods. "I've been trying to figure out where to start." She squeezes my hand. "The forest is the right place since it's where Elizabeth's story begins. But first, I must explain a little of how I ended up there."

18

Hedy

Lausanne
July 1944

Hedy sat at the front of the classroom, perched on the edge of her seat. Watching the door, she worried Joseph might not come. Today marked the end of term; exams loomed next week. Hedy would have no way to contact him until classes resumed in the autumn, and she was desperate to speak to him now.

Two weeks had passed since she'd smuggled her first airman, and she couldn't understand why the network hadn't contacted her to continue. Emboldened by her success and inspired by the Allies' landing in Normandy, she wanted to do more. Maybe the flyer had been caught by a Swiss patrol before reaching the Maquis on the other side of the lake. But how could that be her fault? She had done her part in guiding him to the boat. She wanted to find out if he had made it to France, and Joseph was the only person she could ask.

Even with the windows open, the air in the classroom was thick with summer heat. Professor Hassig, adjusting his tie, prepared to start the lesson. He was known for his strictness—after the door closed, no one was allowed inside. Hedy held her breath as the professor neared the door. She heard the hinges creak, but just before it shut, Joseph slipped in and took an empty seat.

"Now that everyone is present," Professor Hassig said, clearing his throat, "let's start by reviewing the meaning of time in Eliot's first poem in the *Four Quartets*." He glided around the desks, returning the marked essays from last week before circling back to the front.

"Joseph, since you were the last to arrive, why don't you read the four lines at the end of the poem's first section to refresh us?"

Joseph didn't look up. His behavior was puzzling. He seemed distracted, avoiding eye contact and keeping his head down.

"Joseph?"

"Yes, sir, I'm sorry." He finally looked up. Dark circles ringed his eyes.

Something was wrong. Hedy wondered if there had been another crisis at the refugee camp. After class, they would talk and she would find out.

"I'll read it now," Joseph said.

Hedy liked poetry, but she wasn't sure about Eliot. Because he was a devout Catholic, she wanted to dismiss him. The world had plenty of religious men, like Pastor Rolle, instructing people, especially women, on how to live. But she couldn't deny that sometimes the clarity in Eliot's words drew her in.

Joseph stood, the paper crinkling in his hand. He read too fast, stumbling over the lines.

Professor Hassig crossed his arms at his chest. "Can you tell the class what those lines mean?"

Joseph shuffled his feet, gaze fixed on the floor, seemingly lost in his thoughts. As the moment stretched into a long silence, the tension in the room grew, and the professor's patience thinned.

"Come on, young man. This isn't physics!"

"I'm sorry, sir." Joseph hung his head. "I'm not feeling well today."

"All right, sit down." A little knot formed in Hedy's chest as the professor approached her desk.

"Hedy, would you like to give it a try?"

She sat up straight. Professor Hassig didn't have the kindest manner, but he was fair. If she made a reasonable effort, he wouldn't fault her. Her eyes fell on the opening line about dawn, and the image that came to her was of a pink-and-orange sky holding a promise, an excitement about the day ahead and all that would unfold.

"Maybe Eliot warns against wasting time," she said, tipping her head to one side. "That no matter where the morning wind takes us, out at sea or on land, we shouldn't lose sight of what's important."

"What do you mean by important?" he pressed her.

"Our duty?"

"Good. Let's dig deeper on the word *duty*—perhaps his meaning is closer to destiny, what the Greeks called *telos*—fulfilling our destiny."

Hedy glanced at Joseph, but he still wouldn't meet her gaze.

"The last line of the poem, 'In the beginning,'" the professor said, looking out at the class to address them all. "Is that clause not odd to come at the end? Does anyone remember the famous line from the opening of the *Four Quartets*?"

A young man raised his hand. Professor Hassig called on him.

"It was about distractions, sir," he said.

"Correct," the professor said. Light shone in from the window. Standing near it, he tilted his head toward the glass like an old crow leaning into the sun as his shiny black eyes scanned the students.

Suddenly, the line that had calmed Hedy in Vevey station—*At the still point of the turning world*—made sense. Eliot meant that the world turned with distractions—newspaper articles, debates on immigration, the government's blackout regulations—diverting people from relying on their own abilities to determine right from wrong. People would think clearly without these distractions, and war might be avoided. She couldn't imagine anyone willingly wanting war.

After the class finished, Joseph got up and spoke with Professor Hassig briefly, then darted from the room. Hedy hurried after him, running to catch him on the steps outside the building.

"Joseph, how are you?"

He kept walking. Had he not heard her?

"Wait a minute," she said, following him.

"I'm busy. I have to go."

"I need to speak with you."

"I can't talk now." He quickened his pace.

She was nearly running, her heart pounding with the urgency of what was inside her. Joseph was the only person she could talk to about the airmen. "It's important."

He stopped and faced her. "What?"

"I want to continue to help," she blurted out, then looked around and lowered her voice. "I guided one pilot with success. But it's been two weeks, and no one in the network has contacted me. With the Allied landings in France, there must be more I can do."

"They will come to you if they need you." His eyes narrowed on her. "Be careful what you ask for."

"What does that mean?" She no longer saw the confident man who had told her to be strong and admired the circle as the ancient symbol of truth.

"Nothing. Forget it."

He'd lost weight. His face was leaner, his cheeks and jaw sharper. "Tell me what has happened?"

"It doesn't concern you." His voice was tight as a drum. "I've got to go." He turned to leave.

Hedy grabbed his arm, and he swiveled to face her. "Let me help you," she pleaded.

"Not with this. It's too big."

"Is it an airman?"

He ran a hand through his dark hair, hesitated, then nodded. "An American." She stepped closer. "Shot while escaping." His hand trembled slightly. "I'm hiding him until he's strong enough to row across the lake."

A beat of silence as she took in the import of his words. "Who shot him?"

"Our soldiers."

She lifted her shoulders. "Where are you hiding him?"

"In my dorm room. I have a fire escape outside my window to bring him in and out and a toilet in my room. I thought it could work. But now he can't stay."

Joseph rubbed the side of his face with his still-shaking hand. He must have been gnawing his nails all night because the skin on the stubs of his fingers was raw.

"Why can't he stay?"

"Yesterday, I received notification from a colonel in the army that I must report for six weeks of military readiness training."

That's why he'd spoken to Professor Hassig after class—to inform him he couldn't sit the exam next week. Military training superseded work or studies. One was called up with a few days' notice and had to drop everything to serve.

"I could help while you're away. Bring the airman supplies. Stand in for you until your return."

"Too risky. Everyone will know I've gone off for military training. No matter how quiet he tries to be, he'll be heard flushing the toilet or running the water. The caretaker has a key to my room. He could open the door at anytime. Without me there to smooth things over, he'll be discovered. The pilot said . . ."

"What?"

"This is his second attempt. He'll be sent to a military prison camp until the war ends. I have to move him somewhere fast."

"What does your contact in the network say?"

"He's gone quiet." Joseph frowned. "Either he's been arrested or is under suspicion and wants to lay low. It's a mess. I don't know what I'm going to do."

She thought for a moment. "How long until the airman can row across the lake?"

"The doctor says he needs ten weeks to recover."

Two and a half months. Until late September. She could hide him. She knew the perfect spot. "There's a hut that belongs to my father in the forest, not far from my house. No one goes there." The words came out as they formed in her head.

"Maybe you don't want to get involved. The risks—"

She leaned forward. "Can he walk? He'll need to walk in the forest to reach the hut."

Joseph nodded. "I've got access to a car." He touched her elbow. "Think carefully. You'll be—"

"When do you report?"

"Tomorrow."

"Then we move him tonight."

"I can't . . ." He shook his head. "You shouldn't do this. It isn't fair to you."

"What isn't fair is that our soldiers shot an innocent man fighting on the right side of this war." Her mind was already spinning with everything she would need to do to get the hut ready. "Drive to 9 Piguet-Dessous in Le Brassus. Past it, and not far along, you'll find logs stacked off the side of the road where there's a sawmill. I'll be waiting there. After I see your car lights, I'll come out."

He nodded. "Midnight?"

If she was fast she could get the hut ready by then. Her father visited it once or twice a year. It was where he stored his wood to dry before making his violins. It would be dusty but there was a stove that he lit when he first stacked newly cut wood inside to cut the dampness. "Right."

"Thank you." He took her hands in his. "Not many people would be willing to take such a risk."

Hedy didn't believe that. Hiding a pilot didn't measure up against the great battles in the air and on land, but it was something. And now, more than ever, she wanted to do her part.

The sky had blackened by the time Hedy stepped off the train at the station in Le Brassus. Her mind buzzed with the tasks at hand. She had to stay focused and not let anything divert her from the preparations or she'd be late for the handover of the airman tonight.

As she left the station, Franck came up alongside her. "How are you, Hedy?"

She stiffened. "Busy, studying for my exams."

"I've brought you a surprise." He held out a small paper bag and opened it. A sweet odor hit the air. Inside the bag, she glimpsed white crystals. Sugar. She didn't want to ask him how he got it. He'd probably stolen it from his father.

"It's for you and your mother. Here, take it."

"You don't need to give us anything." She stepped back.

His dark eyes stared hard at her. "Take it."

Her mother's warning not to upset him flashed in her mind. She reached out her hand.

"Don't you want to know what I've been doing for the last weeks?" he asked. "I thought you might have missed me since our dinner."

"I need to get home. My parents are expecting me and I'm already late."

"I've been working on something for Pastor Rolle." He straightened his shoulders. "He relies on me. But I'm less busy now. Shall we have dinner at a restaurant?" He swallowed, and she watched the Adam's apple rise and fall through the skin of his throat. "Why not tonight? You would like that, wouldn't you?"

"I can't. I've got my exams next week."

"Then, when your exams are over." He stepped closer and touched her arm.

Her skin bristled, and beads of sweat on her palms dampened the paper bag. She shouldn't have accepted it, and she wanted to give the bag back and tell him that she couldn't see him again. But her mind was so full of what she needed to do that she didn't have room to consider Franck. "I've got to go," she said and hurried off.

At midnight, she sat on a pile of logs, the scent of freshly cut wood strong in the air. A breeze ruffled the birch and willow leaves, lulling her to close her eyes and rest in the darkness. She'd walked three hours, with more still to go, but she'd achieved what she set out to do.

She'd swept the hut, made a bed of blankets behind two wood piles and filled the stove with charcoal, ready to light when they arrived. She had taken food from her mother's pantry—a tin of green beans, a portion of Gruyère, strips of dried beef, a few potatoes—along with knives and forks, a candle, tea and the small cooking pot at the bottom of the drawer, which her mother never used. She told herself it wasn't stealing and that one day, when the war was over, she would thank her mother and tell her of her secret sacrifice that saved a pilot's life.

Only after she'd left the hut and was walking through the forest on her way back home did the reality of what she was embarking on sink in. Two and a half months. Ten weeks. Seventy days. No matter how many times Hedy turned it around in her head, she couldn't figure out how to feed a man with only her ration card. The scarcity of supply and rationing of essentials, even if her country wasn't fighting in the war, was a heavy burden. Meat. Bread. Butter. Oil. Sugar. Tea. Rice. Soap. Cloth. Shoes. Everything was rationed based on one's age and profession. Ration cards had to be presented and matched to identification papers. As an unmarried female student, her rations were just above a child's. The black market was possible, but she needed money, which she didn't have.

Hedy was acutely aware that her mother would notice any further depletion of the pantry. A pang of guilt struck her. It wasn't fair to exhaust their family's winter stockpile, especially after her mother's hard work growing and canning the vegetables. The war would likely continue for another winter, and they would need this food. She remembered the brown bag full of sugar and the water-glassed eggs. Franck could help. She could tell him her family needed the extra food—but her parents had already said they had enough supplies. He would either become suspicious or feel she owed him something in return. No, she didn't want to go to Franck, but she might have to if it could keep the pilot alive.

Two beams of blue light pierced the darkness. Hedy leaped down from the log pile, signaling the car to leave the road and enter the sawmill. The engine shut off, and the light disappeared. Metal doors creaked open, and footfalls resounded on the dirt.

"Hedy," Joseph said, "this is Samuel."

She could make out a white triangle, likely the bandages wrapped around his hand and arm. He stepped closer, and she felt a rush of air.

"Pleased to meet you, Hedy," he said, his voice carrying a distinctly American lilt.

Sensing he was extending his good hand, she reached for it and found a firm, confident grip. She felt an unexpected heat, like a spark, from the touch of his skin against hers, in a moment so vivid and sharp that she didn't want to let go.

19

Samuel

La Forêt de Risoud
July 1944

Samuel watched her. All he knew was her name. Before they set out on foot, Hedy and Joseph had exchanged a few words in French. He didn't know what about. Then she told him, in perfect English, that they must walk in silence because they weren't far from the French border. Army night patrols. They wouldn't be safe until they reached the hut in the middle of the forest.

He knew something about army patrols. One had surprised Peter in the church in Kublis. His mind replayed Peter running, arms tight at his sides, to reach the safety of the forest where Samuel waited, a Swiss soldier like a Boche with his low helmet chasing him. One. Two. Six shots. Blood gushed from Peter's chest, then a deadening thump as he went down. Two of the bullets meant for Peter hit Samuel in his left arm and hand. The soldier hadn't seen him. All Samuel could remember was running, the burning on his left side, and blood pouring out like melted wax. Luckily for him, the contact had been waiting, and once the soldiers left with Peter's body, he'd brought him to a doctor.

Samuel looked down and checked Peter's watch. He couldn't get over how he'd given it to him right before he went into the church. Had he sensed something might go wrong? He made Samuel promise to keep the watch safe. Samuel was determined that his friend's death wouldn't be in vain. He and the watch would survive the war.

They'd set out an hour ago, and his eyes had long since adjusted to the darkness. Despite being told so little, he'd had time to figure a few things out about Hedy. She was clearly from around here—where moss and leaves softened the ground, and the air smelled of spruce, pine and sap. From the dirt track they walked on, just wide enough for a truck, he understood they were moving through an old forest that was logged from time to time but mostly left alone. He could tell by how high the trees went because it was possible to compare shades of darkness to distinguish canopy from sky. The trees had to be hundreds of years old to reach that height. Forests don't survive unless they've served a purpose. Perhaps an ancient fortification, a natural barrier against cavalry coming over the border from France.

She could reckon by the stars because he watched her glance up, keeping Polaris in her sight. Since Samuel tracked it, too, he knew they were heading north. She was attentive not only to the sounds around them, holding out her arm once to alert him to halt so they could listen before determining it was safe to move on, but also to him. He'd lost a lot of blood. He was slow. His hand and arm throbbed. The surgeon who fixed him up told him he needed rest and shouldn't do anything strenuous.

If Samuel's breathing sped up, she slowed down to give him time. She was strong, too, because he couldn't help her carry the bag of medicine and bandages the doctor had given him, along with the jars and pans rattling gently inside the pack on her back. Hedy had said only a handful of words to him, but already he knew these things about her.

She led him off the dirt track onto a narrow trail. The forest canopy was denser and blocked out the stars, forcing her to slow down a little, yet she seemed to know exactly where she was going. He followed, grateful for her slower pace as they navigated the uneven, rocky terrain. She helped him climb over a low stone wall, its surface covered in a layer of moss. Finally, they arrived in a small clearing, where a humble hut stood, its presence a stark contrast to the dense forest.

She opened the door. "We're here."

Pitch-black inside. He felt the room spin as he heard her slide the pack to the ground. She lit a candle. He shivered in the cold and damp. She moved to the stove. He could see a pile of blankets in a corner. His head was fuzzy. Mouth dry. He would have liked some water, but that seemed a luxury. If he could only reach the blankets before he tumbled. On his knees, he crawled to the corner, curled up on his good arm, saw coal or charcoal glowing in the stove, and closed his eyes.

Hedy

She worried she'd gone too fast. The pilot, she must call him Samuel, had nearly collapsed after entering. Maybe the eight kilometers to the hut was too far for an injured man to walk. As she lit the stove, her worry grew and she went over to him, listening. His breathing was steady. She considered preparing tea, but he looked so peaceful she decided to let him rest.

His boots were muddy, so she untied the laces and slid them off. Outside, she knocked the heels to remove the mud and turned them upside down. A wad of Swiss francs tumbled out. She gathered the bills and tucked them back inside his boots, turning them the right way up.

After cleaning her shoes and putting them next to his, she drank a little water and settled on the other side of the hut with a blanket. She should sleep before trekking the eight kilometers back to her house. But it was her first time alone with a man at night. A man she knew nothing about.

When she had asked Joseph how he supplied food for the pilot, he said the network had planned to give him cash to buy supplies on the black market. However, after paying the surgeon and purchasing medicine, nothing was left over, so he had no choice but to steal eggs from farmers.

Did Samuel know about Joseph's desperate measures to keep him fed? If so, why wouldn't he share his money? But even with the money, it wouldn't be enough to feed him for two months. Would she, too, become a thief? Hedy had never stolen anything in her life. And yet, wasn't hiding the pilot an infraction greater than stealing? What had seemed so straightforward and clear to her in the light of day had turned gray and confusing by night.

The hut was now lovely and warm. Despite her reservations, she felt herself drift off to sleep.

At some point, she awakened to sounds coming from outside. Soft rustling leaves. She sat up. Too light to be a man's footsteps. Maybe grouse or deer. She used to hunt grouse with her father, so she listened and recognized their call. Strips of light slipped between the seams in the wood planks. Her parents would be up in a few hours. She needed to get going. She stood, took her shoes, and opened the door.

A thin fog hugged the ground. Pink sky in the distance. Her legs were stiff from all the walking, and one arm ached from using it as a pillow. She put on her shoes and went behind a tree to relieve herself.

She wished she'd brought paper and a pencil to write him a note. It would be hard for her to get away tonight. She wouldn't be able to come back until tomorrow. She hoped he would understand. There was plenty of food, though she would need to bring more water. She took her empty pack and left.

That night at dinner, Hedy's thoughts kept wandering back to him. She worried he wouldn't ration the water, expecting she would return right away. She'd sensed him watching her the entire time they'd walked side by side. Did he doubt her? Or maybe he didn't trust her. She couldn't blame him after what he'd been through. But she felt it was more than that—like he was trying to figure her out. She'd even thought he was observing as she navigated by the stars. Her brain flickered back to the sawmill and the burst of heat when their hands touched.

"Are you ready for your upcoming exams?" her mother asked.

She looked up. "Not yet. But with classes over, I've got a few days to concentrate on studying."

"So you won't be going to Lausanne for the rest of the week?"

"No." Hedy immediately regretted saying that. What if she needed to buy food? She only had one ration card, which wouldn't be enough. She'd have to try to buy food on the black market and it wouldn't be safe to do it here in Le Brassus where everyone recognized her. "Well, I might still go, to use the library."

"I saw the bag of sugar on the counter," her mother said, passing her the potatoes. "How did you get it?"

"Franck was at the train station. He said it was for us. I didn't want to take it, but he insisted."

"He's a strange young man," her father said. "My advice is that you keep your distance."

"He could get angry," her mother warned.

"Who cares if he becomes angry? The next time I see him, I'll tell him." Hedy noticed the jar of eggs was gone. She could have given some to Samuel. "Did you give the eggs away?"

"Yes, two families were grateful to receive them."

She wanted to ask her parents about the black market and how it worked but feared raising their suspicions. Her mother passed her the bowl of carrots, and Hedy added another serving to her plate.

"Hungry tonight?" Her father's eyes narrowed on her.

"It's the studying." She hated lying, but she had no choice. "Speaking of studying, could you make an exception and allow me to take what's left on my plate to my room? A little food helps me to stay awake."

Her mother frowned, but her father added more cheese to her plate before her mother could say no. "Go on. Get back to your books. I'll help your mother with the dishes tonight."

"Thank you, Papa."

Back in her room, Hedy wrapped the potatoes, carrots, cheese and a slice of apple strudel her mother had made for dessert in a cloth and put it in her bag. Tomorrow, she planned to fill up her thermos and one of her mother's big canning jars with water. She would tell her parents she was going to the library to study, but she would see Samuel instead.

Hedy sat at her desk and tried to concentrate on the questions Professor Hassig had said might be on the exam, but her thoughts kept returning to Samuel. She was sure the walking had exhausted him. All that medicine and materials for his wounds—what if he needed help with the bandages? The more she thought about it, the more she considered going back tonight to check on him after everyone had gone to sleep. He was utterly dependent on her, but she had no idea what he needed.

If something happened to him, she would be responsible. Hedy got up and paced. She could go tonight, bring paper, maybe a book for him to read. What would he do all day in the hut? She went to the bookshelf that held her collection of English novels from school—Shakespeare, Dickens, Austen.

She grabbed the Shakespeare, some paper and a pen and put them in her bag. Now, she could finally still her thoughts enough to concentrate on her exams.

When she heard the grandfather clock in the hall strike midnight, she put her pack on her back. The house was still and quiet. In summer, she left her window open to bring a cool breeze at night. Rather than using the front door, which might wake her parents, she lifted the blackout blind and crawled outside. She went to the vegetable patch, a little way from the house, and used the watering hose to fill her thermos and the canning jar, then she was off.

She made good time, moving at a faster pace than the previous night. She guessed it was about one-thirty when she scrambled over the stone wall, came upon the hut and opened the door.

"Samuel?"

Inside was dark. Quiet. She couldn't hear him breathing. She waited one beat. Two. "Samuel?"

The ache in her gut told her he wasn't here. A bolt of fear burned through her chest. What if an army patrol had taken him?

"Hedy?" A man's voice.

She turned. Samuel was standing outside. "Where were you?" Irritation ripped through her voice.

"Outside. It's a swell night."

"You can't sleep outside."

"Why not?"

"I warned you about the patrols. If you're caught I'll be caught too. This hut belongs to my father." Her pulse raced. "They would make the connection between us."

"I'd never tell them about you. I give you my word. I'd say I escaped into the forest and found this place. I'm inside all day, Hedy. I can't be in there at night too. It's suffocating. I need air. And look at the stars—they're stunning."

She took a deep breath. Maybe he was right and she was overreacting. She suddenly felt foolish. "I brought you water and more food."

"I sure could use some since I ate everything you left. I guess all that walking made me hungry."

She put down her pack and started unloading the items.

"Let me help," he said, coming alongside her.

Other than her father, she'd never stood so close to a man before. He smelled of citrus mixed with pine, as if he'd been sleeping against the trunk of an old spruce. "I'm lucky you aren't a city boy."

"I'm lucky you're a brave woman."

It was too dark to see him. She could grasp only a rough outline of his shape, but she imagined his movements—bending an elbow, turning his head and shifting his shoulders—because they sent a ripple of warmth between them.

"Could you look at my hand?" he asked. "It's burning and itching."

"What did the doctor say?"

"Arm's not bad but the doc said the hand needs to be disinfected and the bandage changed every other day. Joseph cleaned it once but it's been a few days. Would you mind?"

She'd never cleaned a wound. "You'll have to tell me what to do. Let's go inside. I'll light the stove and we can use the flames along with the candle to see."

"The doc gave me iodine. He said to put a few drops in water and clean the wound, then let it dry and put fresh bandages on."

Inside the hut, she filled a bowl with water and added the iodine drops. She had to hold his hand close to the stove to benefit from the light as she unwound the white gauze. His skin was hot to the touch. She worried there might be an infection. Holding his wrist, dipping the cloth into the orange iodine water, then pressing gently on the brown threads stitched through his skin, the soft vibration of his pulse on the pads of her fingers stirred something inside her.

He winced.

"I'm sorry." She looked up, realizing she'd been pressing too hard. In the dimness, all she could see was the shape of his face and the beard that grew on his chin. She thought if he started talking, it might get his mind off the pain. "Did you escape on your own?"

"I was with another fellow, an RAF pilot." Samuel moved his other hand and the flames from the fire glinted on the metal watch at his wrist.

"Where is he now?"

"Dead." His voice broke. "A Swiss soldier shot him in the chest. He gave me his watch just before he went into the church . . ." His voice trailed off.

"That's terrible." An awkward silence followed. They sat still, waiting for the wound to dry before she wrapped a fresh gauze over it. When she finished, she looked up at him. "How does that feel?"

"Better, thank you." He turned his hand slowly to look at how she'd tied the gauze. "You'd make a first-rate nurse."

"Thanks."

"Can I ask if the food you brought me tonight comes from your home?"

"Yes, it was left over from dinner."

He made a clicking noise with his mouth and shook his head. "I won't have you stealing from your family on my account."

"It's not stealing," she lied.

"Yes, it is." He took her hand and opened it. "Here's some money from the salary they paid us weekly." He placed the folded bills on her palm, closed her fingers over them with his hand and didn't let go. An electrical charge shot along the underside of her arm, aimed at her heart.

She withdrew her hand, still warm from his touch. "I can't buy beyond what is permitted on my ration card, but with your money, I could go to the black market where the vendors won't ask for the ration coupons."

"Is that legal?"

"No."

"What if you get caught?"

"I won't."

"I can't have you do that for me." His voice sharpened. "It's too dangerous." He leaned forward. "Have you done it before?"

She shook her head. "But I've never hidden an American pilot either."

"I'm serious. I can hunt. There's bound to be deer in this forest."

"You need a weapon. And with only one arm I don't think you'll have good aim."

"I know how to make a fishing rod. If you bring me to a river, I'll catch something. I'm one hell of a fisherman."

"The river is down in the village. You can't go there. People will see you." She could feel his gaze upon her, burning like the flames from the fire.

He shifted his weight. "There has to be another way."

"Let me try the black market. I'll be careful, I promise."

Hedy didn't stay long. She put Samuel's money in her bag and headed home. Climbing over the limestone wall and wading through the undergrowth, she smiled. They hardly knew each other, but she couldn't deny something existed between them. Wasn't that how it had happened with her parents—*un coup de foudre*—love at first sight, as her mother always described it? Perhaps her emotions were heightened by all the secrecy and danger, and once the novelty of hiding him wore off, her feelings for Samuel would, too. But the farther she went through the forest and away from him, the more she desired to return to his side.

It struck her that she didn't know the color of his eyes because they'd always been together in the dark. Next time, she'd come during the day. She wanted to see what Samuel looked like.

20

Hedy

Lausanne
July 1944

Hedy stood across the street from the butcher shop. It was early afternoon, and a knife seemed to cut the street in half: one side sparkled in sunlight, the other obscured by shade. The butcher shop sat on the sunny side, its red awning shading the window. Waiting for the woman inside to leave, Hedy figured she'd have more success purchasing meat without a ration card if the shop was empty. The glass door finally opened, and Hedy, feigning calm, stepped on the hot asphalt and crossed the street.

She scrunched her nose at the sour smell inside. He must be slow-cooking a ham bone in cabbage in the back. Eyeing the columns of raw meat arranged under the glass—pink pork, pale chicken, red beef and lamb, dark innards—she found what she wanted. Behind the counter, a stout man with a burly mustache pounded a knife into a rack of ribs. Seeing her, he stopped.

"Good afternoon, mademoiselle. How can I be of service?"

Hedy stiffened. *Don't think, just ask.* "I'd like four cured sausages, please." She took a breath. "The large ones."

He nodded and put them on the counter. "Will that be all?"

"Yes."

She held her breath as he made the calculation. "Three francs."

Opening her bag, she took the money and handed it to him.

"I'll need to clip your ration cards."

"Of course," she said, pretending to look for them in her bag. "Oh no, I must have forgotten them at home. Could you make an exception?"

He scowled, placed the sausages behind the glass, and returned to pounding the bony rack.

She tried another four butchers. Same objection every time. One even threatened to call the police. Her feet ached from walking on the hard sidewalk. The sun shifted away from the lake toward the mountains in the west. Evening was coming on. Now, every butcher shop was packed with customers. Weekly, there were articles in the paper about illegal slaughterhouses and butchers distributing unregistered meat. The black market existed. Hedy just had to figure out how it worked.

She paused at the end of the street before a corner shop displaying cakes and white meringue in the window. Her mouth watered. She wanted to linger, take it all in, forget about the war, ration cards, and the impossibility of feeding a pilot on a young woman's rations. She hadn't considered any of this before agreeing to hide Samuel. When she stepped back, a woman dressed in a white apron with flour on her face ran into her.

"Sorry," the woman mumbled, then moved on.

Realizing the woman had come from the back of the shop, Hedy suddenly had an idea.

She walked to the next butcher shop until she reached the cross street, turned, and turned again to enter the alley behind. She counted the doors until she was sure which was the butcher's and waited. The alley was in the shade, and she was the only one in it. She'd been foolish to think she could buy meat illegally in a well-lit store with windows. No one knew her; of course they wouldn't trust a stranger. But she might have a chance here in the alley, with no one watching.

The door opened. A woman stepped out and lit a cigarette. Hedy's insides squeezed. She didn't want to say anything wrong but had to seize this chance. She took a step forward.

"Do you have cured sausages to sell?"

The skin on the woman's bony face tightened. "Am I right that you don't have ration vouchers?"

Hedy nodded.

Crossing one arm at her chest, the woman rested the elbow of the other arm on her hand, with a cigarette dangling between her fingers. She inhaled, tilted her head back and blew smoke in the air. "My husband plays by the rules, even if half the butchers in Lausanne don't. He wouldn't hear of it."

"But other butchers do?" Hedy said, leaning in.

The woman lowered her head and looked pointedly at Hedy. "Try Rémy at Rue du Simplon. Go to the back door and knock. Tell him Eva sent you."

"Thank you."

"Be careful, you can't trust anyone these days."

Hedy found Rue du Simplon in no time. It was nearly five o'clock. The shops would soon close. She still needed to catch the train back to Le Brassus. She couldn't waste another minute and knocked on the back door.

No one came. She raised her hand, ready to knock again, when the door cracked open.

"Who is it?" A man's rough voice. He stepped into the alley. His graying hair suggested he was in his late fifties.

"Eva sent me."

"What for?"

"Cured sausages—four, please."

He looked her up and down. "You're a friend of Eva's?"

"Yes."

"Ten francs." He held out his hand. "Pay now, and I'll be back with the sausages after I finish with the customers out front."

Hedy hesitated because the price was excessive. But if Samuel was economical and ate a few slices daily, one sausage could get him through the week, especially if she supplemented it with items from her mother's pantry. "Are they the large ones?"

He nodded. "I've got customers waiting. Ten francs."

Eva's warning about not being able to trust anyone troubled Hedy. What if he took her money and never came back? It wasn't like she could go to the police if he didn't hold up his end of the bargain. Her insides squeezed even tighter.

"Waste of time," he said, turning away.

She pulled the money from her bag. "Here."

He yanked it from her hand and slammed the door.

There was nothing to do but wait. If he cheated her, she could try to go inside and demand her money back, but it would be his word against hers. After all she'd been through this afternoon, she had to believe Rémy was different. He never said a word about ration vouchers. He didn't need to since Eva had referred her. It didn't make sense for Eva to send her to a place where she would be cheated. Hedy paced the cobblestone alley. He would come back, she told herself; *be patient.*

The door cranked open, and she held her breath. Rémy threw a brown butcher bag in the air. She caught it.

"Don't go telling nobody where you got it."

Her heart leaped. "I won't."

He snapped the door shut.

She tucked the meat in her bag and hurried toward the train station.

21

Samuel

La Forêt de Risoud
July 1944

Dawn arrived. It took Samuel's breath away. The light—amber, plum, jade—brought the forest into focus in increments, the way a photograph develops slowly in a darkroom. He glanced at the rock near his foot, the one on which he'd carved a single jagged line with the knife Hedy had left him, marking a day since she'd gone away.

His father's voice came to him. *There is always something that needs doing, and there's peace in the doing.* Samuel hadn't minded the army with all its rules and training. Some men couldn't abide by it, didn't want their minds trained to think a certain way. For them it was like losing a limb that just kept aching. Not Samuel. The hard part was being thrown from that regimented world into this one. Even the hotel in Davos had structure—roll call in the morning, lights out at ten at night. But here, he had no one to answer to other than himself and the girl.

He thought about her a lot. Had there been trouble at the black market? Was that why she hadn't returned? He imagined her in the prison cell they'd thrown him in. She didn't deserve that, not for helping him. And if she wasn't in trouble, what was she doing now? Maybe she'd decided she'd done enough. He wouldn't blame her if she changed her mind. She wouldn't be wrong to think she'd already risked plenty by bringing him here. Perhaps she wouldn't come back. His thoughts turned into an endless swirl of confusion. His father's voice urged him to do something.

His eyes shifted to the hut. Concrete blocks in the corners cleared it from the ground, allowing the air to circulate under the floor. He couldn't see to the other side because of all the twigs, sticks and leaves the wind must have heaped there. Two wooden steps led to the door. A pitched roof with a protective awning prevented the snow from piling in front of the door in winter. Walls of reddish-brown planks, weathered ash gray near the base. She'd said it was her father's hut. From how the trees had grown around it, he guessed it was a generation older than her father.

He went inside, turned on the stove and boiled water for tea. He'd nearly run out of what she'd brought. Then he went outside and walked around the hut. Scattered on the ground were blocks of wood. He guessed her father must have cut the logs out here before stacking them in the hut to dry. He kicked the blocks with his foot—some were a good size for whittling. He smiled. It would be nice to give her something.

Samuel got the broom, and though it wasn't easy with his left hand bandaged, he eventually cleared out all the twigs under the hut, swept away the leaves and stacked the branches in a pile. He sat down on the bottom step to catch his breath. There must have been fifty sticks of varying sizes. Then, he sorted them in a line from tallest to shortest, took a medium-sized one, then another. He hadn't been sure what he was doing until the twigs formed into the shape of a hut. He spent all morning snapping their ends to add the steps and pitched roof. It got his mind off his grumbling stomach. At midday, he stood and stretched. Still, no Hedy.

In the afternoon, he rummaged through the understory looking for something to tie it all together. He found vines that he twisted into twine. The uneven gaps between the sticks bothered him. He made another cup of tea.

By the time the sun descended and the air buzzed with the sounds of night, he got an idea for how to fill those gaps. He gathered the moss from the stone wall that felt as soft as cotton in his hand. He would have added flowers if there were any but the forest was all moss and trees. He stuffed the house with moss and put a red ash leaf for a door. As the sky turned black, he carried the miniature hut inside and placed it on a wood pile so he wouldn't step on it in the night. He lit the stove and made a cup of tea with all that was left of his water. His left arm and hand burned. He should clean the wounds and change the bandages again soon, but he would need Hedy. Leaning against the wall, he closed his eyes and tried not to think.

Hedy

At breakfast, Hedy told her mother she would be going to Lausanne.

"Back to the library?"

"Yes, some classmates have formed a study group to prepare for the exams." She felt a small pang of regret about lying. But last night, she'd been too tired to trek through the forest, and she knew that Samuel would be out of food and water by this morning. She had to go today. "We'll study together all morning and I'll be home in the afternoon."

A knock at the front door stretched across the house to reach the kitchen.

"Who could that be at this hour?" her mother said on her way to the door.

Hedy snatched the boiled egg from her plate, slipping it inside her dress pocket. She would add it to what she'd already packed in her schoolbag: a thermos filled with water, a baguette and the sausages.

Her mother returned to the kitchen with Madame Jadot trailing behind her.

"Off to Lausanne today, Hedy?" Madame Jadot smiled. "I'm glad I didn't miss you."

Hedy lifted a shoulder. "That's right, I'm going to the library. Has something happened?"

"I'd say." Madame Jadot sat down. Her hair was raked back from her face into a tight bun, making her mouth scowl. "Madame Borel, you'd better join as you'll want to hear it, too."

"I'm just getting a cup for your tea."

Hedy watched her mother go to the cabinet with glass doors and lift a Limoges porcelain cup with a fine gold handle and matching saucer. She didn't understand why she treated Madame Jadot with the respect she reserved for Hedy's father's clients who came to collect their violins. As she filled the cup with steaming hot tea, Madame Jadot steepled her hands and waited for her mother to join them.

"All the trains today have been canceled!" Madame Jadot announced.

Hedy blinked. "What?"

"I passed the station master on the street early this morning, and he told me that if I was on my way to the station, I might as well turn around and go home because a tree fell on the tracks overnight."

"My goodness, was anyone injured?" Hedy's mother asked.

"No, but think how many would have been if the tree had fallen on a train full of passengers during the day. As soon as

I heard, I had to come." She cut a look at Hedy. "I don't think you'll be going to Lausanne today."

Hedy clutched the mug, trying to think through how she might still be able to get out of the house to see Samuel. "Surely they will have a replacement bus."

"It will take another day to organize." Madame Jadot blew on the tea to cool it. "The station master said that after clearing the tree, someone must inspect the tracks to ensure the rails aren't damaged. Depending on what they find, it could be up to a week before the line is operational."

A wave of unease rose in Hedy's stomach. She should have gone to the hut last night, but she'd been exhausted after walking all over Lausanne. She didn't want Samuel to go hungry or to believe she hadn't returned because she'd failed at the black market. He would have to wait until tonight when she could sneak out without being noticed. But as her gaze fell on the red-and-white checked tablecloth, she felt a spark of disappointment because she'd been looking forward to seeing him in the daylight, if only to discover the color of his eyes.

"You'll have to study at home until the tracks are repaired," her mother said. "Hopefully it'll all be sorted in time for your exams in a few days."

Hedy nodded and sipped her tea.

"I always wonder how university can keep young women so busy." Madame Jadot pulled a face of doubt. "You should spend more time at home, helping your mother."

Hedy flinched a smile. "Once my exams are over, I'll be at home all the time." She stood. "I better get started on revising." She topped up her cup with more tea, thanked Madame Jadot for coming to alert her to the problem with the train and hastened to her room.

Sitting at her desk, she opened her books. The earliest she could get away safely would be eleven tonight—fifteen hours from now. She hoped Samuel would be all right. She should have brought more supplies and planned it better to get him through the periods when she couldn't come every day. From her window, she observed Madame Jadot move down the path to her house. Hedy felt better knowing that her neighbor was gone. There was something about the way she involved herself in their lives that troubled Hedy. Her mother said it was due to loneliness after losing her husband, but Hedy felt it was more than that. Why had Madame Jadot appeared pleased that she couldn't go to Lausanne? She disapproved of women earning their living outside the home. But then a darker thought came—might she be suspicious of Hedy? Could she infer she was breaking the law, even hiding an American pilot?

Hedy looked out the window. A pear tree stood like a dividing line between her house and Madame Jadot's. As a child, Hedy marked the seasons by that tree, listening to the buzz of the bees in spring as they hopped from one white blossom to another, seeking shade under its glossy green leaves in summer, then marveling in the blaze of red-and-orange foliage that spun like raindrops falling on the ground in autumn. But now the tree seemed to be in perpetual winter, thin like an older man bending to one side, with only a few branches still reaching for the light. As a result, there weren't enough leaves to block the view of her window, which faced Madame Jadot's front door. Could she have seen Hedy slipping out at night? No, it was too dark. But what if she heard her open the window and jump to the ground? Hedy doubted Madame Jadot would be awake so late or that the sound of her moving around would travel the two hundred meters to her house, but still, she would be extra careful tonight. She'd take her shoes off and jump from the windowsill barefoot to not make a sound.

After dinner, as Hedy cleared the table, there was a knock on the front door. Her father got up to answer it. Hedy and her mother could hear men's voices talking in the hallway, then the door closed, and her father returned.

"Who was it?" Hedy noticed a tightness in her mother's voice.

"Pastor Rolle." Her father's gaze fell on Hedy. "He came to make sure you were here."

She shivered with raw fear. "Me?" Had Madame Jadot told Pastor Rolle she'd seen Hedy climb out of the window at night? She clutched the sink to steady herself.

"A young woman on her way home was attacked tonight."

"Oh!" Her mother cupped her hands to her face. "Is she all right?"

"She got away, though she suffered nasty bruising on her face. It happened on one of the side streets off the main road. They haven't found the man who did it. Pastor Rolle came to alert us that a predator is out there."

Hedy's mother threw a worried look at her. "That woman could have been you. I've been warning for months that the blackout regulations make the streets unsafe for women to walk alone at night."

"Until they find the perpetrator, the men have organized a night patrol to protect the women in the village." A wrinkle crossed her father's forehead. "He wanted to tell you that Franck is part of the patrol and he'll be watching over our house."

Hedy felt a shadow of fear steal into the room and loom over her. "Does the patrol start tonight?" she asked, trying to keep her voice steady.

"Yes." Her father stepped closer. "No need to worry. You're safe inside."

But that was the problem—she had to bring Samuel food and water. And she *wanted* to see him. Maybe she could wait until well after midnight. Franck wouldn't stay up that late when he had to rise early to milk the cows. But what about the man who had attacked the poor woman near the village? Would he be in the forest, and would she be putting herself in danger by going out at night? Unlike the lake, the night sky didn't frighten her; the stars she used to find her way were familiar and reassuring, and the darkness cloaked her from prying eyes. But now she was no longer sure.

Back in her room, Hedy decided that she ought to press on with her plan. When the clock struck midnight, she removed her shoes, turned off the light, grabbed her pack and lifted the blackout curtain. But instead of being met with darkness, she noticed an amber glow that flitted like a firefly. She dropped the curtain and stepped back.

She counted to ten, then looked again. The light was fainter and farther away, but she could see it swaying like a swing in the darkness. It had to be the patrol. She couldn't risk running into it after Pastor Rolle had come to the house to warn her father of the danger. Samuel would have to wait.

Putting her pack down, she stretched out on the bed. He'd be sleeping now. That's what she needed too. In the morning, she'd have a clear head to think things through. One thing was certain: she couldn't allow another day to pass without bringing him food and water.

When she woke up in the morning, her parents had left. She checked her father's workshop, but he wasn't there either. Hedy decided to write a note—*I've gone to make inquiries at the train station; perhaps the line is working from Le Sentier*—and left it on the table. Then she wrapped the hard-boiled egg her mother had left for her, along with some bread and jam, and filled the thermos with fresh tea.

Deciding not to take any risks, Hedy made as though to go to the train station. After she was far enough away from the house and Madam Jadot's prying eyes, she crossed onto side streets and turned back toward the forest. She worried that Samuel, concerned that something untoward had happened to her at the black market, might leave the hut and try and find help elsewhere. She hoped he would trust her enough to wait. A car passed Hedy on the road, causing her heart to jump. But it kept moving, and so did she.

Bounding over the moss-covered wall, she ran to the clearing. He was sitting on the steps outside the hut. He must have heard her approach because he lifted his head. Hedy's breath caught at how the light sparkled in his blue eyes.

22

Samuel

La Forêt de Risoud
July 1944

Samuel's heart leaped with joy and gratitude when he saw her climbing over the stone wall near the hut. He longed to express his relief but didn't want her to misinterpret his concern for her safety as lacking faith in her abilities, so he breathed in and held back his words. She came up and sat on the ground next to him, her breath slightly labored.

"I wanted to return last night," she said, flustered. "But I worried someone might be following me."

"Who would follow you?" He felt terrible that he'd been the cause of making her so anxious and fearful.

She lifted a shoulder. "A young woman was attacked last night. The men in the village organized a patrol. I couldn't risk them seeing me sneaking out of the house."

"Was she hurt?"

"Luckily, she got away. But the blackout blinds make it easy for predators."

"You need to be careful." He leaned toward her, wishing he could protect her when she wasn't with him. "Tell me what happened at the black market."

She looked up at him, and he felt his head swoon like he was flying into the sun. It was the first time he'd seen her in daylight, and her brown eyes with specks of gray were the color of the Arkansas River at twilight when he and Tommy waded in, casting their fishing poles in the water. Her radiant brown hair with tints of red dangled in two plaits on either side of her sharp shoulders. Her skin was the same pale peach color as the roses his mother grew on either side of the farmhouse's back door. He could smell the roses now—pungent pear mixed with citrus. He breathed in and held that moment, not wanting to let it go.

"I found a butcher who sells meat without ration cards," she said, reaching into her bag. "Four sausages. I've got an egg, bread and cheese, too. I'll put the water on for tea."

"Rest for a moment. You must be tired."

She raised her knees and put her chin on them. "I worried you'd think I wasn't coming back." She looked straight at him.

His insides ached. He wanted to say she was the only one he trusted. But his thoughts were running fast, following the rhythm of his heart, and he struggled to reconcile them. How could it be that her countrymen had imprisoned him, killed Peter, and tried to kill him, but she risked her life to save him?

"Here," she said, pouring water into a cup from the jar in her pack and handing it to him.

The water felt cool on his dry throat. He hated that she had to carry so much for him. He remembered he had something for her and got up. "I have a surprise for you."

He carried the miniature house dangling from the twine like a Christmas ornament. She smiled when he gave it to her, and he thought he saw warmth flash in her eyes.

"It's all I could do with one hand," he said.

"It's beautiful. I want to hang it." She looked around, stood and looped the twine on a nail in the awning. "It brightens the place up, doesn't it?"

He wanted to say she brightened the place, but he kept that to himself. "I wish I could do more."

She stood. "You need to eat. I'll make tea."

That sounded just fine. He got up to help. She propped the door open with a stone and lit the stove.

"You cleaned out under the hut," she said, her quick, sharp eyes darting around.

"I figured it needed doing before winter."

"Maybe the doctor would prefer you rest."

"Sawbones ain't here."

"Sawbones?"

"Army slang for surgeon."

Hedy smiled. "After we eat, I'll change your bandages."

She brought the tea mugs outside. Then she took the egg, bread, cheese and sausage from her pack and put them on the step, arranging it all as if they were in a restaurant, and the bottom step was their private table. Samuel's mouth watered as she peeled the egg and cut it in two.

"You must be starving," she said. He watched her slice the cured meat into thin strips and then peel away the white casing on each.

He devoured everything she gave him. Sweetness like the perfume of wildflowers lingered on his tongue, and he didn't know if it was from the meat or cheese but he remembered all those cows grazing in the meadows, their heavy bells clanking across the valley. There were so many things he wanted to know about her. Did she have brothers and sisters? What did her parents do? What did she think about the war? What did she want to become after it was over? It didn't feel right to ask her directly. He wanted to find his way into her world.

He lifted a wood block from the ground and showed it to her. "This has the same tight rings as the logs drying inside," he said, tossing the block in the air and catching it with his good hand. "Your father must make something special with it."

"Violins. Papa carves the soundboards from the spruces that grow here."

Samuel couldn't imagine what sort of skill a man must have to turn wood into music. "I'd like to hear that music."

Again, he threw the block up in the air, but this time, Hedy reached across to catch it, and their shoulders touched. A shudder ran down his spine. Had she felt it, too? He noticed tiny red dots like berries rising along her neck. He wanted to touch each one with his finger, as if tracing their connections might reveal the map of who she was inside. Their eyes met. A voice in his head whispered that he shouldn't, but it was too faint for him to heed. Samuel bent to kiss her, and when her softened lips met his, he tasted a mix of floral and earthly flavors like a perfect cocktail he could drink forever. His one good hand cupped her face. Then he pulled back to look at her to ensure that this was what she wanted.

"That was short for a first kiss," she said, moistening her lips with the tip of her tongue.

He didn't know if she meant *their* first kiss or *her* first kiss, but he took it as encouragement. "Does that mean I have permission to kiss you again?"

"Yes."

Samuel leaned in, and the moment their lips touched, time seemed to slip and slide back to the world as it had been before the war, when he and Tommy ran barefoot in the forest, the soil rising between their toes, and they'd fished and laughed and skipped and kissed girls behind the airfield where they learned to fly. As her arms stretched around his neck, her fingers rifling through his hair, he forgot about all the death he'd seen and the men he'd killed. The war had yet to happen. Like Hedy, he was innocent.

Then, with a jolt, his thoughts returned to the harsh reality. His presence in her life was a stain, a mark of his selfishness. Because of him, she had resorted to theft, risked her life for an escaped prisoner, and put herself in danger. Samuel had robbed her of her innocence, and now he was on the brink of taking her love. It was a cruel twist of fate, an unfair burden he couldn't bear. He wouldn't do it, not when he had no intention of staying. She was risking all for him, and in return, he would soon be gone, leaving her alone to face the consequences.

The voice in his head no longer whispered but shouted: *she deserves better*. He pulled away, removing her arms from his neck. "Hedy, I don't know what I was thinking. Forgive me."

Confused, she stared at him with those brown eyes that made his heart pound.

"I've miscalculated," he said in a voice that took all his control to keep steady. His words must have felt like spears stabbing at her heart, but it was his duty to protect her. "We must not do this again."

Hedy

Unable to look at him, Hedy turned to the hut with the moss house hanging from the awning. No one had ever made anything like that for her. He was thoughtful and gentle, and she'd melted like butter under the heat of his kiss. But why had he pulled her in only to draw away?

Maybe it had been wrong to tell him this was her first kiss. He must doubt her maturity. Did he think she was too young for him? And yet, she sensed they were not so far apart in age—both in their early twenties. Perhaps the kiss had failed to live up to his expectations. Samuel likely had experience with numerous women. He must view her as an unrefined girl from a remote mountain town. A disappointment.

But didn't he realize all the trouble he was causing her? He shouldn't have cleared out the leaves and branches under the hut because now she would need to tell her father why she'd felt compelled to clean the space. Did he know that his actions, even good intentions, only complicated her life? *Miscalculated*. She felt unnerved and angry, like he no longer treated her as the woman who had saved his life but as a dial to adjust on his plane's instrument panel.

Her passion of a moment ago hardened into fury. She didn't want him to kiss her ever again. Hedy, not Samuel, had miscalculated, and now she was determined to set things right.

She cleared her throat. "Before I go, I'll change your bandages," she said in a voice harder than she intended. But she needed to be firm. She was too open and naïve, confusing her duty with notions of love. She stood and went to the hut to get the iodine and bandages.

Unwinding the bandage on his hand, she pushed aside the feelings of warmth that swelled inside her from before, when they touched, and she cleaned the wound like a nurse treating a patient. She was glad to see the swelling around the stitches had gone down, but plenty of bruising remained.

"Hedy, could we talk—"

"Did the doctor say how long until you can use your arm?"

"Part of the bone fractured, so the doc said it needs three months to heal." He looked at her. "I'm sorry, I only—"

"It's fine." Joseph had told her two and a half months. The extra weeks would keep Samuel in the hut until mid-October. It would be cold but possible, as long as he was gone before winter set in and the snow made the forest impassable. Once she'd finished with his hand, she shifted to the arm. The bandage had been left too long, so the cotton threads had melded to the wound and surrounding skin. Every tug to remove it made Samuel wince. In a way, she didn't mind. He deserved it. By the time she'd finished, she'd left a pink and raw patch on his skin.

She dabbed the iodine water on the wound, cleaning the brown thread that snaked from the inside of his elbow to the middle of his forearm. It was rough to touch, like the fishing wires her father had attached to the hook on his rod. Her mind slipped, imagining Samuel fishing with her father in the Lac de Joux, catching *féra*, a whitefish she and her mother would fry in butter with roasted almonds. But she dreamed of what could never be—unless the world changed and he returned. Why would he? Not for her. He had told her that a moment ago when he pulled away. She willed her mind to be strong and focus on the task. She was helping a pilot, not falling in love. Finding a tube of ointment in the bag with all his bandages, she applied it to the wound to keep a barrier between the skin and the new bandage.

"I'll clean it again in two days," she said, standing. "Just so you know, I won't come tomorrow. I have my exams during the day." She took a deep breath. "And at night, I'll meet a pilot at the Lausanne station and escort him to a boat along the lake." She'd been relieved to finally receive the instructions at the end of term.

His gaze met hers. "You've taken enough risk. Don't—"

"I've given my word."

"Tell them you can't."

She wanted to say that she wasn't like him, changing his mind every minute, and it was none of his business. Having experienced how easily an airman could stumble into trouble, she had to be there. Samuel wouldn't understand that it was more than returning the airmen to their squadrons to continue fighting. She was making up for her country's indifference. Her private war against the intolerance and lack of empathy of people like Franck. Samuel's insistence that she shouldn't go annoyed her. She gathered up the items and put them back in the bag. "Done."

"What do you have to do?" he asked, looking at her.

He had no right to question her, especially after his humiliation just now. He was probably only thinking about himself, worried that if something happened to her, he'd be in trouble. But nothing would happen. She'd done this before.

The pilot would follow her. They wouldn't speak until they got close to the lake. She would make sure no one was following. She could do this. He had no right to tell her she couldn't.

"I better get going," she said.

He grabbed her hand. "Wait—"

"What if you were that pilot tomorrow night?" she said. "Would you want me to abandon you?"

"All I'm saying—"

"That's it's OK for *you* to take risks, flying a plane and dropping bombs, but not me?"

"I'm a trained soldier. And I don't drop bombs. I deliver equipment, radios, guns, bicycles and men to support the French Resistance."

"The Maquis?"

He nodded. His bright eyes were on her like a target, making her heart bounce. *Forget him,* she told herself firmly. *He doesn't want you.*

"You're already doing more than you should," he said.

"Don't worry." She lifted her chin to mask the rip in her heart. "I'll be fine."

23

Hedy

Switzerland
July 1944

At home that night, Hedy tossed and turned, unable to sleep. Her thoughts twisted like a mountain path, switching back and forth between Samuel's humiliating rejection and his warning that she was taking on too much risk. Self-doubt gnawed at her as she struggled to understand why he had kissed her, only to toss her aside. She must have disappointed him, but how? And if he was right that hiding one pilot while smuggling another left her overexposed, could his caution augur trouble to come?

She must have dozed off at some point because she awoke to a light streaming in from the window. She checked the clock: 7:30, giving her only twenty minutes before the train left, if the service was up and running. *Mince!* She'd intended to get up early in case she needed to take a bus or walk to another station. She threw on her clothes, grabbed the toast her mother had set on the table and slipped it into the side pocket of her bag before running to the station. There wasn't time to brush her hair or teeth or to stop to hear what her mother was saying as she rushed out the door.

Out of breath, Hedy reached the station with a few minutes to spare. A wave of relief washed over her as she saw the train waiting at the platform.

Adrenaline got her through the morning exam, and she finished the last question with time to spare to review her answers. But the exam in the afternoon was more challenging. The day turned hot, and the cavernous exam hall reeked of sweat. Luckily, her desk was next to a window, and a light breeze spilled through the opening at the top. She wrote slowly, resting her hand between questions, distracted, her thoughts drifting back to Samuel. It took all her effort to focus, and she left the final question half-answered.

Afterward, she went to a café, and reread the only instructions she'd received for tonight, which had been written on the last page of a book left in her locker. *At nine o'clock, wait on platform six with a book in your left hand, and go to the lake address provided, where a boat waits in the back.* Though her limbs rattled with exhaustion, she forced herself to scout out various routes from the station. The most direct, along the main street, would take her and the airman no more than ten minutes to reach. She wasn't nervous like she had been the first time. She felt ready and like she knew what to expect.

A few hours later, the rain fell hard as Hedy stood outside the Lausanne station. She snapped the umbrella down, and water droplets sprayed her clothes and shoes. Before entering, she shook the umbrella to dry it then wiped the water off her dress. Inside the station's echoing hall, plenty of people were milling around, putting her at ease. She glanced at the clock: five minutes to nine. As she shouldered through the crowd, her damp leather soles squeaked on the tile floor, mixing with the rush of voices from people hurrying to catch their trains.

She took the stairs to platform six, carefully holding the book away from the umbrella to keep it dry. The night was gloomy and damp. Murky coal smoke drifted in the air, carrying the stench of creosote as the train on the platform opposite left the station. Fiddling with the umbrella, she watched the rain fall on the tracks.

Two men hurried down the stairs, joining her on the platform to wait for the train. They stood off to the side, smoking and glancing in her direction.

A bright light and a whistle announced the train entering the station. Hedy held the book up against her left side so the airman would see it. The doors clattered open, and the men on the platform flicked their cigarette stubs to the ground and boarded the train. She waited and watched, leaning forward, but only two women and an older man got off. The doors rattled shut, the train lurched forward and an uneasy feeling overtook her. Shuffling her feet, she waited. But there was no one to meet. Maybe a mistake had been made, or the train had switched arrival platforms. She went up the stairs and crossed the hall, scanning the crowd for a man standing alone.

She thought about Samuel and what he'd told her of the trouble he'd met in Kublis. Anything could have happened to prevent the pilot from catching his train. She didn't want to abandon him, but there was no point in waiting for someone who wasn't coming. She circled the hall again, stopping at the newspaper stand to buy the evening paper, then went outside.

A relentless rain fell. She walked around the station in case he'd somehow slipped by her and was outside. The umbrella kept her dry as she held the book close to protect it. But the rain, overwhelming the drains in the road, flowed through the street and water seeped into her shoes. She waited another hour, hoping the pilot might appear on a later train and come out to look for a woman holding a book. But he never showed. Hedy went back inside to catch the next train home.

The exhaustion she'd been fighting all day overcame her on the train, and she fell into a deep sleep. At Le Brassus, the conductor's voice roused her from her slumber. She stumbled off the train in a haze and lumbered along the platform.

A thick darkness cloaked the town, the rain still falling but lighter than in Lausanne. She passed the schoolyard and the empty playground on the other side of the stone walls. She'd always thrived at school. Looking back, she realized why—the lessons produced a single correct answer with no gray areas to debate. But her experience outside the classroom was nothing like that. The school gate was closed, all the windows, along with those of the houses and shops on the street, blacked out. She hurried along the unlit street, wanting to escape the darkness and the oily puddles on the asphalt. Turning off the main road, she took a smaller path that wound through a beech tree copse—a shortcut to reach her house.

"Hedy." Franck's slippery voice came at her in the darkness.

She heard his heavy steps behind her. Her house wasn't far. If not for the blackout curtains, the lights would be visible. She doubled her pace, sliding on the wet grass.

He grabbed her elbow and jerked her back. "Why so fast?"

"What are you doing?" A clamp of fear in her chest as he spun her around.

"I'm on patrol. Come . . . here . . ." he slurred, pulling her close, his hot sour breath on her face.

She began to tremble—first with disgust, then fear—as her internal alarms fired at full throttle. Then her fear turned to anger, and with it, a surge of courage. She yanked her arm free and stepped back, hitting something hard. She stumbled and fell, landing on one side of her face. A sharp pain pierced her skin and something warm oozed from her cheek.

"Franck," a man's voice called out as a light flashed through the darkness, "let's go."

It was only a second, but it gave her the time to stand and run.

She skidded on the wet ground but stayed upright, her breath coming hard. The rain fell in jagged swells, stinging the gash on her face, while anger, like a fire, blazed inside her chest. Arriving at her father's workshop, she tried the door, but it was latched. She pushed up the hill to the house and tried that door. Also locked. She reached up to the lintel and felt around the cold stone until she found the key. Hands trembling, she fumbled with the lock until it finally clicked open.

"Maman, Papa?" she called, her voice cracking with panic.

No response. She slid the metal bolt, locking the door behind her, and hurried to her parents' bedroom. Empty. Where were they?

24

Samuel

La Forêt de Risoud
July 1944

That night, Samuel couldn't sleep. He didn't know if it was the rain drilling like a jackhammer on the hut's tin roof or the guilt still nagging at him for what he'd said to Hedy. Watching her brown eyes dart around, unable to settle, he knew his words had hurt. He had done it to protect her, making her believe their kiss meant nothing, though each time her arm or fingers brushed his skin, he felt a flash of desire. She was strong and fearless. But what would happen if the Swiss authorities caught on to the network? She could be hurt or thrown in prison because of him. What troubled him most was that he wouldn't be able to save her the way she had saved him.

The charcoal in the stove burned slowly and steadily, creating a cozy fug inside the hut. He wished she could be here with him now and not out in the rain helping a pilot. In a way, that was what he adored about her—how she would step up and risk her life to benefit a stranger. He hoped it had gone well and she was safe from danger. He ached inside to know how she was. All he could do was wait. The waiting made him crazy.

He leaned his head against the wall and tried to string together all the moments that had brought him here. Crashing his plane. His first failed escape. Those ten awful days in Wauwilermoos. Meeting Sam Woods. The Swiss soldiers who'd killed Peter outside the church in Kublis and wanted to kill him, too. Joseph, the kid who was part of Woods' underground network and who'd hidden him in his dorm room. And now Hedy. What were the odds that a boy from Kansas would meet a beautiful girl halfway around the world, and she would risk her life in the middle of a war to save him? Another sliver of guilt caught in his throat for arguing with her yesterday before she left. He had only wanted to warn her of the danger. Was it more than worry? Maybe he was jealous she might fall for a man other than him.

He rubbed his forehead to get these crazy ideas out of his mind. They could never be together because he wasn't sticking around. He aimed to get strong enough to row across the lake and reach the Maquis in France. Nothing could distract him from that goal, not even a beautiful, brave girl like Hedy. If Colonel Fiske wouldn't let him fly again, he'd still prefer to return to the squadron. The world he understood, the only place he belonged.

He loaded more charcoal into the stove and boiled the water. As he made tea, his mind spun back to her. From the moment she'd led him through the forest in the darkness, he couldn't stop thinking about her. Every time she appeared, goose bumps crawled over his skin. She moved like a gazelle, climbing over the stone wall in a dress. He loved her dresses. Long cotton shirts, cinched at the waist with a leather belt, billowing to the knees and sleeves pitched to her elbows. She wore them in two colors—olive green and ruby red—and looked swell in both. Was he falling for her?

Maybe. He missed her. Tomorrow seemed a long time until he would see her again.

He finished the tea, dried the cup, and focused on something else. Woods' shiny black Opel. He hadn't looked inside the car but imagined it would have red or black leather seats. Samuel had only ever driven his father's Mack pickup truck—an old thing with a fierce silver bulldog rearing like a stallion on the hood. He loved that truck. It was a world away from the Opel. Then he remembered what Woods had said: *something's out there waiting for you.*

He glanced at the watch: 0200. And it took him back to that morning—when the two bullets aimed at Peter hit him, and his body slammed hard against a tree, squeezing the air from his lungs. He hadn't been sure if he would survive as he slid slowly to the ground. He recalled Peter's last words. *When I get back, I'll tell you a story about this Rolex, but until I do, take care of it because it means the world to me.*

Though he would never know the watch's history or why it meant so much to Peter, he would honor his friend's last wish. One day, he would find Peter's family in England and return the watch to them.

Thump. Thump. Samuel straightened his back and listened. Sounds came from outside, like something heavy falling on the steps. Maybe a fox had curled against the door to shelter from the rain, or a branch knocked by the wind had landed there. Another thud. His throat tightened—too heavy for a fox, and a branch wouldn't fall twice. Perhaps Hedy had decided not to help the pilot, and returned to tell him. But she wouldn't trek through the forest in this rain.

The door opened, and Samuel's heart jumped against his ribs. By the flickering light from the stove, he saw a tall man enter and stop. Samuel placed his good hand on the floor, ready to brace himself to sprint outside.

"*Qui êtes-vous?*" the man asked.

In his gut, Samuel knew the game was up. But he didn't care about what would happen to him. All he could consider was what might happen to Hedy.

Hedy

After removing her wet clothes, Hedy hung them in the bathroom to dry. She put on her pajamas and sat on the sofa. The grandfather clock rang the hour—midnight. Where were her parents? In the rush to catch her train that morning, had she missed them telling her they'd be away tonight? She touched the swollen skin on her face and shuddered, feeling Franck's menace like a second person stalking the room. She realized he'd wanted her that first night he came to dinner, and she feared that, like a hunter after his prey, he wouldn't give up.

Hedy stretched her body on the sofa and closed her eyes. She fell into a deep sleep and was awakened many hours later by a persistent knocking.

She sat up, thinking the soft tapping was the rain on the roof. Then she remembered her parents and rushed to the door. Opening it, she found her father, clothes dripping, carrying her mother on his back.

"Papa, what's happened?"

"Close the door," he whispered, hurrying inside. "We don't want to wake Madame Jadot."

"Ouch," her mother cried as her father placed her on the sofa, a trail of water in their wake.

"I'll get towels," Hedy said. "Then you must tell me where you've been." Returning, she handed the towels to her parents and waited.

"Your mother had an accident." Her father had brought a chair for her mother to elevate her leg and unlaced her boot. "She's sprained her ankle."

"I heard an awful crunch when I slid on the mud," her mother said, wincing as the boot came off. "Hedy, bring me some dry clothes."

Hedy found her mother's pajamas under the pillow on her parents' bed. Helping her mother change, she asked, "What were you doing outside in this weather at such a—"

"Your face." Her mother touched Hedy's cheek. "What happened to you?"

Hedy looked down. "I fell."

Her mother motioned that Hedy should sit down on the sofa, and her father knelt beside them, touching Hedy's chin and tilting her face to examine the cut.

"How did you fall?" her mother asked.

"Running away from . . ."

"Who?" her father asked.

"Franck."

His face twisted. "He did this to you?"

She shook her head. "He followed me from the train station and caught me at the short cut through the beech trees. I think he was drunk . . ."

"Did he hit you?"

"No. He . . ." She couldn't say the word because that would give it weight, make it real. "I fell trying to get away." She hesitated at the notion that had formed in her mind, but now that it was there, she couldn't shake it. "What if he's the man who attacked the woman the other night?"

Her parents exchanged a look. "Did anyone else see you together?" her mother asked.

"No. I should report him before he hurts someone else."

"I'm sorry this happened," her mother said, feeling gently around the cut on Hedy's face with her fingers. It bled slightly and she pressed the towel against the cut to stem it. Hedy winced. "Luckily, it isn't deep, and you don't need stitches, but you'll have a bruise." She asked Hedy's father to get the bottle of iodine, a cloth and some water.

"I want to report him," Hedy said.

A line of worry crossed her mother's forehead. "Under the circumstances, I'm not sure that would be wise."

"What do you mean?"

"You have the American pilot to consider."

Hedy clamped a hand to her mouth. A wave of panic ripped at her heart. "Where's Samuel? Has he been arrested?"

"He's safe." The lines around her mother's eyes tightened. "But hiding him isn't. Do you want to tell us what's going on?"

Her father returned, placing the items her mother had requested on the sofa and bringing another chair for him to sit on. "Your mother and I want to help, but first, you must tell us what you're involved in."

She hesitated. She'd promised Joseph to protect the network by never speaking of it. But now that her parents knew about Samuel, weren't they complicit? "Papa, please don't turn Samuel in. He needed—"

"We would never turn him in."

She took a breath and relaxed a little. Once she started talking, the panic subsided, and she couldn't stop. She told them about Joseph, the first pilot in Vevey, Samuel, the pilot who never showed up in Lausanne and even how she bought meat on the black market. When she'd finished, she sat back, exhausted but relieved, like a weight had been lifted. Her parents stared at her in disbelief.

"My goodness, Hedy, you've been busy," her mother quipped.

"Have you told anyone besides us?" her father asked.

"No." She sat up. "How did you find Samuel?"

Her mother glanced at her father, then turned back to Hedy. "I guess it's time we told you about our secret."

Hedy blinked. "You have a secret too?"

Her father nodded. "Let's get our story straight first. We must tell Madame Jadot and anyone else who asks that your mother fell in the bathroom. The truth is, while you were in Lausanne waiting for the pilot who didn't show, your mother and I guided three Jewish children across the border in the forest. The rain made the route slippery, and she fell."

Hedy felt light-headed. Too much was happening all at once. Staring at the white towel on her mother's lap, she tried to take in what her father had just said.

"I was in a bind because I needed a safe place to keep the children," he continued. "I went to the hut. It scared your pilot when I opened the door." He grinned. "Luckily, one of the children speaks English, and she translated. He readily agreed to keep the children overnight while I returned to get your mother to carry her home."

She looked up. "The children are with Samuel?"

He nodded. "Two girls and a boy. They walked from Bordeaux after a raid at the orphanage they were hiding in."

She felt a spike of exhilaration at the idea of her father and Samuel reaching an accord that had nothing to do with her. Remembering the moss hut Samuel had made for her, she knew the children were in good hands. "Did you tell him you're my father?"

"No, but maybe he figured it out." Her father rubbed his palms together. "He never mentioned you, said he stumbled into the hut for shelter after crashing his plane." Her father laughed. "Poor man doesn't realize the impossibility of that story since the valley is covered in forest—impossible to land a plane. I knew he had been brought here by someone but I didn't press him. I got the sense he wanted to protect you."

"I see." Hedy could feel her mother's gaze on her. "What happens now?"

"Tomorrow morning, we will conceal the children in Monsieur Glauser's milk truck and bring them to the refugee camp in Geneva."

"Does Franck know about his father's involvement?"

"No, and he must never find out."

"That's why he talked about his father secretly hoarding food in the cellar," her mother said. "Do you think he suspects?"

Her father shrugged. "He said his father was selling it on the black market when he came here with those eggs, so let's hope he doesn't deviate from that line of thinking."

"Maman, is that why you thought we should invite him? Was it because you didn't want to raise his suspicion?"

She nodded. "I'm sorry. I fear it has caused you trouble. But we didn't want Pastor Rolle or Franck to think we had something to hide." She motioned to the desk in the corner. "Can you get me the notebook and pen in the drawer?"

Hedy went to the desk and, after opening the drawer, found a worn leather notebook, small enough to fit in a handbag. She brought it and a pen to her mother.

"Thank you. I must write the names before I forget them."

"What names?" Hedy asked.

"The children from last night."

Hedy watched as her mother wrote the date at the top of the page in a tight, neat script, followed by three names: *Rachel, Adi and Chai.* Her mother flipped back a page to a list of more names. "Good." She looked up at her husband. "Forty-five." She smiled.

"You and Papa have smuggled forty-five children through the forest?"

Her mother nodded. "They've all lost their parents. Some are with siblings, but most are alone. I keep a record for the future. Someone might want to know one day after this terrible war is over."

Hedy felt tears in her eyes. She had been wrong to think she was wiser or better than her parents because of her education. They knew right from wrong—just as Joseph had said, the circle represents eternal truth, what we all find inside ourselves. She leaned over and hugged her mother. "I'm so proud of you and Papa."

"Oh, Hedy, we are even more proud of you."

She stayed in her mother's embrace, safe and warm. But her father's voice stirred, calling her back. "Hedy, there's something I'd like to ask of you."

She pulled away from her mother. "Yes?"

"I've received word from our contact on the French side that another group of children will arrive next week. I never know what condition they'll be in. Some will have come far, walking all the way. Your mother cannot help with her ankle. I fear one person isn't—"

"Of course, I'll be there."

"This won't be like anything you've done before. It's at night, without torches. A cliff on the French side where the German Army regularly patrols. It's not without danger. On the border, the soldiers shoot on sight."

"If Maman can do it, I can."

He cradled his hand on the side of her face that wasn't injured. "You've been brave. But in this, you must follow my instructions exactly. Do you understand?"

She nodded, and an easy silence settled around them. She felt nothing could pierce the unity and strength of her family. Her thoughts skipped to Samuel and the conflicted feelings fluttering inside her. She could still feel the warmth of his kiss and the helpless connection they seemed to share, the one she felt the moment she'd wrapped her arms around his neck. All she wanted was to find that feeling again. But he didn't want her.

Her father put his elbows on the table and leaned forward. "How did the pilot receive his injuries?"

"Our soldiers . . . they shot him."

"Why?" Her mother's voice tightened.

"For escaping the Allied internment camp in Davos. He was lucky. They killed the English pilot who was with him."

Her father rubbed his temples as if it might help him make sense of what she'd said. Her mother leaned forward and took Hedy's hands. "You could have turned away from him in his time of need, but you didn't. I'm proud of you."

"May I go with you tomorrow to meet the children?" Hedy asked.

Her father nodded. "I'd like that."

25

Hedy

La Forêt du Risoud
July 1944

Hedy and her father set out at dawn. The cool scent of a rainstorm rose up from the forest as dew seeped into the dark soil and the limestone crevices underneath. Smoothing the wrinkles in her dress, she held it up so the tall understory wouldn't dampen the hem. She wished she'd spent more time and care braiding her hair this morning because strands had slipped loose and hung about her eyes and mouth. It wasn't like her to consider her appearance, but this morning she felt off-center, as if she'd unexpectedly lost the straight line that her body constantly rotated around.

Scrambling over the stone wall, she saw four figures in the clearing outside the hut: two girls, a boy and Samuel. The boy, sitting on Samuel's shoulders, held an airplane made from sticks in his hand, which he glided through the air.

"Whoosh, whoosh," Samuel said, circling the hut. "Coming upon the zebras. How many down there?"

"*Onze!*" The boy grinned.

"I'll circle back and make another pass to see if the lion cubs need help."

"*Allez plus vite!*"

One of the girls waved her hands. "Any cubs with broken bones?"

"*Oui.*" The boy nodded. "*Deux!*"

The other girl jumped up and carried a stretcher—a tea towel tied to twigs—which held small rocks.

"*Appelez le docteur!*" the girl said.

An urge to join in their childish game overcame Hedy. Returning to the stone wall, she removed some moss and brought it to the two girls, dividing it between them. "Apply this medicine to the lion cubs to heal their bones." She nodded at them.

The girls' eyes opened wide. "*Merci, Madame.*"

Samuel, eyeing Hedy, came to a sudden stop.

"*Continues!*" the boy commanded.

"Chai, we have visitors." Samuel bent down so the boy could slide off his shoulders.

Hedy's father put the pack on the ground. He then introduced Hedy to the three children: Rachel, the eldest, who translated for Samuel, Adi and the boy, Chai.

"Is your wife OK, sir?" Samuel asked.

"Yes. She's sprained her ankle and must stay off it for a few weeks. Please call me Alain. We're no longer strangers."

As Hedy translated, Samuel's gaze on her felt like a hot wind warming her body.

"Can we stay another day?" Rachel asked. "We like it here."

Hedy's father shook his head. "A dairy farmer waits with his truck to take you to a children's refugee home in Geneva."

Rachel pulled a face. The other children did the same.

"Chai, take this airplane with you," Samuel said, grasping their disappointment. "Make sure to fill a sack with twigs from the pile near the hut so you can make more planes with the new friends you'll meet where you're going."

After Hedy translated, Chai looked up at him. "Are you really a pilot?"

"I am."

Chai hugged Samuel's leg as Samuel stroked the back of his head. Hedy noticed red stains on Samuel's bandage.

"Looks like you might have overdone it," she said. "I'll have to change them for you."

Adi must have noticed the blood, too, because she took all the moss Hedy had given her and brought it to Samuel. "Monsieur, put this on your arm."

He bent down. "I will. *Merci*, Adi."

Rachel pointed to the hut. "Why is all the wood inside? Back home, Papa stacked wood outside to dry for the fire-place."

"This wood isn't for burning. It's special. I'm a luthier." He traced the shape of a violin with his hands. "The trees that grow in this forest have lived here for centuries, and their wood is extraordinary. I keep it inside the hut to dry and protect it."

"What's a century?" Adi asked.

"One hundred years," Rachel said, before turning to Hedy's father. "I played the piano at home . . . I wish I could still . . ." Fragile lines appeared at the edges of her eyes.

Hedy had asked her father if she could bring the music box since she remembered Samuel's wish to hear the wood's unique resonance. She removed it from her bag and wound the music box's curved metal handle. The notes whispered, the sound unable to reach them. Then she rewound it and placed the metal box on the thin spruce plank from her father's workshop. The notes expanded like a bird taking flight, each distinct in a simple phrase that alternated and repeated like a question being asked.

"Beethoven's 'Für Elise.'" Rachel recognized the piece as her fingers traced the notes in the air.

Hedy's father nodded. "Correct."

The children and Samuel stared wide-eyed at the power of the wafer-like plank. Hedy could remember calling it the magic wood as a child. What the forest had nurtured for centuries, her father transformed into something of beauty.

The music came to an end.

"Can you rewind it?" Rachel said, her voice ringing with longing.

Hedy let the music flow again, aware that it gave the children hope. The thin plank was a reminder that men had a choice: to craft something of beauty over the destruction brought by war. As Rachel's eyes widened and a smile came across her face, Hedy cut a look at her father. Seeming to grasp what this small box could mean for a girl who had lost everything, he nodded his approval.

Hedy turned to Rachel. "The box is a gift for you. You'll be able to play it at your new home."

Tears streamed down Rachel's face. She hugged Hedy, then her father, and finally Samuel. "I will keep it always, I promise. Thank you."

Adi shuffled her feet, trying to be brave and hold back tears. Maybe she feared she'd been forgotten. Hedy moved toward her, but Samuel was already on it. He went to the nail, where the house he'd assembled for Hedy from sticks and moss hung, and handed it to Adi.

"Will you take care of this for me?" he asked. "It's a special house that needs to be with someone special too."

Adi couldn't understand until Hedy translated; then, she grinned.

After more hugs and goodbyes, Chai even cried a little, Hedy and Samuel waved goodbye as her father led the children away.

Once they were alone, an awkward silence fell, which she was the first to break. "How did you . . . I never thought I'd find you playing with the children."

"Me neither." He shrugged. "The boy had awful nightmares, kept calling out for his Mama. Rachel told me his mother is dead." He tugged at his beard. "I told him a story about a man I met at pilot school who used to fly around Africa with a doctor looking for injured animals. He liked that and wanted me to tell him more so I made up stories about the lions and elephants the man had saved. He asked if we could play that in the morning. I wanted to help him forget about the war and be a child again, if only for a morning." He nailed her with a stare. "What happened to your face?"

She touched the scab that had formed overnight. "I fell running . . ."

He leaned forward. "Running from someone?"

"Franck."

"Who's Franck?" His voice hardened. "And what did he do to make you run?"

She told him how Pastor Rolle had introduced them, the awful dinner at her home, how Franck had approached her afterward and she'd dismissed him, then the encounter last night when he seemed drunk, and how she feared he was the one who had attacked another woman in the village a few nights ago. "I want to report him to the police, but my parents say we can't."

"Why not?"

"His connection to Pastor Rolle and with me hiding you and my parents smuggling children, we can't risk drawing the attention of the police."

Samuel's body angled away like something was in his path that he wanted to avoid. He reached into his boot and pulled out a small knife. "Then you must carry this to protect yourself."

She shook her head at the shiny silver blade. "I don't know how to use it."

"Grip the handle and plunge the blade into whoever tries to hurt you. The key is to keep it on you. Tuck it inside your boot the way I do. If he tries it again, you can injure him enough to distract him and give you time to get away."

Like the voice in the dark last night that had given her those precious seconds to escape. She reached for the knife, and their fingers touched, sending a ripple of warmth through her. "Papa must have given you a fright arriving in the middle of the night."

"I thought I was done for when he spoke to me in French." He shook his head and laughed. "Then Rachel stepped into the hut behind him, her clothes dripping, and said in nearly perfect English, 'We need to hide here overnight.'"

"Did you know it was Papa?"

"Once I saw him up close, yes." He dropped his voice. "You share the same brown eyes."

Hedy felt her cheeks blush and got up so he wouldn't notice. "I'll get the iodine and bandages."

They settled around the bottom step. As she unwound the bloodstained bandage on his hand, he asked about last night.

"What about the pilot?"

"He didn't show." She saw that a stitch had torn away from the skin on his palm and it oozed blood. "I won't help the pilots anymore. With Mama injured, I need to support Papa."

"Phew, that's reassuring. But does your father expect more children?"

Hedy cleaned the skin around the stitch and pressed down on it. "Does that hurt?"

He shook his head, and put his hand gently on her shoulder.

Outside, alone among the trees, she felt they were connected; that he understood her. "Next week another group will come and he needs my help." She applied cream and fresh gauze. "Let me do the arm now."

Samuel hunched forward. "I have enormous respect for your parents. How they saved those children and many others . . ."

"Mother has a book with all the children's names. Forty-five in total."

"Remarkable. But the thing is, everyone's luck runs out after a while. I found that out the hard way when I thought my mission was a milk run—" she looked at him with a raised brow "—it means it was as easy as buying milk at the corner shop." He took a breath. "Reality suddenly hit hard: my copilot was dead, the rest of the crew were bailing out over France, and I ended up interned in Switzerland." He gave her a tight smile. "Your father has had a good run of luck. Maybe it's time to take a break for a while."

Hedy was glad she hadn't mentioned the German patrols or how worried her father seemed because that would just add to Samuel's concern. "Lives are at risk. Children's lives."

Silence. Samuel didn't have an answer to that. He looked at the bits of wood scattered on the ground. "I still can't fathom how your father transforms the wood . . ."

"It's not Papa but the forest that does it."

His face screwed up into a question. "What do you mean?"

She rubbed her shoe over the soil, revealing white rock underneath. "This forest has a thin layer of soil, below is all rock."

"Limestone. We have it back home."

"The trees have had to adapt to survive. Instead of pushing their roots deep, they extend them horizontally and grow slowly to share the thin soil with the rest of the plants. Papa says the slow, steady growth produces the tight rings in the wood."

Samuel's eyes skimmed the forest. "So in all these spruce trees, the sound magically reverberates through the wood?"

She laughed. "Of course not. Trees are like people; no two are the same." She was surprised to hear her father's voice in her own. She'd accompanied him so often into the forest that all the things he'd taught her had naturally fused with her understanding of the place. "Most trees are anxious to survive so they angle and curve to find the light. But a rare few, only one in ten thousand Papa says, have the patience and confidence to wait for the light to find them, and they grow straight. It's only the straight ones that have the tight rings that produce the resonance for his violins."

"One in ten thousand." Samuel smiled, and whispered something to himself that she couldn't catch.

"How does that feel?" She pointed to the new bandage, hoping she hadn't wound it too tightly.

He looked at her, his eyes shining with affection. Brotherly affection, Hedy thought.

"Promise me that when you go out to help your father, you'll be careful."

"You worry too much," she said, missing the warm touch of his skin as she gathered up the items and brought them inside the hut.

26

Hedy

La Forêt de Risoud
August 1944

A week later, Hedy tried not to make a sound as she knelt alongside her father on the plateau's edge. A light southerly wind floated over the trees, and the crescent moon cast a faint light on the ground.

They'd climbed over the stone wall, marking the border with France. Her father had warned they would be most exposed to German patrols on the plateau. They must remain silent, their ears tuned to the direction of sound—the crunch of leaves from below meant refugees, and the same sound on this level indicated a military patrol. Hedy worried she couldn't discern the direction and would get it wrong. Her father told her if a patrol came, he would signal, and she must lie flat, hold her arms around her head, and roll down the Gy de l'Echelle.

The Gy de l'Echelle was a steep five-kilometer descent to level ground. The Germans avoided it, taking the longer route to reach the plateau, which was why the Gy was the preferred passage of the smugglers. "And the best place for us to hide if a German patrol passes," he said. "Gravity will ensure they won't be able to get a bead on us. We'll sound like deer passing through the trees."

Her father tapped her shoulder and pointed downward. He'd already told her that if the French smugglers didn't appear on the plateau, it meant they'd encountered trouble bringing the children up, and he would descend to help. He motioned with his hand that Hedy was to remain. A shiver of cold ran through her, but she gave a thumbs-up.

Alone on the ridge, she listened to the swish of leaves as her father disappeared. Maybe her mother had sprained her ankle rolling down the Gy de l'Echelle on that rainy night. Hedy wondered if her mother had been in danger from the soldiers. How many nights had her parents been here in darkness without the benefit of tonight's moon or in heavy snow in the winter? It wouldn't be possible to scale the Gy de l'Echelle in ice and snow, and she imagined they would either shift farther west toward Chapelle-des-Bois or east toward Le Mont d'Or. Her parents had experienced many things she knew nothing about. She regretted that they'd kept secrets from her. She vowed to tell her children everything. She didn't want to live in the shadows like her parents had.

If her father had gone the five kilometers, he would need two hours to get there and back. Maybe the French smugglers had made it halfway up the cliff; if so then he'd return in an hour. She didn't have a watch, but she guessed an hour had gone by. Arching forward, her body rigid with anticipation, she listened to the hoot of an owl, the rustle of a fox, the whoosh of a branch knocked by the wind. She even heard the rush of her breath, drawing in and out.

Crackle. Her pulse hammered. *Swish.* Blood pounded in her ears. Should she lie flat, cover her head, and disappear down the cliff? It took all her will to hold back and wait. She pressed her palms on the ground, expecting the vibration of heavy boots. When they didn't come, she exhaled, leaned over the ledge, and waited.

"Ssh," her father's voice drifted in the air.

An urge to call out to him came over her; sucking in a breath, she pressed her lips together.

Her father's gray shape crested the ridge. A child in his arms. Breathing fast, he handed her the boy and disappeared back down the cliff. She guessed the child was five. He whimpered, and Hedy regretted they'd left the pack with food and water on the other side of the border. But her father had said it would make noise and wasn't worth the risk. Kissing his pale forehead, she swayed silently from side to side. Some instinct told her that a steady and smooth motion would comfort him. Maybe his mother was now making her way up the cliff. Her father had likely taken the child from her arms to lighten her load. Then a darker thought came at her—what if he no longer had a mother and was alone?

Not long after, her father reappeared with a girl. He motioned with his other hand that Hedy should take the two children and cross back to the Swiss side. She didn't want to leave him alone, but he insisted, his firm eyes guiding her to understand that the children would be safer once they were over the stone wall.

Hedy bent down to look at the girl's face. There was a dull shine in her eyes, as if she was tired. Cuts scraped her chin, and dirt marks smeared both cheeks. Hedy held a finger to her lips to warn the girl not to speak.

Crossing the plateau, Hedy thought of the night she'd brought Samuel to the forest, how she'd listened to his breathing, careful of his wound. She now did the same with the girl. At the low stone wall marking the border, she guided her over it and squeezed her hand, hoping she would know her next steps would be more secure and safe in Switzerland. It wasn't until she found the pack with food and water that her father had hidden behind a tree stump that Hedy dared to speak.

"We'll wait here for the others to come," she whispered, opening the bag with one hand, her other holding tight to the boy sleeping against her arm. "Are you hungry?"

The girl nodded.

Hedy pulled out the thermos and poured water into the cup. Then she unwrapped the slices of meat and cheese and put them on the tree stump. The girl ate as they waited.

Her father arrived carrying a second girl on his back.

"Is everything OK?" Hedy said.

"Yes, although getting up the cliff with these three wasn't easy. The girl has twisted her ankle and is unable to walk."

"Are you hungry?" Hedy asked the other girl.

"Yes," she whispered.

Her father gently placed her on the ground next to the stump. She reached for a piece of cheese, a gleam of yearning in her eyes, and then, like a squirrel, grabbed as much of the food as her small hands could carry.

"What's next?" Hedy asked.

"Monsieur Glauser waits on the woodman's road not far from the Chalet de la Thomassette. If you can help me bring them there, we'll hide them in the back of his truck among the milk bottles. I'll sit up front to help him bring the children to our contact in Geneva." He reached over and cupped his hand on Hedy's face. "I'm proud of you. Then you must go home and rest."

But Hedy had another idea. She would pass by the hut on her way home to let Samuel know that all had gone well. He'd been worried ever since she'd mentioned it to him, with his talk about running out of luck, and she wanted to prove to him that luck had nothing to do with it.

They set off through the forest. Hedy carried the young boy in her arms, and her father carried the older girl on his back. The other girl walked between them, sometimes clutching Hedy's hand, other times her father's. Hedy squeezed her hand, hoping to convey that everything would be fine.

It was still dark when they came upon Monsieur Glauser's truck parked on the woodman's road. He unrolled the canvas cover, revealing dozens of tall metal milk jugs. Unfolding a step, he placed it behind the truck for the children to use. He whispered that they should hide among the milk jugs. Once they were inside, he rolled the canvas cover down, put the step away, and turned to Hedy.

"I want to apologize for my son. Your father told me what happened. Franck's gotten his head mixed up with the wrong men at military training. I will speak with him and send him to work on my brother's farm near Lucerne for a month." He wiped his mouth with the back of his hand. "If it weren't for what we're doing here, I'd go to the police now and have him arrested."

"Thank you," she whispered.

"Are you sure you can find your way home?" her father asked.

"Yes." She wanted to say that she knew this forest almost as well as him, but he'd already hopped into the passenger seat and closed the door.

As the truck rumbled away, Hedy turned back into the forest. The soles of her feet ached, and the hilt of the knife rubbed against her talus bone. Like a protective brother, Samuel had given her the knife. She couldn't imagine using it, but if it made him feel better, she would keep it. Once she reached the hut, she might remove her boots and rest for a while before returning home. She had time—no more classes to worry about or lies to invent for her parents. Her shoulders loosened, and her body relaxed.

She walked through the understory, avoiding the well-trodden path because there was less chance she'd run into a patrol, and it provided a shortcut to the hut. Her father had shown it to her on previous walks through the forest so she knew how to recognize it—marked by a fallen spruce and a handful of beeches growing nearby. He'd said it was a deer and wolf track, and part of her felt safer walking where men didn't.

The one thing she'd forgotten to do was get the children's names to add to her mother's book. Maybe her father knew them. Tonight, the number of lives saved had increased to forty-eight. Though it was a drop of water in the ocean of lives lost, she found solace in the image of her mother sitting at the table, writing each child's name down.

In the distance, the trees thinned, and she could make out the white limestone wall leading to the hut. Breathing in the sharp scent of spruce on the night air, she wondered if Samuel would be sleeping outside. Maybe she would find him against a tree and surprise him. She left the understory and stepped onto the dirt path that would bring her to the limestone wall. She took a few steps and heard a movement behind her. She started to turn, but a hand clapped over her mouth and another one around her neck.

"I've been waiting for you." Franck's voice. A sharp tug of panic in her throat as he tightened his grip around her neck.

He dragged her off the path toward the wall. She raised her arms to pull his hand off her mouth. He grunted, releasing her neck and pinning her arms behind her back, holding them there with his sweaty body. He tore the front of her dress, groping her breasts before his hand found its way to her neck and compressed her throat, making her eyes water. Fear roiled through her, but she wouldn't give in. She went deep inside to find her mettle. Twisting, she struggled to get free, but his grip was too powerful.

At the wall, he let go of her mouth, and in that instant, she shouted, "Help!" Franck pushed her face against the rocks and pressed his weight onto her so that she had no air in her lungs.

"No one can hear you." His hot breath on her neck reeked of alcohol. "It's just me and you."

Winded, chest pressed into the rocks, she concentrated on the knife. He lifted her dress from behind, tore her underwear, and pressed his body on her. He started moving up and down, his breath fast and hot on her neck as his hardness grew. She brought her knee up and reached into the boot, the cold hilt on her fingers as she pulled the knife out. With both hands, he lifted her hips, ready to enter her, but she stabbed the knife into his thigh. He howled and stepped back.

"Bitch!"

She scrambled over the wall. With one hand, he yanked her down to the ground, striking her chest with his knee and holding it there so she couldn't move. He pulled the knife out and threw it over the wall. She spat at him. He slapped her face and lifted his knee. She tried to kick free, but he spread her legs and knelt on the ground, then he suddenly went still. She heard a gurgling and felt a warm liquid on her face and chest. His hands released her and went to his neck. She shuffled away just before he fell, knocking his head against the wall.

A hand touched her shoulder. She screamed.

"It's Samuel. He won't hurt you again."

She folded against his chest.

27

Hedy

La Forêt de Risoud
August 1944

"What do we do now?" she asked, trembling.

"Bury him."

"Did you stab him?" She couldn't figure out how she'd gotten out from under him.

"I found the knife after he threw it over the wall. I must have hit a jugular vein. There's blood everywhere." He lifted her chin from his chest with his hand. "Are you OK?"

She couldn't answer. She felt broken. Her mind blanked out like the attack had shut it down, and she had to find a way to restart it. The sour smell and heat from Franck's breath haunted her, as did the crush of his weight. Her body ached all over, but under the pain, sizzling and seething anger burned—how had he come so close to taking from her what she would not willingly give?

Samuel gently pulled away. "Wait here."

Alone in the darkness, she felt the air shuffle and heard the branches break. "What's happening?"

"I'm moving him away from the path. Then we'll go to the hut, and I'll clean you up and find some clothes. Is that all right?"

She looked down. Her dress, torn at the front, dangled off both shoulders. The skin on her knees burned and her arms and hips ached. She wasn't sure she could walk. She felt unsteady and leaned against the wall but shuddered when her skin touched the hard rocks.

"Samuel?"

"Yes, I'm here." He reached over and took her hand, brought it to his lips and held it there. "I'm so sorry," he whispered. "Hold on while I hide him out of the way, then I'll take care of you."

He let go of her hand. She listened to Samuel pulling Franck's body away from the wall and out of her life. She stood suspended in time because she couldn't go to the part of her brain that was logical and wanted to know what would happen next.

"I'm back," Samuel's soft voice reached her in the darkness. "I'm going to climb over the wall, hold out my hand and help you over."

The strength of his grip, guiding her over the rocks and down the other side, reassured her. And the gentleness in his voice and touch slowly brought her back to who she'd been before the attack. Then he wrapped his arm around her waist and led her to the hut.

He brought out a bucket and poured water in it with a pitcher he filled daily from a nearby stream. She listened to his boots on the steps as he went inside and came back out, then a hefty fall of items on the floor.

"I'll clean you," he said. "I won't be able to see anything. Is it OK if I unfasten your belt and remove your dress?"

"Yes."

"Tell me if it hurts." She felt the torn cloth rake over the open cuts on her knees. "How are your ribs?"

"When I move on the left, it's hard to breathe."

"He might have fractured one."

Gently, Samuel washed her as she stood in the clearing. She was shaking but he murmured how brave and bold she was to fight, that he was proud of her, and her body went still. She was grateful for the crisp scent of soap on her skin that washed away Franck's blood and sweat. Samuel patted her dry, slipped one of his shirts over her shoulders and helped her into a pair of his trousers, which he cinched with a belt around her slim waist. Then he helped her inside and poured a glass of wine from a bottle her father had brought to thank him for looking after the children. "Here, drink this."

She took a sip, and the sudden heat at the back of her throat awakened something. Anger. "I'm glad he's dead. The world is better off without him."

"You're right about that." Samuel rubbed his beard, and she glimpsed his knotted forehead in the candlelight as he pondered his next steps. "With that rib . . ." He looked at her. "If you don't return home, your father will come looking for you here, right?"

She nodded, though every movement hurt. "Yes. But he won't come for a few hours, until he's back from Geneva."

"This is what we're going to do. You will sleep and rest until your father gets here. Then he and I will bury Franck." He paused. "Am I right that it's Franck?"

"Yes."

"That's what I thought. Then, your father will help you walk back home with that fractured rib. And no one will ever know what happened."

"But he'll be missing. They'll look for him."

"Don't worry. Your father and I will sort it out." He adjusted the pillows and the blankets and helped her to sit down. "I'm going to move him again to be sure he can't be seen from the path once it's daylight."

"Will you come back?" Though she felt it, she didn't want to say she was afraid.

He hesitated. "It can wait." He sat down alongside her. "It won't be daylight for a couple more hours." She leaned into his warmth, her head on his chest. "Sleep. When you wake, you'll feel better."

But she couldn't sleep. Fear overtook her, and she needed to talk. "Are you ever afraid?"

"Heck, yes. Everybody's got something that gnaws at them. Even the bravest pilot carries fear inside. It's how he handles it that matters."

"Tell me." She needed to hear a voice other than the one inside her head.

"You'd be surprised by the internal terrors going through men's minds. They don't talk about it, but by paying attention, you get glimpses."

"The bomber pilots are afraid?"

"Yes. I remember this kid, probably only nineteen. He was claustrophobic, and he was a ball turret gunner. It's the most terrifying place in a plane—a glass ball suspended near the wheels. Every time he scrunched his body to slip inside the turret ball, I could tell from the way his jaw tightened that he fought with himself to take those first steps." He shook his head. "Everyone struggles with fear. I certainly do."

"Really? You're sometimes afraid?"

"Heck, yes. For me, it's flying through clouds. I don't mean a few scattered ones but a block that turns the sky into a slab of white marble." His voice went cold. "Just thinking about it is enough to conjure panic in my chest."

"Why?"

"There's nothing for the eye to grab a hold of. No depth or perspective. It's pure terror. I don't know where I am, and I can easily convince myself the plane will drop to the ground."

"That's awful. What do you do?"

"I look at the instrument panel to remind me I'm still moving. But panic has a way of overtaking rational thought. All I can do is grit my teeth and hold on to the steering wheel with the belief that if I keep moving, I'll make it through the clouds to clear sky."

"I wish I could be as brave as you."

He stroked her back. "I'd say you're braver than me. There's something I need to confess." A quiet fell between them. "But let's save that for another day when you're stronger, and all this is behind you."

"Something for me to look forward to?"

"Yes. Now, sleep. You need rest."

His words died away, and the silence between them grew and expanded. Closing her eyes, Hedy finally felt safe.

Light streamed through the cracks in the wall. Though it hurt to move, Hedy sat up, hearing voices outside. She stood slowly and opened the door. Her father and Samuel were together.

"How do you feel?" Her father came to her. "Samuel told me what happened. I'm sorry. I should have acted, done something about Franck and this wouldn't have—"

"It's not your fault," she said through a lump in her throat. "I don't think he would have stopped. Where is he?"

"We've moved him off the path, and tonight—"

"You didn't bury him?"

Her father shook his head. "Tonight, I'll bring him over the border, leaving him in France with some cash in his pocket and a carton of cigarettes nearby. The authorities will think somebody killed him because of a smuggling deal gone bad." He threw Samuel a look. "I'll never be able to thank you enough for having the presence of mind to give her a knife. It saved her from that brute."

Samuel leaned back on his heels like he was trying to balance his weight. "Your daughter saved my life." His voice was thin, like it stretched long with feelings she couldn't read. "I just wish I could have got there earlier."

"You did more than enough, son." Her father turned to Hedy. "Let's get you home."

A few days later, Hedy emerged from her room to find Madame Jadot in the kitchen with her mother. A trill of panic at the base of her throat as she considered pivoting on her heels to return to the safety of her room. She'd yet to face the outside world and she wasn't sure she was ready. But Madame Jadot's gritty voice shot like a cannon across the kitchen, hitting her in the chest.

"Where have you been?" She waggled a finger in Hedy's direction. "I haven't seen you for days."

"I—"

"Hedy had a bicycle accident," her mother cut in. "She fractured one of her ribs. Per the doctor's orders, she has been resting in bed."

Madame Jadot's dark eyes moved over Hedy. "Isn't that a shame. I do hope you'll feel better soon." She waved Hedy over to the table. "It's good that you're up because there's something I've learned that you will both want to know."

"Come and sit down." Her mother stood and went to the shelf above the sink. "I'll get a cup and pour your tea."

Cautious steps brought her to the table and the empty chair next to Madame Jadot. Once she had settled, Madame Jadot inclined her head gravely, fixing Hedy with a long stare, and then said, "It's about Franck Glauser. He's missing."

Hedy's throat went dry as she tried to shake off the grainy image of Franck grasping his neck. Madame Jadot had enunciated that final word so clearly Hedy was convinced she'd done it on purpose. But to what end? Maybe she knew more than she was letting on. Did she suspect that Hedy was somehow involved or culpable in Franck's disappearance?

Across the room, her mother broke the awkward silence by clapping her hands. "Oh!" she said, returning to the table. "What do you mean missing?"

"He hasn't been home for two nights," she continued briskly. "His father reported his absence to the police. They're searching everywhere."

"How awful," her mother said, frowning. She glanced at Hedy, as if reminding her to speak up.

The ache in Hedy's chest stabbed harder, but she found the strength to speak. "I hope he's all right. Are there any leads?" She brought the cup to her mouth and blew on the tea. "When was he last seen?"

"With Pastor Rolle two evenings ago. The pastor is most distressed as he relied on Franck. The two are quite close."

Hedy slowly set down her cup, spilling tea on the table.

"Surely he will soon turn up," Hedy's mother said. "Perhaps he's just gone out of town for a few days and forgot to notify his father."

"Well, well." Madame Jadot's gaze shifted between Hedy and her mother. "Time will tell."

Sunday, a week later, Hedy sat on the bench alongside her mother at church. Her ribs had healed, though her left side was still tender, and any sudden movement hurt. The sun shone through the closed windows like spotlights, exposing the dust floating in the air. While waiting for Pastor Rolle to appear at the dais, she overheard whispering voices. *He was found in France. Stabbed twice. Over cigarettes. It must have been a smuggler. The poor family.*

Hedy held her breath, straining to hear more. But the speakers had moved on to a new topic.

Pastor Rolle dedicated the service to Franck, saying he was the victim of violent smugglers and that the police would track the killers down and they would be held responsible. Hedy's pulse raced as she tried not to fidget but she couldn't sit still. She was sure the pastor was staring at her as he spoke. Maybe Franck had told him about his obsession with her. If he'd been following her into the forest, had he seen Samuel? But if Pastor Rolle knew, he would have sent the police to search the hut. As his sermon droned on about other matters, her heartbeat slowed and she convinced herself that whatever evil drove Franck to follow and attack her, he kept it a secret from everyone, including Pastor Rolle.

Samuel had been right: no one will ever know. She missed him. It had been a week since that fateful night. Her father had been bringing him food and water while she recovered. Each time he returned from the forest, he said Samuel had asked about her and hoped she was well. Now that Hedy felt strong and Franck had been found and neither she nor her family were implicated in his death, she could return to thank him for all he'd done to save her.

She found him outside, leaning against the beech tree at the edge of the clearing. It was dusk and the clouds shimmered orange and pink from the low sun. He must have heard her approach because he stood and went to her. They stared at one another, the light from the sky warming the space between them.

"How are you?" he asked, taking her hand.

"Better. They found Franck's body. Everyone believes he was killed by smugglers."

"Your father knew what to do."

"Has he brought you all that you need?"

"Yes." He let go of her hand and reached up to touch her face. "I have all that I want now that you're here."

A warmth rose in her cheeks, and she pressed her hand over his and held it there. She wouldn't let the memory of that terrible night take over. Instead, she remembered their kiss, her first, that had stayed with her all this time. It had sat next to her through the long day of exams, stood in the rain alongside her on the platform as she waited for the pilot at the Lausanne station, walked through the forest with her as she crossed the plateau to wait at the Gy de l'Echelle, and perched on her shoulder like a guardian angel as she fought off Franck. Their kiss was a beacon in the darkness of war, a moment beating with possibility even after he pulled away. And now she'd come back to claim it. She wasn't going to let something that good slip away.

"You said you had a confession to make."

He laughed. "My confession: I love you."

"Then why—"

"Because I didn't want to hurt you. I was determined to return to the squadron in England. I had no intention of staying here and it didn't seem right to put you in danger and allow you to believe that we might have a future together."

"And now?"

"I love you, Hedy, and I'm not going anywhere. You're stuck with me, if you'll have me."

She felt a line of heat spiral up her neck to her chin from the muscle throbbing in her chest. He kissed her hand, and the air buzzed with an invisible charge. Then he leaned in, his lips touching hers. She tensed for a second, remembering, but his touch was nothing like the crushing weight that had meant to hurt her. Samuel's mouth hesitated, like a question waiting for her response. When she exhaled, their breath collided, and his tongue gently opened her mouth. She could feel a vibration roiling down her jaw and spine, rattling every bone in her body just from the touch of their lips. He pulled away, and she wanted him back, close, without anything between them.

"Hold on," he said. "Are you sure about this?"

She nodded. Every fiber in her body stirred with yearning and the voice in her head whispered: *love him now before he's gone.*

His finger traced a line down the back of her neck, and her skin tingled as it wound its way forward to her clavicle. She shuddered as he pressed lightly on the indent between her shoulder bones. Then, he leaned down and kissed her there, and a warmth flooded through her body.

Slowly, he guided her down to the forest floor. He kissed her neck, then her chin and mouth. But when his breath touched her lips, he pulled away. She wanted him back and tugged at his shirt to bring him close, but he held his distance. His blue eyes were on her like a target.

With one hand, he slowly undid the buttons on her dress. She shivered as each one loosened, and a swoosh of air skimmed her skin. The cotton dress slid off her shoulders. He kissed the upper curve of her arm, the inside of her elbow, the edge of her wrist. Her blood flowed warm, and her limbs felt loose. She didn't feel awkward or self-conscious like she thought she would, and she wasn't afraid. His finger traced a line down the center of her body, and she imagined it was the line his plane made in the sky, banking left then right, climbing for another pass before descending.

Hedy was no longer in the forest but up in the sky, gliding high above the trees, soaring through the blue with Samuel. She would fly with him forever. He was the one—the only one—the man she loved, the man who made her feel like she was entirely herself, the one who had saved her life and cleaned the dirt, blood and pain from her body. She would never want anyone else. Together, they had made it through the clouds to find a clear sky.

28

Samuel

La Forêt de Risoud
August–September 1944

Summer was drawing down, the nights turned shorter, the air sharp and crisp. A thin layer of frost hovered on the ground in the mornings. For a fortnight, Hedy, his beloved, had come daily. It had been the most beautiful two weeks of his life. His heart warmed, recalling the days they never left the hut, too enamored with exploring each other's bodies.

Today, he was waiting for her like he did every morning. But as the season shifted, Samuel sensed their time together might be coming to an end. He couldn't say why, just a niggling at the back of his brain. He should shut it down because it might bring bad luck to think like that. Their love was fierce but fragile, and like his B-24, he worried that something could come along and crush it as a burst of flak had shattered the plane's window.

A light wind ruffled the understory as she approached, a basket on her arm. The scent of pine and spruce filled the air. She glanced up at him, her eyes sparkling with anticipation. The breath left his lungs at the sight of her rosy cheeks. She'd been walking fast. A newspaper and bottle bounced against the basket's rim. She bounded over to where he was sitting and set the basket down.

"It's finally happened." Her voice trembled with excitement as she unfolded the paper and held it up, her eyes shining with joy.

He couldn't read the headline in French, but the black-and-white picture of General Charles de Gaulle walking down the Champs-Élysées said it all.

"Paris is liberated?"

"Yes!" She flipped the paper around to translate. "Under General Philippe Leclerc, the French 2nd Armored Division entered Paris to the loud cheers of Parisians. The German commander, General Dietrich von Choltitz, signed a surrender at Montparnasse station in front of General Leclerc and Colonel Rol, commander of the Forces Françaises de l'Intérieur of the Paris region. At 1900 local time, General Charles de Gaulle—leader of the Free French who has been living in exile in London since the Fall of France in 1940—entered the city."

The wind rasped through the trees. It was too matter-of-fact, Samuel thought, like reporting the weather. He wondered if it had been intentional to edit out all the blood, pain, destruction and death that had brought the war to this point.

"It's nearly over!" Hedy's voice rattled with excitement. She held up a bottle of wine. "Let's celebrate."

He took the paper and studied the tall general wearing a box-like hat. In the background, he spotted American troops with their round helmets, straps undone, dangling under their chins.

"Maybe it's only the beginning of the end," he said with a tinge of uncertainty.

"Why not the end?" She went into the hut and returned with two tin mugs.

"The Krauts have given up Paris. But they've got bases in southeastern France that they won't give up without a fight, let alone the rest of Europe."

"How much longer can it go on?"

He set the bottle between his legs and opened it with one hand, and the pop of the cork echoed off the trees. In a few more weeks, he'd have the use of the other one. He hadn't made up his mind about what he would do after his hand and arm healed, other than remaining by her side. Maybe he could speak with Woods and get a job helping him at the embassy.

"You'd be surprised how stubborn men can be about fighting one another. Hard to start, slow to stop." He tipped the golden liquid into the mugs and a waft of citrus like a burst of sunshine hit the air. They clinked the tin mugs as if they were crystal coupes.

"To the liberation of Paris," Hedy said.

"To the beginning of the end."

The wine felt cool on his throat. No label on the bottle. Only a waxy white script on the green glass: *Petite Arvine.*

"And then what happens?" Her breath hitched. "Between you and me?" She looked deep into his eyes.

"I'm staying here with you as long as you'll have me," he said, his voice filled with unwavering commitment. "Including tonight. We'll face whatever comes together."

She'd told him there was another group of refugees expected and that she would help, even though her mother's ankle had recovered.

"Your arm hasn't fully healed."

"It's healed enough."

"I told Papa and he doesn't like it. He said to think of the trouble if we're stopped by a Swiss patrol."

"I'll disappear. Or pretend I don't know you."

She emptied the mug. He refilled it.

"Even with Paris liberated," she said, "we still need to be careful. This part of France remains under German occupation."

Samuel didn't tell her that was what troubled him. The German soldiers patrolling the border would see it was the beginning of the end for them. Desperate and angry, they had nothing to lose. He wanted to be there with her, just in case. He couldn't bear the thought of losing her now.

Hedy

The wind cut through the trees, and the branches creaked and swayed as Hedy, Samuel and her parents made their way to the French border. At first her father had resisted Samuel's participation but Hedy's mother, sliding an arm around her husband's waist, convinced him. "An extra pair of hands, even if only one, is always useful. Let him join us. He can wait with me while you and Hedy go over the wall to the French side." It was three against one so her father consented. Samuel would remain on the Swiss side with Hedy's mother as a lookout. He was told to hoot like an owl three times if a patrol came, so Hedy and her father would know to keep below the ledge.

They walked in silence, her parents in front, Hedy and Samuel behind. Through the canopy, she could see thick dark clouds blotting out the stars. She slipped her hand into his, and his warm fingers laced through hers. After an hour of walking, they saw the white stones of the border wall up ahead.

Hedy's father slid the pack with food and water off his back, handed it to her mother, and motioned for her mother and Samuel to remain hidden behind the trees. Then he pointed to Hedy to follow him down the Gy de l'Echelle.

The incline was steeper than she had imagined. It felt like she was on top of a rolling wave in the dark and feared sliding off the crest. Then she remembered how her father had told her to take little steps to slow the descent. Soon, she found her bearings, the steepness receded, and she could pick up the pace.

Her father stopped. Sweat beaded under Hedy's arms. She peered at the darkness, trying to see what had drawn his attention but only heard the leaves rustle. He situated the direction of the sound and headed toward it.

They came upon an older woman and a child hovering behind a tree—the whites of their eyes fearful in the gloom.

"Are you the only ones?" Hedy's father whispered. "Where's the smuggler?"

"Maman," the boy said, pointing down the cliff.

"My daughter is with child," the old woman said, breathing heavily. "She's slow, so the smuggler left us."

Her father turned to Hedy. "You bring them up. I'll find the boy's mother. Do not come back down."

Hedy nodded. She took the boy's hand; his fingers clamped and held on tight. His grandmother followed. After a while, the woman slowed, leaving a distance between them. Hedy told the boy to wait. She went to find the grandmother, who had stopped to rest.

"Come," Hedy said, urging the woman up. Fear pumped through Hedy's veins because she knew they couldn't continue moving this slowly.

"Hedy," Samuel whispered, his hand touching her back. "I'm here."

She couldn't believe he was standing beside her, the boy on his back like he'd carried Chai. He motioned that Hedy should help the grandmother.

Hedy put her arm around the woman's waist and guided her up. The woman leaned on her for support. They didn't speak. Hedy listened carefully, attentive to the noises beyond the crack and snap of the branches underfoot. She worried a patrol would hear them. Samuel put out his hand at the top of the ledge for them to wait. Then, they moved as quickly as they could across the plateau, climbed over the low wall, and reached her mother.

Hedy rested her hands on her legs to catch her breath. Samuel tapped her on the shoulder and pointed at the cliff. "Back down," he whispered.

"Papa said not to go back down."

"I'm going. You stay here with your mother."

The wind cut little eddies through the trees, stirring the branches. If it was only one woman, wouldn't her father be able to bring her up alone? How long had he been gone? In the dark, it was hard to make sense of time. If Samuel was right that her father needed help, she wanted to be there. She grabbed his hand, and they made their way across the plateau.

They let go of each other on the way down, taking little steps, one after another. She knew it would soon even out, and they could go faster.

A sharp sound reverberated in the air. Hedy wanted to stop and figure out the direction, but Samuel kept running. Branches scratched her face and hands. A metallic odor hit the air and she recognized it as the smell her father's gun made when she went with him to hunt grouse. Her lungs burst with panic.

Samuel stopped and dropped to his knees. Hedy gasped at the sight of her father on the ground. Samuel pressed his good hand on her father's chest to stem the bleeding that gushed like a geyser. Hedy put her hands on his face.

Her father shook his head. "Leave . . . now."

"Samuel will carry you," she said, holding back tears.

Her father grabbed Samuel's shirt with his hand. "Save . . . them both."

Hedy saw the woman from the corner of her eye, a large belly protruding under her skirt. Sweat slicked down Hedy's back.

"Your mother . . ." Her father gulped for air. "Go . . . protect her. I love you both."

She bent down and kissed her father's forehead. "I love you, Papa."

Samuel pulled Hedy by the collar and dragged her away. The woman had already gone ahead. Hedy looked back, the whites of her father's eyes on her. She stumbled. Samuel picked her up and pushed her forward.

Shouts in German whizzed and echoed. The burning panic spread from her lungs to her legs. She ran up the last stretch while Samuel helped the pregnant woman, dragging her heavy body up the plateau. The acrid taste of gunpowder sunk deep into Hedy's lungs. She felt her body crack down the middle as she climbed over the ledge because she knew her father was dead.

They stumbled across the plateau. Her mother's eyes, wide and desperate, locked on Hedy's. She, too, must have heard the shots and seen the blood. Hedy's heart ripped with sadness. Her mother held her arms out, searching. Unable to find him, she clenched her fists and fell against Hedy's chest.

She folded her mother in her arms and gently pulled her forward. The German patrol could be following closely behind. They had to move away from the border. Samuel gathered the others. She wanted to tell her mother what had happened but needed to find the right words so the crack inside wouldn't break her in two.

29

Hedy

La Forêt de Risoud
September 1944

Hedy's chest bled with sorrow as she held her mother's hand.

"Papa didn't suffer. He was at peace with his decision to save the woman with child."

Her mother stared straight ahead. Samuel, who walked alongside, put a hand on Hedy's shoulder. She was grateful the darkness hid the blood that had begun to dry on his skin.

"Let's rest," Samuel suggested.

Having walked far from the border, they felt stopping was safe. The boy sat down on the ground. His dark eyes darted between the adults.

Samuel checked his watch. "It's four. Perhaps you should bring them to the dairy farmer now and I'll take your mother to the hut."

Hedy, still in shock, couldn't grieve or cry. She had to complete what her father had started. She turned to the pregnant woman, noticing her ashen face and the blue circles ringing her eyes. "We have farther to go. Will you be all right?"

"I don't want to cause more trouble for your family." Her voice quivered. "I'm so sorry."

The boy stood and went to his mother's side.

"It will take an hour and a half to reach Monsieur Glauser," said Hedy. "We need to keep moving so we don't miss him. He starts his rounds at six." After the French police informed their counterparts in Switzerland about her father, the entire village would be more closely watched. If the milk didn't arrive on time, like it did every morning, it could cast suspicion on the farmer. She couldn't risk putting another life in danger.

"Have a quick drink and something to eat before we continue," Hedy said, trying to open the pack, but her hands fumbled with the cord. Samuel reached over and opened it for her, placing the items on the ground. Then he held her hand.

"We'll need to talk back at the hut," he said. "You and your mother must be ready when the authorities come to the house with questions."

Hedy worried her mother might stumble over her answers. "How much time do we have?"

"A day, maybe two if the German administration isn't efficient. Make sure you warn Monsieur Glauser the police could be coming around." He touched her cheek. "Don't worry, we'll figure this out together."

"I'm glad you're here." She squeezed his hand, and Samuel pulled her close.

"Your father was a wonderful, brave man." His voice cracked. "Go now. I'll take care of your mother."

As she approached the dairy truck, parked in the same place as last time, Hedy's knees began to buckle. She'd held herself together walking through the forest, her mind focused on getting them all here. But now that she'd arrived, her throat turned raw and ragged. She dreaded facing the man whose son had attacked her and the moment she would have to tell him about her father.

Monsieur Glauser unfolded the step and positioned it to help the boy and two women mount the truck at the rear. He looked beyond Hedy, perhaps checking to see if her father trailed behind. She almost turned to look for her father too, wishing that if she only willed him to be there, he would appear, as he had so many times. How could everything be the same, yet different? It struck her that with each person who didn't yet know and she would have to tell, her father's death would hit her anew.

"Hide behind the milk jugs." He motioned to the family. Then he rolled the canvas cover down and folded the step. "Where's your papa this morning?"

"On the . . . Gy de l'Echelle . . ." there was a break in her voice ". . . a German patrol . . . killed him."

"*Oh mon Dieu!*" His voice faltered as he stepped back and raised his hands to his face. "A damn good man, your father . . ."

A steely silence fell as Hedy squeezed her arms tight at her sides.

"He will be missed. Condolences to you and your mother. We must be careful now."

"The police will come around asking questions."

He put the step in the truck and turned back to Hedy. "You get your mother ready. Your father would want her safe." His eyes were clouded over with shock. "He was a good and honorable man. Don't let anyone tell you differently. I better get moving. We must act normal, like any other day. After things settle, I'll check on you and your mother. Be careful, Hedy." He got in the truck, started the engine, and left her alone.

She turned back to the forest. Her legs were tired now. The dew on the undergrowth had seeped through her shoes, and soaked her toes. Alone, the weight of her father's death made her stumble. It took all her effort to drag her feet forward.

She wanted to return to Samuel and her mother, but grief dragged her down. As she fell on her knees, tears flowed in uncontrollable gulps. She sank against the earth and hugged her knees in a tight grip.

Drained, she sat on her haunches and looked out at the forest. A ray of light fell on a wispy sapling growing out of a felled spruce. It was the length of Hedy's forearm, and she guessed it was three years old. She wouldn't know anything about trees or undergrowth if her father hadn't brought her on many of his walks through the forest. So much of who she was came from the time she'd spent with him. As the soft edges of the morning's light spread through the forest, Hedy realized that her father hadn't left. She would carry him in her head and heart for the rest of her life, just as the sapling emerged from the tree on the forest floor.

She stood and wiped the dirt from her face and dress. Walking, her legs felt lighter and more robust. She thought about how the spruce and beech had survived by supporting one another, sharing the resources, growing slowly. Why couldn't men and women do the same? What use was there in studying poetry, philosophy and literature if it didn't stop people from killing one another? Then her father's last words rattled through her head—*protect your mother*. Had he been warning of the immediate danger from the patrol or a broader threat looming?

As she walked, her mind rolled through the questions the police would ask. She and her mother would deny any knowledge of her father's smuggling. There was no evidence to link her mother to her father's actions unless Madame Jadot had seen her going into the forest with him, but it would be Madame Jadot's word against hers. She would tell the police that they had both been at the house all night. She wasn't aware her father had gone out. And this morning, they thought he'd woken early to go to the workshop, as he often did. If the police didn't appear by the end of the day, they would report him missing. No evidence could prove they'd been involved in smuggling children from France.

Suddenly, she came to a stop, and the air rushed from her lungs. There *was* Samuel. The police would come to search the house *and* the hut her father owned in the forest—especially the hut. A crushing weight on her chest. Then, a quiet clarity. She realized what her father had meant as he lay dying: she and her mother were in danger because of Samuel.

Hedy ran. She didn't know how much time they had, but she feared it wasn't long.

Samuel

At the hut, Samuel made tea for Hedy's mother. He wished to say something to console her, but he'd only picked up a few words in French. As he went over everything that had happened, he said a prayer of thanks to whatever God existed out there that had given him the foresight to go with Hedy. He couldn't think about what would have happened to her if he hadn't been there. He'd already lost Tommy. He couldn't risk losing her. He would stay by her side until the war ended. Then they could decide together where to live. Either here or in the U.S., Samuel didn't mind. It was up to Hedy and her mother. All he wanted was to protect them.

Samuel looked at his watch: 0800. Hedy should have been here by now. He got up and paced. Maybe the dairy farmer had decided it was too risky to bring the refugees to the camp, and she'd had to bring them here and move at a slower pace. Perhaps the Germans had called the Swiss Army and sent a patrol into the forest.

When, at last, he saw her running toward the hut, he sighed in relief.

"You OK?" he asked.

She didn't look at him. "Monsieur Glauser took them." Her voice sounded different, as if she was forcing brightness into it. "How's Maman?"

"Quiet. I made her tea."

"Papa's death changes everything," she said.

"I won't let anything happen to you or your mother." He wanted to tell her he was more convinced than ever that he'd found his purpose in this tiny hut in the middle of the forest.

"You must leave." Her tone turned sharp like a biting wind. "Tonight."

"Where do you want me to go?" He thought she would suggest another hiding place.

"To France."

He shook his head at her. "I'm staying here with you."

"The hut is registered in Papa's name. The police will search it. You're putting us in danger."

A thousand protests rose inside him. He couldn't abandon her, not now that her father was gone. Who would protect her? There had to be another way. "I'll hide elsewhere. Find another hut, then return here after things cool down."

"I'll still need to bring food to you. And they'll be watching me." She looked beyond him, her gaze like cracked glass, and all he could think was that the weight of her father's death had splintered her world into pieces that she couldn't put back together. "If you stay, all three of us will be caught."

He didn't want to accept that. They'd created a beautiful place where he felt he belonged. He knew one day he would have to return to the world out there. But when that time came, he planned to bring her with him.

"Hedy's right," her mother said in English.

He'd never heard her mother speak English. She stood and came alongside them. She and Hedy spoke in French.

"Maman agrees that you must go. She wants us to clean out the hut. There can be no trace that you've been here."

Samuel stared at her in silence, his expression drawn with anguish. He felt a gut punch to his stomach. Would his and Hedy's relationship disappear without a trace, too? He couldn't bear that. "I can't—"

"You can, and you must," Hedy cut in. "Maman will return to the house in case the police come."

Hedy's mother opened her arms and embraced Samuel. "Goodbye, American pilot. Be safe."

He held back from arguing and looked down at his arm. He wasn't sure he'd be able to row across the lake. Maybe she would listen to that and allow him to hide elsewhere. If caught on the lake, he'd be sent back to Wauwilermoos.

After Hedy's mother left, he said, "I won't be able to row the boat."

"I will row for you."

"But you can't."

"Why not?"

"You told me you're afraid of water."

"Papa said one day I would have to face my fear. That day is here."

The ground shifted. Samuel realized that if she was willing to row at night to get him safely to the other side, she saw no other way forward. He had always trusted her, and she'd never failed him. As much as it hurt him, he had to trust her now, too. He hated leaving her alone to face the police, but in his heart, he knew she was right. Him remaining here increased the danger for her and her mother. They didn't need to suffer any more pain than they'd already experienced tonight. Accepting her decision, he resolved to give her the strength and confidence to row back to the Swiss side of the lake alone.

"OK. We'll do it together. I'll help you."

She stared into his eyes. "I love you, Samuel. Our time will come, just not now."

30

Hedy

La Forêt de Risoud
September 1944

Many hours later, after clearing the hut out and the sun had set, Hedy and Samuel left the forest. While emptying the stove and rearranging the wood piles in the hut, she'd worked it all out in her mind. To guard against someone recognizing her, she wouldn't take the train at Le Brassus. Instead, they would walk farther west to the station at Le Pont and keep on the small roads between the forest and the Lac de Joux.

It took three hours to reach Le Pont. They waited in the dark on an empty platform. Once they boarded the train, Samuel pretended to read a paper. They got off at Lausanne. Hedy retraced the car's route all those months ago with the American pilot. After another short walk, they came to the house along the lake and waited in a field across the street. They left the field at midnight, entered the driveway, and descended to the lake.

She heard the choppy water, like glass breaking. The wind roared strong. Crests of white foam on the surface. Dread overtook her arms and legs so that she couldn't move. She would never be able to get in the boat.

Samuel sensed her fear. "You can do this," he whispered, leading her to the boat that sat on the shore. A long wooden paddle poked up from the hull. He lifted the bow and dragged it down to the water. "Put your foot in the center. Once you sit down, I will push off."

Hedy blocked out the choppy waves and put one foot in the boat, then the other. The air in her chest felt tight like a hand squeezing her lungs, and there wasn't enough to breathe. She concentrated on every movement, believing it was the only way to prevent a fatal mistake. The boat teetered with her weight. She gripped the metallic sides to steady herself. Samuel slid the hull into the water and climbed in.

Her fingers gripped the paddle's flat handle. She sunk the blade in the water, and the lake grasped it like a hungry animal. Hedy seized up, fearing the paddle could slip from her hold, and gripped tighter. She pulled, and the boat glided forward.

"That's right," Samuel said. With her father's compass, he guided her to maintain a southern direction. He taught her how to turn. "Make a wide sweeping arc with the blade." And how to maintain a straight line. "Keep the blade in the water close to the side of the boat and switch sides every two pulls."

Hedy did as he said. Drops of water drenched her dress each time she switched the paddle from one side to another. Her knees rattled from the damp and cold. She tried not to think about anything other than the next pull of the blade. She looked ahead: all was darkness except for ghostly ripples breaking on the water's surface. The stars and moon hung like cobwebs in a far-off corner of the sky, barely visible. On shore, the blackout blinds swallowed the light.

"You're doing great," Samuel said.

Her chest constricted, not from panic, but from the thought that she would no longer hear his voice after tonight.

She pulled the paddle through the blustery water and held it close to the side of the boat, the wind at her back.

A light suddenly flickered on and off in the distance.

“Lie flat,” Samuel commanded.

She lay down, and Samuel did the same. Their heads touched. Extending his hand, he laced his fingers through her hair. French-speaking voices drifted on the wind. Might the current carry their boat into the patrol? Hedy didn’t want to imagine what would happen. She shut out the expanse of dark water under her and the police patrol on the surface, focusing instead on the sapling she’d seen in the forest that morning. She wanted to believe it was a sign sent by her father, that some part of him was still here, watching over her. After a while, her pulse slowed, and she breathed easier.

Samuel let go of her hair. “They’ve gone.”

She raised herself, returned the blade to the water, and pulled.

“Can you see the shore up ahead?” he asked.

The moment she’d been dreading was soon upon her. She carried a secret. It didn’t have to do with her father or mother. It was between her and Samuel. She wanted to tell him, but he wouldn’t go if she did.

The boat thumped and stopped on the pebbly shore. Hedy wanted more time. Since she’d decided Samuel would have to leave, every moment had been filled with activity—cleaning out the hut, putting the blankets and all the items in her house, walking to Le Pont, taking the train to Lausanne, rowing across the lake. Somehow, all that action had kept the ache of their looming separation at bay. But now that she’d reached a standstill, she felt her heart breaking. Once she was moving again, Samuel would be gone.

She turned around in the boat to face him. “I’m sorry.”

“You’ve done nothing wrong.” He took her hands.

Tell him, a voice whispered in her head.

But if he stays, none of us will be safe, she answered back.

"Listen to me." His breath brushed her face. "You'll be rowing into the wind on the way back. It will be much harder." She felt something cold and heavy in her hand. "I want you to have it. If we weren't at war, I'd give you a ring, but the watch will do until we are reunited."

He looped the leather band around her wrist and cinched the metal pin in the hole. She looked at the black dial with luminous, wafer-thin lines and spots that glowed like green stars in a glossy sky. It was 2 a.m.

"Head north. Hold the compass close to the watch to read the direction using its light." He placed both her hands against his chest. "You can do anything, my love."

She wanted to believe him, but she wasn't sure.

"Promise me you won't be afraid. You have the compass and the watch. Imagine I'm sitting right behind you, no matter how bad it gets."

"Yes." A sob wound up in her throat.

He kissed her. "I love you, Hedy, the girl who saved my life." He got up.

She pulled him back. *A little longer. Hold him before he goes.* "I love you too." She squeezed her fingers against her palms to quell the urge to tell him of the joy and pain interlaced in her heart like two veins pumping blood through her body. She didn't want anything to sit between them. She had no choice and pressed the secret deep in her chest to wait until his return. What harm could there be in telling him later? It was only time.

He pulled away. "Turn around, face the lake, and I'll slide you back out on the water. My strong, brave Hedy." He leaned in and kissed her for the last time. "I'm with you, always."

She turned and held the paddle. Her body rattled with sorrow. She could still turn around and tell him not to go. Then, in her mind, she saw the woman with child that her father had saved, and she knew she was doing what had to be done. The boat slid away from the shore. She dipped the blade in the water and pulled.

The wind blew hard, and the water turned solid like she was rowing through a brick wall. It took strength to pull the paddle. She gripped it tight and kept on, stopping only to check the direction with the compass. But each time she did, the current carried her off to one side, so she felt she was slipping back rather than sliding forward. Soon her arms burned from the effort. Every time the boat rocked, and water splashed over her dress, she feared it could tip over, and the lake would swallow her, and she'd sink to the bottom. When trepidation overtook her so that her hands and arms shook and she couldn't move, Hedy looked at the watch. She heard Samuel's voice—*keep on, you can do this.* Adrenaline squeezed through her veins. She returned the blade to the water and pulled. No different than walking in the forest, she told herself. Instead of a green understory, there was blue water. If she just kept pulling, she'd reach the other side.

The farther she went, the more drenched her dress became. She regretted not having brought a sweater. Her hands swelled red and stiff from the cold. An unease that she couldn't maintain her grip on the paddle spread through her. If the paddle sunk into the water, she'd drift with the current and never reach the other side.

A light flashed up ahead. Another patrol. Maybe the same one they'd come across earlier. Hedy squatted and squeezed her body down into the hull. She brought her knees up to her chest. Out of the wind, she felt warmer. She took quiet, steady breaths. Exhaustion came over her. She and Samuel had rested for a few hours after cleaning out the hut, but other than that, she'd gone two nights without much sleep. If only she could rest her eyes for a few moments, it would do her good. Her body melted and drifted with the current. She closed her eyes, wanting to sink into a deep sleep.

Something startled her awake, and the watch's dial, glowing the time, 3 a.m., warned of danger. *Get up*, it urged. No longer was her mother the only one needing protection. Over these last weeks, she'd slowly realized there was someone else she was now responsible for—the child growing inside her. It had taken Hedy a while to figure it all out. The first time she'd missed her monthlies, she thought it could just be running late, as sometimes happened. But when her monthlies didn't return, her gut told her it meant something. A part of her had wanted to tell Samuel, but another part reasoned there was no harm in waiting a little longer, just to be sure. It was too big of a thing to be wrong about. The moment she saw the woman in the forest heavy with child, Hedy knew in her bones that she was pregnant and would look like her one day.

She'd decided to tell Samuel once they were back in the hut. He would be happy. But then her father had been killed, and there wasn't time. Now, she had to protect her mother. If Samuel knew about the child, he wouldn't go.

She sat up and faced the darkness. No lights flickered. Only the wind thumping, like a sheet blowing hard on a clothesline. She checked the compass—south—made a wide scooping arc with the paddle and felt the boat slide in her desired direction. With the light from the watch, she again read the compass. North. Hedy looked ahead, muscles taut, hardening herself for all that would come next.

31

Gina

Le Brassus
October 2018

I stare at Mamie for several quiet moments, unable to speak. The restaurant is empty, and the fondue pot and plates have been cleared away. I perceive Lily, the owner, hovering not far off with the bill, but I'm still riveted to the past, trying to get my bearings.

"Grandfather was a prisoner of war in Switzerland with other Allied pilots?"

She sighs. "Yes."

"And you risked your life to hide him, and that's how you fell in love?"

She nods as her crooked hands smooth the creases in the white tablecloth.

I want to say that's a massive piece of our family history to leave out. "Why didn't you tell us? Did Mom know?"

She signals to Lily to bring the bill and turns back to me. "No, I never told your mother."

"Mamie—"

"Your grandfather was ordered by the army never to speak of his experience in Switzerland." Her hands rise in the air in her defense. "An order isn't something you can ignore. So, we didn't talk."

Lily brings the bill, and Mamie slides it across the table to me. I pay with the dollars I changed to francs at the airport. Something chilly settles in the air between us. Mamie tilts her head to one side and looks out the window. "I'm rather tired," she says. "Perhaps we can stop and resume tomorrow."

I reach over the table and take her hand. "Of course." It must be hard for her to relive her father's death and Franck's brutal attack. I know what it is like to watch a parent die, to question all the choices you make on their behalf, thinking that if you'd pursued a different one maybe the outcome would have been better, and you could have saved them. It's not just grief that haunts you afterwards, but guilt, too. And what woman hasn't experienced a form of sexual assault, though not always with the violence Franck afflicted on Mamie? I swallow, pushing away a black memory. That's a wound that stays for the rest of your life.

"Thank you for sharing your story," I say. "The things that happened to you must be difficult to discuss, even after all this time. You're incredibly courageous, and I want you to know that I'm honored to be here to help you find Elizabeth."

Mamie squeezes my hand. I want to ask if she was carrying Elizabeth when she rowed Samuel to the other side of the lake. She intimated that she was pregnant, but she didn't come out and say it. I have so many questions, but she looks pale and old in a way I've never seen before. Both eyes are bloodshot, and her drooping lid curls farther down. Yes, she must be suffering from the long trip and jet lag, but I can't help thinking that revisiting the pain in her past is having a physical impact on her body. I don't want to push her. It's taken her over seventy years to open up. I can't expect her to tell me everything in one night. Luckily, the hotel is across the street. I help her to the door and hold her hand as we leave the restaurant.

Outside, the wind blows, carrying a wild forest smell. Mamie lifts her head and breathes in the cool night air. She touches her fingers to her lips, and a smile crosses them.

In the morning, I awaken to a text from Kai. *Received records from Rolex.*

I ask Mamie if she wants to go with me to see what Kai has discovered in the Rolex archives, but she prefers to stay in bed and rest. After I get dressed and tie Mom's scarf around my ponytail, I bring her a croissant and coffee, then put the "do not disturb" sign on the door handle before leaving.

When I arrive at Kai's, he buzzes me in, and I slip off my shoes and head upstairs. No music this time. He's on the first floor, sitting in an armchair before the fireplace. Flames roar behind the hearth's glass door.

"Nice fire," I say, edging toward it and holding my hands out to warm them. "It's colder today."

"October is when the first snow arrives."

"The town and forest must be beautiful, all in white, but I hope it doesn't snow because neither Mamie nor I have the clothes for it."

He tilts his head. "I didn't realize you're here with your grandmother."

"She was born here. We've come back for a visit." Why am I lying? Mamie has been hiding this for too long. There's no reason for me to do the same. "We're trying to find someone."

He leans forward. "Does the Rolex have something to do with who you're looking for?"

"Maybe. I don't yet know." The fire cracks and pops. "All Mamie has told me is that she wants to give the watch to her firstborn daughter, whom she lost decades ago, and we're here to find her."

"I see. Would you like a coffee?"

"No thanks, I just had one and won't stay long." I rub my hands on my thighs. "I don't want to leave Mamie alone for too long."

"Nice scarf," he says, noticing my ponytail. "Yesterday, you wore it on your wrist."

"It's sentimental, belonged to my mother."

"I like the way you mixed it with the watch. The yellow against the black dial. That was cool."

"Thanks." I feel my cheeks growing warm. Is it because of how he's looking at me or the heat of the fire? "What did you find out from Rolex?"

"Well, I'm not sure it makes sense because you said your grandfather was American. The original owner of the Monoblocco was James Lindsay, a British pilot."

He lifts a paper from the table beside him and passes it to me.

MONTRES ROLEX S. A.
18, rue du marché
GENEVE
GENEVE, le 30th March 1942

Lieutenant James Lindsay (Army)
Gef.Nr. (VII c)
Oflag VII-B

Rappeler réf: HW/MC

Dear sir,

We beg to acknowledge receipt of your order dated 10th March 42, and in accordance with your instructions we will supply you with 1 Chronograph Oyster No 122.

This watch costs today in Switzerland Frs. 250, but you must not even think of settlement during the war.

As we now have a large number of orders in hand for officers, there will be some unavoidable delay in executing your order, but we will do the best we can for you.

Meanwhile, believe us to be,

Yours truly,
Montres Rolex S.A.
Director
H. Wilsdorf

Mamie didn't mention James Lindsay last night. I glance at his address. "What is Oflag VII-B?"

"It was a prisoner-of-war camp in Germany holding Allied pilots."

Another POW camp? That's odd. Could the watch somehow connect the two camps? The idea is loose, but I let it roll around in my head. "Why was Rolex sending watches to Allied pilots in German camps?"

"I asked the archivist about that. Hans Wilsdorf, who signed the letter, was the founder of Rolex and an Anglophile. Once he heard that the Germans confiscated the watches from captured airmen, he promised to send any airman in a POW camp a watch if they wrote to ask for one."

I look again at the letter. "James Lindsay must have written to him requesting a watch."

He nods. "The Monoblocco, made of a single piece of steel, is very solid, so it makes sense that's what Rolex sent to a POW."

"But if the German guards confiscated their watches, why would they allow new ones into the camps?"

"The archivist said Rolex used the International Red Cross to hide the watches in the rations they brought on prison visits. The records indicate Rolex sent three thousand watches to Oflag VII-B! And you have one of them in your possession." He sniffs like a hound onto a good scent. "A story like this, with the papers to back it up, increases—"

"Mamie isn't selling."

"Right. Sorry, I forgot."

"Maybe the watch connects the two POW camps?"

"Sorry, you've lost me." He frowns. "There's only one camp."

"My grandfather was a POW held in a camp in Switzerland."

He cuts me a look of doubt. "I don't know who told you that, but it's wrong. Switzerland was neutral."

I lift my shoulders. "Mamie told me. She would know because she was here."

"What did she say?"

"That Grandfather was shot escaping from a camp in Davos, and Mamie hid him in a hut in the forest outside of Le Brassus."

At this, his eyebrows lift. "That's crazy." He stares at the fire and then turns back to me. "I'm not saying your grandmother is lying, but maybe she's confused."

"You don't know my grandmother. Her mind is sharp."

"Well, only one way to find out." He stands. "Let's check the computer; if it's true, we'll find some evidence."

I follow him up the stairs and settle on the stool beside his chair. As he turns on the computer, I take in the view through the window: a vast blue sky and rolling hills covered in trees. It's breathtaking, but he's already typing, and my attention snaps to the search engine: Allied pilots, Switzerland, 1944.

He scans the results and clicks on a link to a book. I lean close, reading the title: *Shot from the Sky: American POWs in Switzerland* by Cathryn Prince.

"I've lived here ten years . . ." He trails off, looking stunned. "No one has ever mentioned this."

I think about Mamie and how she couldn't tell us about Elizabeth. "Maybe it's not talked about because they're ashamed."

He nods and clicks on the link to the book. The Naval Institute Press published it in 2003, nearly sixty years after the war ended. He opens a sample and scrolls to the introduction.

> *In 1944, as the Allies began to achieve air superiority, the U.S. Army Air Force was responsible for most airspace violations over neutral Switzerland. The country's proximity to critical German targets made it an attractive alternative to German-occupied territory for disabled Allied planes seeking safe ground on which to land. But choosing Switzerland as a sanctuary was not always the wisest course. Once Switzerland chose to define its obligations as a neutral country to include armed opposition to territorial and airspace violations, its military shot and forced down crippled Allied planes that had entered Swiss airspace because they were unable to return to their bases in England.*

Kai cups his hand to his forehead. "They shot down damaged planes?"

> *Once the airmen landed, they were sent for the duration of the war to internment camps where the Swiss were to provide shelter, food, and medical care. The servicemen's own government would be responsible for paying for these services. In September 1944, there were 1,036 American, 78 English, and 4 German military internees.*

Kai leans away from the computer, folding his hands at the back of his head. "I can't believe it." Then he turns to me. "Why do you think the watch connects the two camps?"

"Mamie said Grandfather escaped with his roommate, Peter, an RAF pilot. He's the one who gave Grandfather the Rolex just before he was killed by a Swiss patrol in Kublis."

Kai taps the table with his fingers. "Maybe—"

"What?"

He picks up the paper from the Rolex archives. "What if James Lindsay had a brother, Peter, who was also a pilot? Then the watch would have passed to him upon James's death." He swivels back to the computer. "Let's see what we can find."

He opens another tab and types: *Lieutenant James Lindsay, His Majesty's Royal Air Force, 1942.*

Multiple results appear, including many black-and-white photos of pilots standing before massive airplanes that must have been the one my grandfather flew. He stops scrolling at an official-looking website: *The National Archives . . . how to look for records of Royal Air Force personnel.* He clicks on it, enters the same information, and hits return. We both lean forward to read what appears.

> *Lieutenant James Lindsay died in service to his country as a prisoner of war in Bavaria, Germany, on 12 December 1942. He was survived by his parents, Mr. and Mrs. Henry Lindsay, and his brother, Peter Lindsay.*

I stare at the screen. "James never made it out of the German camp, but his watch did."

Kai nods. "It would make sense that his brother Peter received it as a part of James's items after his death."

Little pricks rise on my neck at how close I feel to my grandfather. Then something Mamie said last night niggles at the back of my mind—*your grandfather was ordered by the army never to speak of his experience in Switzerland.*

I turn to Kai. "Can you go back to the book?"

"I'll buy it."

"Oh, I didn't mean—"

"I want to read it." He downloads it and opens the appendix. "What are you looking for?"

"Mamie said Grandfather was ordered not to discuss his time here. Is there anything on that?"

Kai flips through the book and points to a page. I lean forward and read it.

> *Many among the hierarchy in the U.S. military had encouraged the idea that the American fliers landed in Switzerland to escape the war, especially as in March and April 1944, fifty-five American planes landed. After the war, the U.S. government refused to grant pilots interned in Switzerland prisoner-of-war status, hence they were not eligible for medical and financial benefits. American veterans' groups have largely ignored the former internees, viewing them as little better than deserters. One reason the story of the Swiss internees has remained in history's shadows is because they were ordered not to discuss their internment with anyone once they were repatriated.*

I look out the window at the wooded hills stretching in the distance and the dark shadows cast by the clouds. Everything Mamie told me suddenly feels real and alive.

"It sounds like the only one who cared about your grandfather was your grandmother." He takes a breath. "Did they get married in Switzerland?"

"I don't know." I stand. "Thank you for this. I would never have made the connection between Peter and James without you. I've got to get back to Mamie."

He smiles. "Good luck. Keep me posted, and if there's anything else I can do to help, let me know."

When I return to the room, Mamie is dressed and ready to go. I warn her about the cold, and she reminds me that she grew up here and knows it well. She says there's a bench across from her house, just before the forest, where she'd like to sit for a while.

"I want to be close to the trees. Did you hear the rain last night? Now that the sun is out and the forest is warming, the trees will release their oils. I miss that smell."

After we're outside walking arm in arm on the main street, Mamie asks, "What did your watchmaker learn from Rolex?"

"Peter got the Rolex from James, his brother who died in a German POW camp."

She squeezes my hand. "Your grandfather would be happy to know that. After the war, he went to England to find Peter's family, but they had all passed. He never knew the story behind Peter's watch, but now you've uncovered it."

"Kai helped me figure it out." I smile.

"He sounds like a nice young man."

"He is. Will you tell me what happened to you after Grandfather left for France?" I hope this time, she'll talk about Elizabeth.

She motions to the bench up ahead. "Let's sit, and I'll continue where I left off."

32

Hedy

Le Brassus
September 1944

The rays of the early morning sun warmed Hedy's back as she pulled the boat up on the shore. She dragged it along the beach and checked Samuel's watch: 5 a.m. Wringing the water from her damp dress, she ironed out the wrinkles with her hand. She planned to catch the first train from Lausanne, disembark at Le Sentier, and walk the rest of the way home. She'd arrive before the church rang the midday bells if she could make good time.

At home, her heart contracted as she opened the door. It was the first time in the house since her father had passed. Her mother sat at the kitchen table.

"Is he gone?" she said, looking up.

Hedy felt her legs loosen. She reached the chair just as her knees buckled. "Yes."

Her mother put a hand on her arm. "I'll make you a cup of tea."

Hedy's palms were swollen with blisters from the hours of rowing. But the pain was nothing compared to the hole inside her heart. She had lost the two men who meant everything in her life. She tried to imagine Samuel now—had he already found the Maquis? Maybe he would soon be on his way back to England. But that brought another worry—what if his squadron sent him over the English Channel to continue fighting? His plane could be shot down. No pilot, even one as brave and skilled as Samuel, could survive that a second time. If he died, Hedy would never know, nor would he know of the child he'd left behind.

Her mother's hand touched her back. "Drink."

The milk in the tea made Hedy's stomach turn. She edged away from the table. "Has anyone come?"

"No." Her mother sat next to her.

"Is there anything in the house or Papa's workshop that could link you—"

"We have always been careful so as not to endanger you. There is nothing, *ma chérie.*"

Hedy reached over and took her mother's hand. "I'm sorry about Papa." She wished she could undo what had happened in the forest or find a way to bring him back. She couldn't change the past, but she was determined to keep her promise to her father. "You must say you knew nothing about the smuggling."

A shaft of light fell on her mother's forehead. "What if they don't believe me?"

Hedy leaned forward. "You will make them believe you."

At three o'clock in the afternoon, a heavy knock on the door woke Hedy. She dragged herself from the bed and straightened her dress and hair. Her mother waited in the hallway. Hedy nodded, and her mother opened the door.

"Madame Borel, we are from the cantonal police." Two men in blue-and-black uniforms, one tall, the other short, pushed past her. They tracked in mud on their black boots.

A flash in Hedy's mind—her father's body in the forest. Had they just returned from there?

"What's going on?" her mother asked.

Their square-brimmed hats bobbed as they swarmed through the house, checking each room to see who else was home. Hedy undid the watch, slid it from her wrist, and tucked it in her pocket.

"When was the last time you saw your husband?" the tall one with beady black eyes said, standing before her mother.

"At dinner last night." Her mother held her hands still at her sides. "He said he had something to finish in his workshop and stayed up late."

"And this morning?" The short, stocky gendarme, eyes murky brown, stared hard at Hedy.

"He left before we got up. Please tell me what this is all about. Is Alain in trouble?"

The men went to the kitchen and pulled open the drawers. Metal cutlery clacked against the wood, and the porcelain plates and bowls in the cupboards rattled from the banging. Hedy didn't know what they thought they might find in the kitchen, but they tore through the pantry, knocking a jar of strawberry preserves that splattered red all over the white pantry door. When they finished, everything hung open and exposed. Then, they proceeded to the main room and turned over the cushions on the couch.

"What are you looking for?" her mother said, dragging a hand across her apron.

"Last night, your husband was caught smuggling refugees from France. He attempted to evade a German patrol and was shot and killed."

Shaking, her mother covered her face with her hands and stepped back against the dining table. Hedy went to hold her for support.

"It's all right, Maman, I'm here."

The short gendarme snorted. "He got what he deserved."

Hedy didn't know if the gold bar insignia on his arm indicated he was senior in rank, but she sensed it from his tone.

"Keep them both here while I check the other rooms," he said.

"What do you want from us?" Hedy said.

"We must determine if your father acted alone," the other said, drawing out the last word. "Or if he had help . . ." he stepped closer ". . . from the Anglophile in the family?"

Like a warning, Hedy's heart beat very hard. "I'm an English major at the University of Lausanne. Is that what you're referring to?"

He removed a small notebook from his back pocket. "You've made statements against the government."

"What statements?"

He thumbed through the pages. "A denunciation was made to our office in March regarding your questioning General Guisan's order on blackout blinds."

Her mind went blank, but then she remembered Madame Jadot's warning that she would report Hedy. Was one person's interpretation of an act sufficient for the police to classify her as disloyal or a criminal?

"It was a misunderstanding," Hedy said tightly, trying to calm the fear mounting inside. "One night, I'd been doing my homework and had forgotten to put up the blackout blind. It could happen to anyone."

"I've found something," the senior gendarme said, returning to the main room. "Have a look." He held up a small leather book.

Hedy started, raising her eyes at her mother, who wouldn't meet her gaze.

"Where was it?" The gendarme opened the book.

"Under a mattress."

Hedy's heart raced. The officers' words cut through her ears like a hot knife. Why hadn't she remembered the book where her mother recorded every child's name and warned her of the danger? She had to have known they would find it. The sharp point of the knife spread to her neck and chest. Her body burned with dread.

"Here's the last entry: 11 August: Bordeaux: Rachel, Adi, Chai," the gendarme said. "All Jews! It goes back to '41."

Hedy wanted to step forward and protect her mother. She could say the book belonged to her, that she had been the one to assist her father. But a terrifying thought rose in her mind. What if she was carrying Samuel's baby? Didn't she have a responsibility to protect that life, too? She looked at her mother; this time, her mother looked back. Without uttering a word, Hedy understood that she had never intended to destroy the book, even if Hedy asked her to. Sweat covered Hedy's back. Her entire body was on fire.

"There's plenty of proof," he said, waving the book before them. "I can arrest you both for smuggling Jews into the country."

Hedy's mother stepped forward. "It is me you want. After helping my husband guide them over the border from France, I wrote the names down. I accept full responsibility for my actions. I will confess everything. My daughter wasn't involved. She's innocent."

"Don't," Hedy said, her eyes wide and searching. "It was all Papa." Her hands shook, and she put them behind her back so the officers wouldn't see.

Her mother touched her cheek and held her hand there. "It's all right, *ma chérie*. I knew what I was getting into. No regrets." She smiled. "Next to you, this is what I am most proud of. Your father felt the same. I couldn't destroy the book. I love every one of those children as if they were my own. To live by truth is to be exposed. I wouldn't have it any other way."

Hedy stood there, looking into her mother's gentle eyes, willing the moment to go on as she pressed her face against her mother's hand.

"Come along, Madame Borel," the gendarme said, pulling her mother away. He handcuffed her. Then his murky eyes locked on Hedy. "We'll keep investigating. If it turns out that you were involved or assisted your parents in any way . . ." his face hardened ". . . then we'll be back."

Her mother's shoulders curled forward like she was steadying herself to bend over, but it was due to the shackling of her hands in front of her. She managed to turn back and look at Hedy one last time. With tears in her eyes, she whispered, "Be strong, my daughter."

"Maman, no!" Hedy's voice quivered as she stepped forward, but an arm came down before her, like a barrier that forbid her crossing.

"That's enough," the gendarme said firmly, stopping her.

Hedy could hear her father's voice echoing in her mind: *protect your mother.* A terrible darkness overcame her, and she felt a shiver of foreboding as the door slammed shut.

She listened to the car engine and the crunch of gravel outside, staring at the mud left by the gendarmes' boots until it turned to dark spots on the edges of her eyes, and the world went quiet.

She walked into her parents' bedroom. The mattress had been overturned, and the chest of drawers filled with pressed shirts lay strewn across the floor—shirts her father would never wear.

Then, she went and sat at the kitchen table, as she had done every day with her parents, and gripped the wooden edge to ground herself. The cupboards and drawers were all open, forks and knives scattered on the counter alongside broken cups and chipped plates. The kitchen towels her mother had embroidered with clovers, pears and apples had all been pulled out of the pantry and thrown on the floor. There wasn't one thing in its place. But she didn't have the energy or will to put it all back together.

Staring at the empty chairs where her parents should be, she had never felt so alone.

33

Hedy

Le Brassus
October 1944

Setting a hand on her belly, Hedy watched the first snowfall of the season. She considered all she'd done to prepare for the winter, knowing that this coming springtime, she wouldn't be alone. There was no longer any doubt in her mind that she carried Samuel's child, and for that, she was grateful. The baby gave her strength and resolve to face an uncertain future.

She was on her own in a way she'd never been before. After learning her parents had engaged in the illegal smuggling of Jewish children across the border, family friends and former schoolmates shunned her, shifting their gazes as she passed them on the street. Upon entering a shop, the customers stared at her as if their steely glares could cause her to leave. And when she ignored them and made her way to the counter, she would discover that the goods she asked for were not available. But as she turned to leave, she overheard the requests of the next person in line, and the goods were provided. Hedy had become a threatening infection.

As she followed the trail of gray smoke churning out of the chimney from the fire she'd lit in the hearth, she went through all the steps she'd taken to prepare for her first winter without her parents. She'd first called the luthiers in Geneva and Lausanne, offering to sell them the wood, tools and inventory in her father's workshop if they came to collect it. Though it was hard to part with the items she'd spent her lifetime around, she sensed her father would understand and approve. Then, she only shopped in Lausanne, where she was a stranger, and people left her alone. She bought chickens and built a coop in the garden at the back of the house. During the last warm days of September, she tended to the vegetable garden like her mother always had, canning the beans and tomatoes and planting onions and garlic. She collected the hazelnuts and walnuts that fell from the trees and lined them up to dry before storing them.

She would need to be resourceful and self-reliant. Once the baby bump showed, she couldn't risk being seen and would have to remain inside during the day. Unmarried pregnant women weren't allowed in society, and she shuddered to think what would happen if anyone discovered she was carrying a child. Anticipating the days she would be confined to the house, she stored cheese and cured meat in the pantry, as the villagers did a century ago. She hadn't figured out who could help with the delivery, but that was still seven months away, and she was sure a solution would come. The war might be over by then, and Samuel would return. As the snow fell harder, she kept telling herself that each day that passed brought her closer to the day they would be reunited, and she could tell him about their child.

A knock came at the door. Hedy got up from the sofa, wondering who it could be. Since her mother's arrest, she'd only been visited by the police following up with questions about her parents. Not even Madame Jadot had come over. She opened the door.

"Hello, Hedy. May we come in?" Pastor Rolle's breath misted in the cold air.

She wiped her hands on the apron at her waist, trying to push away the memory of Franck and that terrible night in the forest because she could not separate these two men. They existed as one in her mind. Hovering behind him, Madame Jadot peered over his shoulder. Hedy hesitated, unsure of what she should do.

Pastor Rolle smiled. "We've come to see how you are."

In this weather, closing the door and not inviting them in would be rude, so she stepped back to let them enter. The pastor removed his black felt hat and leather gloves and shook the snow off his coat. His head inclined to a hook on the wall. "May I?"

She nodded.

He hung his coat and hat, and Madame Jadot did the same. Hedy led them into the kitchen. Her mother would offer tea, but something inside her warned against it. They were not here as friends. She would be polite and listen, but no more. She motioned to the table, where they all sat. Hedy placed her hands in her lap.

"What is it you want?"

Pastor Rolle smiled again. "We've come to see how you are getting on in this big house."

She straightened her back. "I'm fine, thank you."

"Pastor Rolle and I were just saying that this house is too big for one person." Madame Jadot thrust a shoulder forward. "Perhaps it's time to consider moving elsewhere."

So, that's why they were here. "The house belongs to my mother, and once she returns, she will live here again."

"Speaking of your mother." Pastor Rolle fixed her with a hard stare. "Yesterday, her sentence was passed down."

Hedy's upper body tipped forward. Since her mother had confessed to smuggling with the book of names providing evidence, a trial wasn't held. Unable to see or correspond with her before sentencing, Hedy feared the worst as she held her breath and waited.

"Five years in prison."

"Rather light," Madame Jadot huffed, "for what she did."

Hedy looked out the window at the falling snow, like shattered porcelain, and imagined her mother watching it through the cold metal bars of a prison window. She couldn't understand how her mother's liberty was the price for saving innocent lives. Hadn't the slogan been *saving the upcoming generation*? Was it all farce? As her mother's dark fate settled around her, she felt a looming danger staring at her from across the table. She'd failed to protect her mother but wouldn't fail to protect her baby. Her instinct had been right about the pastor, and now it told her that she should never have let him into her home, just like her mother never should have invited Franck to dinner. Evil existed. She'd experienced it that night in the forest. Pastor Rolle had sent Franck to her. Now, he wanted to take away her home—the only sense of security she had left. She looked away from the window to the pastor's dark eyes.

"Thank you for coming," she said, standing. "I'll see you to the door."

"We're here to help." His slippery voice sent a cool shiver through her. "Consider what Madame Jadot suggested. A young, unmarried woman shouldn't live alone in a big house. We think you'd be more comfortable elsewhere." He stood.

Hedy was already at the door, turning the handle, grateful for something solid to hold on to as the pastor put on his coat and hat.

"Think about what we've discussed. This house should be given to a good family loyal to the country." He stretched his fingers into black leather gloves. "Since it wouldn't be appropriate for you to come to the church, tell Madame Jadot when you've decided to move out. Don't wait too long. I'm confident you're smart enough to know where you do and don't belong."

"I've always been a friend to your family," Madame Jadot added.

"Goodbye." Hedy closed the door behind them.

An eerie silence descended as she leaned against the door, trying to get her bearings. They were gone, and the house quiet, but the threat remained, beating in her chest.

She put on her boots and slipped into her father's padded overcoat with deep pockets to keep her hands warm. Whenever she needed to think clearly, she went to the forest. Immersing herself in the natural world and away from people always helped her to see things as they were and not as she wanted them to be. She didn't mind the snow or cold; walking would keep her warm. Despite her mother's voice ringing inside her head, holding out the hope that the war wouldn't last another year and Samuel would be back, she had to rely on herself to find a way forward.

Her breath misted as she trudged up the hill to the Chalet de la Thomassette. She could see Madame Glauser chopping items on a wooden board through the kitchen window. The earthy smell of chicken soup seeped through the door and reached her outside. Hedy hunched forward and continued.

Of the two choices facing her—staying in Le Brassus or leaving for France and then England to find Samuel—she had to consider which one held the greatest peril. Until today, she hadn't doubted that her family home provided the safest place to bring a baby into the world. That was why she'd spent every day preparing it. She had plans to reinforce the coop for the chickens from some of the leftover wood in her father's workshop. She would have fresh eggs daily if she could keep them warm through the winter. She often went to the forest to collect fallen branches to dry for kindling. But this morning's visit filled her with doubt. What if it wasn't enough that she'd lost her parents and been outcast from society? Would they insist on taking her home, too?

She breathed in deeply. The oils rising off the spruces and beech mixed with the energy in the woodland, filling the air with a powerful scent that helped her think. Could the visit have been a tactic to scare her? Her parents had no debt, and as long as Hedy conserved the money she'd earned from selling what was in her father's workshop and paid the bills on time, the pastor had no grounds to kick her out. The law would protect her. That was what it was there for. And when she saw it from that angle, it became clear that their visit was intended to frighten her. Maybe they wanted her to do something reckless to use against her.

Besides, with the war ongoing, Hedy couldn't risk entering France and joining the streams of refugees seeking food and shelter—not when she had them here. She didn't even know the name of the squadron that Samuel belonged to or where in England it was located. How many thousands of American airmen must be there—how would she find Samuel among them?

Dusk was coming, and the snow was beginning to turn a menacing blue-gray. She decided not to go as far as the hut because she wanted to return home before the snow iced over. The smell of the soup from Madame Glauser's kitchen made her think of dinner. She would make a vegetable soup with potatoes. That would warm her up. She couldn't forget to grab the bundles of thyme and bay she'd hung in her father's workshop to dry as they would add to the soup's flavor. She had watched her mother make soup every winter for her and her father. Now, Hedy would do it for her unborn child. Her mouth watered as she turned for home.

Four months later, the baby's kicks woke Hedy early. Stumbling to the bathroom, she checked Samuel's watch: 5:30 a.m. She lifted the blackout curtains. The sky was still dark.

She boiled water and added roasted barley with a sprig of thyme. The chickens clucked in their pen. Since the baby often woke her early, she would chat with the chickens in the warm coop during the quiet morning hours before anyone else was awake. She always wore her father's overcoat, buttoning it up in case someone saw her. But today, the buttons wouldn't fasten, and she smiled at the healthy baby growing inside. Carrying the mug and last night's scraps—carrot peelings, breadcrumbs, an apple core—she put on her boots and went outside.

Overnight, the snow had hardened. She had to be careful not to slip while crossing the garden. She was proud of the coop she'd built from wire mesh bought at the hardware store. She'd sunk it deep into the ground to prevent foxes from tunneling their way in. Then, she covered the wire with felt, pine branches, and cardboard layers. It was often warmer inside the coop than in the house because she could only afford to heat her bedroom. She checked the bowl of water. It hadn't frozen during the night.

"Adi, Rachel," she called out.

The hens scrambled out of the hutch and down the wooden ramp she'd made from the planks in her father's workshop. Excited to see her, the hens clucked and gathered around the scraps she scattered on the ground. Hedy checked for eggs, found one in the hutch, and slipped it into her coat pocket.

Her stomach was too big to squat on her haunches to stroke Rachel, who liked to follow her around. Instead, she settled on a low stool in the corner facing the door. Rachel hovered between her boots.

"I'm happy to see you too," Hedy said, stroking Rachel's ermine feathers. Adi came by and cooed as if Hedy's presence pleased her. "I need you both to be especially productive in May with a big haul of eggs for the baby."

A May baby. She could hardly believe she'd made it this far. She'd had no more visits from Madame Jadot or Pastor Rolle, which confirmed her decision to stay had been the right one. She was a little lonely as the hens were her only friends. She looked forward to visiting the coop daily to see them and discuss her concerns. The baby kicked. Hedy put her hand on the side of her belly. Like with the hens, she could feel her baby's bones through her skin, thin and delicate but strong.

"Good. Keep kicking," she said aloud, rubbing the spot, and the baby kicked back. She laughed. Adi stopped pecking at the apple core and looked up at her. Hedy couldn't remember the last time she'd laughed out loud.

Outside, she heard snow crunch under heavy boots. Hedy leaned forward and turned to the door. It was slightly ajar, and a pale light streamed through the opening.

"Hello?" she called out. Who would be there at this hour?

The hinges on the door squeaked. A woman's figure entered the coop. Hedy's heart hammered.

"Madame Jadot, what are you doing here?" She snatched the coat to cover her belly.

"I've been watching you," she said flatly. "Why don't you ever leave the house?"

A memory of Franck hit her, and a chill ran down her spine.

"Please leave," she said. "You haven't been invited."

"Invited? Your parents are traitors, loyal to foreigners over their own country!"

The hens scrambled up the plank and into the hutch at the screech of her voice.

"Pastor Rolle warns that a good tree cannot bear bad fruit and a bad tree . . . you are the seed of a bad tree." Her face twisted. "Now *you're* trying to hide something, is that it?"

"I don't know what you're talking about." Under Hedy's dress, the baby turned jerkily as though it sensed her fear.

"Stand up," Madame Jadot commanded, wiping her hands on her apron. "Show yourself!"

"This is not your property and you have no right to be here."

She smirked. "It won't be yours for much longer."

The panic in Hedy turned up a notch, vibrating like a metal rod drilling through her blood and bones and along her spine. She couldn't stand. "Get out!" she shouted.

Madame Jadot gripped her arm, yanked her off the stool, and kicked it over. As Hedy stood, both sides of her father's coat slipped to her hips. The cotton dress stretched taut over her swollen stomach. Madame Jadot stepped back, satisfaction and scorn glinting in her eyes. Hedy lifted the coat to cover herself.

"You're a whore," her voice rattled.

"Wait, let me explain," Hedy pleaded.

"You disgust me." She spat in her face, spun around, and left.

34

Hedy

Le Brassus
February 1945

Hedy's hands shook uncontrollably as she wiped her face. The air in the coop felt thick and suffocating; her sanctuary, once a place of solace, had become a trap. She stumbled outside, the cold air cutting through her like a knife. Her boots slipped on the snow as she hurried back to the house.

She went to the kitchen and washed her face. Soaping it twice, she still smelled the sour saliva. What had she done? Panic ripped through her. She couldn't stop shaking. She rewashed her face and hands, and finally, the smell was gone.

She sat down at the kitchen table. She'd gotten rid of Madame Jadot's scent but felt her presence, like a lump of rage standing in her path. She couldn't fall apart and panic. She needed clarity. She put her head in her hands and slowly went through it all. And like a map in her mind, she saw how the last six months had brought her to this point. Shunned and ostracized, she was on the outside of society, and it had been done for a purpose. She could see that now. They'd killed her father and imprisoned her mother. It was only a matter of time until they came for her. They just needed a reason. And Madame Jadot had found it: her baby.

What had she been thinking all this time? She'd been foolish and naïve. The day her mother was arrested, she should have left and gone to France. Could she row across the lake now, as she'd done with Samuel? But the lake was so cold in winter that a body couldn't survive more than a minute in the water. She feared she couldn't keep the boat steady with the extra weight from the baby. Remembering how raw and stiff her hands had been holding the paddle in summer, she worried the winter cold would freeze her fingers, and she'd never reach the shore.

The other option was to walk through the forest. Since most of France had been liberated, except for holdouts along the Atlantic coast, she doubted there were still German patrols. But the snow was heavy, and the steep Gy de l'Echelle posed a problem. She could take a longer route, but at night, she might fall in the snow and not be able to go on. There were snow shoes in her father's workshop; they would stop her boots from slipping. She'd carry them on her back until she reached the part of the forest where the snow was the heaviest. She would prepare a pack with food and water and layer her clothes.

Hedy tried not to think about the uncertainty of what awaited her in France. She wanted to believe that she would find kindness among strangers and that people would help her, just like her parents had helped others. She clung to this hope, her only lifeline amid despair.

Despite the overwhelming odds against her, Hedy was determined to protect her unborn child. She would rest all day and set off at dusk, avoiding the main road and disappearing into the forest. No one would think of looking for her there. She was confident that if she kept moving, her body would stay warm, and she and the baby would be safe. She clung to this plan, a flicker of light in the darkness.

Hedy locked the front door and trudged through the brown sludge on the side of the road. Her mother had always been the one to cut her hair, and over the many months she'd been gone, it had become long and unruly, and she'd taken to arranging it in a milkmaid braid at the back of her head. Despite wearing layers of clothes and a full pack on her back, she moved swiftly, passing the sawmill on her right. It seemed like another lifetime when she'd sat on the logs waiting for Joseph to bring the injured American pilot.

She was leaving her mother and her home for an uncertain future. But in her heart, she knew it was the only path, and she looked straight ahead at the tin sky and the wooded hills stretching in the distance.

The sound of tires rolling over asphalt came at her. A car approached from behind. Tension knotted in her chest, and her pulse pounded. Up ahead, she could see the snow-covered path off the side of the road that led into the forest. Just a little farther, and she would be there.

Slowing, the car came up alongside her. The engine rattled, and the air filled with an acrid stench.

"Hedy Borel?" a man's deep voice called out.

She turned and saw a man wearing the blue-and-black uniform of the gendarme.

"No," she said, pulsing blood in her temples as she increased her pace.

He cut the engine and got out of the car. Hedy again looked at the path up ahead. An urge to run overcame her, but the snow was thick. She might slip and fall. And he would surely follow.

"Come with me," he said, grabbing her arm.

She pulled away, mouth dry, the pounding now in her throat. "What is this all about?"

He locked an iron handcuff on her wrist. "The Commune has instructed us to take you off the street."

Her body stiffened. "I haven't done anything wrong."

His eyes fell on her stomach. "Get in the car."

A spear of fading light glinted on the car's black metal door. The handcuff dangled loose from her wrist. She was still free, and the forest wasn't far. She could try to run there, hide in the hut, and cross the border to France. From there, she'd find her way to England and Samuel. She twisted away from him as if to test the possibility, and the buttons on her coat snapped off. Cold air seeped through her sweater. Even with the layers, it chilled her bones. He tightened his grip, and her arm pinched with pain. Then, she glimpsed the gun on his hip.

Everything inside her warned not to get in the car, but she could see no other option. To protect her child, she obeyed.

Two hours later, the car rolled through a wrought-iron gate. Hedy read the name etched on a stone pillar—Hindelbank. She'd never heard of this place. The car stopped, and the gendarme opened the door, unlocking her wrist from the handcuffs. She rubbed the skin where the metal had dug against the bone. She stepped out of the car; the gravel rasped underfoot. She stopped and stared at the Baroque-like castle with towers, walls and iron bars on the windows. She entered, was led through a narrow gray door, and told to sit on a wooden bench.

During the drive, all she could make out from the small window in the back seat was that they were heading east, away from the fading light. They came to a large lake and followed it for some time. She knew it had to be the Lac de Neuchâtel. Hedy had only seen it once before: from the top of Mount Tendre after she'd climbed the peak with her father, and he'd pointed out the three lakes of Léman, Joux, and

Neuchâtel. As she stood inside Hindelbank's cold interior and heard Swiss-German echoing down the hall, she understood she'd left the French-speaking cantons behind. She felt like a foreigner in a world that she knew nothing about.

"Mademoiselle Borel," a man's voice. He was middle-aged, wearing thick black glasses and ironed trousers with sharp creases. "Come with me."

She followed him into a sparse office. He sat in the chair at his desk, a window behind him. There wasn't another chair. Hedy stood with her arms at her sides.

"Welcome to Hindelbank, the Women's Penal Institution of Bern."

Her breath caught. "This is a mistake. I haven't committed a crime." She was surprised at how steady her voice sounded. Inside, her muscles quaked with rage. There was no way they could know about her hiding Samuel. He'd been gone for five months. "What right do you have to take an innocent person off the street?"

He looked up. "Upon learning of your licentious behavior, the officials at the town hall, for the well-being and stability of the community," he snorted, "decided to place you in administrative detention."

Madame Jadot had told them. She could see it now. But what was administrative detention? "How long will I be here?"

"That will be up to the discretion of the elected officials in your town." His eyes went to her stomach. The bulge was impossible to hide. "Who is the father?"

"None of your business." Hedy's mouth went dry. Only men had the right to vote and stand for office—she didn't have a chance.

He cleared his throat. "Your attitude of opposition . . ." he glanced down at a file on the desk ". . . seems to run in the family—both parents involved in the illegal smuggling of Jews." His arms rested on the desk on either side of the file as he rubbed his thumbs against his index fingers. "I bet they made a fortune."

She swallowed back the urge to defend her parents. She was in a world of trouble, and all effort had to be spent finding a way out.

"Being a prostitute, it's no surprise you don't know the father's name."

"I'm not a prostitute," she shot back. "I have a right to defend myself in a court of law."

He shook his head. "There are rules at Hindelbank, and failing to obey them will result in punishment. You are not permitted visitors for the first month and will only be allowed to write and receive letters after the second month. Every morning, the wake-up bell rings at 6:20. Ten minutes later, at 6:30, the cell door unlocks, and you must be dressed and out in the corridor for roll call."

Hedy's knees swayed. She needed to sit down.

"The philosophy at Hindelbank is reform through work." He glanced at the file. "You have been assigned to the laundry, where you will iron uniforms and bedding for the women's hospital in Bern. At 8 p.m., lights are turned off, and the cell door is locked."

He couldn't go on much longer. What else was there to say? She felt pressure in her pelvis and squeezed her legs together.

"Sign on the line," he said, holding out a black pen that shimmered in the light like the police car's metal door.

She hesitated. "What am I signing?"

"Your acknowledgment that you have been read the reason for your detention and that you understand and will abide by Hindelbank's rules and regulations." Samuel had been through prison—ten days. They might let her out after ten days if she did everything they asked. She signed.

The director rang a bell. A woman in a brown uniform, her dark hair pulled back tight, entered.

"Please proceed with the check-in for Mademoiselle Borel. Tomorrow, she will see the doctor."

"Yes, Director Schneider," the woman said, then turned to Hedy. "Come along."

She was grateful to be out of his office. She asked the woman for the toilet, and alone in the stall, she finally sat down and tried to figure her way out of this. Maybe she could return to Director Schneider's office and persuade him she wasn't a prostitute. Perhaps her mistake was not giving him the father's name. She could make one up, then maybe he would let her go. But what if they checked? And if she gave them the name of a man she knew, like Joseph, she'd only be getting him in trouble, too.

She glanced at the watch partly hidden by her sleeve. Samuel had told her that the POWs in German camps had their watches confiscated. Now that she was in prison, she feared they would seize her watch, too. She couldn't bear to be without it. But where to hide it? Maybe in her shoes. No, they would search them just like they'd search the pockets of her dress and coat. Her mother's voice as she brushed her hair before bed came to her: *it's thick enough to hide a family of mice*.

A knock on the metal door. "Hurry up," the woman said.

"Coming." Hedy's steady voice masked the turmoil twirling inside her. First, she removed the pins holding one of the braids in her hair and perched them between her teeth. Then she unwound the strands so they hung loose. After she removed the watch from her wrist, she intertwined it in the strands of hair and redid the braid.

"Now," the woman commanded.

"OK," Hedy said. Slipping the pins into the braid with the watch inside, she attached it to the back of her head, tucking it under the other braid to hide it from view. Then, she flushed the toilet and went out.

The woman brought her to a room with benches and lockers.

"Undress," she said.

Hedy removed her coat, shoes, dress and stockings.

"Everything," she said sourly.

Hedy pulled her undergarments down to her ankles, then slid them off with her feet.

"Turn around," she said, snapping rubber gloves on her hands.

Hedy froze. Was this an examination because of the baby?

The woman jutted her chin and spun her hand in a circle. "Turn around. Body inspection."

"Where?"

She stared hard at Hedy. "Hands on the chair, and bend over."

Hedy did as she was told and winced as two fingers entered her. Then she gasped and blinked back tears as the woman forced her fingers into her anus. She thought she would be sick.

"Get dressed," the woman said, handing her a pile of clothes.

She put on the uniform: brown wool stockings, a brown dress and a brown apron. Then, she was given bedding to carry and followed the woman down a long corridor. They crossed an open courtyard. Hedy looked up to an empty square of gray sky. She missed the forest—the rich, earthy smell and vibrant green color that warmed her body and gave her strength. It was cold, gray concrete here, where life couldn't thrive.

Keys jangled at the woman's waist. Since none of the doors had handles, the woman lifted the keys to open them. Hedy winced as the last door slammed shut behind her.

That first night, she couldn't sleep. Unfamiliar sounds vibrated on the other side of the wall. Shouts, cries, metal doors shunting back and forth. She stared at the full moon through the narrow bars on the window. Samuel might be flying tonight. She hoped he was safe. She had no idea how long she would be here or if they would ever let her out. At least her mother could appear before a judge and defend herself. Hedy had been denied a voice. She didn't even know what evidence was used against her. Was Madame Jadot's testimony that she was with child enough to lock her away? How did a pregnancy prove that she was a prostitute? She thought about all the things she would say to a judge in her defense—she had never received money in exchange for sex, a man wouldn't be jailed for sleeping with a woman before marriage, and she had no criminal record.

Then her thoughts shifted to the hens. She'd debated whether to open the coop door before she left. They might not survive the night if a fox got to them, but she didn't want them trapped inside, where they would starve. In the end, she'd left it open. She hoped that Madame Jadot would take them in.

In the morning, the bell rang, and the doors unlocked with a crushing metal thud. Hedy stepped out into the gray corridor. She was joined by women who also exited their cells to her left and right. Had they been the ones crying through the night?

A female guard passed along the line and called out names. "Borel, Hedy?"

"Yes."

After the roll call, they proceeded to the canteen for breakfast.

The irons were heavy and hot. Hedy had never handled a box iron. Each one was hollow inside to hold what the women called a slug—a piece of clay put directly on the fire, removed with a long hook, and inserted in the iron to supply the heat.

She struggled with the iron's handle. It was too hot to touch without a cloth, but since sweat dripped off her hands, the cloth quickly slipped off, and the handle seared her fingers. It wasn't easy to get the slug out, as it sometimes got stuck. Once, she had to force it out and burned her thumb.

The women gave her advice, which she tried to follow: "Dampen those sheets more." She sprinkled them with water to make it easier to remove the creases. But, if she added too much water, the women admonished her: "Those sheets will crease once they're dry, and you'll need to redo it, wasting time."

The heat was the worst. The laundry was in the basement, without windows. A large oven ran all day for the slugs, constantly shunted between the irons and the fire. Hedy couldn't stop sweating. Water ran down every part of her body. Even the soles of her feet were wet, and she slipped in the brown wooden clogs that were part of her uniform. She was thirsty, her lips bone-dry. Seeing Hedy was with child, the older women gave her the uniforms because they were more straightforward than the sheets, which required lifting and hanging on a line before they could be folded. She passed the box iron over the blue lettering embroidered on the pocket—*Frauenspital*—and tried to imagine who would wear it. Nurses, doctors, orderlies, cleaners. Hope pumped through her veins. She envisioned slipping a tiny note inside the pocket so they might know about her. Were they even aware that female prisoners pressed their uniforms week after week? Maybe they wouldn't care. As the morning wore on, her mind grew numb and tired, and she forgot about the note.

The bell rang for lunch. Hedy was grateful for the break.

In the canteen, she sat next to a woman wearing a brown uniform. They were the only two in the laundry—all the other women had blue uniforms.

"Why are the others in blue, and we're in brown?" Hedy asked.

"Blue uniforms are for women convicted of a crime." She rubbed her nose. "The way I see it, they're the lucky ones."

"Why?"

"They know when they will get out." She looked at Hedy. "You and I don't."

35

Hedy

Hindelbank
April 1945

The days blurred into one another. Ten-hour shifts, six days a week, ironing Frauenspital uniforms. Hedy's hands turned red. The skin between her fingers cracked. Knobbly knuckles, raw and ragged. But at night, alone in her cell, she found solace from the watch's dial glowing in the darkness. She touched her belly and imagined a son or daughter with Samuel's straw-colored hair.

In the laundry, she hid the watch under her sleeve, away from the wolfish gazes of the blue-uniformed women. She'd heard them yell and call each other lying thieves. If they saw the watch, they might try to steal it from her. And she couldn't let that happen. The watch got her through the nights in the cell, alone in the darkness. When she looked at the dial, the light of the hands pushed back the walls and lifted her out of the eight square meters. She reunited with Samuel in the hut, where she could feel the rise and fall of his chest as she slept alongside him. Sometimes, the watch took her and Samuel far above Hindelbank; in his plane, they flew together and free.

She made a friend. Lucie, the woman in the cell next to her. Among the prisoners, talk was forbidden except on Sundays, when the women were allowed outside to walk in a courtyard bound on four sides by white brick walls. Lucie had been the one to approach her, coming alongside as she walked.

"Are you doing all right?" Lucie's small black eyes glanced at Hedy's belly.

"Yes."

"Here's a biscuit." She passed her a napkin.

Hedy slipped it into her pocket. "Thank you."

"You're in the laundry?"

She nodded and held out her raw, red hands. "You?"

"The kitchen. The guards watch us all the time."

"The only good thing about the laundry is that it's too hot for the guards."

A wind whipped, and they moved closer to the wall.

"Do you have visitors?" Lucie asked.

Hedy tightened her collar against her neck and said nothing.

"Me neither. I've been here a year. They should let me out soon, don't you think?"

Hedy wanted to give her hope. "I would think so."

"Can you feel the baby move?" Lucie came closer.

"All the time. It's a good sign."

"Can I feel?"

She felt sorry for the poor girl, who seemed a little younger and had already been here a year. Hedy glanced at the guard, who was talking with a prisoner. She undid one of the buttons of her cotton-padded coat. Lucie put her hand on Hedy's belly.

It didn't take long for the baby to kick. Lucie's eyes went wide. "I can feel it."

Hedy redid the button, and they continued walking.

"What are you here for?" Hedy said.

"Running away."

"From home?"

"I don't have a home." Her gaze hardened. "My mother died when I was ten. Father couldn't look after me, so I was sent to a foster family."

"I'm sorry." Hedy touched her arm. "You didn't like the foster family?"

Lucie wiped her nose on her sleeve. "I hated it. They didn't want a daughter, only someone to milk the cows in the morning. The first time I ran away, the authorities brought me back. The second time, the farmer said he didn't want me. Father wouldn't take me either." Lucie swallowed. "I guess that's why I'm here."

"But it must have been better than Hindelbank?"

"The farmer was a bad man. He hit me." She twisted the edge of her coat between her thumb and forefinger and looked up at the sky. "There's no good place anywhere but in heaven. I hate the nights, the crying, and the slamming of doors. Do you hate the nights, too?"

"I'm so tired, I fall asleep." Hedy didn't have the heart to tell her that being alone with the watch and Samuel in the nights got her through the days.

Hedy was brought from the laundry two weeks later to Director Schneider's office.

"We need to prepare for the baby's future," the director said.

There was a chair for her this time. She sat across from the director, expecting he would tell her that she and the baby would be released after the birth. It had to be that way. The only logical conclusion was that they would both be freed. The doctor had told her she was due in May and that if the kicks came hard and in regular intervals, she should alert the guards to bring her to the infirmary.

The director studied her file. “Do you have a job waiting for you in Le Brassus, Mademoiselle Borel?”

“I was a student at the University of Lausanne.” She lifted her chin. “I will find work.”

“What type of work?”

“At a shop.” She thought of Lucie. “Or a farm.”

“And the child?”

“I will work *and* look after my child.” Women had always found a way to do that.

“Most young mothers have support from family. You won’t have that.”

Her throat chafed, and his words felt like a rope strung around her neck. She raised a hand and rubbed her nape.

“I fear you and your child will become dependent on the state.” His eyes fixed somewhere on her face, carefully avoiding her gaze.

“I won’t depend on anyone. I have a home and a garden. I will supplement what I grow with food I buy from wages earned from—”

“Prostitution,” he said, no longer avoiding her gaze.

The rope scraped and burned Hedy’s skin. “No.” She struggled to breathe. “I will never do that.”

“A baby needs a stable environment. No honest man would want to be with you.” He examined his nails. “Give your child up for adoption.”

She shook her head firmly. “Never.”

“It’s the only way your child can have a good life in a stable environment with a real family.” He looked down at the paper.

Hedy kept thinking about the farmer who beat Lucie. She would never give her baby up to strangers. Hedy stood. Her legs shook with the weight of her belly. She bent her knees and leaned forward. “I’d like to return to the laundry.”

"Think carefully about what we've discussed. Next time, I hope you'll agree that I am correct."

That night, when the bell rang for roll call, Hedy stood outside her cell. As she waited for the guard to pass, Lucie scuttled across to her, slipped a folded paper into the pocket of Hedy's apron, and returned to her cell. The guard's keys clinked as she rounded the corner.

"Borel, Hedy?"

"Yes."

"Christen, Lucie?"

"Yes."

The two women glanced at one another. Hedy patted her apron in recognition of the note, but something about the look in Lucie's eyes troubled her. Hedy wanted to call out and ask what was wrong. In the morning, she would speak with her. Entering the cell, she flinched as the metal door closed behind her.

She reached into her apron and pulled out the paper. Wanting to unfold it and read the message inside, she saved it instead, like when she was little and waited to eat a morsel of chocolate or a slice of her mother's apple strudel. Now, she could look forward to reading Lucie's message by the glow of Samuel's watch.

Hedy hoped it would distract her from the director demanding she give away her baby for adoption. His insistence that she could not provide a home for a child left her unsettled and anxious. It didn't help that crouching at the back of her mind were doubts about how she would earn money to buy food and pay the bills without family support. There was some truth in what the director had said. But she had her parents' house, the garden, and chickens. It wouldn't be long before Samuel returned. Once the war ended, he would help. The image of the woman in the forest appeared in her mind. Hadn't she made it through worse than Hedy was facing now? She could hold on until Samuel was back. Once they were together, all would be fine.

She cracked the window open. The cold air gave her hope, reminding her of the world outside waiting for her. As she crawled under the thick wool blanket, the lights went out. A cindery darkness settled over the cell. She was glad she'd waited to read the note—a bright spot in the dark night.

Unfolding the paper, she held the watch's green light close to Lucie's childlike script. *Thank you for being my friend. Goodbye.*

A hollow ache formed at the base of her throat. She had to stop herself from opening her mouth and screaming. Was Lucie going to kill herself? She got up, went to the wall, and touched it.

"Don't give up hope," she whispered. "You will get out. We will talk tomorrow and find a way." She hoped Lucie could hear her.

There was no reply.

Later, Hedy shifted back and forth in the narrow bed. It took a long time for sleep to settle over her. Even the light from the watch couldn't put her restless mind at ease.

36

Hedy

Hindelbank
May 1945

Hedy's ears burned from the grinding metal when the cell door shunted open in the morning. She stepped out to the hall and joined the women for the morning roll call. She didn't have the strength to turn and look at Lucie.

"Borel, Hedy?"

"Yes."

"Christen, Lucie?"

Silence.

Hedy watched the guard step inside Lucie's cell, and just as quickly, she stepped out and shuffled down the corridor.

The silence was foreboding. Maybe Lucie needed medical attention, and the guard had left to get help. Hedy wanted to do something. She looked down the corridor. The prisoners were standing outside their cells, waiting for instructions. She moved in the direction of Lucie's cell. If she was fast, no one would see. At the door, an odor hit her—pungent, familiar—the metallic stench in the forest. When Hedy entered the cell, her clog slipped and she looked down. A track of blood made her freeze. She followed the red line to Lucie on the floor, arms outstretched, cuts to both wrists, eyes open, looking up for the sky.

A wave of nausea hit her. She stepped back into the hallway. Clanking keys and ringing footfalls warned the guards were returning. She felt dizzy, but she had to return to her cell door. *I'm sorry. I'm so sorry.* Fingers of dread stabbed at Hedy. She felt them pounding on her back and chest. She reached her cell door and leaned against the wall to get out of the way of the guards running past with a stretcher. Then she ran her hand over the curve of her stomach and looking down, she saw a red imprint left by her clog on the floor from Lucie's blood.

A week later, she dreamed she was in the laundry, and sweat dripped down her legs. But when she woke in the infirmary, she found her nightgown drenched. Then came a sharp and sudden cramp. She took short breaths as the nurses had advised her to do: *when the time comes, concentrate on your breathing until the pain subsides.*

She glanced at the watch. Five in the morning. She hadn't wanted to come to the infirmary. But after Lucie's death, Hedy was again brought to the director's office. *You are incapable of taking care of a baby properly.* This time, she didn't argue back. There was no point. She didn't answer when the director asked her to sign a paper giving her permission to put her baby up for adoption. She refused to take the pen. Then he told her she would no longer be required to work in the laundry and sent her to the infirmary.

Hedy had asked if she could stay in her cell, but the director insisted she be placed under supervision. Maybe he worried she would try to kill herself, like Lucie. He didn't understand the difference between them. Hedy had everything to live for. Not just the baby but Samuel and her mother. She had a family waiting for her return. Lucie had none of those things. His cruel voice haunted her. *Your child will have a far better future with a real family.* Her family was real; it was simply injured, not destroyed.

Another surge of pain. Hedy breathed through it. The director's voice pounded against her temples: *you must act for the good of the child.* She didn't want the nurses to know the baby was coming. She had no plan other than to bring this child into the world without them knowing. It made no sense, for what would she do once it was born? With every pang and twist that roared through her body, this moment called for her to be quiet and to do this alone.

The throbbing eased, and she listened to the noises of the night. The breathing of the other women in the ward, the creak of an iron bed, the sounds from outside the walls that passed through the heavy brick. Was it wind or rain? She didn't know. Sharp throbs came and went like the waves on the lake the night she rowed Samuel to safety. She had no idea then what danger awaited her. Should she have known? Maybe all this could have been avoided if Samuel had stayed. But wouldn't the police have come for him like they did for Hedy and her mother? She had no idea if she'd chosen the right path. With a finger, she traced a circle on her belly—the circle of love that she and Samuel had shared.

Through the night, she concentrated on her breathing, counting each exhalation in whispers: *one, two, three.* She let the pain ripple through her body, knowing that without it, the life she and Samuel had made wouldn't find its way into the world.

On the morning rounds, a nurse walked by her bed. She must have heard Hedy's short, sharp exhalation because she came to her and touched the wet sheets. Hedy was moved to a separate room. Daylight streamed through the window. She watched the fast-moving clouds in the sky, and her breath skipped between them. The throbbing in her stomach came swifter and more frequent. She checked the watch. Two o'clock. It couldn't be much longer. The nurses were helping now, telling her to push.

"It's over! It's over." A man's voice broke through the women's talk. He looked down at her. She recognized the doctor.

"What's over?" she said.

"The war!" he said, clapping his hands. "Now, let's get this baby out."

Had she heard wrong? "It's over?"

"The German forces signed a document of surrender at Reims," he said, smiling, "after Hitler shot himself in the head. Come on, it's a good day for a baby to born. Push."

But hours later, the child still wasn't ready. Hedy kept thinking that despite the war being over, the little life she and Samuel had made must have sensed the danger that awaited in the world and wanted to stay inside longer. It wasn't until the blue sky was swallowed by dusk, and a tarry light seeped through the window with knife-like shadows that Hedy felt it was near.

"One more push," the doctor said, "come on, come on."

Hedy pressed her hands against the bed. Her lungs exhaled with all the air they held, and she felt something slide out of her body.

"Good. The head is clear."

She leaned back and caught her breath.

"You're not done yet." A woman's voice in her ear. "One more."

Hedy leaned forward, and the baby slid out with a single focused push.

"It's a girl," the woman said.

"Elizabeth," Hedy whispered, falling back on the pillow and exhaling with relief. Her mouth was dry. It was hard to speak, but she wanted to say her daughter's name, wanted the nurses and doctor to *hear* it—the name she'd chosen, Samuel's mother's name, the name she gave their child. "Can I hold her?"

"The nurses must clean her first." The doctor's quick look at the nurse sent a ripple of fear through Hedy's exhausted body.

"Will you bring my daughter to me?" Her chest was tight and heavy. "Please let me see her. I beg you—"

His hand pressed on her shoulder. "Calm down, Mademoiselle Borel. Everything will be fine."

How could she be calm? Nothing was fine. It never would be. They weren't going to bring her daughter back. "Elizabeth," she shouted between gasps of air, "Elizabeth."

"Nurse, prepare the injection. For her health, Mademoiselle Borel must be sedated."

"I don't want an injection. I want my child. Elizabeth . . ." She tried to swing her shaking legs to the edge of the bed. *Find her. Don't let them—*

The nurses pinned her down, and the world went dark.

37

Gina

Le Brassus
October 2018

I sit on the bench, gazing at Mamie with shock and dread.

"How could they steal your child after putting you in prison for being pregnant?"

"*Unmarried* and pregnant. That was a crime in my time."

"I can't believe you never told us." I hope she doesn't think I'm accusing her. I feel so much sorrow at what she went through and regret that Mom never knew how courageous her mother was—fighting to save Grandfather and keep Elizabeth. Mixed emotions flow through me—empathy and affection for Mamie and anger for those who did this to her.

She lifts a shoulder. "I thought that putting it behind me would be the way to cause less pain and hurt for everyone." Tears roll down her cheeks; her arthritic fingers reach up to wipe them away. I put an arm around her. She taps her forehead. "Elizabeth has always been in my mind." She presses her chest. "And in my heart." The weight of her pain, carried for decades, is palpable. I feel a deep sympathy for all that time Mamie lost with her daughter.

I have so many questions I want to ask, but we've been sitting for hours, and I'm cold, so she must be, too. She looks thoroughly worn out from talking and reliving the heart-breaking memories she shared. I don't want my questions to put her through more distress.

"The wind is picking up. Let's go back to the hotel."

She squeezes my hand. "I'm tired."

"I'll call a taxi." I pull out my phone.

"*Non, ma chérie.* The doctor says I lose muscles if I don't use them, so walking is good for me." She sighs. "I could walk all day in the forest and never be tired. The ground is as soft as carpet. If I can lean on you . . ."

"OK." I help her up. "We'll take it slowly."

She looks at the house with the red shutters, once her home. I want to ask if she ever returned to live there, but fearing that will dredge up more grief, I hold back. "What would you like for dinner?"

She shrugs. "I'm too tired to go out. You go ahead without me."

"Why don't we order room service? I saw fries and hamburgers on the menu."

She smiles. "A change from fondue."

At the hotel reception, a woman informs us that a delivery arrived earlier. She goes in the back to get it. I turn to Mamie. "The town hall file?"

She nods.

"Here it is," the woman says, placing a box on the counter. "Would you like someone to bring it up for you?"

Across the top of the box, I read in faded black ink: *Famille Borel.* I'm disappointed at how light the box feels; it doesn't match my vision of the extraordinary lives she and her parents led based on what she's told me. "No, we're fine, thanks."

Once we've ordered room service and settled on top of our beds, I open the box and find a jumble of frail brown folders inside. Wiping away the dust, I arrange them on the desk by year. I place the earliest files, dating 1880, near the window; the others surround it. The last one, marked 1945, is the thickest, and I put it on the chair.

In 1880, Emile Borel immigrated to Switzerland from France. A carpenter, his skills were needed in the watchmaking workshops in Le Brassus. He married Bettina, who died in childbirth in 1894 but was survived by her son and my great-grandfather, Alain. Alain apprenticed with his father and then moved to Austria to apprentice under a luthier. He returned to Le Brassus two years later and opened a luthier workshop. In 1918, he married Ariane, who, in 1925, gave birth to Mamie.

When I reach the pile in the middle of the bed, I learn Mamie was the only woman among five men from her gymnasium class in 1943 to enter the University of Lausanne. A single sentence, and yet it's enough to turn back time so that I catch a glimpse of Mamie as she was then—the redness in her eyes disappears, the deep lines etched in her forehead smooth out, and her wispy white hair turns brown with shimmering red highlights. She was even younger than I am now, struggling against all those men who didn't think she belonged there. Why hadn't she ever told me about this time in her life? But wasn't I too occupied with my own to ask?

1944. The papers stack up tall. Alain Borel, caught smuggling Jewish refugees into Switzerland, was killed by German officers on the French border. I stop. My fingers tremble with the story she told me—that my great-grandfather was a *passeur*—smuggling people for money. And I feel the pain she experienced witnessing her father's tragic end, just as I did Mom's. Time can't wash it away; it stays with you forever.

The doorbell rings. It's room service. I cut Mamie's hamburger and add ketchup to her plate for the fries. She takes one. "Oh, that's tasty," she says and eats more.

I take a bite of my burger and continue reading. A wind blows, knocking the glass pane in the window. I look up to watch the fading light and plunging shadows. In the forest's deepest part, I imagine Mamie's father, the luthier with agile hands, saving those the world had given up on.

"Have you found any reference to Elizabeth?" Mamie asks.

I pick up the last two sheets from 1945. My expectations are high—I'm sure I'll find something, but after reading through it all, I realize Elizabeth hasn't been mentioned. I reread a terse document stating that in February 1945, Mamie was placed under administrative detention and sent to Hindelbank Women's Prison. No reasons are given other than a reference to general terms like *moral lapse, deficiencies of character, grossly violates expectations.* My blood boils. Nothing about Elizabeth, as if she never existed.

"No. Only that you were placed under administrative detention and sent to Hindelbank." I take another bite of the burger. "What does administrative detention mean? I've never heard of it."

She shrugs. "Just some legal term that gives powerful men the authority to lock people up." She rubs her eyes. "I'm exhausted. Time to brush my teeth and then to sleep."

I clear away her plate and help her get ready for bed. Then I turn off the light and grab my laptop. Since Elizabeth was born in prison, maybe if I research Hindelbank, I'll find something to help me trace her. I type Hindelbank Prison, Switzerland, in the search bar. It's the only women's prison in the country. Scrolling through pictures of women wearing orange jumpsuits, I find a promising link to the Swiss Federal Council's website: *Reparations for women subject to administrative detention in Hindelbank Prison from 1942–1981*, and click on it.

In the period between 1942 and 1981, a large number of women were subject to "administrative detention" and sent to Hindelbank Prison. Most of these women were detained under the cantonal public law or federal civil law at the time, without ever having committed a crime. Illegitimate pregnancy, for example, was a common reason for administrative detention. Administrative detention has two distinctive features: firstly, it was not possible to request a court hearing; and secondly, the facilities were not suitable for the intended "education measures". At Hindelbank, the women subject to administrative detention were not separated from criminal offenders.

It wasn't just Mamie but many women. Administrative detention only ended in 1981. It's hard to believe unmarried pregnant women were still locked away in Switzerland just ten years before I was born. Now I understand why she never wanted to come back. Fear and shame. But it gives me an idea.

I type in the search bar: administrative detention, Switzerland, and click on the first result: "Shut out and locked away: how and why." It's a website dedicated to researching and understanding the use of administrative detention in the country. There's a video. I grab my headphones, scroll down and click on the arrow that starts the video. The scenery is beautiful—cows in a field, birds piping—and reminds me of the idyllic landscape I saw on the train on my first day in Switzerland. Then, the camera slowly pans across to a massive Baroque building. A woman's trembling voice says, "*Administrative detention was an abuse of power over human beings.*" My chest burns. The place is oddly familiar, as if it's in my blood. Hindelbank.

Unsteady voices, some angry, others confused, speak. Men and women switch between Italian, German and French, telling their stories. Each voice is distinct, yet all carry a slow-burning tremble, like an ember of trauma rising from darkness to light.

"We were wrongly imprisoned. If you weren't in the norm, they took you away like a package no one wanted. Society decided to remain silent. I always had the feeling it was my fault. I'm to blame. I'm stupid. Ashamed, I kept it a secret and told no one."

My phone buzzes. I pick it up, hoping it hasn't woken Mamie. But she doesn't stir. I put it on silent mode and then check the text. It's from Kai.

I took the watch apart. Would you like to see it?

The mainspring pops in my mind, along with what I now know about the emotional weight the watch carries for Mamie—from the moment Grandfather gave it to her on the boat, to how she relied on it to get through the dark nights at Hindelbank.

Yes. Can I bring Mamie?

Come by tomorrow at ten. Yes, bring Mamie.

Thanks. See you tomorrow.

Returning to the screen, I realize that Mamie's done her part—she opened up to me about the pain in her past. Now it's my turn. Like a beating pulse, I can feel Elizabeth is out there waiting—if I can only find her.

At breakfast, I tell Mamie about Kai's invitation to see the parts inside Grandfather's watch. "He asked me to bring you."

Mamie stares at the window. A light rain falls and a wraith of white mist hovers around the forest. She turns to me and as the arc of her eyebrows knit I wonder if she's not still in the past, reliving all that happened. "I think I'll rest this morning." The lines around her eyes and mouth deepen.

"Are you sure?" Maybe I pushed her too hard to talk. I should have given her more time.

"Tell your watchmaker I look forward to seeing the Rolex once the hands sweep over the dial, the way they used to." She smiles. "I found great solace in that movement."

"OK. I'll tell him. And I won't be long."

"Enjoy yourself. I'll be fine."

Outside, the mist clings to my puffer coat as I walk to Kai's. This time, when I ring the bell, he doesn't buzz me in but comes downstairs and opens the door.

"Hi," he says, his eyes searching behind me. "No Mamie?"

"Too tired. She's resting at the hotel."

"Let me take your jacket." He hangs my coat on the hook in the hall, then unlocks the door next to the stairs and stands back so I can enter first. "This is my workshop." The room is divided in two. On the left, a wooden bench extends the length of the wall with lathes, mills and other machinery on it. Under the bench narrow drawers resemble antique apothecary cabinets, and thin metal shavings, like bits of wool, huddle on the floor beneath the machines.

A pungent odor, like a tomato vine, hits me. It's familiar but takes a moment for me to place—the smell of Dad's garage after oiling the break lathes on the Mustang.

The other side of the room has a large working table set against the wall. On it sits the disassembled Rolex. All the pieces, including the long metal spring curved in a spiral S, are on the table, and like there's a tide pulling me in, I go to it.

"It's beautiful," I say. "So many components."

"That's the chronograph."

I remember the first day in the museum when I heard *chronograph* but didn't know what it meant. I feel as though I've learned a lot since but haven't come any closer to finding Elizabeth.

Kai settles on a stool and motions for me to take the other one. He reaches for a loupe on a wooden stand, slips it over his right eye and examines a mechanism through the magnifying lens. His black T-shirt is snug on his body, tucked into khaki trousers.

"Did you figure out how to fix it?" I ask.

He nods. "Just waiting on parts from Rolex."

I'm mesmerized by the movement of his long fingers as he uses a fine instrument to lift a tiny mechanical wheel.

"Why did you react strongly over the phone when I said I wanted to restore the watch?"

"Restoration is what happened in the eighties and nineties. Watchmakers replaced all the old parts with new ones, but it took the life out of them. Scratches and dents tell the story of the people who wore the watch." He pauses. "Perfection is meaningless. It isn't real."

I think of Mamie losing Elizabeth. It's left a gash deep inside her, like me losing Mom. The difference between watches and humans is that when the former breaks, it can be repaired, but we keep reliving our pain.

He spins a holder with screwdrivers of various lengths, reaches for one, and sets about lifting a bolt from the back of the metal case with surgeon-like precision.

As he works on the watch, I tell him what Mamie told me, how she ended up in Hindelbank because she was unmarried and pregnant and that they took her daughter away.

He slips the loupe off. "That's awful. How are you going to find Elizabeth?"

I lift a shoulder. "A commission was established to research administrative detention—it only stopped in the eighties. I thought of calling them but they're in Bern."

"That's not far. Why are you hesitating?"

"I don't speak German."

Kai laughs. "Whoever answers the phone will speak decent French or better English. Why don't you call them now? I speak German and can help in case you have a problem."

I smile and pull out my phone. I took a photo of the website with the telephone number and dial it.

"*Guten tag? Wie kann ich helfen?*" a woman says.

"Sorry, I don't speak German."

"*Können Sie später zurückrufen?*"

I cover the phone with my hand and look at Kai. "I think she's saying to call back as she's the only one in the office now."

He takes the phone and speaks to her. I can make out a few words—*Hindelbank* and *Amerika*. Then, he asks for Mamie's full name.

"Hedy Borel."

He's nodding, waiting, then writing something down. "*Danke*," he says, handing the phone back to me.

"What happened?" I stare at his blue eyes.

"You've got an appointment tomorrow at 2 p.m. with Madame Keller. Here's the address." He hands me the paper.

"Are you serious?"

"Yes. They checked their records. Hedy Borel is in the database and they want to meet as many of the victims of administrative detention as they can. When I said you had come from America and were only here for a week, she squeezed you in for tomorrow."

I jump up and wrap my arms around his neck. "Oh, Kai, thank you so much. I can't tell . . ."

He's stroking my back and I realize that I've given the wrong impression. I back away. "Sorry, I didn't mean to—"

"Don't be sorry, I liked it." He smiles.

"Mamie's name is in the database? You're not making that up?"

He shakes his head. "How will you get to Bern tomorrow?"

I shrug. "Not sure. Train, I guess."

"If your grandmother is too tired to walk over here today, she's going to struggle with the train tomorrow. I'll move a few appointments and take you."

"Oh no, Kai, you don't have to do that."

"I want to." He checks his watch. "I have ten minutes left before I go to meet a client. You like the mainspring, don't you?"

I nod. "How do you know?"

"Because your eyes light up when you look at it."

Did he notice that about me? "The spiral shape is stunning. I love it."

He smiles. "Why don't you help me put it back together? It's all cleaned and ready to assemble into the barrel. You can do it."

"Me? No, no, no. I'll mess it up."

"No, you won't. I'll guide you." He lifts a loupe from the stand and hands it to me. "You'll do great."

He's serious. But I don't know if I can. Maybe I'm going to fail. I lean back. "I'm not sure this is a good idea."

He hands me the loupe and rubber finger gloves. "I've cleaned all the parts with alcohol, so these gloves will prevent the oil and dirt on your skin from getting on the mechanical pieces." He smiles. "Just try."

I slip the loupe over one eye and the gloves on my first three fingers and thumbs. My eyes follow Kai as he takes a tool resembling metal tweezers, lifts four pieces, including the S-shaped spring, and brings them close.

"This is all we need," he says. "The metal coiled ribbon, the arbor to wind it around, the teeth base of the barrel that holds it, and the barrel cover. It's simple. Twist the uncoiled ribbon around the arbor into a spiral pattern."

I love his confidence. But the moment he gives me the metal tweezers, my hand shakes. A silence so still falls that even the air around us seems to stop.

"You can do this." His voice sinks into my head, making me believe he's right.

Kai places a long metal ruler on the table. It's edged with teeth-like openings on both sides, numbers running next to them. In the middle are carved hollow circles that increase in size.

"Place the teeth barrel in the circle that seems to match its size."

My fingers tremble as I lift the barrel. I hesitate between the number eight and nine circles on the ruler. I choose eight. It fits.

"Good eye." He removes a metal tool with a thin point from a box. "Now it's time to grease the barrel." He opens a plastic container holding a tacky substance. "Dip the point in there so the grease adheres to the metal."

I cover the tip with the sticky substance.

"This next part is important. You need to apply grease to the barrel." His fingers touch mine, and a frisson of warmth runs down my back. He gently slides the tip back and forth. "The grease breaks the slipping of the spring inside the barrel."

He opens a wooden box. Inside is a long metal tube and various-sized handles that resemble the metal hand crank of an old pencil sharpener.

"Which handle size do you think we need?"

"Number eight to match the barrel size?"

He smiles. "Now take out the metal tube. Put the arbor on the end, then snap and lock on the number-eight handle."

I do as he says. "Excellent. Lift the metal spring and feed it into this opening in the handle. Then crank the handle to coil the spring."

I watch in amazement as the strip of metal disappears inside.

"Almost done. Hold the metal tube down into the greased barrel."

I press a lever, and the coiled spring snaps into the barrel.

"Good." He smiles. "What's next?"

"Put the barrel cover on?"

"That's right," he says, handing me the metal tweezers.

Lifting the barrel cover, I drop it over the coiled mainspring. The top and bottom click like a note resonating on a string. "I will forever cherish this experience. Thank you."

"You have extraordinarily delicate yet strong hands, classic watchmaker hands."

I laugh. "That's an original line!"

"I'm serious," he says, a slight break in his voice. "While you were winding the mainspring, I noticed your fingers are agile, like a surgeon's. Have you ever thought about becoming a watchmaker?"

"Me? I only learned what a mechanical watch was once I visited the museum in Le Brassus. I thought all watches ran on batteries."

"Well, now you know. You should think about it." He checks his watch. "I've got to go. I'll pick you up at your hotel tomorrow at noon."

He stands and ushers me out of the studio. The phone upstairs is ringing. He opens the front door and before I can think twice, I kiss him on the cheek. "Thanks."

"You're welcome. See you tomorrow."

38

Gina

Bern
October 2018

The office for the Commission on Administrative Detention is in a building along a stretch of cobblestone streets in Bern's old center. In the guidebooks, I read about the city's medieval fountains adorned with wooden pillars and carved allegorical figures. Kai drops us off as close as he can get to the building while he runs errands and agrees to pick us up at the same place in two hours. Mamie's excited as I help her up the worn stone steps to the second floor.

Madame Keller, a middle-aged woman with a chestnut bob and burgundy glasses, meets us at the door. She has a warm smile that doesn't quite reach her eyes. We follow her to a conference room with beige walls and glass doors. A window overlooks the street, allowing the sounds of the city to filter in. The décor creates a soothing atmosphere with warm colors and soft textures. Perhaps it's meant to ease the pain of those looking for answers to the questions in their past.

My nerves are on edge. I can't stop tapping my foot on the wooden floor. What if we learn that Elizabeth is no longer alive?

Mamie, sensing my worry, reaches for my hand. "You OK?"

I nod, my thoughts heavy with uncertainty. "How about you?"

"Hopeful," she whispers.

A woman brings a tray with coffee. Madame Keller returns with a file under her arm.

Adjusting the glasses that match the color of her lipstick, she looks at Mamie. "We're delighted that you've returned to Switzerland, and we hope we can answer your questions. I spent some time yesterday pulling all the records I could find on you."

Mamie cups her hands around the coffee cup while I tug at the ends of the yellow scarf, which I slipped through the belt loops on my jeans this morning for good luck.

"Before we go into the specifics of your case," she says, tapping the file with her hands, "I would like to explain the purpose behind the Independent Expert Commission (IEC). Unfortunately, your experience wasn't unique. Though we do not know the exact number of individuals against whom administrative detention orders were issued, it's estimated that from 1930 to 1981, somewhere between twenty and forty thousand men and women were held in administrative detention."

I try to comprehend the enormous number, something tangible to make it more than just a statistic. There were forty thousand students at university—all those faces I passed on the quad, in the library, and filling the stadium at football games. The burden of their lives turned upside down, like Mamie's, weighs heavily on my chest.

"From a twenty-first-century perspective, depriving individuals of their liberty without evidence of a crime being committed and withholding the right to trial are clear violations of fundamental human rights and personal dignity.

After the Swiss Parliament officially recognized the injustices committed against these individuals, the Federal Council appointed the IEC to conduct a historical inquiry into what took place. We've been granted wide-ranging authority to access documentary sources in federal and cantonal archives and to interview victims and witnesses." She takes a sip of coffee. "Any questions?"

Mamie shifts in the chair. "I appreciate the commission's mandate and purpose, but I don't see how research can benefit victims like me."

"The commission can never make up for what happened to you or the thousands of men and women who suffered under the coercive welfare system that existed at that time. The purpose of our work, the interviews and the documentary materials we publish on our website, is to get to the truth so you can tell your story. Not only was your liberty taken, but also your voice, and we aim to correct that. Secondly, we've been asked to make recommendations, which we strongly feel should include financial compensation for the victim's suffering."

"That sounds like a good start," I say, taking a sip of coffee, though I know only reuniting with Elizabeth will ease Mamie's suffering.

Madame Keller clears her throat. "I'm afraid that you were subject to some of the worst practices that existed at the time. Let's go through the timeline. On 5 February 1945, the town hall received an anonymous denouncement that a young, unmarried woman, Hedy Borel, was pregnant. The Commune immediately—"

"Anonymous?" Mamie cuts in. "The accuser remains in the shadows?"

Madame Keller leans forward. "It's not in the records. Do you know who did it?"

Mamie's cup is empty. She puts her hands in her lap. I can see a knot of anger forming along her forehead, the same one that twists in my belly. "Of course I know. Madame Jadot. Add her name to the file."

Madame Keller jots a note on the pad of paper next to her. "I will do that. Thank you for the clarification. Now, based on the denouncement, the officials in the town hall issued an administrative detention order to remove you from the community on the unsubstantiated conviction that you had engaged in prostitution. On 10 February 1945, you were arrested and placed in Hindelbank Women's Prison, a facility with convicted criminals. The file says you were assigned to corrective labor. Do you remember which work unit?"

Mamie stares at her hands. "How could I forget? I ironed uniforms for the women's hospital in Bern."

Madame Keller jots that down, too. "Did you receive compensation for your labor?"

"No."

I wrap my arms around my waist.

"We have here that you gave birth to a girl on 8 May 1945." I slide forward in my chair as Madame Keller looks down at the file and adjusts her glasses. "From my reading of the documents, I believe you were coerced into giving the baby up for adoption. Is that—"

"Adoption? They stole her! I never got to see her." Mamie snaps her a fierce look as the lower lid of her bad eye trembles.

"Unfortunately, it was believed that separation would be easier if a bond never formed between mother and child." She glances down at a piece of paper. "It appears it wasn't only the town hall involved in determining your baby's fate. The church played a role—specifically the Protestant pastor, let me find his name. Here it is, Pastor Rolle."

Mamie lets a curse fly under her breath as she takes the paper that Madame Keller hands her.

Hindelbank, le 30 Mai 1945

Pastor Rolle
Le Brassus, Vaud

Pastor Rolle,

We apologize for the delay in responding to your letter of 10 May 1945, concerning Mademoiselle Hedy Borel, interned in our establishment. It has not been very easy to obtain the consent of the aforementioned to renounce her rights to her child. Despite her vehement insistence against adoption, nevertheless, she did in the end understand that it would be all the wiser to follow the course we recommend, given that she has absolutely no certainty as to her own financial future, let alone that of her child.

According to your wishes, we have not told Mademoiselle Borel the whereabouts of her child.

You will therefore find attached the declaration that Mademoiselle Borel was good enough to write and sign in her own hand. We hope that this official document will allow you to undertake the adoption of the child, and thus to preserve her from an unfortunate fate. Please accept the expression of our respectful sentiments.

Director Schneider
Annex: 1 Declaration

As Mamie reads, I can see her face twist and her fingers tremble. "I never signed any declaration to give my child up for adoption. They wanted me to, but I refused."

Madame Keller leans forward. "I believe you. From my interviews with many women who found themselves in the same situation, I learned that they, too, all refused to sign the adoption declarations that their files contain."

Mamie straightens her back. "Are you saying the declarations were forged?"

"We lack the evidence to prove that. But if we read between the lines, we know that the women signed multiple documents upon entering Hindelbank. The authorities would have known of their pregnancies at the time of their intake. Perhaps one of these documents would later be attached to the declarations for adoption."

"From the moment I entered Hindelbank, the system was against me," Mamie says, her eyes downcast.

"The men in power told themselves they were acting in the best interests of society. If you had family members or people in high standing in society who could fight for you, the outcome might have been different. But I believe your mother was in prison?"

Mamie nods. "For smuggling Jewish children into Switzerland during the war."

"That certainly worked against you. A widely held view then was that non-conformist or bad behavior was inherited, a genetic illness. Hence, your mother's conviction for smuggling served as a mark against you."

A moment of quiet settles in the room. Perhaps Madame Keller senses Mamie needs time to absorb all she's said. I reach over and take her hand. It must be hard to hear this, like reliving it, but I hope it will bring closure and allow her to move on.

Madame Keller clears her throat. "What we do know, by talking with hundreds of women who went through a similar experience, is that they carry an enormous sense of guilt for what occurred. We hope our research will help them to see that none of this was their fault. Even if you don't have the evidence to prove the documents used in your case were falsified, by providing the context of the time, which is often missing, we bring the truth to the surface and help you and the other women to heal from a harrowing period in your lives."

Mamie smooths her skirt. "No one heals from Hindelbank."

"I understand. I'm very sorry." She shuffles through the papers. "There is no record of your release date. Would you like to share that part of your story?"

Mamie looks at her. "You mean how I got out?"

"Yes."

Mamie turns to me, her eyes rheumy and red but still clear enough that I can read the message in them: *you, I will tell you.* Then, she glances at Madame Keller. "Perhaps we can discuss that during another interview. What I would like now is to meet my daughter. Will you help me find Elizabeth?"

Madame Keller folds her hands and takes a breath. "I'm not sure Elizabeth will agree. Many of the adults who, as children, were given up for adoption, find it too painful to revisit their past. They don't consider these women their mothers or even a part of their family."

"I understand. I want to try."

She rifles through the papers. I hold my breath and hope that she'll give Mamie this chance.

"I'll have to check the database. We have a list of all the children born to women in administrative detention and the families they went to. Our policy is to not give out the personal information of these individuals without their consent. All I can do is contact Elizabeth, explain the situation and see if she would be willing to meet. I'll need about fifteen minutes. Do you both want to wait?"

"Yes," I say, my throat tight.

After Madame Keller leaves, Mamie whispers, "What will I do if she doesn't want to meet?"

I take her hand. "Let's not think that way."

Through the glass doors of the conference room, I watch Madame Keller at her desk, phone in hand. *Please, Elizabeth,* I whisper, *your mother didn't abandon you. She never would have done that. She's come all this way to tell you that and more. Don't let this opportunity go by. Give her a chance.* I watch Madame Keller nodding her head while she talks. Pen in hand, she's writing on a piece of paper.

I turn to the window. The sun shines bright on the fountain outside. The carved sculpture on the pillar is a gold and pale blue Lady Justice. She's at the level of the window. Blindfolded, in her right hand she holds a sword and the golden scales of justice in her left. I tap Mamie on the shoulder so that she will turn and look at it. She scoffs.

"I know justice doesn't seem possible," I say, "and that nothing can give you back the seventy-three years you lost . . ."

The door opens. I turn and try to read the expression on Madame Keller's face. She's holding in the balance all that Mamie has come here to find.

"I spoke with Elizabeth. She's a doctor of oncology at the University of Geneva. Quite an accomplished woman." Mamie smiles, but her mouth quickly turns down. "At first, she said she had no time. But I explained the situation, the role of the IEC, and why it's important to help the victims heal. Ultimately, she agreed to meet your granddaughter at her offices tomorrow at 1 p.m."

"Me?" I say.

"She wants to take it slowly. Just find out a few things about her birth mother before deciding to go farther."

Mamie turns to me. "Will you?"

"Of course, I just hope—"

"Don't raise your expectations too high," Madame Keller cuts in. "This will be hard for Elizabeth. She's willing to talk to you, but she was very clear about not meeting her biological mother just yet. You must persuade her."

Pressing my hands against my sides, I have no idea how to do that, but I'll figure it out like everything else on this trip. Then I see the paper on the table and an idea comes to me.

"Do you think I could have a copy of the letter from the prison director to Pastor Rolle? It would show Elizabeth how much Mamie wanted to keep her."

Madame Keller hesitates. "For privacy reasons, I'll need to black out the names to protect the individuals mentioned. I'll take care of that now."

To protect them? What about Mamie? Who protected her? It's not fair that these men can hide behind their positions after all this time. I turn to the window and glance at Lady Justice. "Maybe there isn't just one type of justice. If you reunite with Elizabeth, you'll thwart that awful pastor's plan to keep you apart."

"Seventy-three years too late."

"But it's still righting a wrong."

Mamie sighs. "It's all that's left to me."

Madame Keller returns. "Here you go." She hands me a copy of the letter with the names redacted. She turns to Mamie. "When you're ready to tell your story in full, I'd be honored to interview you for our final report."

Mamie nods, but I can see her hesitation. "After I get my daughter back."

"My deepest hope for you is that something good can come from all of this."

"Thank you."

39

Gina

Bern
October 2018

Outside Madame Keller's office, Mamie and I settle on the bench near the fountain and wait for Kai. Sunlight filters through the plane trees lining the cobblestone street, and yellow leaves fall and twirl in the water.

Mamie sits still. I take her hand. It must have been hard for her to learn that Pastor Rolle was behind what happened to Elizabeth in Hindelbank. Squeezing my hand, she turns, eyes heavy with sorrow and hope. "Tomorrow, you'll meet her."

"I'm not sure what I'll say." My throat is dry and gravelly.

"Just be yourself." She leans close and kisses me on the cheek. "You remind me of Samuel."

"I'm not even half as brave as Grandfather or you."

A beat of silence.

"You're good-hearted the way he was. It's OK to be unsure. Everyone is afraid sometimes, even your grandfather."

"From what you've told me, I can't imagine he was afraid of anything."

She points at the sky. "When he flew, he used to be terrified of heavy clouds that could turn the sky into a slab of white marble. He said he sometimes panicked, fearing he would lose his way."

"What did he do?"

"He kept going, believing he'd eventually reach clear skies."

"What about you? Were you afraid of something?"

"Oh yes. For me, it was water."

"But you know how to swim."

"Before your grandfather, I couldn't. My father tried to teach me in the lake near our house, but I panicked and froze. The first summer we arrived in the United States, he took me to the pool daily until I became a strong swimmer." She sighs. "He was a gentle soul and patient. We didn't have many years together but made the most of what we had."

"How long were you together?"

"Twenty years."

"That sounds like a lot."

She sighs. "When you reach my age . . ." She snaps her fingers like those twenty years passed in a few seconds. "It feels short. He died too young. A car accident only five years after your mother was born. He was overjoyed when she arrived. I honestly thought my childbearing days were over, and then she was a beautiful surprise that brought us so much joy." Mamie's lips are red and dry. I hand her the water bottle I brought, but she waves a hand and shakes her head. I don't press her.

"What are you afraid of, *ma chérie*?"

"Being without Mom." The raw and honest words rasp from my too-tight throat. "I don't know how to find my place or where I belong. At university, the students and professors seemed to exist in a big, bright place full of light while I stood outside in the dark. I wanted to join them but couldn't find a way in. My college roommate said I didn't get it." The guilty threads of that day still haunt me.

"Didn't get what?"

"You know, when things happen, what I should do, or how to act."

"Tell me," Mamie says. "I've told you my secrets. You can tell me yours."

Tugging at the scarf belted around my jeans, I take a moment to gather myself. Mom is the only one in the family who knows. But I want to tell Mamie because I feel closer to her than Dad or anyone else. I'm the only one she's trusted with her long-buried secret. And after what she's been through, I think she will understand. "A professor, the head of the architecture department, invited me to his house to discuss my essay. He said I deserved an internship at a top firm over the summer and that he would help me to get one. We were on the couch . . ." I can still conjure his garlic-infused breath and the sweat glistening on his forehead.

"He suddenly leaned forward and kissed me—hard. I didn't realize that deserving the internship had a catch. What angers me is that I didn't instantly pull away, like how you fought Franck. Instead, I froze and kept thinking, this can't be happening. To protect myself, Mom always insisted I carry pepper spray, never walk alone at night and go out with a group of girls. But when it's someone you know, a professor you respect—his classes were my favorite—it's like the world is suddenly out of sync. I somehow disconnected from my core self because I couldn't act."

Mamie squeezes my hand.

"It wasn't until he touched my breast and dragged my hand over the lump in his trousers that I unfroze." I can still hear his insistent words in my head: *make me come*. "Finally, I reconnected and pulled away. Then he flipped and called me a *fucking* tease. He said I went to his house willingly; it would be his word against mine. I got up and ran."

"I think your reaction is understandable and normal, *ma chérie*."

I turn to her. "He was right: I willingly went there. Even worse, I *let* him kiss me. I could have shut my mouth and slapped his face. He said the gauzy blouse and a short jean skirt I wore to class signaled to him that I wanted him. I'm ashamed that he saw me that way. If only I'd—"

"No. You did everything right. A man who has power over you wants to hide his abuse of that power by blaming your willingness to trust him, and your clothing. Pure manipulation."

"But shouldn't I have reported him? He must still be doing the same thing to other female students."

"Yes, that's true. But look at me. It's a struggle to hold powerful men accountable. What you can't do is let his actions shape your choices. Is that why you came back from university?"

"Partly. I wanted to help Mom."

"I know you did, and it was beautiful for her to have you there."

"But it's true that I didn't fit in at university." I take a breath. "Maybe if he hadn't, I would have stayed and tried harder."

"Keep searching for your place. You'll find it."

My phone pings. I look at the message. "It's from Kai. He's stuck in traffic and won't be here for another thirty minutes. Shall we get a coffee?"

"I like it here, in front of the fountain."

"Me too. You looked at me when Madame Keller said there's no record in the file of how you left Hindelbank. I got the sense . . ."

She nods. "I want to tell you before I tell her, a stranger." She tilts her head back and stares at Lady Justice above the fountain. "Do we have enough time before Kai arrives?"

"Yes."

"I remember every detail of that day. The weather was similar to today, a crisp chill in the air, but behind those thick prison walls without sunlight to bring warmth, it felt bitterly cold . . ."

40

Hedy

Hindelbank
September 1945

Hedy put on a white long-sleeved blouse under her brown uniform. She was always cold, even with two pairs of socks and working in the laundry with the hot irons. No matter how many layers, Hedy felt numb.

She crawled under the bed, as she did every morning, and gouged the wall with the curved edge of the spoon she'd stolen from the canteen. She carved at the drywall until the grainy plaster slid between her fingers, and a cavernous line appeared. On the nights when she couldn't sleep, she knelt under the bed and counted with her finger until she found the deepest groove etched there and in her heart: the day Elizabeth was born.

Today was the one hundred and fifteenth day since they stole her daughter. With every step, she felt an emptiness. She would never be whole again.

The cold had come that first week after giving birth. On her way to and from the laundry, she'd ask the guards if she could speak with the director, but her request was always denied. None of the women asked about her baby. They left her alone. But she saw them staring at the cloudy stains on her uniform as milk seeped from her breasts in uncontrollable waves. That was when the cold first hit her—a tremor down her back as if a snowball had slipped under her collar. She held the iron handles steadily and slid the slugs easily into the fire. She was drawn to the red and yellow colors dancing and crackling with warmth. The fire was her only friend. She searched it for the faces of her parents, and for Samuel and Elizabeth. Sweat dripped down her legs, but she shuddered as if she'd been sealed in a block of ice.

Hedy wasn't giving up. Like a hibernating animal, she burrowed deep inside herself and crafted a plan. The day she was released, she would go to every orphanage in the country, starting in Bern, and ask about a baby girl born on the day the war ended. She was sure that if she kept searching, she would find her. This possibility got her through the frosty spring and bitter summer. And now that the weather had turned, it would get her through an icy autumn and bone-chilling winter.

Director Schneider appeared at the laundry on the one hundred and fifteenth day and asked for her. The other prisoners looked at him. Hedy read the question in their eyes—hadn't he already taken everything she had to give? She removed the slug from the metal iron, clacked it on the stove, wiped her hands on her apron, and stepped out into the hallway.

She figured a guard had found the gashes on the wall, and now she would be punished.

"Is there anything you need from your cell?" he said.

They were moving her, maybe to a cell with cinder block walls. She would find a way to carve the days into them. Hedy kept her eyes down.

"Mademoiselle Borel, did you hear me?"

The director's voice seemed to come from afar, like it moved through water. Maybe this was what it felt like to slip into the lake as her father had done when trying to coax away her fear. He'd say she was a complete failure if he was here now. He would never forgive her for not protecting her mother and Elizabeth. "I'm sorry. What did you say?"

"Is there anything you require from your cell?"

Fingering the pocket in her apron, she felt the watch. "No."

"Very well." He turned. "Follow me."

They walked through a maze of interconnected buildings, their shoes echoing off the concrete floor and walls. The director paused at each steel door to take a key and unlock it. Perhaps he would bring her to a part of the prison Hedy didn't know about, where she would be left alone. After a while, he stopped before a room and turned to her.

"Here we are," he said, his right hand twitching as he nodded to the guard, who stood on duty at the door. A clink of metal in the air as the guard put a key in the lock, and the door opened.

Hedy turned. A tall man stood inside, a gray felt hat in his hand.

"I don't understand," she said.

"This gentleman has come to collect you."

The man stepped forward and extended a hand. "I'm Sam Woods from the American Embassy."

Her ears popped at the sound of English. She rushed through the door, convinced he had news of Samuel. But when the door slammed with a thud behind her, dread crept over her shoulders. "Has Samuel been shot down?"

"No, miss, nothing like that. Second Lieutenant Reardon is fine. He's waiting outside in the car for you."

"He's here?" Hedy could hardly believe it. Her Samuel, here at last.

"Yes, miss. And your mother is in the car, too. I had a helluva time getting you both out."

"But Maman—"

"I have some pull, well, more than some. I called in a few favors to get your mother's sentence commuted to one year for good behavior."

The hate against Hedy's family had been so strong that she never imagined a day like this could come.

"Thank you, thank you so much." She took a breath. "I need to find my baby."

He reached a finger in his collar, pulling at it as if it was too tight. "I assumed you'd been imprisoned for smuggling airmen, but when they told me it was for prostitution and you had had a child in prison . . ." He took a breath. "I figured it must be Samuel's. I went to every high-level contact." He pointed his hat at the door. "But that son-of-a-bitch Schneider, excuse me, miss, but there is no other word to describe a man like him, said you could be set free, but the baby—"

"Where did they send her?"

"She was adopted three months ago."

His words stopped Hedy's breath for a moment. She had imagined a temporary orphanage where Elizabeth would stay until Hedy was released. But adoption was permanent. She would be raised by a family that wasn't hers. Hedy and Samuel were her parents. She took a deeper breath and looked at the man from the embassy. "Are you sure?"

"I'm afraid so. I asked which canton, thinking I could track her down, but he wouldn't reveal anything. I'm afraid . . ." He looked at the hat as if he could find the right words printed on the brim. "You'll have to put it behind you. The United States has issued you and your mother two American passports to emigrate."

"I won't leave without my daughter."

He shuffled his feet.

"I want to see Samuel." She would tell him about Elizabeth, and he would help her persuade this kind man that she couldn't go without their daughter.

"As I said, he's in the car. We will go there, but I need one moment with you first." He cleared his throat. "Director Schneider showed me a document you signed giving up your rights to the baby. Even if you did find her, you have no legal basis on which to claim her."

"I didn't sign that document. He wanted me to, but I refused."

"I'm not saying you did sign it. But the document exists. You have no legal recourse to get your daughter back. I'm sorry."

Hedy's teeth chattered. "I need to speak with Samuel."

"Yes, miss, and you will. I'm terribly sorry. None of this is fair. I want you to consider Second Lieutenant Reardon for a moment. Since returning from France, he's called my office every day to ask for help finding you. He doesn't know about the baby, does he?"

She shook her head.

"I didn't think so. Otherwise, he would have asked me to find her, too." He rubbed his chin. "What good will it do telling him now?"

No secrets between us. Hedy lifted her hands to cover her ears.

"I'm sorry, miss. I know you've suffered a terrible loss, but why put him through that, too? You'd be torturing a poor man who won't be able to find his daughter. And he will soon be facing tough days."

She let her arms drop. "Samuel—why?"

"The army doesn't want the fliers talking about what happened here. They're painting them as cowards, undeserving of POW status, even going so far as to say they're deserters."

"Samuel's not a deserter."

"No, he's not. None of the fliers who ended up in Switzerland are. But my government doesn't want the public finding out that they paid the Swiss to keep their airmen in prison and out of combat."

So, they would denigrate Samuel, just like they had done to her father and mother.

"You saved Second Lieutenant Reardon's life; in my mind, you're a hero." He put his hat on and motioned to the guard outside to open the door. "That's all I wanted to say. Now, you go meet your beau and your mother. Tell them what feels right for you. They sure are eager to see you."

She turned and stared at the open door and the rectangle of sunlight passing through it. In the distance, a shiny black car waited. She stepped toward it. The bright light hurt her eyes, so she held up her hands to shield them. The car door opened. Samuel came rushing over, picked her up, and twirled her in his arms.

"I love you, Hedy, the girl who saved my life," he said, bringing her down to the ground and cupping his hands on either side of her face. "It's over. We made it through. It's all clear skies ahead."

The way he was looking at her, as he had looked at her on the boat when they'd parted. It was as though, for him, nothing had changed, and yet for her, everything had.

"Your mother is in the car. Tomorrow, we have a flight to the U.S. The three of us." He was out of breath, his voice full of promise. "We can leave the past behind and start our lives new." He held her close. "I promised you I'd come back. It's all over. You're safe now."

She saw her mother in the car, staring at her through the open window. Her face was thin, her hair brittle and white.

"Samuel, there's something I must tell you."

The crunch of gravel came to her. It was Woods walking over and opening the door. Seven months before, when she stepped out of the police car and entered the prison, Hedy had made that same sound under her shoes. Then she'd carried Elizabeth. Woods fixed his eyes on the gravel.

"What is it?" Samuel looked at her.

"One hundred and fifteen days."

He tilted his head to one side. "I don't understand."

"Hedy?" Her mother's voice rang sure and strong.

"There will be plenty of time to talk," Samuel said. "Let's get out of here. Forget about this awful place." He hugged her close and helped her into the car.

41

Gina

Geneva
October 2018

I'm on the correct street: Avenue de la Roseraie. Elizabeth's office is in a warren of gray hospital buildings. Eventually, I find the one for oncology, push the glass and steel door, and take the elevator to the second floor.

The receptionist smiles. "How can I help you?"

"My name is Gina Carlyle. I'm here to see Dr. Elizabeth Faber."

"Do you have an appointment?" A green-and-blue light reflects in her eyes as she searches the computer screen. "I can't find your name."

"I'm here on a personal matter. Dr. Faber asked me to come to her office at 1 p.m."

"Please take a seat. I'll tell her you're here."

I glance at the patients wearing knitted hats, and my memory reels back to all those chemotherapy sessions Mom went through. I tug at Mom's scarf around my ponytail. There's a row of seats along a side wall, and I choose one at the far end. Black-and-white photographs of sand dunes, snow-capped peaks, leafy jungles and ocean waves hang on the walls. Peaceful landscapes meant to reassure and calm the patients whose bodies are torn apart by the treatments. When a female doctor in a white coat passes in the corridor my pulse jumps, and I sit up straight. Then I realize she's too young to be Elizabeth.

I've yet to fully work out what I'm going to say. On the train to Geneva, I tried to organize my thoughts, but it felt like I was either saying too much or too little. Do I tell her what Madame Keller told me—that unwed pregnant women placed under administrative detention often had their adoption papers falsified and Mamie had no control over what they did with her baby? Maybe that would raise additional questions, and I wouldn't have the answers, causing Elizabeth more pain. Shouldn't Mamie be the one to explain what happened? I could keep it simple and say that her mother has returned to find her, hoping it will be enough.

"Gina Carlyle," the receptionist says, "please follow me."

Walking along a gray corridor, we pass examination rooms on both sides. She motions to an open door on the left. I take a deep breath and enter.

A woman with soft, silvery hair sits at a desk before a computer. She wears a bright blue dress under a white doctor's coat. When she looks up, my stomach shifts. Elizabeth's hazel brown eyes resemble Mamie's, but the rest of her—the angular cut of her chin, the way she holds her shoulders back, and the swift, confident stride as she steps forward—is all Mom.

"Come in," she says, motioning to the gray leather chair near her desk. "My next appointment is in fifteen minutes." She sits down and crosses her legs. "I'm not sure I'll be able to help you. As I told the woman on the phone, I'm not interested in meeting my birth mother."

"She's come all this way to find you," I say, leaning forward. "She was born in Le Brassus. That's where we're staying, at the Hotel de la Lande. Will you please come and meet her?"

Elizabeth uncrosses and recrosses her legs. One hand tugs on the stethoscope coiled around her neck. Her eyes glance at me, and I catch a flash of pain in them before she looks away. It strikes me that she is usually the one to deliver unforeseen, life-changing news. Now, she's on the receiving end. She holds her hands in front of her, palms up as though warding off a frontal attack. "Does she want money? Is that why she's here?"

"Oh, no. She wants to give you a watch. A valuable one."

"A watch?"

"It's your father's watch. She wants you to have it."

"My father?" She lifts a shoulder the way Mamie does when she doubts something. "My mother was a prostitute. She didn't know who my father was."

"She wasn't a prostitute." I shake my head. "She was in love with him and still is, though he died a long time ago."

Shifting her weight, she recrosses her legs. "I don't want anything from her." She pulls the stethoscope off and puts it in her lap. "Tell her she did the right thing by giving me up. I've had a much better life with my adoptive family than I could have had with her." She glances around the office as though the glass table on which her computer sits, the bold abstract painting of blue-and-red squares above her desk, the overflowing bookshelf in the corner, and the plants spilling over the windowsill—spiked aloe vera, ponytail palm and purple violets—all back up her point.

"She's not well," I say. "Will you—"

"No." Elizabeth sighs and puts the stethoscope on the table.

"Why?"

"She had seventy-three years." She wraps her arms around her waist. "Why did she wait?"

I don't have an answer. Maybe it took losing Mom for Mamie to confront the past and find the daughter she left behind. All I know is that I need to figure out what Elizabeth feels inside to change her mind. I fiddle with the ends of the yellow scarf. It's been six months without Mom, and the pain, though less searing and raw, is still there every day. What must it be like to live with that loss for seven decades? Loss changes with time. Maybe it hardens like cement until there's no way to get through it. Elizabeth's sense of not being wanted; she needs to know it wasn't abandonment. Mamie had no choice. I reach for the letter in my bag. Once she reads it, she'll understand. But I hesitate. A part of me worries that even the letter won't be able to get through the cement wall she's built to protect herself.

I take a deep breath. "Mamie had another daughter, Elaine, who was my mother."

A quick smile comes, then goes.

"She died six months ago of esophageal cancer. She was fifty-nine."

"That's a difficult cancer to treat."

"She suffered a lot." My voice cracks.

"By the time symptoms appear, it's often too late." Elizabeth leans forward like she's on familiar ground and more at ease. "I'm sorry for your loss," she says.

Tears suddenly stream down my face. I don't want to cry, but being in a doctor's office brings back all the things that were done to Mom, each one signed off by me because it held the promise of her survival. I realize now that I doubted myself so much that I didn't have the courage to let her go. "She had a feeding tube in her stomach. They kept her alive, but everything they did added to her suffering. I blame myself for not saying no to all the interventions. I just didn't want her to die."

Elizabeth glides her chair closer. "Modern medicine is blessed with wonderful cures, but they can come at the cost of prolonging lives that we should let go."

I wipe the tears away with the back of my hands. "I have a picture. Can I show you?"

She nods and I pull out my phone. There's an image of Mom before she got sick that I've set as my screen's wallpaper. It's how I want to remember her—eyes bright, face smiling, hair soft with a hint of silver like Elizabeth's. I hand it to her.

She takes the phone and stares at the image. Her lips press together. Does she see herself in Mom? "She must have been a wonderful mother."

"Yes, she was."

"Did she teach you French? I'm impressed by your fluency."

"My grandmother taught me."

She hands the phone back to me and silence returns. There's a warning in my head that I'll lose her if I don't keep talking.

"Since Mom traveled a lot for work, Mamie took care of me most afternoons. We would read her favorite weeklies together—*Paris Match* and *Point de Vue*."

Elizabeth smiles. Then, her phone buzzes. She lifts it from the pocket of her white coat.

"Yes? OK, send him over." She stands. "My next patient is here."

I pull the letter out of my bag. It's folded and crumpled. I should have put it in a plastic sleeve or envelope to protect it. "This is for you," I say, handing her the paper. "It's from my grandmother's file."

"I told you, I don't want anything from her."

"Please." I hold it up, waiting for her to take it, but she keeps her hands at her sides. "Once you read it—"

"Hello, Dr. Faber." A young man is at the door. His face is gaunt, but his eyes brighten upon seeing her.

"Daniel, how are you? Come in, we've just finished."

I put the paper on the glass desk. She can read it later after I've left. Then she'll know what they did to Mamie. But Elizabeth swoops it up, places a hand on my back, and guides me to the door. "I meant what I said. It was nice talking with you." Somehow, Daniel and I have exchanged places. "Goodbye, Gina. Good luck to you." The door closes.

I'm standing outside her office. And the paper from Mamie's file, the one that was hidden from the public, the one with the names of the men blacked out to protect them, the one that shows how hard Mamie fought to keep her daughter, the one that can reunite them after seventy-three years, isn't with Elizabeth but is still with me. How did that happen? There's a pounding along my spine. I can't leave without giving it to her. I bend down and try to slip it under the door, but a rigid rubber strip attached to the bottom won't let anything pass.

My fingers leave damp sweat marks on the corners. I could prop it against the door handle so she can find it there. But her name isn't on it, and if it falls to the ground and someone, a cleaner or a nurse, comes by and picks it up—then no one will know who it belongs to, and she will never see it.

"Can I help you?" a voice says. I turn. It's the woman from reception.

"There's something I need to leave for Dr. Faber. I forgot to give it to her."

"You can give it to me." She carries a stack of folders. "I'll make sure she gets it."

The pounding has spread from my spine up to my neck. "I haven't put her name on it." My voice rattles. "Do you have an envelope? I want her name on it so it doesn't get lost."

"Come with me to reception."

My legs feel like lead as I walk the short distance, passing all the calming photos on the wall.

She hands me a brown manila folder. "Will this do?"

I nod, put the paper inside and hand it back to her. She writes Dr. Elizabeth Faber on the front then smiles. "I'll make sure she gets it."

Maybe I should stay and wait until she finishes the meeting with Daniel. Then I can try one more time to give it to her.

"Is there anything else?" she asks, glancing beyond me to the elevator.

"No, thank you."

42

Gina

Le Brassus
October 2018

I can't remember walking to the train station or buying the ticket, but clearly I did, because as the train shuffles through the tunnel and emerges on the other side, the sunlight slams into my eyes. It's windy and blustery, so I pull Mom's scarf from my hair and wrap it around my neck.

I keep replaying every detail of those fifteen minutes. What could I have done differently? Given her the letter first and insisted she read it. Make sure she knew Mamie had wanted her. I should have explained how the whole system was rigged against an unwed pregnant woman, told her about Grandfather, how Mamie had saved his life, and they'd fallen in love, and that she wants to give her his watch before she dies. But I only said some of these things, not the most important ones, and now it's too late to go back and fix it. I shouldn't have worn that gauzy blouse and short jean skirt to class or gone to the professor's house. Mamie's wrong: it is my fault. If only Mom was here—she would have persuaded Elizabeth.

I reach Lausanne and my phone buzzes. It's Kai.

"I've got the Rolex working," he says, his voice brimming with excitement. "I can hardly wait to show it to you."

I'm thrown back to the day in the museum when I imagined the graceful second hand sweeping across the black dial as if flying through time. Kai can bring the watch back to life, but turning back time doesn't change things. People are made of muscle and flesh, and they can't be fixed once they're wounded.

"Gina, are you OK? How did it go with your aunt?"

"I'm on the train, just left Lausanne. We can talk when I get there."

In the carriage, a group of university students are giddy with laughter, happy to be out of class. I think of Mamie, seventy-three years ago, taking the same route home after her classes and risking her life to help Grandfather in the forest.

Maybe Dad was right and no one gets anywhere by looking at the past. I never should have come because I've made things worse by giving Mamie false hope, letting her believe it's possible to reunite with the daughter she left behind.

Stepping onto the platform at Le Brassus, I see Kai before he sees me. His blond hair ruffles in the wind, and the weight pressing on my chest lifts a little. He catches my eye, and we move toward one another.

"You didn't have to come," I say, smiling.

"I wanted to." He kisses me on the cheek. "Let's find a place to talk."

The restaurants won't open for another two hours, so we go to the hotel bar and settle at a corner table away from the men drinking alone. Kai orders a beer, and I choose a white wine.

"I take it the meeting with Elizabeth didn't go well." His quick clear eyes appraise me.

"She's angry, said seventy-three years is too long to wait."

The drinks arrive. My hand shakes a little as I reach for the glass.

"You told her about what they did to your grandmother in Hindelbank?"

"I tried," I say, dipping my head, wishing I could disappear. "I had fifteen minutes. It went by so quickly. I tried to talk about Mamie, but she pushed the subject away. Then, like an idiot, I only remembered to give her the letter at the end. I should have held my ground, insisted—"

"Don't." He reaches for my hand. "I'm sure it went better than you think." He takes a beat, then presses on. "So, what did you talk about?"

"Mom. I thought if I mentioned Mom's cancer—" My throat burns. I haven't told Kai what it was like to care for Mom—the double-sided coin of those twelve months. Yes, it was an honor to be there for her, but it was also how I hid from my fear of the world and of failing to live up to be the strong woman she was. All this time, I've been hiding behind Mom's illness because it's easier than facing the challenges out there.

He sips his beer. "Well, how did Elizabeth react?"

"She knows about esophageal cancer." I reach for Mom's scarf. "But I think I made an idiot of myself because I cried."

"Crying doesn't make you an idiot."

We sit for a moment in silence, sipping our drinks.

"So, let me summarize," he says. "You told her why you're here, and she shot down any possibility of meeting her birth mother. Then you talked about your mom, and maybe . . ." he leans in as if to get my accord ". . . you bonded with her over your mother's illness?"

"Bonded is a stretch. She's an oncologist, so she talked to me like she would with anyone who has experienced cancer up close. But her eyes did sparkle when she looked at Mom's photo. There's a striking resemblance between them—I think she saw it."

"It sounds like a beginning," Kai says evenly, then smiles.

"More like an ending." I take a gulp and finish my wine. "I don't think I'll see her again."

Kai raises a finger to signal to the bartender and then points at our empty glasses.

"Did you tell her about this?" He places a green felt bag on the table.

"The watch?" I nod. "She's not interested; she doesn't want anything from Mamie. One of her patients arrived, and I had to go. She still doesn't know that her father was an American pilot."

"That might be a reason to see her again."

The plan was for Mamie to tell her and give her the watch. But I've ruined that. The waiter brings our drinks. I look out the window. Dusk is falling fast. The sky is lichen gray, like the trunks of the spruces all over town.

"Give me your wrist," Kai says.

I hesitate. I don't feel I've earned the right to wear it. I don't have my grandparents' courage or resourcefulness.

"Come on," he insists. "What do you think of this new strap?"

He reaches for my left arm, and the cold steel case touches my skin. Kai cinches the clasp, and the gray suede draws my eye. Soft as cashmere. "I love the strap. It gives it a modern touch."

I turn my wrist clockwise to look at the dial, and a thrill shoots up and down my spine at the third hand skating across the darkness. This must have been how it looked when Grandfather wore it in the forest, the black dial blending with the night, protecting him. Maybe it reassured him when he was alone in the hut, as it had reassured Mamie during the long nights at Hindelbank.

"No words?" he says.

"None that could give it justice. You've truly brought it back to life."

"It was an honor to repair a watch that belonged to such brave individuals." He looks at me. "Including you."

"Me?" I look down. "I'm nothing compared to James, Peter, Grandfather or Mamie."

"That's not true. Not many people would drop everything to help an ailing grandmother repair the broken threads of her life." He reaches over and lifts my chin with his fingers.

I want to tell him that it's not courage but fear, how it's easy to drop everything when you're running from yourself. "Honestly, I've made the threads unravel more."

He frowns. "You're too tough on yourself—you found Elizabeth."

"But I couldn't persuade her to meet Mamie." I take a breath. "Nothing else matters."

He stares hard at me as if he's pulling my layers back, seeing into the hopeless and powerless depths of who I truly am. I shudder to think what that must look like.

Condensation rims the bottom of his glass and gathers on the table. He wipes it away with the edge of his hand. "Remember that you put the mainspring in there. It's your repair work, too." He takes a slow breath. "We make a good team. Maybe we could collaborate again."

He's trying to cheer me up, but what he's saying can never be. "This is my only watch." I laugh. "And it's not even mine." I hold up my wrist and smile, but my heart aches inside. "Maybe there's no point in understanding the past if it doesn't improve the present."

"Not everything we do is going to work out. What's important is to be strong and daring enough to try."

"But this was Mamie's last chance. So much was riding on it, and for Elizabeth to reject her . . ." My gut twists.

I could have righted a wrong, given two people what was stolen from them—the time to know one another. Now, they'll never have that. I reach into my bag, pull out the wad of bills, and hand them to Kai.

"Thank you for all you've done," I say, gulping down the rest of my wine.

"What are you going to do now?"

"Tell Mamie." My voice is tight. "And bring her home."

"What about . . .?" He puts the crumpled cash in his pocket.

He's left out the last word—us.

43

Gina

Le Brassus
October 2018

That night, I can't bring myself to tell Mamie. I leave a message at reception for her, saying I've been delayed and she should go to bed and not wait up for me. I spend the rest of the night walking outside, trying to get my thoughts clear before coming to bed at midnight.

The following morning, I wake up and go downstairs to get her a coffee and croissant.

"How are you feeling?" I ask when I return to the room. It's windy and blustery outside again so I tie Mom's scarf around my neck.

"I must have been asleep when you came back yesterday," Mamie says. "What happened with Elizabeth?"

"I went to her office at the University Hospital of Geneva. We didn't have a lot of time. She's busy with all those people who need her."

"What's she like?"

"Tall with silver hair, she wore a blue dress under her doctor's coat. She's a mix of you and Mom." I take a breath. "She's definitely your daughter."

Mamie looks at me. "Why?"

"She's got the same spark in her eyes that you do. And she's fiercely committed to her profession."

Mamie smiles. "I can hardly wait to meet her."

Now, the hard part. "Elizabeth was told a story that wasn't true. I tried—"

Mamie nods and looks away. "I see. It's OK."

"No, it's not OK. None of it's OK." My voice is loud and angry. "What they did to you was wrong. And she doesn't know. I should have talked about the damn letter. Instead, I spoke about Mom and cried."

Her gaze turns back to me. "I'm not sure the letter would matter to her."

"Of course it would."

Hedy tilts her head and looks up at the ceiling. "He wanted me to sign. I didn't."

I come close and touch her knee. "I know. You would never sign your daughter away."

She puts her arms around her waist.

"Shall I get you a blanket?"

She shakes her head. "Tell me again what she looks like?"

"Like you and Mom, especially Mom. She's got the same strong way of holding her shoulders upright."

"That's your grandfather. Even the army couldn't take that away from him."

"But she's built a protective wall around herself. She didn't want to know about you, Grandfather or the watch. So, all I could talk about was me and Mom." I sigh. "I should have made her read the letter in front of me, then—"

"Come," she says, lifting her arms to embrace me. "You have done a wonderful kindness for me."

"No, I—"

"Thank you for trying." Mamie's voice cracks as she points at her chest. "I have to live with my mistake."

"What mistake?"

"I should have fled before."

"Where would you have gone?"

"To France."

"The war was still on. Something even worse might have happened."

"Nothing could be worse than what happened."

"What if you'd lost the baby during childbirth? You did the right thing by staying. You kept her safe."

She puts her hands on her face. "I don't know . . ."

"Do you remember when you said that what happened with the professor wasn't my fault? What happened to Elizabeth isn't your fault. You saved a pilot, fell in love, and he gave you his watch."

She drops her hands and smiles. "Rolex Oyster Chronograph."

I reach for my purse and bring it out. "Kai's repaired it. I'll put it on you."

She's smiling as I attach the gray strap around her tiny wrist. Kai must have awled an extra hole in the suede because it fits her perfectly.

"Gorgeous," she says, rubbing a finger over the soft suede. She looks at the dial. "It saved me twice."

"How?"

She wipes a tear from her cheek. "When I rowed Samuel across the lake to France and came back alone." She swallows and points at the numbers. "It was my light in the darkness, a beacon that helped me find the way."

"And the other time was when you were in prison?"

Her lips fold inward. "In the cell, at night." She brings the dial close to her heart. "It made me feel less alone because it reminded me of what your grandfather used to always say about flying through the clouds into clear skies. All I had to do was hold on and wait for the clear skies to come."

"You were fearless."

She shrugs and looks at me. "I had found my purpose, and that gave me courage." She holds up her wrist. "We'll still give it to Elizabeth. It's hers. She was with me both times. She gave me strength and purpose."

"OK. I'll figure out how. Maybe I can bring it to—"

The telephone rings. Mamie and I look at each other and shrug. I go to answer it.

"Hello?"

"You have a visitor downstairs," the receptionist says. "Shall I send her up?"

"What's her name?" I ask, and wait.

"Dr. Elizabeth Faber."

I straighten my back. "We'll come down." My heart races. "Please tell her we're coming now." I hang up the phone and turn to Mamie.

"She's downstairs."

"Who?"

"Elizabeth."

"Oh my goodness, that's wonderful . . . frightening too."

"Are you ready? Let's go."

Mamie doesn't hesitate. This is the moment she's been dreaming of. I grab the room key and help her out the door. She doesn't want to wait for the elevator, so we take the stairs. We enter the lobby and I spy Elizabeth standing near the window, uncertain about her next move. Mamie must recognize her because she squeezes my arm and I can hear her breath catch.

"Hello, my child." Mamie's voice cracks.

Elizabeth takes small, awkward steps as we approach.

"Thank you for coming," Mamie says.

I motion to the armchairs and we all sit down. The hotel reception is busy, people are checking in and out, and the clatter of dishes reaches us from the restaurant. But neither

Mamie nor Elizabeth pay attention to any of these sounds, as I watch them focus on one another.

"What made you change your mind?" I ask. "The letter?"

She tilts her head. "What letter?"

"The one I gave the receptionist."

"Oh, I read that," she says, shaking her head. "But it was hard to understand with the names of the people blacked out." She rubs her hands together. "It was you who changed my mind."

"Me?"

"After you left, I couldn't stop thinking about this grieving young woman who came all the way here to find me. Last night, I kept going over all that you said, how you and your grandmother used to read *Paris Match* together and how she cared for you after school. I realized that you share a special bond, something I've never . . ." She breaks off, staring ahead of her.

"What is it, my child?" Mamie asks.

"This might sound strange, but I wondered if you and Gina coming here was meant to help me find the thing I'm missing." She looks at Mamie. "Does that make sense?"

"Yes, it does," Mamie whispers. "You've been missing a mother's love because we never had a chance to be together. It wasn't fair."

"I know." She stands. "I'm here now. I'm sorry about what happened to us."

"Me too."

They embrace for a long moment. Elizabeth wipes her eyes and brushes the tears away from Hedy's cheeks.

"I didn't need the letter. I could see it in Gina's love for her mother and her love for you. If you were someone who didn't care about me or didn't know who my father was—you never would have built a family on a foundation of such deep love. That was the moment I realized I'd been lied to." She clears her throat. "I wanted to come here to learn the truth."

Mamie reaches for Elizabeth, and they embrace again. "You are loved. Always have been. I'm sorry I never could tell you."

"I thought you didn't want me. I thought there was something wrong with me. I've always struggled to be close to people. Afraid I'd lose them the way I lost you."

"You never lost me. I always held you here . . ." Mamie touches her chest ". . . in my heart."

Now I'm crying, too, and Mamie signals for me to come over. The three of us hold hands.

"If only Mom was here," I say.

"She is here." Elizabeth smiles. "I feel her presence in you. She'll always be with you. Love like that doesn't die." She squeezes my hand. "It lives on within us."

"I'm so glad you changed your mind," I say. "We defeated those men who tried to keep us apart." I look at Mamie. "Didn't we?"

"It took seventy-three years, but we did it." Mamie smiles.

A woman in a hotel uniform approaches, holding a large cardboard box.

"Am I interrupting? I can come back later."

"It's fine," I say. "What is it?"

"We are collecting our annual winter clothing donations for those in need. If anyone has items that they would like to give away, this is the box we will leave at reception." She holds up the cardboard box for us to get a clear look. Inside, I glimpse sweaters, scarves and gloves. Mamie's gaze shifts to me. She doesn't say anything, but I can sense what she's thinking. It's been on her mind since I made her all that crème caramel, and she asked me to come with her to Switzerland. I feel something inside me shift.

"I have an item to donate," I say.

"We always need new things."

I untie the scarf and hold it in my hands.

"Oh—what a striking color. Are you sure?" the woman asks.

I look at Mamie. She nods. "Yes. It's time for a change. I don't need it anymore." I let the scarf fall from my hand into the box—a golden ribbon among all the gray sweaters.

"That scarf will be a ray of sunshine for someone. Thank you."

A gift from Mom and me to someone in need. "I'm happy to do it."

The woman leaves. Mamie and Elizabeth have a lot of lost time to catch up on, and there's someone I want to see. "I'm going now," I say.

"Where to, my dear?"

"I'd like to tell Kai how much you appreciate his work."

"Who's Kai?" Elizabeth asks.

"A watchmaker," I say.

Mamie touches the Rolex and looks at me. "Can you help me with this?"

I unhook the strap and hand it to my aunt.

"This belonged to your father," Mamie says, "it's for you."

"It wasn't working when we arrived," I explain. "Kai repaired it."

Elizabeth stares at the watch as if she's not sure.

"Go on," I say, "put it on."

"I've never had something grand and big like this!" She holds up her wrist and flashes a small quartz watch.

"Well, it's about time." I turn and kiss Mamie on the cheek.

"Thank Kai for me," she says. "Tell him the watch is perfect."

"I will."

"Bring him next time?"

"Yes."

Elizabeth secures the watch and stares at the black dial. It fits her perfectly, as though it was always meant to be on her wrist.

"Mamie has a lot of stories about that watch," I say, hugging her. "I think you'll love it even more after you hear them."

"Goodbye, Gina, and thank you."

Outside, the cool air feels good on my face. I decide to walk. The low clouds are layered with shades of blue I've never seen before. I don't realize I'm smiling until I catch my reflection in a shop window. I hardly recognize myself without Mom's yellow scarf. It's taken me a long time to realize I don't need it anymore. Elizabeth is right. Mom will always be within me.

A swirl of emotions hit—I suddenly can't wait to see Kai. I run past the shops on the main road and the big white building that houses a famous watch school, then along a park, and finally down a country lane with cows in a green field. I wave at them when they lift their heads to watch me dash past. I push myself harder because I don't want to lose another minute.

When I reach Kai's house, I ring the buzzer and put my hands on my knees to catch my breath.

"Who is it?" he asks on the intercom.

I lift my head and shout, "Gina."

The door buzzes open. I run through it, and halfway up the stairs, Kai is already on the white carpet waiting for me.

"Is your grandmother OK?" He looks worried.

"Yes, she's so happy. Elizabeth came. She's with Mamie now. You were right. I didn't do so bad after all."

He hugs me. "I knew it!"

"Yes, you did. There was something else you said . . ."

"I don't remember, what?"

"About collaboration? Is that still a possibility? I mean, it could be that Mamie and I are staying."

"In Le Brassus?"

"Yes."

"Carlyle and Grueinger. How does that sound?"

"Perfect."

"Will we specialize in pilot watches, exclusively Rolexes, or broaden the category to all military uses, including diving watches?"

"Whatever you want to do. I'm up for it."

"You'll have to learn many things and work extraordinarily hard; watchmaking is precise and unforgiving."

"I think I can handle it."

"I know you can. And you're in the right place."

"Yes, I've found my purpose and am exactly where I should be."

44

Hedy

La Forêt du Risoud
October 2019

On a crisp fall day, a car stops at the Chalet de la Thomassette, where the road ends before the forest. The doors open, and Hedy, Elizabeth and Gina get out. They walk hand in hand as a warm wind, perfumed with pine, blows the leaves from the trees. Hedy glances up at the cloudless sky and smiles.

It's been nearly a year since she reunited with Elizabeth, and since then, she's spent every day in Le Brassus. After Madame Keller wrote a detailed report on her case, the Commune returned one of the apartments at 9 Piguet-Dessous to Hedy as compensation for the pain and suffering she experienced. Hedy lives there with Gina, who is in her first year at the École Technique in a three-year program in watchmaking. Her granddaughter is learning the same techniques watchmakers studied two hundred years ago. Every weekend, Elizabeth comes from Geneva to spend time with them. Kai often joins, and they all talk about the Rolex watch and why pilots like Samuel needed them.

The asphalt hurts Hedy's joints as she walks, but once they reach the woodland, the ground turns soft, and she feels like she can walk forever. These last weeks, the forest has been calling for her. Earlier in the summer, Hedy went with Gina and Elizabeth to find her father's hut. Gina wanted to use her phone to navigate their way, but Hedy would have none of that. The route from her house to the hut in the forest is forever etched on her heart.

It was bittersweet to climb over the stone wall, though she struggled and had to rest and lean on Gina to make it. She felt the moss through her fingers and saw the clearing and the beech tree; all took her breath away. She could still hear Samuel's voice calling out to her, as it had when they sat at the bottom step, and she changed his bandages. The gray walls are more weathered, and the roof with the awning is falling apart, but the hut still stands. She thinks the trees know how to take care of a place that belongs to the forest.

Hedy feels a lump lodge in her throat as she observes Elizabeth gazing at the Rolex on her wrist and admiring its sleek black dial. The simple act of having her eldest daughter walk by her side means the world to Hedy. She no longer thinks about what she failed to do or what she could have done differently to keep Elizabeth with her. These days, her thoughts are on Samuel. She recalls how, that first year in America, he brought her to the Arkansas River—the place he loved because it held the memories of his brother. Maybe that's why Hedy wants to return to the forest—where her memories are the strongest.

To Hedy, life feels like a river; she floats on the surface, carried by the current underneath. Sometimes, the river churns with adversity and heartbreak; other times, it flows with joy and wonder. She's learned that she can't change the current; all she can do is keep moving to make it through.

"Were you never afraid to walk here alone at night?" Elizabeth asks as they go deeper into the forest.

"No, I always felt safe. There is nothing to be afraid of here."

The air shifts with a sudden coolness, a precursor of change. She takes a deep breath. "Can you smell the pine and spruce resin as the trees release their oils?"

"Yes," her daughter and granddaughter say in unison.

Maybe they're tired of her stories. She wants to tell them again about her father's wood and the one in ten thousand spruces that produce the resonance for his violins. But her breath slows, and her forehead aches. She's dizzy. "I don't know how far we've gone . . ." Her legs feel heavy. "Shall we rest for a moment?"

The girls help her sit down on a moss-covered stone along the path. Hedy marvels at the different shades of green on the forest floor.

"Would you like some water?" Gina asks.

Hedy nods. As she takes the bottle from Gina, she sees her granddaughter's red fingers. "What are you doing to have fingers like that?"

"Turning a lathe, and I love it." Gina laughs. "How could I have known that when you asked me to come to Switzerland, I would discover the profession I love." She feels Gina's warm lips on her cheek. "Thank you."

"You always were a clever girl. You just had to find your passion." She touches Gina's face with her hand. "And you found Kai too?" She can feel the heat rise in her granddaughter's cheeks. "Tell me again about the engagement. You said he gave you a watch and not a ring?"

Hedy feels the air move. Maybe Gina's showing her the watch, but her eyesight is so weak that she can only make out a blur on her granddaughter's wrist.

"When I told him that Grandfather had given you the Rolex on the night you brought him to the other side of the lake, he thought it was romantic. This watch is German, an A. Lange & Söhne, with a stunning open heart dial. Every time I glance at it, I see the rotation of the balance spring."

Hedy doesn't know what this means, but she likes Kai, and that's all that matters.

"What about your father? Has he accepted your engagement to Kai?"

"Dad promises to come to Le Brassus for the wedding, but it won't happen until I finish my studies."

Hedy wonders if she'll still be here then. She notices that Gina no longer wishes Elaine was here. Maybe she's learned to accept that loss is a part of the river of life, and what matters is how you fill that loss. In Hedy's mind, Gina is filling it right.

She drinks, swirling the water in her mouth before swallowing. She turns to Elizabeth. "What have you decided to do with the Rolex?"

"It means so much to me," Elizabeth says. "If it weren't for the watch, I never would have known the truth about my heritage—"

"I never would have met Kai," Gina cuts in.

"It also allows me to connect with my patients on something other than their illness. It's not just the men but many young women like Gina who are drawn to the watch. They all sense a story behind it and ask me how I got it. I take the time to tell them about my father and how he met you and fell in love. It makes me feel close to him, as if he is still alive. All my patients love the story, and they forget they're sick and maybe dying, if only for a few magical moments."

"Like Chai," Hedy whispers.

"The boy your family saved, right?"

Hedy nods. She sees Chai on Samuel's shoulders, the airplane in his small hands stretching up to the sky.

"But I'd like your and father's story to be more widely known, and I'm exploring how to do that. Maybe the watch is the right vehicle."

"How?" Hedy asks.

"Kai has contacts at Rolex. They've offered to buy it from me."

"Will you sell it?" Hedy's voice rises in surprise.

"I would consider selling it to them if they meet my conditions."

"Oh. What are they?"

"The proceeds go to a fund to help the needy families of the pilots interned in Switzerland or the brave individuals who chose to help them escape. I don't understand why both groups suffered; they tried to do the right thing. Maybe the watch can help rebalance things in their favor."

"A wonderful idea," Gina says. "We could even put up a sign outside the hut explaining what happened here with the names of the saved children."

"We've got to find the book of names," Elizabeth says excitedly. "I will call Madame Keller and ask if she can search the police archives. Imagine if we can find some of those children and bring them and their children and grandchildren back to the forest as a remembrance?"

Hedy wants to tell Elizabeth and Gina that their ideas are lovely, but the words slide like marbles on her tongue. She struggles to speak, and something pinches her chest. She opens her mouth to get air and lifts one hand, but even that is a struggle. Suddenly, the brightness of the day is lost. She knows she should get moving because they still have a long way to go. Hedy wants to walk one more time with her daughter and granddaughter deep into the forest, climbing over the wall to the hut.

"Mamie, are you OK?" a voice calls to her from some distance.

"Yes," she says, finally. But all is quiet, as if they can't hear her.

She smells the cool scent of the spruce behind her and slides back to rest her head against its old gray trunk. She looks up; the light curves and cascades through the canopy like water falling to the ground. Her fingers sink into the dirt as her body melts against the soft earth. After all that walking, the forest is a warm blanket to rest on. But something inside presses her to get up and continue. The moss-covered wall can't be far. She used to love to walk with her father through the meadow and the river running through it, the ground sloping and speckled with white limestone and green understory. She spent hours by her father's side as he moved among the trees as though they were his family—he knew their ages and their personalities—now she's with him again, passing birch and spruce and ash until he stops, touches an old trunk's gray grooves, looks up, and tells her this is the one.

She hears a sob and feels a warm hand touch her cold face. Someone is calling her. Is it Samuel? She wants to go to him, lean against his chest and tell him about Elizabeth and Gina and all that has happened since he left. He must be with Elaine and her parents. Together, they're all waiting for her. She senses it's time. The river is flowing, and she feels the current churning and changing. She's done what she had to do here; now it's time to move. She trusts that wherever the river carries her, it will be with Samuel to clear skies.

Acknowledgments

To Anna Klerfalk, my agent, thank you for believing in this story and for your direction on revisions.

Thank you to the team at Embla Books, especially Stephanie Carey, who championed this novel from the start and Emma Wilson and Chelsea Graham, who worked so hard to bring it into the world.

To Lisa Ireland and Fiona McIntosh, two excellent writers who read parts of the novel, thank you for sharing your knowledge and encouraging me to keep revising.

To my writing group—Nola d'Enis, Teresa Hardy and Mike Lawson—thank you for reading every chapter and providing insightful feedback, suggestions and support.

To Edward McManus, thank you for fact-checking elements of the story and Steve Prokaskys, a former naval aviator who flew with my father, thank you for reading Samuel's chapters and for all your suggestions.

Finally, I couldn't have written this without the loving support of my family—my sons, whose passion for watches led me to this story and my husband, for everything.

A Note from the Author

This book began as a whisper of an idea when my sons, home from university during the pandemic, suggested we visit the newly opened Audemars Piguet Museum in Le Brassus. It was the first time I'd seen the inside of a mechanical watch, and from the moment I set my eyes on the mainspring—the thin metal ribbon that powers the movement—I knew I wanted to write about one.

Though I have kept as close to the historical record as possible, the pandemic travel restrictions in effect the year the museum opened meant that for the sake of the story, I set the museum's opening in 2018 rather than the actual opening year of 2020.

The museum inspired me, but I had a watch without a story. To find one, it would take many visits to Le Brassus, wandering around the town and through the forest. On the wall of the Protestant Church, I came across an engraved plaque: *1939–1945, Despite Our Infidelities, God with His Almighty Hand, Protected our Country, To Him Alone the Glory*. What infidelities, I wondered? I'd read about the Bergier Commission tasked in the 1990s with "conducting a legal probe into the fate of assets which reached Switzerland as a result of the National Socialist regime." However, the plaque hinted that something specific might have occurred in Le Brassus during the war, which the town's residents seemed to regret.

I researched Switzerland during WWII and discovered that the forest behind Le Brassus—La Forêt de Risoud—was a major smuggling route for bringing Jewish children from Europe to safety in Switzerland. My husband and I went on the annual hike along the old smuggling route to commemorate the brave French and Swiss men and women who were arrested or killed for engaging in this illegal activity. I also came upon the declassified files at the U.S. National Archives of the American pilots interned in Switzerland during World War II. That led me to Cathryn J. Prince's *Shot from the Sky: American POWs in Switzerland*, a rigorously researched account of the American aircraft, sometimes shot down over the country, and the airmen imprisoned in Swiss internment camps. Now, I'd found my story.

But the Switzerland I've lived in since 2007 seems so remote from its past that I didn't feel the story would be complete if I left it entirely in the 1940s. I wanted to explore how the country has changed. Around 2014, I remember listening to the car radio on school runs, and there were interviews with women who had gone through traumatic experiences as young adults. I wasn't sure why their stories were suddenly coming out, and I didn't yet understand what Administrative Detention was about, but the pain in their voices has always stayed with me.

The watch allowed me to pull these storylines together. I imagined some trace of Samuel's soul, and his love for Hedy remained on his Rolex, which his granddaughter Gina could feel over seventy years later. And, of course, the scars of what happened to Hedy, like the women I heard telling their stories on the radio, lingered over her and society today.

I loved researching and writing this story, and I hope you've enjoyed reading it. If you did, I'd be grateful if you could take the time to write a review online. Your review can help other readers to find my books.

If you'd like to get in touch with me—I love hearing from readers—you can find all my contact details at cynthiaanderson.co.uk. You can also sign up for my newsletter to learn about what I'm reading and to receive a notification when my next book is released.

About the Author

Cynthia Anderson was born in California and has degrees from the University of Colorado and the London School of Economics. *The Pilot's Wife* won a Bronze Medal in the 2024 Historical Novel Society First Chapters Competition. She is based in Switzerland with her husband and their labrador.

About Embla Books

Embla Books is a digital-first publisher of standout commercial adult fiction. Passionate about storytelling, the team at Embla believe our lives are built on stories – and publish books that will make you 'laugh, love, look over your shoulder and lose sleep'. Launched by Bonnier Books UK in 2021, the imprint is named after the first woman from the creation myth in Norse mythology. Embla was carved by the gods from a tree trunk found on the seashore; an image of the kind of creative work and crafting that writers do, and a symbol of how stories shape our lives.

Find out about some of our other books and stay in touch:

X, Facebook, Instagram: @emblabooks
Newsletter: https://bit.ly/emblanewsletter